LORNA GRAY

Lorna Gray is passionate about understanding the past and takes much of her research from spoken history. She loves the fact that writing gives her the excuse to ask people about their memories, and treasures the unique little insights that every new conversation has to offer. She is also a published illustrator and her work has featured in a number of archae-ological reports, children's books and non-fiction titles.

Above all, Lorna loves a good adventure. She doesn't mind whether it comes in the form of a good book, a film or rambling about the ruins of a castle as long as it is guaranteed to have a happy ending.

http://www.saltwaydesign.com/
@MsLornaGray

In the Shadow of Winter

LORNA GRAY

Harper*Impulse* an imprint of
HarperCollins*Publishers* Ltd
77–85 Fulham Palace Road
Hammersmith, London W6 8JB

www.harpercollins.co.uk

A Paperback Original 2015

First published in Great Britain in ebook format by Harper*Impulse* 2015

A catalogue record for this book is
available from the British Library

ISBN: 9780008122737

Automatically produced by Atomik ePublisher from Easypress

For Mary Stewart

Chapter 1

The Cotswolds, England. 1947

I suspect that my impression of the past is something akin to a soldier's image of his homeland – all improbable blue skies and greenery like a treasured souvenir postcard where the colours have been painted in. That being so, I can only sympathise with all those war-wearied men who, instead of returning to find the picture held dear in their imagination, discovered a land brown with the stain of bombed-out buildings, plain rationed clothing and the soot of struggling industry.

Not that the land was brown at present, admittedly. If snow was good for something, it could be said that it was at least *clean*.

Right on cue, the first hard spikes of a fresh storm flung themselves against my cheek. Reaching for the last two buckets, I hurried, or at least hurried as much as a person can in a foot or more of drifted snow, across to the house before Freddy could return. It only felt like a moment ago that we had put the poor ponies out to wade about in the valley but it appeared to have been a pattern of the past two months that the hours of every day would vanish in a blur of turning ponies out or bringing them in again, mucking them out and feeding them. Although, just for a change, the last hour in particular had been filled with endlessly lugging water across the treacherous roadway.

It is tempting here to launch into an explanation of the past weeks of hardship and isolation, and the conditions of our ceaseless battle against the bitter wind but I have never yet heard anyone describe this unnatural winter, a year into peace, without making it seem exaggerated or even simply downright invented. What I will say however, is that entire crops of winter vegetables were frozen uselessly into barns and with animals dying in herds at a time from cold and malnutrition on the whitened hillsides, these hard facts do perhaps begin to paint the right kind of picture. I know of at least one local farmer who, defying regulations, butchered his own sheep to feed his stranded neighbours.

For me, it was the addition of water to this list of deprivations that formed my most immediate difficulty. Like most of the Cotswolds, we had no mains water but the trusty hilltop spring, which normally supplied my hairy menagerie, was buried several feet beneath a hard cap of snow and ice and now only the rustic pipes that some former landowner had laid deep underground from pond to house could still be relied on to flow. It did seem particularly perverse that wherever I went I should be surrounded by great powdery heaps of the stuff.

I had actually finished the present watery mission however, and brought in everyone from the upper slopes before I finally caught the rough sound of Freddy's return. The ponies were blowing hard and hurrying out of the narrow valley when they ought to have been walking and, instantly dropping whatever I was doing, I stepped quickly across the yard to meet whichever miniature disaster had happened to the boy this time. It was beyond me to guess how he had somehow managed to turn even this mundane task into yet another adventure but there he was, fiddling about with the valley gate and standing at the centre of a sweating and excited cluster of tossing manes; bothered, overheated, but perfectly unharmed.

Getting him to speak was the next challenge. The boy was so excited and so agitated, and so very desperate to tell me about it that his words kept coming out in the wrong order, and sometimes even the letters too. Only then he finally managed it and any habitual urge to scold him abruptly evaporated.

His tale must have demonstrated every one of the usual inconsistencies inspired by his wonderfully overactive imagination but it would have taken a harder woman than me to ignore the underlying thread of genuine alarm. Even then, I probably could still have dismissed it as fantasy and, thanks to his appalling lack of self-confidence, he almost certainly would have believed me. But his description of the moment of spotting someone floundering on the furthermost slopes with its madcap image of that same foolish soul trying to force their way uphill through deep shifting powder was inescapable and, in the end, I found it unavoidably convincing too.

And so that was how I found myself first prising a pony from its hay to reluctantly accompany me out into the disorientating amber light of a thickening snowstorm. Then, with the dark shadow of a hedge as my only guide, why I set about blindly tracing a path along the ridge top until yards felt like miles. And why now, nearly an hour later, I was standing cold and painfully breathless while the wind carved white spirals around me, dispassionately staring. At a dead man.

He was sitting unnaturally slumped and motionless in the lee of an old dry-stone wall and with wind-driven drifts already beginning to claim his silent body, he was rapidly becoming nothing more than a misshapen extension to the shade. If I had been any later I might never have seen him at all. Everything about him was adding weight to the appearance of habitual vagrancy and where his head had sunk down onto his chest, I found that I could see very little of his face beneath the tattered and filthy remains of a scarf that may once have been patterned. His stained coat had a gaping tear to the seam of one sleeve and, lying half-propped against the hard frozen support of the tumbled stones, he had one hand jammed into the buttons near his chest, presumably in a useless quest for warmth. The other, just visible as white lifeless fingers within the swathes of a fraying cuff, had slipped from his lap to rest among the exposed stones by his side. It seemed to me that he must have made that same cruel mistake experienced by many other homeless people before and, having failed to beg his way into the cover of a dry barn and a hot meal, had chosen to pause and catch his breath for a while in the comparative shelter of this old stone wall. And then, with energy and resources at their lowest ebb, he must simply have, tragically but inevitably, expired.

So it came as a surprise when the pale frozen hand suddenly tightened gruesomely upon the rock by his side to thrust him awkwardly to his feet.

I had been creeping closer with that macabre curiosity of one who needs to at least be sure before turning for home so it only took one staggering plunge forwards in a search for balance for him to crash blindly into me. I gave a yelp, mainly at finding a corpse becoming suddenly very much not a corpse, but he, poor man, found the shock of impact infinitely worse. Meeting someone at all in a whiteout was obviously utterly unexpected, and to find them standing silently and unmoving just above him was quite simply far too much. His strangled cry echoed back off the swirling barrier of icy wind; the momentum, which had carried him so suddenly and forcefully to his feet, made him rebound off me again and he stumbled, flailing backwards until he was brought crashing painfully down once more onto the hard frozen ground.

There was a brief moment of silence while I recovered my balance and my poise and the poor tramp simply lay there. He was as still and as silent as he had been before and I wondered if I really had killed him this time. But then in the next moment I saw him breathe and I was suddenly kneeling in the rubble by his side, putting a reassuring hand on his ragged sleeve and gabbling apologies and explanations like an anxious idiot.

He hadn't moved from his crumpled heap, head concealed in the curve of his arm and a liberal dusting of windblown snow. In fact, he seemed completely insensible to my jumbled words and I was just mumbling something along the lines of "sorry, sorry. I'm so sorry" when all of a sudden he moved again. As before it was entirely unexpected and again he made me yelp and flinch away but this time, instead of plunging to his feet, he twisted round onto his back and took hold of the hand that had been steadily giving his shoulder a little shake.

For a man on the edge of existence his grip was surprisingly firm but what was more startling was the speed with which he snatched aside my other hand. It had instinctively reached to push at his chest so that I would not topple forwards onto him, I think – not hard, in spite of the sharply muttered exclamation it had drawn from him – and my mind was just beginning to make the first uncertain move from confusion into alarm when all of a sudden, quite simply, it just froze.

The hoarse voice was mumbling something up at me, a garbled torrent attempting to form an angry accusation. It sounded like he was questioning my morality and made absolutely no sense whatsoever, but I was not listening to that. All I could think of was the numbing discovery that this was no strange vagrant.

The man's weary tones were curt and altered, and it had been a long time since I had last heard him speak, either in irritation or in friendship. But regardless, the voice was inexplicably, indisputably familiar – I *knew* him.

In an instant the urge to draw back evaporated. "*Matthew?*"

My enquiry was as hesitant as it was incredulous and it had to be repeated five or six times before my words finally filtered through his rage enough to at least silence his ranting. In defiance of his evidential fury, my voice was astoundingly steady as I persevered:

"Matthew? It's me ... Eleanor."

The dark eyes that were marked and shadowed by the hollow strain of exhaustion wavered for a moment before abruptly focusing to fix upon mine. They were staring at me from behind the tattered mask of the scarf and I could see where the fabric was moving in and out over his mouth to the draw of his rapid breathing.

"Matthew?" I repeated, trying not to give in to the appalling rush of concern that had accompanied that first wild unrecognizing glare. I believe I even tried to smile.

His breathing checked.

Suddenly he moved again. It was with that same uncontrolled urgency that had startled me before. I flinched aside, raising an arm instinctively as he leapt to his feet only to realise even as I did so that he must have let me go. There was a sharp crunch of snow behind me and a rapid scattering of loose flakes. Then, irregular and stumbling, the uneven steps accelerated and diminished.

In an instant and without so much as pausing for thought, I had twisted to my feet. I could still make out the weaving shadow of the departing figure and, racing over to the sulkily waiting pony to snatch up his rope before dragging the reluctant creature after me, I set off again across the field in pursuit of the hurrying man.

Even with the handicap of a stubbornly protesting animal, I was still able to gain on him before we had travelled many yards and as I drew alongside and then began to pass him, it was easy to see why. His head was down as he forced himself onwards and it seemed to me that he was only managing to do so at all by drawing on some last deep reserves that had nothing to do with muscle or physical strength. The tatty scarf had fallen away to expose a grimy unshaven jaw and his breath was coming in short laboured puffs that misted in the air around him before being swept away by the ceaselessly bitter wind. He was clearly floundering but I didn't dare touch him again and he seemed to have no intention of stopping until either snow or exhaustion forced it.

In desperation I dragged the pony round to partially bar his path and cried, "Matthew! You're going the *wrong way!*"

For a moment I thought he might try to break his way past but then, with a short agitated cry that seemed to come from somewhere between impatience and despair, he abruptly stopped and stood before me, swaying gently.

Then he lifted his head once more and where the shadowed eyes stared watchfully out at me from beneath frosted brows, I was startled to realise that his dirtied cheeks were actually streaked with tears.

"You were going the wrong way, Matthew," I repeated gently, by way of an explanation.

There was a very, very long silence when I thought he had not heard. But then, in a voice that was so faint that it almost seemed to be coming from somewhere else entirely, he finally whispered, "The wrong … way?"

The question was vague and flooded with uncomprehending weariness, and it made my heart ache. "My home is that way." My voice was soft and steady like a parent talking to a frightened child and, being careful not to startle him, I lifted a hand in an imprecise indication of its direction.

His gaze wavered briefly as he unwittingly turned to look, not that we could see more than twenty yards from our feet let alone all the way down to the farmhouse. But then his gaze snapped suspiciously back to my face, filled with hard distrust in case I had moved, only for the expression to fade again to guilty abstraction as he remembered who I was.

"Your home?"

"Home," I said firmly and then, in the manner of a casual afterthought, added; "Would you like to come?"

Chapter 2

It was lucky that I had thought to bring the pony; I would never have got Matthew back on my own. It was almost as if in that instant of deciding to accept my help, however reluctantly, all of his remaining strength had been spent and for a few horrible long minutes I had feared that even maintaining a grip on the pony's mane as it towed him steadily along was going to be a demand too far.

If I had thought that task difficult however, getting him to relinquish it for an arm about my shoulders and from there steering him into my house proved even more of a challenge. He had neither spoken nor moved from his hunched position since we had started for home and as I set about tugging him along the path, it became horribly apparent that he must have been wandering about out there for far longer than just a few hours. In truth he was barely conscious and although he was obviously trying to spare me as much as he could, he very nearly crushed me when we finally attempted to coordinate a sort of crabwise shuffle into the house.

Freddy, however, was utterly amazing. The boy had already appeared noisily by my side before I could have possibly expected him and, as soon as Matthew and I had set off on our unsteady way, had whisked the tired pony away to hay and a dry stable, only to rush to the door before we had even made it around the side of the house, still talking ceaselessly. He was there now, ahead of us, pushing the door open and dragging it wide so that we could slowly shuffle our way into the short passage by the kitchen.

Even with the boy's help, the doorway was still very narrow and it took some manoeuvring to ease us both through. I suppose if I had thought, I could have got Freddy to run and open the more impressive – and therefore much wider – front door but as with all farmhouses, the kitchen door was the one that we used on a daily basis and I wasn't even sure if the thick ancient bolts could be drawn back on the other.

It had been my intention to cross the wider space from kitchen to stairs, and from there take Matthew up to a bedroom where he could rest and recover in relative comfort but Matthew himself forced me to swiftly abandon that idea. I had managed to get him this far by taking his right arm heavily across my shoulders while his other groped drunkenly from handhold to handhold but whether it was from the blaze of unaccustomed heat or the unexpected realisation that his ordeal was nearly over I do not know, but all of a sudden his remaining ability to support himself abruptly vanished. Entirely without warning, his fingers fell short from their reach towards the tabletop and then his head drooped. He had already been testing me pretty near to my limit but this sudden collapse took me far beyond tolerance and we were very lucky that I even managed to get him as far as the living room settee, let alone all the way upstairs to my bed.

A peculiar pause followed this where, after my abrupt release from such a heavy burden, the sensation of being airborne was so strange that the force of it nearly finished what Matthew's weight had begun. My face burned from exertion and, added to the heat of the fire at my back, it seemed to take an eternity before my aching lungs could adjust to breathing warm air. But then, in the next instant, normality reasserted itself and I had time to wonder that it was Matthew Croft of all people who had been found lost in a snowstorm. And then to notice almost immediately afterwards that the voluble enthusiasm, which had been an almost constant backdrop to our journey across the kitchen, had faded sharply to silence.

Freddy's delight at his part in an apparently heroic rescue ought to have been inexhaustible; I quickly turned with a smile and encouragement so that the boy would be protected from understanding the full urgency of getting the object of his adventure warm but he wasn't looking at me. Freddy was staring with eyes fixed wide at the man who was sitting slumped before us and blinking blearily at the threadbare carpet by our feet.

I took a steadying breath. "Freddy, will you fetch some of my father's old clothes? We'd better get him into something dry." My voice was bright and carefully filled with that lively tone of artificial cheer that was usually the reserve of matronly housekeepers but I might as well have said nothing for all the notice he took.

"Freddy," I said sharply, "did you hear what I said?"

Then I turned my head and followed his gaze.

Matthew was still sitting exactly where he had landed when I had clumsily surrendered him to the settee except that now he was making an ineffectual attempt at unfastening the buttons of his soaked jacket. Finally able to see it properly, the jacket looked like it was made from a kind of stylish brown wool and would have originally been better suited to a walk through town towards his office than across country in the snow. Whatever it had once been however, now it was only disgustingly grimy and the torn seam on his sleeve that had been noted before had since parted even further so that it was now exposing a large expanse of lining.

I suppose it was because of this obvious damage to one shoulder that I had not noticed what had happened to the other.

The stain had spread from his collar down towards the elbow of his left sleeve and it was entirely different to the multitude of scuffs and scrapes of mud and filth that coloured the fabric elsewhere.

"Here, let me." The quickly delivered request was tinged with disbelief as I leant down and reached for the sodden jacket.

His numbed fingers surrendered the task of fumbling with the buttons readily enough and then in a few short seconds I was pulling the icy flaps apart.

"Oh, good God."

Blood had soaked through the shirt onto his woollen jumper and from there spread in an ugly stain across his chest, and it was very clear to me now that there could be no ordinary explanation for what I had found out in the snow.

"Good God, Matthew!" I said again. "What has happened to you?"

He looked up at that and gave me a faintly blurry smile. "Pay no man, isn't that what they say? No, hang on, that isn't it – what's the saying ...?" He was speaking with the careful enunciation of one who was not in nearly as much control of himself as he would have liked to have been. He blinked and then added, "Ah yes, owe no man. But that isn't fair; I don't think he can have meant for it to turn out like that ..."

Then his expression clouded as if he knew he was wandering and, with an obvious effort, he bit off whatever else might have followed.

Freddy must have moved behind my shoulder because Matthew's eyes suddenly snapped past me. He stared up at the boy for a moment, the heavily shadowed eyes widening in alarm before travelling jerkily back to my face. Then, with a blur of movement that was startlingly reminiscent of the precision I had seen out in the snow, he reached out and took a tight hold of my hand.

"Don't tell them." His voice rose anxiously as the draw on my arm forced me to bend awkwardly down towards him. "You won't tell them about me, will you? Please?"

I shook my head, trying to discreetly prise my wrist free only to feel a cold stab of apprehension as he begged again, "*Please!*"

"I won't, Matthew," I said, not really knowing to what I was promising.

He gave me one long hard look and seemed to believe me.

11

Releasing my hand, he blinked from me to Freddy and back to me again. Then, letting out his breath in a long gentle sigh, he slowly and with about as much grace as a bad actor playing a part, crumpled backwards onto the soft panels of the settee.

I stared down at his prone form for a moment before my brain clicked into gear.

"Right Freddy," I said crisply. "Fetch my scissors, the medical kit – the horse one I mean, we're going to need more than plasters – and some blankets. I'll get some water on the boil."

Freddy looked at me with big scared eyes. "Is he dead?" he whispered.

"No Freddy, he's not," I said firmly. "Now off you go, quickly please!"

When the boy had finished that little task, I would strategically send him on another lengthier errand, this time to the hay barn.

If I had been determined to protect Freddy from further shock and the subsequent bad dreams, I only wish I could have extended the same courtesy to myself. Patching up the various wounds that the horses have presented over the years may have trained me in all the practical skills, but nothing could have prepared me for the emotional horror of having to cut away his shirt and examine the twelve or so shotgun pellet wounds that had splattered across his upper arm and chest. None of them had gone deep, he must have been hit at the very edge of the gun's range, but blood still oozed sickeningly from the wounds as I carefully eased the pellets free.

Blessedly, he was still unconscious as I dressed the wounds with iodine solution and gauze; it seemed to take forever to strap it all firmly into place with the thick rolls of bandage when I had to deal with the leaden weight of his body on my own. But then at long last it was finished and I could place bandages, wounds and everything safely out of sight under the great stack of blankets which would slowly but surely bring him back to vital warmth, and pause a while to gather my thoughts.

Many hours later though, and after all that bustle and urgency it was suddenly feeling very much like I was being given rather too much time in which to think. Freddy had been fed and dispatched off to bed long ago and with the wind outside picking up little gusts of ice and sending them in a distant rattle against the glass, I was actually for the first time in my life finding the house slightly eerie. The rhythmic hiss and creak of the door beneath the stairs made it sound like I was catching the stealthy betrayal of someone's passing footsteps and with very little else to do now but sit and wait, I found myself wishing very fervently that the back room was not so draughty and my imagination not quite so alive.

Like our water supply, this little corner of the Cotswolds had never been connected to mains electricity either, so the room was merely lit by the inky amber of an oil lamp and the formerly companionable glow of the hearth. This scene was not unique to my household; on the assumption that others were keeping the same late hours, and hopefully for considerably more ordinary reasons than mine, their homes too must be chasing away the shadows with mild lamp light. Across the country, main roads and railways were closed by impossibly deep drifts and after a month when only a few coal trains had managed to reach the power stations, urban homes and even the factories that had managed to labour for years under the most fearsome bombardment had no choice now but to at long last fall silent. Here was another reminder that the weather had the power to do what the war had not.

Admittedly, I could not exactly claim this particular shortage for myself or my little rural farmstead, having never had any electric heaters, refrigerators or lighting to worry about. But at this precise moment the background hum from a little domestic machinery might well have made all the difference to the windblown whispers which were presently stalking me across the room.

Matthew's head moved on the arm of the settee and I tensed, thinking that he was awake, but his eyes remained closed. His sleep must have been punctuated by nightmares because every once in a while his breathing would jerk and catch in his throat, and occasionally I caught the low murmur of words uttered in an agitated undertone, but he said nothing I could make any sense of. I put the back of my hand lightly to his forehead; it was warm but not alarmingly hot.

I sat back in my chair and settled to watch as he slept. It was strange to find myself so unexpectedly maintaining this late night vigil over a man I had not seen for years, and who now lay restlessly sleeping on my settee. Earlier, my confusion had fixed itself upon flimsy theories of wandering too far in deteriorating weather, but it was impossible to continue this pretence, especially when I remembered that even in a whiteout Matthew would have known these fields and byways as well as I did, if not better.

He stirred again, uneasily. The features of his face were being drawn into sharp relief by the sooty smear of light from the lamp behind me and beneath the tangle of sandy hair which had been thick with dirt and burrs, I could see scratches on his cheek that were days old. His chest was marked by a darkening smudge of fresh bruises and earlier, while I had been dressing his shoulder, I had noted that there were scars too, a jagged series of lines running lightly across his ribs, whitened with age, which must have been from the war.

I shivered suddenly in spite of the fierce heat from the nearby fire and, tucking my legs up under myself, I turned my head aside to fix instead upon the shredded remains of clothing which were laid out on the hearth beside me. Most would be burnt as soon as they were dry enough and only his boots and trousers had been cleaned and hung out with more care. Torn and battered though they were, I suspected he would be too tall for my father's old clothes and with no hope of getting more from elsewhere, I could not possibly discard them.

His breathing changed and I did not need to see the eyelashes flutter on his cheek to know that he was awake. Silently, I slipped across to the fireside hotplate where I had set some broth to warm and, tipping some into a bowl, I slowly turned back to face him once more. His eyes were glinting in the firelight, following me as I carefully drifted closer. Although they ought to have been a dark hazel with flecks of deeper brown, under the light fever of exhaustion they were paler, almost amber.

"Are you hungry?" I asked. He didn't answer and just lay there, staring at me.

"Come on, let's get some of this into you," I said brightly and, firmly ignoring the foolishness that tried to make me clumsy, knelt by the settee before helping him to spoon some of the warming liquid into his mouth.

For a little while he gulped it down hungrily but then, unexpectedly and with surprising force, he pushed my hand away as if the thin meal suddenly disgusted him. He must have noticed my flinch because he quickly apologised.

"Thank you," he said softly, allowing his head to fall back onto the cushions. His voice was weak and quiet as though the effort of speaking was almost too much for him but I was relieved to note that there was more colour in his pallid cheeks.

"Don't mention it," I replied lightly.

He shut his eyes, "I'll be on my way again in the morning."

"I'm sure you will." He looked like the idea of even sitting up was beyond him.

He gave me a little smile, eyes still closed, and suddenly looked more like the man I knew.

"How did this happen to you?" I asked gently as I climbed to my feet. When I looked back, he was staring at me with an expression strongly reminiscent of the one I had first seen in the snow, but I was determined not to let the opportunity pass this time. "Who did this to you, Matthew?"

His head moved awkwardly on the arm of the chair and I thought for a moment he was going to try to get up. "I don't … I can't seem to remember," he whispered helplessly.

"It's all right," I said quickly, guiltily covering the rush of concern

15

that filled me. "It'll keep until morning I'm sure."

"You won't tell them I'm here, will you?" His fingers clutched at the blankets and my heart tightened painfully as that same hunted expression beat a return to his pale haggard face.

"I won't tell them, Matthew. Don't worry."

"He ... I didn't mean to ... They're ..." He spoke agitatedly, seeming to be talking more to himself than to me, and I stepped back as he tried to sit up, feeling suddenly nervous as that wild urge to bolt altered his eyes again. His strength failed him however, and slowly he sank back down onto the settee, looking grey and utterly exhausted.

After a while he seemed to fall helplessly into an unmoving slumber and finally I was able to unclench my fingers from the bowl enough to set it down on the kitchen table. His agitation disturbed me and as I gazed down at his averted face from the comparative distance of the other end of the settee, I wondered just what sort of explanation I was expecting him to give, when the morning came.

Would he even be glad when he finally regained his senses, to discover that it was me that had patched and bathed his wounds? So far his reactions had ranged from gentle recognition to horrified aversion, and I really wasn't sure which emotion I could expect to prevail when daylight and lucid reasoning made their return at last.

"Oh, stop it," I muttered to myself, crossly avoiding working this up into a larger complication than it deserved. There were, I was sure, any number of more pressing concerns in the mind of a man who had very nearly died than whether or not the person that had helped him was feeling suitably thanked.

Armed with this fresh conviction, I slipped silently back to my station in the armchair and prepared to watch once more. I was just beginning to doze myself when he spoke again;

"What is your name? I've forgotten it, I'm sorry." His head moved on the cushion as he tried to twist round to look at me but his shoulder must have hurt him because he gave a short hiss of pain before allowing his head to fall back again.

"Eleanor," I said softly from my armchair.

"Oh." There was a long pause and I thought that he had fallen asleep but then he added, "I knew an Eleanor once, but that was a long time ago; before I went away."

I said nothing and just watched the fire as it flickered gently in the grate.

"She was a lot like you, but younger. And possibly a little shorter, although that could just be because you're thinner than she was." His voice was faint as he mumbled dozily and I realised that he didn't know where he was. "Her father died you know. I meant to write and tell her how sorry I was but somehow I just couldn't find the words."

There was another long pause and then I saw his body tauten. "I'm not making sense, am I, Eleanor?"

"You're fine," I replied soothingly. "Just go to sleep."

For a while I thought he had, but then in a stronger voice he asked, "What did he die of?" He turned his head to look at me and I saw that this time he knew who I was.

"Something with a long unpronounceable name, but basically it was his breathing again," I said quietly. "He lasted a long time, much longer than the doctors said he could. But he went peacefully, and at least it wasn't a shock."

"And you nursed him to the end." It was a statement, not a question.

"Yes," I said quietly.

"No wonder you look so …" He stopped.

"So what exactly? My weather-beaten exterior is confusing you," I supplied lightly.

I think he might have even given a faint chuckle, "I was going to say careworn, but weather-beaten will do."

For some unfathomable reason, given that I had started it, his evident amusement irritated me and I really didn't want to think about why. "Go to sleep." I spoke firmly.

"Yes ma'am," he said with a faint hint of the wry humour that had once so typified him. He didn't speak again.

Chapter 3

After a night of dozing fitfully in the armchair, it was hard to gingerly ease my aching joints out of their cramped position, but he was sleeping more soundly now and finally I dared leave him long enough to go about my morning chores.

Yesterday's fresh bout of snow had not ceased with the dawn and it was still falling thickly on the yard. It had long since filled in the areas I had laboriously cleared a few days previously and the barbed wind was picking it up, tossing it about so that flakes curled around me in little flurries as I sleepily scrunched my way across to the stables. The inmates must have only managed about two hours of escape before the weather had put an end to their liberty once more but judging by the chorus of whickering that met me as soon as I began rattling about in the feed bins, they were all contented enough with their return to confinement, particularly when it meant they got breakfast.

Leaving my assortment of horses and ponies happily munching their meal, I trudged with a relative contentment of my own across the yard and ducked into the goat house. This odd little building had probably had a previous incarnation as a bull house back in the days when this had been a dairy farm, but now it was simply a rough tin roof set on thick stone walls with a small improvised pen area so that they could exercise when the weather was better.

Three cheerful faces greeted me before trotting eagerly over the rough cobbled floor of their house to perform a little boisterous tap-dance about my feet as I tipped out their feed. Laughing, I swept up the small amount of mess they had made and then fetched a milk pail while they ate. Myrtle was a good goat and very docile, and she did not even pause in her steady chewing as I relieved her of her burden of milk. If I had time, I would make butter later.

There was just one animal in my collection that did not inspire quite the same degree of affection and this was the cockerel. He, being a very brave sort of creature, had a habit of feigning indifference until the very moment that my back was turned only to then, with a flurry of feathers, make a wild dive for my ankles. It was always a remarkable coincidence how as soon as I turned back again, he would be intently pecking at the dirt as if nothing had happened. Today, however, he must have wisely read that confrontation would rapidly lead to a close encounter with a cooking pot and as I carefully carried the precious milk back to the chilly gloom of the dairy, he chose to simply fix his beady eye upon me in a disdainful glare before losing all of his sophistication and joining the girls in a frenzied pecking of the kitchen scraps from their feeder.

Freddy was up and making a pot of tea when I reappeared in the kitchen, kicking the snow off my boots and trying to breathe some warmth back into my hands. He looked sleepy but nothing compared to how shattered I felt.

"Eggs for breakfast?" I asked only to smile as he nodded enthusiastically. Clearly there was no need to worry that the upset of the previous day's events would have affected his appetite. "All right then, what sort? Fried, poached, scrambled or boiled? We've got a bit of bread left from yesterday for toast."

Freddy thought for a moment. "Scrambled, I think."

"Right, scrambled it is." I cheerfully returned his grin and it almost seemed for a moment that we could forget the other silent presence in my home. My memories of the past day seemed so unlikely now that it felt as if I had simply experienced an exceptionally bad night with an exceptionally bad dream, and had it not been for the long absent figure from my past currently deeply asleep on my settee, I would not have been able to convince myself that any of it had really happened at all.

Freddy set the table and poured the tea while I juggled eggs and toast, which respectively tried to weld themselves to the pan or spontaneously combust. Finally, however, we were able to sit down and eat and, despite a certain hint of carbon, it was delicious. It was a relief to feel little warming tendrils of energy begin at long last to make their return to my weary limbs.

"Do you think I could have some of that?"

A faint voice from the fireside made us both jump. Feeling strangely guilty again, I looked over to see that Matthew had managed to shuffle himself up to be sitting propped against the arm of the settee. His face was deathly pale and with his dishevelled hair and the scruffs and scrapes on his skin he could still have convincingly passed as a vagrant, and not, as he actually was, a reasonably well-to-do local man. But although his cheeks were sunken and he looked very fragile under the scruffy fuzz of growth on his jaw, the eyes that were cautiously smiling at me from beneath the mask of pain and weariness were calm and disconcertingly familiar, and it was hard to believe now that he was the same person that had been found stumbling about in that blind manner across my land.

He gave me a warmer smile as I abandoned my breakfast to pour him a cup of tea, putting several spoonfuls of sugar in it to help him regain his strength. I was feeling an odd sensation that could best be described as cheerful uncertainty as I approached to hand him the cup and I was relieved to find that I was able to greet him quite easily after all; only to ruin the effect by flinching stupidly as his fingers accidentally pressed over mine. He blinked in surprise, but said nothing.

"What do you want to eat?" I asked, more sharply than I

21

intended.

"Toast?" he said hopefully.

His quick grin was so easy and relaxed that the momentary tension evaporated abruptly, and I couldn't help breaking into a smile myself as I dragged a table over to him and set a plate down by his side. It was a relief to have him so swiftly establish the tenor of our renewed acquaintance, and still more of a relief to see him reach eagerly for the toast. I had feared that his wounds allied with the extreme exhaustion would have brought on a fever but he seemed well enough, or at least not in any great danger.

He managed to eat most of the plain breakfast before grimacing suddenly and thrusting the plate rather quickly back onto the table. In an attempt to suppress the urge to fuss, I had been trying to concentrate on the remains of my own meal but I heard his pained sigh as he settled back against the arm once more, and I could not help watching as he tucked the blankets up under his chin to cover his bandaged chest in what was a very telling mark of vulnerability.

He unexpectedly looked up to catch me staring and I felt myself jump again, flushing as I quickly looked away. It was impossible to know what to say, particularly when I had to wrestle with an overwhelming impulse to gabble idiotic nothings at him, but he must have misunderstood my meaning because I heard him draw a little breath before saying rather hurriedly, "I'm sorry to put upon you like this. It's very good of you to have taken me in."

I did look up at him then, shyness instantly being replaced by a sort of offended irritation as I wondered exactly what else he would have expected me to do. My mouth curled into a brief impression of a smile.

"What actually has happened to you?"

It came out like an accusation and even I was appalled by my own lack of grace. My thoughts might well have been occupied by very little else for the past day but even so, I had still intended to start by asking him how he was feeling or by making one of the

22

many other commonplace social niceties that might have done in the present situation. I certainly had never meant to fling his experience at him quite like this.

Equally certainly, he hadn't been expecting it either. He glanced quickly from me to Freddy and the gentle grin that had appeared in response to mine darkened abruptly to that same unspeakable tension that was so unlike him.

"I ... er ..." he began and then stopped. I waited but he didn't continue.

"Look, you don't need to tell me anything if you don't want to," I said hastily as my embarrassment increased. "It doesn't matter, but it might help if I understand a little of what's been happening. Just a very little ...?"

"Eleanor ... I ... I don't think that I should ... You ..." He faltered.

My intense shame clouded to puzzlement then. The contractions of his mouth had already betrayed the pattern of his emotions from surprise through to discomfort and onwards, not entirely unreasonably, to impatience. But in this last awkward hesitation, I thought I saw another expression flicker briefly across his face. It was so swiftly suppressed that it barely registered, but just for a moment, only a brief fleeting instant, I thought I saw guilt.

I watched him run a hand over his face and it shook a little. He tried again, "It's difficult. You're ..."

Then his eyes flicked up to catch mine, crucially, before dropping quickly away again.

"Oh," I said with that odd note of sharpness back in my voice. It could not have been made plainer if he had tried. "Of course. You can't tell *me*."

He didn't contradict me.

"Right," I said in a strangled croak and ignored the pathetically appeasing smile he attempted.

It was a shock to be so emphatically rebuffed. I know that I had been half expecting something like this but somehow the wise thoughts of three o'clock in the morning were no consolation now that it was daylight and he very clearly had not lost his mind.

I turned abruptly away to crash the breakfast things into the sink, setting about scrubbing the dishes as if the boiling water from the pan on the stove could cleanse me of the strain of his unwelcome presence. After all the worry I had expended in the night on his behalf, I had thought that, at the very least, he would owe me a little basic honesty. But instead it appeared that I was to be roughly abandoned to the thin logic of my imagination, understanding nothing except the very bitter sting of his rejection. And knowing all the while that it ought to have been for me to shun *him*.

Apparently, however, this last little truth was not allowed to matter. Instead, infuriatingly trapped within a straitjacket of compassion, I could do little else but maintain an icy silence while the day passed into a blur of keeping him fed, keeping him warm, making him tea; providing, in fact, any one of the many little things that were essential to his ongoing comfort and recovery. He didn't even seem to register the insult contained within his unthinking acceptance of my continued care.

It might have been a little easier if I could have continued my chores in some other room. Unfortunately, however, there were no fires laid in any other part of the house and while I could still remember a time when there had been a wall between kitchen and living room, my father had removed it years ago so that my mother could have one of the new Calor gas stoves that were suddenly all the rage. Her lively presence and divine cooking had left us for higher things in my early teens but the gas oven still lived on and the only boundary that could separate me now from the presence on my settee was the thin join between the red-tinted tiles in the kitchen and the fraying carpet of the living room floor.

For his part, Matthew, in his brief moments of full wakefulness seemed fixed upon giving me glimpses of that same bright meaningless smile which had irritated me before. This was apparently an attempt to conceal the darker moments of being caught looking broodingly thoughtful and intensely fierce but the improbability of a civilised man such as him even bearing such an expression was unsettling enough.

Added to his continued silence, this obvious secrecy was actually making my own show of frosty distance seem absurdly irrelevant and with the acknowledged flaw in my living arrangements to deal with as well, I was forced in the end to spend the rest of the day attempting to take myself as far away from him as possible. In weather such as ours, however, there was only so long that I could bear it and by about eight o'clock I was shattered, slumping defeated in the armchair by the fire, unable to pretend any longer that I was anything but utterly wearied of this act. I would have dearly liked to have abandoned it, but the only thing I could think of was to scream at Matthew to explain what had happened to him. But he had already made it clear that he had no intention of letting me understand anything about his business and so I held my tongue, and kept my stare fixed upon the crackling flames.

"Eleanor?"

"Um?" I responded sleepily, blinking myself out of my stupor.

"You didn't get a doctor, did you? Last night I mean." Matthew had turned slightly awkwardly against the arm of his settee to look back at me.

"Er ...?" My brain was struggling to get into gear.

"These bandages," he gestured to his chest, "did you fetch someone to do them?"

I glowered at him, "No, Matthew, I didn't. It was snowing in case you've forgotten and we're cut off again for the moment; I did them with my own fair hands. I'm sorry if they're not up to scratch."

"No, no," he corrected hastily, "they're very good." He paused, "So no one knows I'm here?"

"No, Matthew, no one knows you're here," I said tiredly, concealing the shiver as I realised that his fears had not just been a symptom of his confused ramblings in the night.

I climbed stiffly to my feet without looking at him, concentrating instead on straightening the cushions of my chair; "Do you want anything else? Only I'm going to bed now."

"No, nothing, thank you," he said, but then, as I opened the door to the stairs, added; "Eleanor?"

"Yes?" I demanded curtly.

"Just …" A pause. "Thank you," he finished gently.

As if to compound my exhausted frustration, the handle to my bedroom door decided this was the ideal moment to come off in my hand. Crossly, I slapped it down on the dresser and as I bent to wedge the door shut with a small pile of books, I had to wonder whether the house had it in for me too.

Very wearily, I peeled off the five or so layers of clothing that were my defence against winter. My fingers were stiff as I fumbled with the buttons and then, as I gave in and drew the shirt off over my head, I suddenly realised that my wrists were aching with far more than just tiredness.

I looked down and it was with a kind of fascinated horror that I observed dark marks encircling each one. They were ugly and tender and I had to spend some minutes just sitting on the edge of my bed. Somehow in the preoccupation of being offended by his determined silence, the whole shocking truth of my discovery out in the snow had faded in my memory to become nothing more than a product of my uneasy imagination. But the bruises were indisputable and, allied with his refusal to make any kind of explanation, I found that as I finally slipped into bed, I was actually trembling.

Chapter 4

His late night comments on my altered appearance had been right; I was slimmer now. I had been a softly rounded teen but the subsequent years of hard physical work made worse by the deprivations of the war had stripped my body down to lean muscle that I suspected was rather boyish, and sadly no amount of dreaming would allow me to pretend that I had magically transformed my baby fat into a model-like elegance. I supposed that I still had hips somewhere, but they were so well hidden by handmade trousers and the loose folds of my thick winter jumpers that I would have been hard pushed to prove it.

Reassuringly, the bruises appeared less substantial in the light of day and as I quietly slipped down the stairs to the familiar sounds of a windswept world dawning to thick snow, I noticed that, like the marks, the concerns which had haunted my night had since faded to become a more reasonable judgement with the morning. So much so in fact, that upon opening the living room door to the predictable discovery that I still had a houseguest, I believe I simply felt a vague sense of relief that the telltale smudges were harmlessly out of sight. They were well concealed by the thick rolls of excess wool at my wrists – this was one of the better results of wearing hand-me-down clothing – and at least now I could be sure that not only would Freddy not see the marks and upset himself, but, almost as importantly, I would avoid the unhappy experience of provoking belated attention from *him*.

Not that there was presently very much danger of anybody being provoked into anything, whether admissions or otherwise. Matthew was asleep.

He was still lying on my settee, his feet hanging off the end in sleeping disarray, and as I drifted silently past the back of his chair, it was impossible not to give in to the daring burst of curiosity that prompted me to pause and examine him.

His mouth was hanging slightly open as he breathed steadily and his relaxed features had softened through sleep to a gentle harmlessness that was a world away from the waking man who showed the taut pallor of exhaustion and a stark tension in every gesture. His expressive face, although currently drawn and rather grey, held a defined structure and pleasing jaw that were undeniably engaging and beneath the disguise of stubble and vagrancy, he still possessed something of his old appeal. Infuriatingly, he did not seem to have had the good grace to prove that my youthful attraction had been nothing more than a figment of my romantic imagination and for a moment I found that, where his short sandy hair was ruffled by vulnerable sleep, I actually had to resist the urge to stroke it back into place.

He moved, only a brief dreaming shift of his cheek on its cushion, but it sharply reawakened me to an unpleasant fluttering of doubts and apprehension as he settled once more, perfectly unaware of my interested scrutiny.

He was thinner than he should have been, much thinner than a few days of this unexplained drama could justify and it both worried and frustrated me that I knew nothing about what might have happened to make him become like this. The shock of his injuries might well serve as a justification for his present loss of charm – not that his charm could still have any effect on me anyway – but even so it didn't seem sufficient to explain how he had altered in the years since we had last met to become tougher and far more remote than even I would have expected. What had changed in him; what wartime tragedy had turned the gentle young man of my teens into this ... this lean stranger?

I sighed inwardly and moved to step away but as I turned, something stirred in the folds of the blanket. Transfixed, I watched as a dark shape moved languorously and separated itself from the shadows.

Meow it said, before lithely leaping over the back of the settee and dashing across the kitchen floor into the small dairy and its shadowy corners beyond. My hand went to my throat in a classic pose of shock and I felt a powerful wave of hysterical laughter rise within me. A cat! Of all the things I had imagined being somehow associated with the turmoil in my mind, one of the half-wild farm cats was not what I had expected. It had obviously sneaked in to seek warmth in the night and I wondered if I was going a little strange myself, given my determination to live like a character from a horror story.

Shaking my head and silently berating myself, I lit the stove and put the kettle on. There was a great pile of washed crockery on the drainer and I tried to put it away quietly so that it wouldn't wake the sleeping man. I would, I knew, have to re-dress his wounds today – it really ought to have been done yesterday – and so a certain level of interaction was inescapable, but if I could just manage to get breakfast out of the way without having to speak to him, I would be a very happy woman.

"Good morning."

I gave a startled squeak and nearly dropped the cups and sugar bowl onto the sideboard. Hastily collecting them together again and feeling strangely like I had been caught in the middle of a guilty act, I took a deep breath, and turned.

Clearly a master of stealth given that I had been moving quietly myself, Matthew was standing by the settee, looking pale, tired and wearing nothing but the tattered trousers that had been drying in front of the fire and the bandages across his chest. To my immense relief, he looked calm and perfectly lucid, although slightly annoyed as if it irritated him that in his weakness, he had allowed me to observe him while he lay in unguarded sleep.

Who could be after him, I wondered; what had happened to make even sleeping a risk? I carefully avoided noticing the lean fitness of his stomach and upper arms and instead set my face into a concentrated frown.

"Sit down," I said in a voice that betrayed me by squeaking. I tried again, finally managing to sound much more convincingly detached and stern. "What can I get for you? Tea? Toast?"

Amusement had flickered behind his eyes at my tone but then, as if to mask the brief spark of old familiarity, the faint lift of his mouth swiftly contracted into a flat line; although this might have been from the sudden discomfort as he settled uneasily into a dining chair.

"Some clothes would be nice, then I'll get out of your hair."

"*Really?*" My surprise came out in another squeak that this time I think I managed to successfully conceal as a cough. My delight was palpable, however, and I couldn't help that the powerful sense of release at his announcement of an imminent departure was making me seem suddenly very cheerful.

"Clothes I can do," I said brightly and had to concentrate very hard on not smiling.

I experienced a faint feeling of something like conscience as I laid out breakfast and then climbed the stairs to rummage through my father's things. Dragging out a pile of old jumpers, I went through them until I found one which was relatively unworn and would probably fit Matthew's rather longer arms. He was lucky; there were still a few shirts left too and, pulling out the two that had escaped either the moths or being altered to fit me, I collected them up into a neat little pile and then shoved the drawers shut again. Unusually, the muted click of wood on wood was repeated by a louder, sharper slam of the front door.

As was apparently becoming the norm for me, I instantly gave a guilty start of surprise and very nearly dropped the stack of folded clothes. Somehow I managed to snatch them back again and barely able to believe that he would leave before I had even properly equipped him for the snow, I hurried, with trailing sleeves flapping madly about me, out of my room, across the narrow landing and down into the gloom of the stairs.

And ran straight into Matthew just as he was stealing silently up them.

He put out a hand to steady me. Knocked out of all restraint by relief and the pain of our collision, I drew a shaky breath to laugh and to tell him about it but before I could even speak a word, I found myself being curtly hushed.

His authoritative grip on my arm made me draw breath in a different way as he leaned in to whisper in my ear.

"Someone's here," he hissed. "Get rid of them."

I shot him a foul look to hide my shock at the unpleasantness of both his tone and his closeness. Then, thrusting the clothes carelessly at his chest, I shook off his hand and marched with perfect icy hauteur down to the door at the foot of the stairs. It only occurred to me as I was closing my fingers over the handle that the rough edge to his temper might not have been entirely without cause, depending on what I found on the other side.

There was suddenly every temptation to turn tail and run upstairs to hide with him, and I very nearly did so. But then a woman's muffled voice hallooed through the living room wall and I recognised the invasion for what it was; just another harmless example of that comforting time-honoured custom that country people have of walking straight in and out of other people's houses, usually in time for tea.

I carefully put my face in order, and opened the door.

Mrs Ford was slightly older than I was, married, and took this as an excuse to be a bit superior and a little snooty. For all her airs I liked her though, and with half my mind still centred on

31

my own concerns, I wondered what was worrying her. She was hovering just inside the kitchen and clutching her handbag to her as if her life depended on it, but it seemed highly unlikely that she was the source of the mysterious threat that had the power to send Matthew diving for cover.

That something *was* worrying her, however, was perfectly obvious. I thought she had smiled cheerfully enough when I welcomed her, but she seemed oddly stiff with me as she refused my offer of a cup of tea and now she was hovering awkwardly by the kitchen table with the prudish air of someone who had just swallowed a very bitter lemon. I wondered whether she had caught sight of a half-dressed man disappearing up my stairs.

"What can I do for you, Mrs Ford?" I asked while sneakily trying to clear away the three sets of breakfast things.

"Well," she began hesitantly, still looking uncomfortable. She stood for a moment staring at the pile of well-thumbed books that Freddy had left abandoned on a chair and fiddled with her handbag again. Then she must have caught my curious look because she seemed to give herself a shake before suddenly brightening and eagerly bursting out with; "Have you heard the news? Isn't it too *awful?*"

"What news?" I asked, confused. Surely she hadn't walked all the way from the village in these conditions just to indulge in gossip.

I was automatically making tea anyway, whether she wanted it or not, but then the flimsy webbing that covered the handle of the battered old tin teapot crumbled and fell away as I touched it, and with a silent curse I snatched up a teacloth so that I could pour without scalding my hand.

I glanced back at my visitor in case she had noticed the tatty state of my kitchenware but she didn't seem particularly aware of anything as she flushed with the excitement; "I'm surprised you haven't heard already – it's been all over the wireless."

I didn't bother to mention that I had sold the wireless about six months ago when Freddy's boots had finally got beyond repair.

"What news?" I repeated.

"About that man over at Warren Barn, Old Whatsit's son, you know; the one with the stammer."

"Jamie Donald?" I supplied. Jamie was a seedy-looking man who made a dubious living by doing Lord knows what surrounded by pheasants in the heart of the nearby country estate commonly known as the Park. He had set up home there after the war and didn't seem particularly fond of human company, sometimes, strategically I thought, adopting the offensive slur of the stage alcoholic as I rode past with ponies in tow. I had seen him do it to others too, so it wasn't just me, but for all his oddities, he had given Freddy some honey once so couldn't be all bad.

"Yes, him, that's right. He's only been *murdered!*" No sign of nervousness now, she clearly relished the horror of it. "Nearly five days ago – the poor man was brutally strangled. It's been on the wireless; it would have been in yesterday's newspapers had it not been for the blizzard. Which killed nearly all the sheep on Exmoor. Didn't you know?"

"No, no I didn't." It wasn't entirely clear to me whether she had meant her question to refer to the man or the sheep; not that it mattered anyway because she had swept on regardless.

"Well —" There was a bizarre moment of suspension where I could see her mouth moving so I knew she was speaking but somehow, hard as I tried, I just couldn't comprehend the words. But then, unhappily, my mind cleared of its numbness and I caught the tail end of her excited rush. "… and the police have had dogs out and everything, and Mr Langton from the Manor lent Sir William some men and they found a scent but lost it in the snow. I must say that I always thought he looked a bit sullen but who'd have thought that he was a *murderer*."

"I'm sorry. Who did you say …?" But I didn't need her answer. I already knew.

Matthew Croft.

For a moment it felt as though the world had actually stopped.

Only that was clearly wishful thinking because then it started again, my heart racing painfully in my chest while those last few words resounded in my head with all the gentleness of a death knell.

So this was his terrible secret, the reason for his silence and the cause of his determined exclusion. But…*why?*

I must have spoken this last question out loud because she gave me a funny little smile that was mainly shocked but just a little bit gleeful. "The men that disturbed him at the scene said that they caught him going through poor Jamie's pockets, so the wireless is saying money, but it's my guess that he came back from the war *damaged* … What's the word? Shell-shocked."

I put a trembling hand behind me onto the worktop. My blood was pounding in my ears and I might have staggered but for its solid support. "Oh my God," I finally whispered and carefully eased myself down into a chair.

She was quick with eager sympathy; "It is shocking, isn't it? The police don't know where he is and Sir William is furious. To think a murder could happen on his estate; it really …" There was a crash upstairs and she broke off, looking startled. "What was that?"

"Freddy, I expect," I said hastily, hoping that she wouldn't notice the way my breath was coming in short panicky gasps. The room was spinning with the horror of it; my frustration at his silence seemed utterly idiotic now, particularly when I realised that while he had hinted at danger and pursuit, he had been carefully neglecting to mention that it was, in fact, the *police...*

Mrs Ford was staring at me with wide-eyed alarm, "But I saw Freddy outside with the ponies." She clapped a hand dramatically over her mouth. "Lord, you don't think …?"

"No," I said firmly. "I do not. It was probably just one of the cats."

"But aren't you afraid?"

"Of what?" I asked, almost impatiently. I wasn't really paying attention as my brain fell back yet again into the search for flimsy excuses in the face of this awful discovery. It seemed impossible, every instinct screamed it must be, and yet cruel logic armed with

34

the evidence of what I had found in the snow quietly persisted in forcing the point home. *This* was the mystery he had tried to hide from me? Impossible, my mind said again, forcefully, but then a memory flashed before my eyes of that first meeting, his hands imprisoning mine and his voice becoming nearly unrecognisable as it twisted into crazed unthinking fury.

I blinked quickly and focused on a bit of dirt on the table.

"All alone here," she said in a low whisper. "With *him* on the loose ... Oh I know you've got Freddy," she waved my objections aside, "but what good is that boy going to be against that ... that *monster!*"

"Oh, Mrs Ford, you do dramatise!" A brittle laugh somehow managed to disguise the trembling in my voice. "I can't see why he would come here."

"Can't you? Time was when you two were rather close as I recall."

"But how did you ...?" I stared at her, shaken out of all appearance of calm, but Mrs Ford was so busy being shocked and appalled herself that I don't think she noticed my change of colour. "I mean that was all a long time ago, Mrs Ford. There's nothing between us now. No," I said firmly into her protest, "I really don't think that he would come here, and if he did, why I'd just send him packing again."

I stood up quickly to cover the lie. I wasn't even sure why I had said it. Over the years I had often fantasised about meeting him again and how my poise and cool reserve would prove to be a rebuke of the most powerful kind. Sometimes, fate being cruel, I had suspected that I would only come across him when doing something unbelievably foolish, forcing me to suffer his sharp wit and blush and stumble my way through our meeting as though I were still an embarrassed teen. It seemed insane that this was the way our little story would end.

A sudden remembrance of a past that could only bring me pain made me abruptly wish to change the subject; it was either that or give way to the rising nausea. I picked up the two forgotten

35

teacups from the worktop and set one down in front of her before reclaiming my seat. "Anyway, Mrs Ford. Don't tell me you trudged all this way through the deepest snow yet just to warn me of something nasty hiding in my woodshed?"

She smiled at my feeble joke. "No, dear." She took a breath and slid into a chair opposite me, only to find that it rocked so violently that she had to hastily transfer herself to another. Kindly, she did not mention it. "I've come to ask a favour."

"Yes? What is it?" I asked distractedly as my brain still span in a desperate rejection of reality.

"It's about the pony. Did you hear that my Simon got his arm shot off?"

"I did, I'm sorry about that."

She shrugged my sympathy aside, "Well, many people lost more, so I just thank the Lord he's come back to me. Anyway the truth of it is, he's not able to work so much now, the pension doesn't go far and things need to be a little tighter. Much as Charlie loves that pony, he's just too expensive." She paused, looking at me helplessly before adding, "I've got a little bit put by but he's eating it away."

I hadn't really been listening and was just slowly nodding my sympathy, but then I gave myself a sharp mental shake and finally I realised what it was that she wanted me to do. "Do you want me to take him back?"

I looked over at her properly for the first time and as my brain cleared, I saw with a jolt that her polite words had been a mask for the grim truth. Anyone could see that she had lost weight, her face pinched and drawn as she doubtless sacrificed her meals for the sake of her son. Rationing was all very well and good, but a family still needed money to buy the stuff.

I stood up crisply. "Of course I'll take him back. How much did you pay for him? Can you remember?" I went to the cash tin on the shelf and lifted it down.

"We paid six pounds, but that was a few years ago," she said sadly, fearing what I would say.

"Right. Well, your lad has done wonders with him, so he's definitely worth more now. I'll give you twelve." I took out what was to me a small fortune and handed it to her. "And I need a rider for the smaller ponies; do you think Charlie will come and exercise them for me?"

Mrs Ford folded the notes and slipped them into her purse. "He'd love to, I'm sure. Shall I send the pony up this afternoon?"

"Yes please, Mrs Ford."

She gave her thanks and we made our goodbyes and then, suddenly, I was alone in my kitchen, standing by the bare oak table and staring blankly at the few notes left at the bottom of the tin. My hands were shaking when I finally lifted it back up onto the shelf.

I waited for a while until the trembling passed and then I went and picked up the telephone.

"Ah, hello, Mr Dixon, Eleanor Phillips here. Yes it is rather snowy again, isn't it … I'm calling about my father's car; I've decided to sell it after all, if you're still interested? Sorry? Oh, you know how it is, the ponies always need feeding. I know, selfish of them, isn't it? Tuesday next week will be perfect, see you then."

Chapter 5

"You take charity a bit far, don't you? I thought you loved that car."

I jumped and span round, the silent telephone receiver instantly forgotten in my frozen hand. My father's jumper must have been larger than I thought because it hung off him, accentuating his lean frame.

Matthew was looking pale again, his eyes gleaming darkly against his colourless face and my first thought was that he seemed unnaturally calm as he lingered there, as though his breathing might have been as fast and as light as mine had he not been forcing it back under control by sheer will alone. My second was that he looked like he ought to have been in bed.

I bent to replace the receiver on its cradle. "Feelings change."

He was standing at the foot of the stairs, watching me and leaning with contrived ease against the door frame quite as if he and I did not both know perfectly well that he had been upstairs only a moment before. He made no reply and for an insane moment I thought we were just going to stand there, staring at each other, trying not to breathe.

But then he spoke. "So they do," he said and moved. Not towards me and where instinct made me step back against the hard edge of the fireplace, but towards the settee where he reached for the folded blanket. He examined it for a moment, testing its fibres between finger and thumb before laying it carefully over the arm again. I could see even that simple movement hurt. I waited.

From my little sanctuary against the wall, I waited for him to speak. I waited for the confession that should have come yesterday, or the day before. It wasn't hard to guess that his panicked flight down the stairs had been driven by a desperate impulse to silence my telephone call. The fact that I hadn't been speaking to the police at all hung between us like a thin joke at our expense. It begged the question; why?

At last he turned. But when he looked at me, it was only to give a brief glimmer of an unfriendly smile. "Well then, Eleanor. What now?"

"Now?" I asked weakly.

"Yes. Now."

Still that same air of cold restraint. Rejection wrapped up in a criminal façade of indifference and it had the same impact as a slap across the jaw. I lost my temper; "Go."

Absurdly, I think my decision surprised him. He stood there, staring; a silent shadow of a man barely able to stand without swaying. I ground my teeth. "Get. Out."

Right on cue, the telephone began to ring.

We both started and then turned to stare blankly at its shrill volume. It didn't stop. I cast a swift sideways glance at the man by my settee and reached out an unsteady hand.

"Good morning ...?"

There was an incomprehensible bustle from the operator before a man's voice erupted loudly into my ear:

"So I've caught you at last. Where on earth have you been hiding?"

"*John!*" It came as an indescribable relief to find myself being greeted by nothing more formidable than the well-bred tones of John Langton from the Manor in the village.

I heard his familiar laugh. "And a very good morning to you too, Ellie. I was beginning to get worried when I missed you yesterday

– Freddy said you were wrestling with the animals. Everything is all right up there, I presume, what with this latest burst of lovely weather and all?"

"Fine actually, thanks," I said carefully, determined if I could to contain my delight to within the bounds of normal pleasantries. "How are things with you?" A snatched glance sideways showed me my companion's face and it wasn't so very controlled any more. I could almost feel his ears straining to catch my friend and neighbour's words.

"Fine, fine," John said shortly. "Now Ellie, I imagine you've heard what's happened?"

A tiny pause as reality hit hard. Then, with an impressive air of calm; "Mrs Ford told me about it just now. How is Jamie's sister doing? It sounds awful."

"Oh, she's well enough." The concern was swiftly dismissed. "I'm actually ringing about you. Has *he* contacted you?"

Another silence while I frantically adjusted my thoughts to this new reality. All I could hear was the faint hiss and crackle on the line and the pounding of my own heart.

"Who, Matthew?"

This was it then. I only had to say one word, I only had to speak. "No."

My voice came out as a hoarse croak. I barely managed to say the next over the rushing in my ears; "Should he have?"

The guilty silence that to me seemed to span several lifetimes must have passed by John in the blink of an eye because when he answered, his voice was merely touched by friendly concern:

"Not as such, no, well that is to say, I know he courted you in the past and I can't help worrying that he might have passed your way. For old time's sake, you know? I know you don't like my fussing but it does worry me that you're all alone there. You've got Freddy of course, but I'm not sure what good he'd be able to do ..." He paused before adding, "You *are* all right, aren't you? Croft hasn't turned up?"

40

Oh God, I thought, here we go again.

"That was all a long time ago, John, nearly eight years," I said firmly. My hand was shaking where it fiddled with the telephone wire. "I can't see why you think he would come to me now."

"So you haven't seen him?" he persisted. "Did Mrs Ford tell you what he's done? I saw Jamie's body and it was savage. He'll hang for sure when they catch him."

I shut my eyes as I prepared to lie again, "No, John, I haven't seen him."

"Good. And you'll call me if he does contact you?" He took my agreement as given. "Anyway, on to a more pleasant subject. They're promising a thaw so the weekend's Dance might actually happen. Would you like to go with me?"

"Oh!" I gasped, taken aback. "I hadn't really thought ... I, um ... I'll think about it. Will that do?"

He gave a laugh, "Yes Ellie, that will do. Just don't keep me waiting too long. Bye, and Ellie?"

"Yes, John?"

"Be careful."

I slowly set the telephone back down onto its cradle. I already knew that when I turned, I would look up, straight into the bare furnishings of an empty room.

I didn't sleep much that night. Nor did I find much rest when I did. Outside, the wind had swallowed what footsteps he had left and I saw no sign as I did my usual tour of the barns at evening stables. I wasn't even sure if that should be a relief.

In my father's day, the farm had been full of young hunters who were being backed before being sent off to their wealthy owners to start their careers. We had farmed sheep too on the steep valley fields which stretched down from behind the house. But then the war had come, my father had died and the horses were taken away to other breaking yards or to play their part in the war effort by working the land. Now Freddy and I scraped by on the small rental income that the pasture fields brought, the price of a few ponies at the yearly sales and my rather doubtful skills as a riding instructor for the local village children. I wouldn't like to imply we were poor hapless creatures, and we certainly fared better than many, but even teaching had dwindled for the moment thanks to the weekend's latest turn of incredible weather.

The next day was no better. The morning dawned reluctantly to yet another dreary day; a blackbird was hopping about amongst the chickens who were waiting impatiently beneath the kitchen window for their breakfast. Its breath was misting in the still air and the cockerel looked too cold to crow.

Behind this faintly pathetic scene, a rickety fence marked the limits of my vegetable garden where repeated hoarfrosts had turned earlier snowfalls to stone. Anything left in the ground was guaranteed to have been ruined but there were a few crates of root vegetables stored in the gloom of the small outhouse; provided that they hadn't been destroyed by frost and, of course, I could actually dig them out.

Turning to the stove, I realised that I might need to now. The dish of last night's stew that marked the remains of our meat ration for the week; the dish that should have fed the boy and me for at least another day, was empty. I bolted the kitchen door after that but it didn't do any good. The next morning another stew and the end of my coarse home-baked bread had vanished too.

That night, I gave in. I left the door unlocked, the bread, plate and cutlery ready on the table and a pile of gauze and iodine with instructions to re-dress his wounds.

Chapter 6

Apparently John's hopes of a thaw by the weekend were not quite as foolishly optimistic as I had thought. Slipping out of the house into the faint grey of early morning, I was amazed to see that there seemed to be a promise of a brighter day ahead; the clouds were lifting at the horizon to show a hint of paler grey here and there, and although the breeze had risen again in the night, it actually felt for the first time as though the steady gusting might be carrying with it a very little warmth.

Encouraged, I decided to risk putting the horses out into their paddocks – they certainly wanted the exercise – and I was going to just turf all the animals out and then get on with the day's chores when something about the way Beechnut sighed as I gave her some breakfast made me sneak back inside to collect her tack. My cosy little yard was silent as I clambered on to the chestnut's back from a convenient wall.

Slithering down the submerged streambed towards the deeper isolation of the valley bottom, trees closed around us absorbing everything until all sounds were muffled except for the regular whisper of unshod hooves over deep wintered ground and the soft collapse of snow falling from a height in the distance. A dry stone wall crept alongside; beyond it, a wind cleared field lay dotted with the hulking mushroom-shaped remains of sheep-grazed haystacks.

It was a different scene from the past years that had found me working endlessly to gather in, to plough or to sow alongside a giggling and yet startlingly efficient army of Land Girls. Then the countryside had been full of flare and chatter and an extraordinary riot of colour and it was a stark contrast to the field's present wide acres which seemed very much to have been painted in tones of muted sepia.

But not quite as muted as it had been, perhaps. As I set Beechnut at the steep banks that lined the valley and back towards home, I thought I heard the faint hiss of water meeting snow over the sound of her laboured breathing. The sound faded again as we reached the top but slowly, as we weaved between the vast drifts that glistened madly and lurked like towering sand dunes along the hedgelines, the light whisper became more regular and when we crossed the wide expanse of wind-cleared hilltop, I abruptly and conclusively found myself being met by the cool unexpected kiss of misted rain to the face.

After all the weeks and months, this was, needless to say, quite a startling development and I was still drifting along with my eyes half shut and a lunatic smile on my face when the chestnut suddenly gave a sharp snort and stopped.

Her ears and eyes were fixed acutely upon the route ahead. She felt as though she might try to turn and run at any moment and automatically putting a calming hand on the suddenly taut muscles of her neck, I peered intently about us trying to make out what she had spotted. An unpleasant recollection was flitting through my mind of one lone man and our last encounter on this hilltop, and I wondered for a moment whether, as my horse watched him, he was likewise watching me.

But then, after a painfully tense pause while I still tried and failed to identify what could possibly have alarmed my brave little mare, I saw movement in the distance.

"Oh my God," I sobbed and urged her forwards into canter.

I arrived back with an angry flurry of hooves to find the yard full of men and dogs. They appeared to be milling about in some disorder and as one they turned to stare when we burst onto the yard in a sweating streaming mess.

"What the hell do you think you're doing?!"

The horse was brought to a slithering halt just inside the gateway. She was plunging and threatening to kick out but the men simply stood there, barring my way and gawping stupidly. Their blank silence was intensely infuriating and, urging the stamping horse forwards once more, I used her as a weapon to force a path through them and retake possession of my yard.

Amazingly, the men parted like obedient cattle. Seizing my advantage, I wheeled the wild-eyed horse about:

"Get out of my yard this instant!"

My low growl was swallowed by the mizzle and banks of hulking snow, and it looked for a moment like they might argue, but a half rear from Beechnut sent them scuttling for the gate. If I was livid, she was raging; she was fighting my hand for control of the rein and much as I valued the effect she was creating, self-preservation made me hastily throw myself down from her back before she could rear again.

Dragging the saddle from her back, I shoved her into a stable where she proceeded to vent her fury on the wall. Then, pretending to be oblivious to the racket behind me, I marched up to the assembled men, stood squarely before them and barked my question:

"Will one of you kindly explain just what exactly you think you are doing on my yard?"

This time the full force of my anger carried into every corner and it was followed by an uncomfortable silence as each man hoped someone else was in charge. Finally, however, one cleared his throat;

"We're on the hunt for Croft, Miss. They reckon he must have gone to ground after all this fresh snow."

Another chipped in with a revoltingly ingratiating tone, "It's all official, Miss. We're helping the police."

This brought a murmur of agreement from the others.

"Are you?" I said acidly. "And that gives you the right to come without permission on to my yard where there is valuable live-stock, does it?"

"We've got to search every farm. Mr Langton said so."

This man's tone was considerably less deferential and I suspected that now that their alarm had abated, my abrasive attitude was making them feel significantly more self-righteous by the moment.

"Oh, he did, did he?" There was a crash behind me as Beechnut started on her door. "And where is *Mister* Langton?"

"In the house ... Miss." This last was hastily added as I glowered.

Sweet heaven, were there traces of his burnt dressings in the ashes?

To the men I said crisply; "Right then. I'd better go and see Mr Langton, hadn't I? In the mean time you may search the barns, but stay clear of the stables and you are not to bring your dogs. I will not have my animals distressed. Do you understand?"

Oh Eleanor, you really are a fool.

I stood there, glaring, as the men sullenly handed their dogs over to a spotty youth and then set about poking into the various corners of my barns. I was thankful to see that they were reluctant to go into the darker niches and when they began half-heartedly probing the haystack, I finally found enough resolve to march away across the roadway and towards my house.

I hardly even knew whether I was doing the right thing in leaving them unattended, and once inside my uncertainty increased horribly when I found only Freddy making a cup of tea for a very relaxed-looking visitor. John was, in fact, looking perfectly at his ease; he was sitting in my kitchen, fiddling idly with a scuff on the well-worn tabletop and apparently totally unaware that Freddy's hands were shaking as they set down the milk jug for his tea – although given that they always shook in John's faintly intimidating presence, this oversight was not perhaps entirely unreasonable.

I, however, was not so oblivious and I couldn't help the questioning look as Freddy thrust a steaming cup at the table and fled silently past me for the door. But thankfully John barely registered the tea or the boy's hasty departure as he politely rose to his feet to welcome me.

I cut curtly across his friendly greeting. "What are all those dogs doing on my yard, John? They're upsetting my animals!"

Settling back in his chair, John simply smiled his warm lazy smile and I had to fight very hard to resist the urge to throw something at him. He was a handsome man and with his blue eyes, dark hair and active sense of humour that sometimes strayed into the roguish he had never lacked admirers, but despite our childhood closeness, or probably because of it, there had never been a hint of anything between us. It was a great relief to me to have a friendly influence in my life who did not seem to have his own personal agenda, and I wondered if he knew how much I appreciated it. Although, of course, just at this precise moment, any particular sense of this long-standing affection was being rather coloured by the shock of finding him in my apparently empty-of-fugitives kitchen.

I noticed then, with that abstraction of thought that sometimes follows a fright, that he must first have sat in the broken chair because it was now resting at a rather jaunty angle against the table, but thankfully he had the good grace to say nothing. Instead he said, with perfect dignity in the face of my agitation:

"Ellie, surely you know we're helping the police to hunt for Croft? That damned man has been on the run for days and it's time we caught him – and if it means searching all the farms in the area, then nothing and no one will stop me from doing it."

"I want to see justice done as much as anyone," I said waspishly, silently congratulating myself on not needing to lie, "but I fail to see how you think this is helping! I've got horses out there going mad in their stables because of your men and their dogs. They

47

were on my yard without permission!"

"But you weren't here, Ellie. And we *are* helping the police."

"I dare say you are," I snapped. Then I wondered suddenly if Freddy was still nearby and could hear us, and so lowered my voice. "But you are *not* the police, and I suspect do not have a warrant. Therefore your men were trespassing. I've allowed them to search the barns this time, John, but I have to say that I am not very happy about being thrust into the thick of this ... this *lynch* mob."

I stopped to collect myself and realised with a painful kick to the heart that he was looking at me curiously. Then his mouth formed a sympathetic smile,

"Lynch mob? I hardly think so, Ellie, dear. If the law chooses to hang him, that's their business; you can't possibly think it is a wish of mine." But then the smile faded and he added slowly. "You're being very defensive. Are you all right? He's not been harassing you, has he? You seem very uptight and I wouldn't want anyone to think that you had anything to hide. People still talk about you and him, you know."

"Well they should keep their thoughts to themselves!" I retorted shrilly and then pulled myself up as I heard the hysterical pitch to my voice. Perfectly genuinely, I started to laugh. "Oh John, don't mind me. It was just a shock coming back to a yard full of all those men. I live a quiet life here – as you know – and I'm not used to seeing so many people at once. I'm over-reacting, that's all."

He grinned, instantly understanding. "I'm sorry too, it must have been a bit of a shock. I didn't think."

There was a pause and I thought for a brief optimistic moment that we could get back onto our usual friendly footing – it was rare for us to bicker like we had as children and I did not like to fall out with him. But this time, instead of the usual friendly giggle at our foolishness, I realised that he was gazing at me appraisingly, and when he next spoke, it was in a tone that showed his distaste at having to delve into a topic that he knew would be difficult for me.

"I'm sorry to have to ask you, but have you really seen nothing of him? No, let me finish – I'm not prying, but after all these years and still single, well, it makes people wonder if you're waiting for something … or someone." He was scrutinising my face for a reaction. "And therefore, with that in mind, it isn't impossible to believe that you might feel you should help him, even after what he's done."

A pause, then: "You are aware of the penalties for assisting a wanted man, aren't you?"

I concentrated on keeping my voice level, carefully disguising the lick of anger that heated my blood. "I'm aware, fully aware. And in answer to your other question, there *was* a war so it was hardly the time to be meeting young men, was it? It is very unfair that a brief romance I had when I was eighteen should still be haunting me now. Just because I haven't happened to marry is not a good enough excuse for all these gossiping idiots to still go on about it: I don't still have feelings for him. In fact, I don't think about him at all."

"Good," John said flatly. "He didn't deserve you then, and he most certainly doesn't now. He always was a smug, sanctimonious b— … sorry … and I'm glad, yes, glad that he's finally come unstuck. Serves him right, the jumped-up little arse."

There must have been something in my expression because John suddenly said, "Poor Ellie, he really did hurt you, didn't he?"

This unexpected sympathy left me feeling absurdly uncomfortable. It was one of those instances when I wished profoundly that he did not know me quite so well. Our friendship didn't usually extend to a discussion of such things and he must have been truly committed to his hunt to have dared mention it now. I never talked about the past, even to John.

I turned quickly aside to busy myself with putting the tea things away.

"There are other men you know."

His tone made me turn back again and I wondered if I had truly grasped his meaning. "Oh, John," I stammered helplessly and cursed myself for being so weak. "I, er – that is to say, I don't ... Um ..."

I floundered, trying desperately to cover my surprise and to find the right words.

"Don't look so scared, Ellie!" He was laughing at me, "You should know by now to disregard anything said by a clumsy fool like me – it was only a casual comment. Oh look, here's Jones. Well, man? Find anything?"

Jones was one of John's grooms, he had worked at the manor for all of my adult life and was one of those timeless people of indeterminate age. His face had been weathered to a rough, creased leather by years of squinting at the sun and it was impossible to judge whether those years amounted to a lifetime or whether he was, in fact, still quite young. Presently, however, he was simply standing awkwardly in the doorway while melt-water ran from his boots to puddle on my floor, fiddling with his hat and looking embarrassed.

"Nothing, sir. No sign of him."

"Well, Ellie," John said, climbing to his feet. "It looks like we've wasted your time."

He gave me a friendly kiss on the cheek in farewell before turning to follow his man outside. "Where next, Jones? Saltershill Barn? Good, the Colonel's been hassling me to drop in on old Marston for weeks. At least someone will be made happy today, although, knowing my father, something will still not be quite right. Ah well, ours is not to reason why ... Look after yourself, Ellie, and don't forget that you still haven't decided about the dance. It will be fun, you know – do you good to get out once in a while."

The door shut behind him and I moved to the window beyond the armchair to watch as the dozen or so men drifted slowly away up the lane. They made quite a comical sight, a rag tag group of farm labourers, grooms and young boys trailing damply behind the impressive figure of John Langton. They seemed more like children, kicking harmlessly through drifts as they tugged their assortment of ill-matched dogs along behind them. And yet the road must have been empty for quite some time before the foul tension of the past minutes finally eased enough for me to be able to notice that there was a man standing in the doorway behind me.

Chapter 7

Matthew was resting a shoulder against the doorframe from the back room – where it appeared he must have been hiding all along – and his complexion was more ashen than ever.

I turned away to collect the forgotten teacup from the table. Placing it into the sink, I said; "My heart nearly stopped when I got back to find the manhunt lurking on my doorstep – thank heavens you managed to find somewhere to hide! Have you been back there all along?" I was speaking with the far too bright tone of one who had just been caught talking about someone they shouldn't. "And would you believe that impressively I didn't actually have to lie once … Was it Freddy that let you in?" This last was as I registered his figure out of the corner of my eye. He had stepped into the room and was now standing about three yards away, across the length of the table. I glanced over my shoulder at him and moved to the stove quickly, mouth already running on to meaningless chatter about chickens, what to prepare for lunch and even, idiotically, the weather.

"Why are you doing this?"

His question stopped me in my tracks.

I hesitated for a moment, mouth suppressed into a tight line. Then I finished filling the teapot with water from the kettle, turned to him and said acidly, "Take a guess."

I marched into the small larder that shared its space with the dairy and brought out the sourdough I had been proving. I made all our bread; I had been lucky in the autumn and had managed to buy a few sacks of coarse flour; and although it was tough husky stuff, it had since proven itself more than a godsend when the nearest bakery was two miles away and, more often than not, half buried beneath the high drifts that regularly closed the Gloucester road.

He waited silently while I wasted time kneading the loaf into life and then thrust it into the oven. The gas lit on the second attempt. Then I took two fresh cups down from the shelf and poured the tea. It was just unfortunate that I forgot yet again about the broken handle.

I gave a scalded yelp and there was a crash as the teapot fell onto the worktop. It instantly began spreading thick brown liquid everywhere and with a badly suppressed curse, I snatched at a dishcloth. There seemed to be gallons of the stuff, running over the worktop and towards the floor and, distractedly, I set about dabbing at the growing lake only to yelp again as Matthew's hand appeared beside mine to join in the mopping up.

I whipped round and glared at him. He seemed taller all of a sudden and even more of a stranger than ever but then, hands up and taking a conciliatory step backwards to reclaim his place by the table, he suddenly decided to speak. His eyes were on the floor as he said in a harmlessly conversational tone, "So what's his beef? He's taking this search a little personally, isn't he?"

It took a moment for me to realise who he was talking about. Those eyes lifted and their expression belied the mild pitch to his voice.

"You do realise that he wants you, don't you? He plans to win you, and I suspect he figures that playing the hero and getting me locked away is his best chance at success."

Then, leaving me stung and searching for a sneering retort, he went to the door and reached my father's heavy black woollen coat down from a hook. "May I borrow this?"

I gaped at him, floundering at this sudden change of tack. "What? Why? Where are you going? You can't just *leave!*" I cast an anxious glance through the far window to check that the road was still clear. It was.

He didn't reply and, feeling like a complete fool, I hastily trotted after him to the kitchen door.

"Matthew!" I cried in exasperation, putting a hand on his arm.

He turned then and the contrived air of concentrated detachment dropped from his face. He covered my hand with his and gave me a very small lopsided smile; "I'm sorry, I really don't have a good way of showing my gratitude, do I? This risk you're taking on my behalf is rapidly proving very thankless indeed, isn't it ..."

I gaped at him mutely, thrown just as much off-balance by this sudden concession as by his accusation. He smiled at my expression and then continued in a voice that was utterly surprising in its gentleness.

"Don't worry, my dear, I'm not too keen on making you contribute to a hanging either. It's just that I'm damned if I'm going to sit about all day while men like him are trying to make it certain. While I'm caught in this hateful net, I can't even begin to combat ... I mean, how can I hope to ...?" He stopped, bit back whatever he was going to say and then added instead, "I'd have to be mad to pass up this opportunity; I really do have to go and have a poke about while those fools are busily looking the other way. And you never know, I may actually find something."

I desperately tried to piece together a more coherent argument than *no, no, no!* while he gingerly eased his arm into the sleeve. But before I could say a word or even work out where he was going, he lifted his hand in a brief touch to my cheek, turned away and vanished yet again through the kitchen door.

Chapter 8

I suppose it shouldn't have been a surprise given the way the morning had gone so far when the crunch of ice under foot betrayed the approach of more people and along puffed a plain-clothed inspector, four uniformed policemen and Colonel Langton. Thankfully the days of my childhood when I had been rendered wide-eyed and speechless by that man's formidable presence were over and I was able to greet him reasonably calmly, although I could see Beechnut watching anxiously from her field and I was glad that I had at least managed to turn her out before they had arrived.

The Colonel was still a fearsomely disapproving sort of person; even as an old man he stood very straight and tall and frowned down his long nose at me as if I were that same little scruffy farm-girl that had stared owlishly at him from behind Mother's skirts. It seemed to me that his presence in the village was something akin to that of an eccentric monarch. He certainly was rather apt to sending the villagers scuttling off to do his bidding based on little more than flimsy whim and a great deal of deference which may not have been entirely deserved, and now he was striding towards me through the thin misting rain with an air of assumed authority which left the policeman to trot along in his wake like an eager puppy.

The pony next to me eyed him warily, no doubt suspecting that this person would be without a titbit. I was standing in the shelter of a stable door with the pony's front hoof resting over my thigh as I carefully rasped the excess growth away, like filing a fingernail, to leave it balanced and comfortable in anticipation of the coming weekend's work. I trimmed all my horses' feet; the ponies had no need of shoes with their hardy little hooves, and of the two horses on my yard, the old hunter was retired, and my mare would never have allowed the blacksmith near her but thankfully did well enough with my careful trimming.

"Now then, Miss Phillips." The Colonel's voice barked as he came to a smart halt before me. "We've come to look for that fellow Croft. Not seen him, have you?"

The grey-haired policeman coughed politely and stepped around the straight-backed barrier of the Colonel. "Good morning Miss – Phillips, is it? – I am Inspector Woods. These are Constables Downe, Smith, Thorne and Fleece." He waved a hand vaguely along the assembled line. "I was wondering if I might ask you to let my men take a look around?"

I set the pony's foot back down on the ground and straightened. The Inspector was rather short with that middle-aged spread running on into what my father would have politely called "well-covered" and his eyebrows were remarkably bushy, almost as if he cultivated them. But as I met his unobtrusive gaze for the first time, I was startled to realise that instead of finding the expected bland obedience hidden beneath, there was something infinitely more subtle lurking within those deep-set grey eyes. He was smiling at me gently and I came to the sudden terrifying realisation that he was anything but harmless.

"Good morning, Inspector. You're welcome, of course, but you're a little late, aren't you?"

"Late, Miss Phillips?"

"Mr Langton and his men have already been here to look around for you."

"Have they indeed?" There was the barest flicker of irritation which was quickly suppressed. "You won't mind if my men take another look, will you?"

"Not at all, Inspector, go right ahead."

Never one to stand around quietly, the Colonel stepped forwards again, his head stuck forwards on a thick neck as he fixed me with a beady eye. "Listen here, Missy, we want to know if you've seen him. My son says that you dallied about with Croft once and so he might come here. You can't hide him, you know, we'll have him in the end and it'll be all the worse for you."

The Inspector looked a little uncomfortable at this speech but I answered calmly enough, "You're about the fourth person now to remind me of my youthful dalliance, as you put it, and it is starting to get a little wearing. Believe it or not I am not in the habit of harbouring murderers."

"There's no use lying, my girl. We know what you're about."

Close to, the Colonel really was a very unpleasant man with little bits of spittle collecting at the corners of his mouth. His face was veined with the signs of his fluctuating temper and all of a sudden I knew that I had never quite done his son justice before. With a father such as this, it was incredible that John was so sane.

I spoke coldly. "Nor am I in the habit of lying to the police."

The Colonel opened his mouth to say something else but the Inspector cut smoothly across him. "Miss Phillips, the Colonel here has been good enough to meet us at the main road and offer himself as our guide, for which we are very grateful, but would you mind just stepping over here so we can have a little private chat?"

Trying hard not to give the Colonel a childishly triumphant smile, I followed the Inspector to the corner where, in more temperate conditions, run-off from the roof would have collected into a large stone water trough. At present, of course, this was simply one great block of ice but the increasingly confident spring-like rain was drifting down into even this little sheltered corner and under its influence, a steady pattern of drips was beginning to wear immaculate hollows into the glassy surface.

The Inspector stared thoughtfully into its depths for a moment before fixing me with his intelligent eye;

"So, Miss Phillips, how well do you know this man Croft? You *were* romantically involved I understand? But are not now?"

"That is correct," I replied, trying to quell my sudden nervousness. The flimsy motivation that had formed my excuse for deceiving friend and neighbour was one thing, but here the consequences of discovery would prove much worse; and cold reason told me that it was a step too far to attempt a lie to *this* man.

He was waiting, looking at me expectantly, and so, reluctantly, I continued, "As everybody seems to be telling you, Inspector, we were courting briefly before the war, but he called it off."

"He did? That's surprising." He must have caught my startled glance because he added quickly, "I mean, surprising given that a lot of people were marrying *because* of the war." He gave a discomfited cough, before getting back on track again, "Have you seen much of him since he was demobbed?"

"No. I heard that he came back just after Easter last year but we didn't see each other. It has been eight years now; there's no real reason to assume we would have anything to say to each other anymore." I paused but then added, "And I gather that he had a bit of a tough time of it, so he probably just wanted some peace in which to recover." I had been speaking quite coolly, concentrating on keeping my manner neutral and my mind clear as I said what was necessary but then, unexpectedly, I had the strange experience of realising that this last statement had the added surprise of most likely being the truth.

"A tough time, you say? How tough?"

"Oh, I don't know, I've only heard this third hand, so to speak. He was in Normandy and then part of the push towards Germany so saw some pretty messy action I believe – although having said that, who didn't?" I stopped, suddenly having the uncomfortable feeling that I was gabbling idiotically. I took a breath and steadied myself.

"Quite. So would you say he came back a changed man?"

I could tell where these questions were leading, "I'm sorry, Inspector; as I've already said, I didn't see him when he came home so I don't really feel I can answer that."

"Of course, Miss Phillips, just a few more questions then. Do you remember him ever showing excessive temper or violence?"

I was suddenly acutely aware of my wrists and smiling innocently I clasped my hands behind my back. "I don't remember anything like that, Inspector."

"Did you know the victim?"

"Not beyond casual pleasantries. I know they both served together."

"Yes." Perhaps judging that this reply was a little terse, the Inspector repeated as if by rote, "Matthew Croft trained as an architect, and therefore had a rather tenuous connection to the world of structural integrity. Mr Donald took sporadic employment as a joiner. This was apparently sufficient for them to be drafted to the ranks of non-commissioned officer and sapper respectively in the engineering corps. Anything to add?"

I shook my head in a negative.

"Good. And finally, given your history with Croft, do you think you would be more or less likely to give him assistance?"

I smiled. "That is a very odd question, Inspector."

"Humour me."

"All right. Regardless of my history, such as it was, with Matthew Croft, I can honestly say that it does not go so far as to condone murder."

As the interview had progressed, his mouth had slowly transformed from a flat serious line to a gentle, amiable smile, and onwards to become a wide grandfatherly beam which was probably meant to be utterly disarming but only made me less trusting in his appearance of benevolent good humour. And when the Inspector then indicated that he had finished with me and turned away, still smiling, to rejoin the others, I could not help having the very unpleasant sensation that I had somehow said far more than I ought.

With determined optimism however, I hoped that whatever might happen later, the Inspector's dismissal would at least mark an end to this particular invasion but clearly the Colonel had not finished with me yet. I had already noted that the cluster of waiting policemen were standing slightly aloof as if they wished to pretend that his steady flow of disdainful sniffs and muttered aspersions were nothing to do with them. He was staring at the hairy little pony with an expression of extreme distaste and when the Inspector quietly slipped past to begin querying the results of their search, the Colonel turned to intercept me with very a stern look in his eye.

"Would your father approve of the way you're carrying on, young lady?"

"Pardon?" I stared at him blankly, completely at a loss as to how exactly my quiet life could be classed as any kind of "carrying on".

"*This.*" He waved his hand airily around my yard, taking in the roughly swept cobbles between great piles of cleared snow, my farriery tools and the scruffy pony which was still standing patiently in its doorway. "I'm sure he had no idea of you carrying on the business after him. The whole place is literally falling down about your ears, or so my son says. It won't be long before the whole place has crumbled away to nothing, my girl, and you'll only have yourself to blame. Can't you get a man in to do it?"

"Where do you think I'd get the money to pay for this man, Colonel?" I asked, relatively pleasantly. "Besides Freddy and I manage well enough between us."

"Freddy? Ah, you mean the *idiot.*"

I choked back a sharp retort and merely smiled serenely. I was actually quite impressed with my self-control.

"And who is this old fellow?" The Colonel had spied the elderly hunter who was snoozing gently with his chin resting on his stable door.

"Harry. My father's hunter." That self-control suddenly seemed rather more precarious as the Colonel woke the poor horse by placing a heavy hand on its nose.

"Send him to the knackerman and you'll save plenty of money. Hell, the man might even pay you for him."

Clearly at this point I was expected to bow and scrape and express my effusive thanks for this suggestion. Instead I looked him squarely in the eye.

"My father was very fond of this horse and he particularly asked me to look after him. He'll go when he's good and ready, and," I determinedly continued across the Colonel's remark, "not a day before."

The Colonel turned an interesting shade of puce. He stared at me for a few moments, a vein bulging in his temple, before turning sharply on his heel with a precision that would have impressed any drill-sergeant.

"Come," he snapped, relegating the Inspector to eager puppy once more. "We can see what my son has found, if anything. I have another son, but he is in the Army. He made Captain recently – very proud moment introducing him at Whitehall last week to my old friend Bernard … ah, I *should* say Viscount Montgomery, Chief of Imperial General Staff, you know."

"Yes, we know," muttered one of the uniformed men who was either Thorne or Smith. "You told us before."

Someone tittered and the Colonel shot them a wild look before striding back out onto the road. Their assorted legs made very hard work of the hill past my house but I barely bothered to watch them go before turning back to the waiting pony. The poor creature had developed a faintly martyred air by now.

I could not help letting out a resigned sigh as I set the pony's foot back down on the ground again. With every man and quite literally his dog turning up on my doorstep, this day was starting to get ridiculous. But dutifully enough, I walked out through the gate and into the house with Freddy to take the waiting call. I could have laid money on who would be on the line.

His secretary sounded harassed but Sir William was oblivious to the pressure on his staff as he finally took the telephone.

"Good day, my dear," he said warmly and I could picture the automatic lift of his hand.

If I had to choose, I would say that Sir William was my favourite of the two elderly Langton brothers, although perhaps it would be more accurate to say he was the one I despised the least. He had at any rate been sufficiently bothered to send a note of regret when my father had passed away and it had been kindly written with some reference to a pleasant shared memory. His wife, an austere woman who was forever to be called ma'am and never by name, occasionally commissioned me to bring ponies up to the house for the entertainment of her grandnephews and nieces and so I had, over the years, built up a certain level of acquaintance with the family. I would never have claimed to be more than an overpaid servant in their eyes though.

Sir William was not as openly sharp as the Colonel but I was not misled into believing that he was any the less calculating in his actions, and there was always the faint possibility that his morals were not quite as upstanding as his brother's. The Colonel had his strict code of honour which ruled, often badly, over everything he did, whereas Sir William had what politely could be called a creative approach and impolitely, a criminal lack of concern for the needs of others. That being said, I had never had anything but politeness from him and I answered him now with perfectly unforced warmth in return.

"Good day, Sir William. How are you?"

"Very well, my dear, very well. I don't suppose the Colonel is still there?"

"You've just missed him, Sir William." It always paid to show him a certain level of deference, even if I didn't feel it. "He went along Bath Lane with the police officers, although given how deep the drifts are at Saltershill, they might have wished they'd cut straight across the fields …"

"Ah," he said cheerfully. "Thank you, my dear. We're on the hunt, you know!"

"So I heard. Goodbye!"

The telephone clicked dead, rattling slightly as I returned it to its cradle, and I shut the door very firmly behind me as I walked back out to the yard. There were few members of the Langton family left to question me now and unless this was going to turn into a complete farce, I doubted very much that I would find his wife interrogating me later.

Chapter 9

The rest of the day did in fact pass rather more calmly. Beechnut, and possibly equally importantly her stable, were none the worse for the morning's upset but I was more worried than I cared to admit when dusk arrived and still no sign of Matthew.

For fear that I would upset Freddy I spent longer than usual out with the horses as I bedded them down for the night. Over the years, their comforting warmth and companionable silence had been my greatest source of support, and now I was standing with my arms slung over Beechnut's withers and my forehead pressed into her warm fur, repeating *you're not just another gullible fool* like some kind of mantra.

Unlike me, Beechnut was now entirely calm and relaxed as she chewed steadily on her hay and we stood in this manner until the drizzling rainclouds had parted and the stars took over the blackening sky. On any other day I might have rejoiced at the sudden shift in the weather which had abruptly given us back some warmth but the budding pleasure of a clean frost and the hope of a brighter day to follow felt presently as far removed as the stars themselves. There might as well have been a forecast of more snow.

Suddenly Beechnut stiffened and threw up her head to look out onto the yard. My mind really could not take any more dramas and, apprehension increasing by the moment, I went with her to peer over the stable door into the silent shadows. I could see nothing. But then she uttered a strange throaty noise and stamped about her box with an agitation that could only mean one thing. A man.

Wary of calling out in case it was some other person I slipped soundlessly out of the stable and, keeping out of the blue light of the waning moon, I tiptoed closer to where I thought he might be. I could see no one but I had not heard anything bar the familiar tramp of heavy feet and subsequent bang of the kitchen door as Freddy finished shutting in the chickens so whoever it was must be still out here. I wondered whether I dared risk calling his name.

"Who is he?"

The low whisper came right behind my ear. I gave a squeak and whipped round, colliding with him in the process.

"Matthew!" I cried in exasperated relief, cuffing his arm, adding; "Ooh, sorry," as he winced in pain at my blow. His rough unshaven jaw was making him look very much the outlaw as amusement glinted down at me out of the darkness.

"Did I scare you?"

"At least I no longer need to worry whether you're still alive. Whether *my* heart is still beating is another matter."

He very gently took my wrist between finger and thumb in a mock test for a pulse. "Well, it's still going, but you might want to get it looked at. It's running a touch fast."

I glowered at him although I suspect my look was lost on him. "Do that again and I'll shoot you myself," I hissed, not entirely jokingly.

"Sorry." He tried to sound contrite. "I couldn't resist. So go on then, who is he?" A longer pause. "Your son?"

I had to laugh, in spite of myself. "Have a heart. He's not my son, he's fourteen!"

Slipping back into the shadows of my stables and taking an armful of hay from the barrow, I moved slowly along the row, nodding in acknowledgement as Matthew stepped aside to let me past. "I know he doesn't seem it but he really is almost grown up. His aunt lives in the village; he was sent there from the city in the usual rush to get the children out, you know how it was. He used to drift up from the village to watch the horses and I let him help with the mucking out occasionally. But then Dad died and he started coming up to help me properly; he just seemed to spend more and more time here. Goodness, sorry." This as a mistimed thrust over a stable door dusted him liberally in blades of fractured hay. "Eventually it simply seemed easier to ask him to stay and I needed the help, so it worked out well for me."

Matthew was listening silently, his head turned away into shadow. The only sign of life he gave was the brief movement of a hand when it brushed the dried grass from his sleeve.

Laying a hand on the soft velvet of the nose belonging to the occupant of the last stable, I went on to describe how the quiet and underfed boy had grown up to be the cheery Freddy that had just gone inside, although admittedly he still looked half-starved however much I fed him. It hardly needed to be said that Freddy was just not the sort to flourish at school; he was of an age to leave and the work with the horses suited him, for now at least; and my quiet little farm must have been a sort of haven for him after what must have been a turbulent upbringing. I had never known for sure but I was reasonably confident that he had been beaten regularly at home and, at any rate, no one cared enough to come and claim him, so here he stayed. And, I admitted, *I* cared very much that he did.

Matthew didn't say anything in response to that so after a few moments of awkwardness that left me wondering what he must be thinking, I finished meekly; "I'd better just go and say goodnight to Beechnut."

He waited for me to reappear before walking back with me towards the house. "Why does she do that?"

Beechnut was stamping around her box once more. I let him open the gate. "Oh, that's quite restrained. She normally tries to break the door down when there is a man on the yard. You should feel honoured." I felt his curious glance; "She was bred to be a hunter, one of John's young projects but she took a bad fall and it knocked her confidence."

"And that caused the behaviour I saw just now?"

"Oh no, it was the rather less than sensitive training methods employed by John's head groom in an effort to get her jumping again. I believe she very nearly killed him. Some horses have a flight instinct, some have a fight instinct; hers proved to be very strongly on the side of fight. At that point they were going to have her shot, but I inherited a little bit of money from Dad and so I bought her. She's a very talented girl and I thought I might as well give her a chance to come good. She doesn't jump any more, but that suits me perfectly."

There was another silence but then, as he followed the path to the door, I heard him say in a tone of private thoughtfulness, "I've been getting you all wrong, haven't I? In fact, I think I'm finally beginning to understand you better – it's been very odd feeling like I ought to know you and yet finding that I don't actually know you at all... You're a kind of earthly St Jude really, aren't you?"

"What do you mean?" I asked, confused.

"You just seem to go about collecting all these tragic little lost souls and nursing them back to health again, myself included."

"You count yourself as a lost cause, do you?" I said with an uncertain smile.

"Why yes, without a doubt. Freddy, Beechnut ... me. But what about you? You collect all these wounded people and animals, and focus all your energy on their needs without seeming to spend much time thinking about yourself." He stopped in the shadow of the kitchen door. "What exactly do you get out of this?"

I looked up at him, feeling extraordinarily unsettled. I found myself on the defensive feeling oddly like I had done something wrong, but without quite knowing what it was.

"I don't know what you mean," I said stiffly.

"Do you not?" he asked. "You do a very convincing act of being all hard and detached, and I almost believed it. But it's not true, not true at all. You expend all this energy helping everyone else and it really is very commendable ... but do you ever stop to think of the consequences for you?"

"So who exactly should I turf out first? Freddy or the horse? And by whose criteria? Yours? Because you can't even bring yourself to admit a few basic truths."

I still couldn't see his face and I shook my head in disdain and pushed past him into the welcoming light of the kitchen. It seemed incredible to believe that yet again he had made a rare effort at communication only for me to find that this time we had strayed into a painful critique of my character. I was beginning to suspect he was doing it deliberately, and I did not like it.

"Eleanor," he called helplessly after me. "I didn't mean it like that."

I ignored him.

I did after all have enough ingredients left to make a meal in the form of a vegetable stew that had spent the past two hours bubbling gently on the hotplate by the fire and a much overlooked can of whale meat now thrown in, literally. I could not help angrily crashing about with the pots; it was easier than talking.

We ate our dinner in silence. Freddy kept looking from one to the other in anxious bewilderment and I wished that I could lighten the oppressive mood, but I was too tired and too wary of starting yet another conversation that would only end in disagreement. Casting little furtive glances at Matthew now that he couldn't hide away in the shadows, I realised that he looked absolutely shattered. Clearly his afternoon adventures had taken it out of him. He looked moody and deep in thought as he chased beans around the dish with the fork in his good hand and, I realised with a painful jolt, he also looked terribly sad.

The bleak tension that still hung about him had pulled at his face to make him look much older than his thirty-four years and there was a stiffness to his shoulder that made me wonder if his wounds were healing as well as they ought. The coarse stubble that was almost a beard by now seemed only to emphasise the current wild nature of his existence, and the paradox of it was, surprisingly, it actually rather suited him.

He ran a hand though his hair and unexpectedly looked up to catch me watching him. His mouth twitched into a sudden smile, making the lines of strain and worry abruptly vanish, and my heart twisted painfully as he became the kind, gentle man I remembered once more. *Sorry*, he mouthed. I gave him a flicker in return before reaching across the table to take his empty plate away.

"Is *anybody* going to tell me what's been going on?" Freddy finally broke the silence with an exasperated shout. He leapt to his feet to carry his bowl to the sink, waggling his spoon as he went. "I've been sneaking food out for no more than a word of thanks and now you've been hiding with the horses all afternoon and he's been off on an adventure. It's not fair!"

This outburst broke the impasse remarkably.

"Steady on, lad!" Matthew flinched back as the rapidly descending jug splashed milk onto his sleeve and he and I were united in protest as cups and teapot came crashing down swiftly after.

"Oh, sorry." Freddy grinned sheepishly, reclaiming his seat, "But won't someone tell me what's been going on? Please?"

I cast Matthew a silent challenge of my own as I passed him a tea-towel.

He reached for the cloth. "All right …"

His attention fixed upon the towel in his hands and if it were possible, his demeanour became even more impassive than before. Even now, it was not willingly that he was divulging his part in this thing.

"Eight days ago I got a message at my office that Jamie wanted to see me and it was pretty insistent, so I went over as soon as

I could, which was probably about two hours or so later by the time I managed to grind my way up the hill out of Gloucester. I've been staying at my mother's for the past month; it's easier when you don't know whether the lanes are going to be hedge-high with snow from one day to the next, and at least it stopped her from worrying …

"Anyway, when I got there, he was lying flat out on the floor and—" A grimace, a furtive glance. "Sorry, the details really aren't for your ears. Suffice it to say, murder was not the first thing that crossed my mind." He had to take a moment to collect himself. Then he added; "So there I was, trying to find a pulse and as I felt his neck, it finally began to dawn on me that this was no accident. But I didn't get much time to think about what it *was*, because at that point something hit me from behind."

His thumb nail was rubbing at a loose thread and I don't think he realised he was working a little hole in my tea-towel.

"I must have been laid out for a little while because when I came round, I was face down in the dirt and my head was hurting like the devil. I tried not to move, but out of the corner of my eye I could see the boots of at least two men and they were discussing what to do with me. Their accents were odd, Irish, I think, but it is hard to be sure. But of this I am sure: one of them picked up the telephone and it was clear I was in for it."

"Why, what did he say?" Freddy's question was anxious. I glanced over at him with a concern of my own but he seemed relatively undisturbed.

"Let's just say that the person on the other end of the line wasn't exactly my friend. They were to fix it that my fingerprints were all over the room, which they were anyway because I'd walked in like a friend, not a criminal. Then he was to put Jamie's watch and money in my pockets and say that he had burst in on me as I was standing over the body. After a brief struggle he was, in self-defence of course, to land an unlucky blow which was to kill me. Nice, eh?"

"But you *did* manage to escape?!" Then, as his eyes lifted, I realised what I had said and muttered crossly to myself, "Of course you did, otherwise you wouldn't be here. Idiot."

He gave a rare smile, "You're not an idiot and yes, I managed to escape. Just about, anyway …"

I could picture the scene. Two men, knowing that one man was dead and believing the other to be at least halfway on the route to becoming the same, were taking their time as they rifled through the corpse's pockets.

"I heard something heavy being lifted. I don't know what it was, a bar of some sort; a lamp stand perhaps. Whatever it was, by some miracle I managed to roll aside just as it came crashing down. Then I rolled back and by a second miracle I managed to bring the fellow to the ground. And then I ran. I ran until my lungs hurt and then I ran some more. They fired a shotgun at me but I was unbelievably lucky and I managed to throw myself down into the streambed. Then, using the stain of frozen water to cover my tracks, I made for the trees. It was dark by then and they couldn't track me so long as I was careful, and believe me, I was very careful – I could have slipped under the nose of a fox, I was moving so quietly. That whole night is just one hideous exhausted blur of motion in my memory now; I didn't dare to rest for even a moment in case they found me."

I asked, "Why didn't you go to the police?"

"Because …" He stopped. Then he shot me an odd little frowning glance. "Because," he repeated carefully, "pretty soon it became clear that the police were on the hunt, too. I would have handed myself in, but seeing all those men and dogs, I didn't get the impression that they were likely to be inclined to believe me – my fingerprints are all over the scene, the house, his things ... and you can be sure that those two villains left no trace of themselves. To be frank I'm not sure *I'd* believe me, my tale sounds pretty fantastical and I'm damned if I'm going to hand myself in to be hanged for something I didn't do."

"So then what happened?" Freddy's prompt was given with all the enthusiasm of a boy hearing an amazing adventure story.

"Well, then I made a mistake. I'd been out there on the run for two nights in this ridiculous weather and I was getting pretty tired and hungry. There's only so much food just lying about waiting to be taken by passing fugitives so as dawn was just coming up I thought I'd drop in on Jamie's sister to see if she could shed any light on this thing. She lives in Miserden, you know? Lord only knows what I was thinking, going there. Anyway, as any fool could have guessed, they were there, waiting for me."

"The police?"

"No, Freddy, the same two men who had attacked me before." He shifted uncomfortably in his chair and I think his shoulder was hurting him. "Luck abandoned me then; I got cornered. They managed to stay out of sight until I was very nearly knocking at the door but suddenly a car's headlights flicked on and I was blinded, pinned against the wall by the light. I didn't wait to see who it was – whether police or crooks – I ran round the building and dived behind an outhouse but they must have anticipated it because just as I ran out the other side, they cut me off. I was forced to jump a wall and scramble across some pretty deep drifts. Until that point I'd had a reasonably good lead but all of a sudden I was exposed; I turned to see where they were and at that moment one of them fired his gun. I didn't even realise immediately that I'd been hit. You don't always …"

I had the horrible realisation that he was speaking from previous experience and suddenly I knew how little my quiet enquiries had told me beyond the information that he had been caught in the bloody retreat through Ypres. It had been an impossible situation, having absolutely no right to the information and knowing how the gossips would get to work if I mistakenly asked the wrong person.

"All I knew was that something had knocked all the breath out of me and I hit the ground hard. But some rush of adrenalin got me to my feet again, and somehow I managed to get far enough under cover of some young saplings to shake them." A fresh grimace. "It was just starting to snow again, I remember, and I was getting pretty panicky by then. I didn't know how badly I was hurt and I didn't want to hole up somewhere for fear that they'd find me, so I kept moving."

"Until I saw you!" Freddy suddenly piped up, "I told Eleanor but she didn't believe me. I was bringing in the ponies that had wandered down to the far fields and I saw you."

Matthew's expression suddenly lightened. "You did, did you? Well, you saved my life, young man. And a second time when you persisted in stalking me in the dead of night and foisting food upon me when I thought I was incredibly well concealed." He ruffled the boy's hair and then smiled as the beaming youth smoothed it down again.

"Oh, well, it was nothing really." Freddy was trying to adopt a cool man-to-man nonchalance which might have worked had his grin not been quite so large. "And Eleanor did her bit too," he added generously.

"She most certainly did," Matthew said, slightly less enthusiastically. And then his expression changed all over again as he added; "So, now you know …"

What an extraordinary mixture of elation and dismay at the sudden release from ignorance. And it still felt rather surreal to be sitting opposite him in the cosy warmth of my kitchen, after all the recent drama, and after all these long years.

I had boiled the kettle; we were all sitting nursing fresh cups of tea looking thoughtful and I caught myself staring at Matthew again, examining his face, trying to understand how he or I were ever going to make sense of this mess. There was still that trace of dark forbidding tension about him and I could perceive now that it was beginning to coil itself around me.

He looked up suddenly and caught my eye before I could look away, and the faint half-apologetic lift that tugged at his cheek made me wonder if he too was thinking that only a few short hours ago he had thought himself alone in this. I wasn't sure if he thought things had yet changed for the better …

He dropped his eyes quickly enough to the teaspoon that was slowly spinning on its heel beneath his fingers but a trace of warmth still lifted the corner of his mouth and yet again it was disturbingly familiar. I felt like demanding: *is this it? Are we friends now?* But instead I took a calming breath and said, "So no prizes for guessing where you went today."

"Well …" Matthew began, glancing from me to Freddy and back again, looking so tired that I couldn't help feeling a fresh rush of concern. Then he shrugged haplessly in the face of my disapproval. "It did seem sensible to take the opportunity of the manhunt looking the other way to go and have a little peek at Jamie's house."

Freddy gasped.

Matthew smiled grimly. "It's all right, I was more careful this time. I have no desire to take any more chances against that gun."

"They were there?" I asked sharply.

"They were there," he confirmed. "Like the last time and if it wasn't too bizarre I'd say they were still waiting for me." A swift glance in response to my exclamation. "Yes, there's little doubt they were waiting the last time. He was quite cold, you see, so he'd been dead for a while. So if they didn't clear out then as soon as the deed was done, the only logical conclusion is that they must have known I was coming and decided to lay a particularly odd trap for me. And that leaves us with the eternal question, why? Jamie may well have been little better than a penniless, workshy criminal living in a crumbling farmhouse but I'm a partner in a reasonably successful architects firm in Gloucester and though I'm not exactly rich, I'm definitely a step above having shady dealings with men like them. In fact, it occurs to me that they were very lucky indeed that I got away."

"Why?"

74

The teaspoon was arrested abruptly in mid-spin by the palm of his hand and it made me jump. "*Why?* Because if I'd died they would have had a hell of a job convincing the police that I'd had reason to rob and then kill him, whereas now they have a ready-made suspect complete with a dramatic manhunt and some very incriminating behaviour!"

The sudden anger of this outburst rang loudly into the silence that succeeded it. Then, looking a little sheepish at our expressions, he added in a considerably more measured tone, "But today, anyway, they were conveniently sitting in a car away from the house and near the barn where they thought they would get a good vantage point. I managed to slip around the back and over the brook without being seen and then I turned burglar …"

"For someone who claims to be so squeaky clean, you seem to have a remarkable number of dubious skills."

Matthew shot me a sudden grin. "Only from my misspent youth, I assure you." He carefully restored the teaspoon to its place near the milk jug before adding, "I hoped to find some clue of what Jamie had been up to so I had a good look around."

"And did you find anything?" Freddy asked eagerly.

"No, nothing, the place was clean."

"Oh," I said in heavy disappointment.

"No, no – you misunderstand me. The house was clean, as in *really* clean. If you had spent as many years stuck with the man as I have, you would know that it just doesn't fit."

"It doesn't?"

"Jamie Donald was the most untidy person I have ever met, and that's saying something." Unconsciously his eyes scanned the room, taking in all the little piles of my accumulated clutter. *Hmph*, I thought. "You know we served together? Well, I even had to put him on report once, it got so bad. No – someone's been in there and tidied up, and I'd cheerfully bet my life on it that it was our friendly Irishmen."

"So you didn't find anything? No letters, no slips of paper with a hastily scrawled note? That sort of thing?"

"You mean anything conveniently naming his attackers? Or explaining how he somehow decided to involve me? Sadly not." He was smiling gently.

"Oh," I said, feeling deflated. "But you seemed so cheerful when you got back."

"That's because I put some more of my misspent youth to work and left our friends in their car a little present. An old trick I've learned from somewhere is to stuff wadding into the exhaust – the car won't start properly and it'll take them a while to figure out why." All tiredness vanished as he grinned devilishly.

"That's awful," I cried. "They might have caught you!"

"That's brilliant," said Freddy, laughing uproariously.

"They were in the house anyway, shouting at each other and spotting my muddy footprints all over the floor so they didn't notice me up by their car. I was tempted to steal it, but I probably couldn't have got it moving and anyway I decided that this little gesture of defiance would be more annoying."

I shot him a disapproving look. "That was still very risky." I frowned. "And that was where you've been all day? It's not that far to Warren Barn."

To my surprise he looked a little uncomfortable. "Well, I drifted back by a long route to avoid leaving a trail for our local manhunt. It's lucky that the woodland is dripping like it is; my footsteps dissolved even as I walked. And then I just sat and contemplated the view for a while."

"Really? Where?" Freddy asked interestedly.

Matthew shifted in his seat before finally replying. "At the bottom of Sixty Acres, the corner that looks out over that odd little cottage and down to the stream at Washbrook. Do you know it? You can see for miles from there and today it was beautiful with mist blanketing the hills and wisps of steam rising from the thawing trees."

I understood then why he had hesitated. I didn't need to hear

76

his description to picture in sharp detail the meeting of three wooded valleys with the straggling cottages of Caudle Green on the far slopes, and a faint outline of the houses of Miserden on the horizon beyond. Only in my mind it was summer, the grass was full of the purple-flowering vetch, a skylark was dancing overhead and the warm breeze was ruffling my hair as I turned with a happy smile towards the sound of a stone turning under foot …

"What were you doing there?" Freddy asked curiously.

"Thinking," Matthew said, looking straight at me. There was a long pause and then, watching me for a reaction, he said carefully, "You won't ask what I was thinking about? I was thinking about you, what I'm doing to you by coming back here, and whether I'm doing the right thing by letting you embroil yourself in my mess. I was thinking about you, as I seem to have been doing rather a lot recently."

I got up so abruptly that I think I made Freddy jump.

"More tea?" I asked with a strangled croak.

"Eleanor …" Matthew began but I ignored him.

I concentrated very hard on the kettle as it boiled. It is amazing how interesting tea leaves can be as they are spooned carefully from the caddy into the pot. And collecting more milk from the dairy for the little jug – which must have been my mother's because otherwise my father would never have tolerated anything quite so floral – was a task that could not be put off any longer.

"Eleanor," Matthew said insistently. "Eleanor? Will you look at me?"

"Stop it," I said quietly to the teaspoon in my hand.

"Pardon?"

"Just stop it," I said again, this time to the teacups.

There was an awkward pause, and then Matthew said levelly, "All right, I can see that you don't want to talk about this now." Then he added very softly, "It's not exactly easy for me either, you know."

The room seemed to shrink and tighten around me, making me feel horribly claustrophobic like I couldn't breathe. If anyone had asked me a week ago how I felt about him I would have happily told them that I was perfectly indifferent but somehow it was as if a switch had been pressed in my brain and suddenly the anger which had lain undetected for years now broke with blinding force. I twisted to face him and found that I was shaking in my fury:

"How dare you? How *dare* you? You have no right to keep pushing me like this! I've already given you shelter and now I'm to understand you've embroiled Freddy. And for what? To sooth your wounded ego?"

"I know I have no right, Eleanor!" He jerked his head in exasperation. "You can't honestly think that I'd fling further demands at you after all you've done so far? That's not what this is about. This is about you and how you flinch like a scalded cat every time I ask you if you're sure you want to be doing even this much – is it really so hard to trust me even a tiny bit?"

He stopped and took a long breath before continuing in a voice that was once more measured and calm. "Look, I'm not trying to upset you; you said yourself that you weren't happy being drawn into the thick of things – yes, you did, you said it earlier, I heard you – and I'm just trying to work out whether this, having me here, risking imprisonment and Lord knows what else is actually what you want?"

"Well, that makes a change," I said acidly, misunderstanding him deliberately. Poor Freddy might not have been in the room for all the notice I now took. "You've never worried about what I wanted before."

"That's not quite fair, Eleanor, and you know it," he said, very softly indeed.

I shrugged off his reproof impatiently and turned back to making the tea as if my hands were steady enough to pour it. With a voice barely recognisable as my own, I spoke with increasing hysteria; "Why are you doing this? You finally start to tell me what happened and I think that perhaps I was mistaken and we could become friends and I can help, and then without warning you twist it and suddenly I'm on the defensive again as if I've done something wrong. *You* wouldn't tell me, remember? You've trampled enough on my…f…feelings… No more, no more, do you hear?!"

I took ragged breath before finishing in a foolish rush. "And anyway, in case you've forgotten, you waived your right to question my choices in life eight years ago." My voice crackled awfully and I stopped in a belated attempt to gather the shreds of my dignity together.

I noticed then, with a twist of something indefinable, that the handle of the tin teapot had been repaired and realised that he must have done it this very morning before the manhunt had appeared. This unfortunate discovery rather took the wind out of my sails but nevertheless I managed to slam the steaming cups down on the table and then glower at him with cheeks that burned with angry heat.

He returned my gaze with infuriating calm. "You're very anxious to avoid a discussion on this, aren't you?" If he had dared to look amused by my outburst I think I might have killed him. Instead he added carelessly, "I notice you were able to talk to the blue-eyed wonder earlier, but then I suspect he's … different."

I gaped at him in confusion. "*Who?*"

"The loverboy who's heroically leading the hunt."

"What on earth has John to do with any of this?" Then suddenly it hit me so that I said with a mocking laugh, "Are you *jealous?*"

He did not reply. He simply raised an enquiring eyebrow which irritated me to an extraordinary degree.

"Oh push off," I snapped childishly, waving farewell to my dignity once and for all. "You think you're so clever sitting there toying with me and baiting me like all this is just a game. Well, it's a living hell for me. My involvement with you begins and ends with preventing another man from going to the gallows; you can stay here until you're free of this horrible thing, and then you're out of my life. Have I made myself clear?"

I still don't really know what made me blow up like that. Murder I could cope with, harbouring a wanted man I could cope with, but being made to talk about parts of my life that I had carefully locked away was more than I could bear. I felt tears prick at my eyes again and I blinked furiously; somehow I had fretted more in the past few days than I had in years.

He was staring at me across the abyss that was my kitchen table. His voice when he finally spoke was cold and entirely detached. "If that is what you want."

"Yes. Yes, it is," I whispered and fled.

It was a long time later that I realised the handle was back on the bedroom door.

Chapter 10

My mother once had to go and sit with an old school friend whose son was to be hanged. She never told me what they talked about, or even if they spoke at all but it is hard to conceive of them doing more than wait in the shrouded embrace of a sitting room until the seconds had finished their dismal climb towards midday.

Last night I closed my eyes to the memories of my last meeting with him; to dream of an eight-year-old argument where a brief romance had ended in rejection and man's denial. This morning I opened them to the realisation that I hated the fact he could still have such a claim on me. And worse, that there was within me a nightmarish impulse to exact the very worst kind of revenge.

The fear lay in the fact that after my unnecessary histrionics of last night, he most certainly knew.

A short while later and still looking very bleary-eyed, I crept stealthily down the stairs. To my dismay, he was already up and sitting at the table, and I braced myself to receive the brunt of his natural scorn. But I ought to have known that he wasn't the sort of man to press his advantage, and instead he was seemingly absorbed in fiddling about with what looked like the remains of my father's gramophone. The crank mechanism had broken years ago; it had lain abandoned in the back room ever since and he had stumbled across it, I presumed, when he had been listening from there the previous morning.

"Fresh tea in the pot, if you want it," he said without lifting his head.

I downed a cup in silence, unsure of what to say. I didn't want to give his knowledge the form of words, that was certain, but I also didn't like this feeling that I had anything to apologise for. I had after all worked hard over the years to create a sense of moral poise and it was most unfair that it had seemingly abandoned me at the first hurdle.

"We need to take a look at your dressings at some point," I said finally, thinking that here at least I could demonstrate something of my regained calm.

He looked up then and smiled gently. "It's fine, I've already done them. The wounds are healing brilliantly, all thanks to you." He was being very kind.

"Oh," I said in a very small voice, and hurried out of the room.

The ponies all greeted their breakfast with their customary enthusiasm and Myrtle could be relied upon for her usual pail of milk but as I handed her a treat, I realised with a fresh pang of worry that we had eaten the last of my usual stores. It meant that we were back to that old favourite of roots and beans and although it might generally be considered normal to enhance one's diet with a bit of illegal bartering, to try to buy more now would be foolish in the extreme. With suspicion already lingering around me, to suddenly use double my week's rations would be dangerously incriminating.

"Well, boys," I murmured. Myrtle's two half-grown sons were nibbling cheekily at my sleeve. "I think I can keep you off the menu for now, but I can't promise anything."

Matthew found me staring sorrowfully down at the chickens; he must have seen me standing there through the kitchen window.

"Are you all right?" he asked tentatively, possibly fearing a ferocious retort.

Glancing around in instant anxiety to check no unexpected passers-by were likely to see, I gave him a quick uncertain smile; "I'm trying to make the cockerel into dinner. I know he's intensely annoying and deserves everything he gets but it's very hard. If I think about it much longer I'm going to end up turning us all vegetarian."

He gave a gentle laugh which did more to ease away my discomfort than any words could do. "Would it help if I offered to do it for you?"

I felt a rush of unexpected gratitude. "Would you? Oh yes please!"

"That's settled then. I do want something in return though … No, please don't look at me like that anymore. This isn't another attempt to force an opinion from you – I don't want to upset you again. It's something I hope you'll find relatively easy, now that you've foolishly committed yourself to my cause." He smiled at my expression, "Really it is. You'll be exercising your ponies today, yes? Excellent. I was wondering if you would mind allowing your course to drift past Warren Barn? I'd really like you to confirm that those men are still there and if they are, see if you recognise them at all. You don't need to go up to them or anything, just look from afar. I'm sure they're perfectly harmless in daylight and if we can start to build a picture of who they are and what they're up to, we'll do a heck of a lot better."

"I … see," I said carefully, thinking fast.

"Don't worry though if you'd rather not," he added hastily, mistaking my hesitation for reluctance.

"No, no, it's fine," I said quickly, "I was just thinking about the logistics, that's all."

"*Really?*" He seemed surprised. "You truly are an unusual woman, aren't you? Most would have quite rightly told me to push off."

I had the distinct impression he was consciously making an effort to be pleasant to me and it looked like he might reach out, but his hand changed direction at the last moment so that he leaned on the hen house instead. I came then to the sharp realisation that the events of the previous night had caused this *politeness* and I was suddenly aware that whatever reaction I deserved from my outburst, this careful handling was not the one I would have chosen.

I smiled grimly at myself as he turned to lead the way back into the house – for someone who had recently confessed to thinking the unforgivable, I was hardly in a position to resent it.

"By the way, I had a thought this morning," I said to the back of his head as I followed him in through the door. "I have a friend in the telephone exchange. She might be able to tell us who your Irishman placed that call to or if she doesn't know, she might be able to ask the girls in case someone else does. I know it's a long shot, but it has to be worth a try."

Chapter 11

The sun was warm on my face as, with a click of my tongue, the ponies set off at a leisurely trot, scuffing across the top of the compressed powder and dodging the treacherous pockets of shade with their concealed slicks of ice. We were following the blurred tracks laid down by fox and manhunt; I was riding one and leading two, which was quite restrained by the standards of the hunt's grooms in the area – they were often seen leading three or sometimes even four fresh hunters out on a hack – and after squeezing through the tall metal gates of the Park, I threw caution to the wind and risked a canter amongst the towering drifts along the wide inviting verge. The ponies were good little creatures and cantered steadily alongside without a murmur before we slowed to a walk and set about slithering down the hill.

The valley was steep here and even this new March sun could not hope to travel high enough in the sky to bring much warmth to this shady little corner. The previous day's rainwater had formed sinuous rivulets through the softening crust before freezing in the heavy night air and we had to pick our way gingerly down to the old stone bridge at the bottom and on through the last gate and out into open fields.

The large house that belonged to the park stood high upon the hilltop and although it was strategically concealed by young trees and the contours of the valley slopes, I still felt the glare of its silent windows. It was an attractive building, very much in the Cotswold style, and it nestled on the crown of the high ridge so that the rear wing gazed out above me over rolling farmland. On the far side, where it faced south to catch the sun, the great gabled windows of an impressive frontage watched over idyllic gardens, bursting in summer with lavender and impressive topiary, before leading the eye down into fresh young plantations and the still waters of the great lake beyond. Now, though, we left the house and its tall gables behind and followed the increasingly slippery track round to the rather smaller farmhouse while my eyes scanned the route ahead. I was looking for any sign of Matthew's two men but I didn't need to search particularly closely – they were clearly still there; their car was nestling in the remains of the drift that had enclosed it outside the tall double doors of the larger stone barn.

The farmyard was just a small collection of buildings, simple and workmanlike, while the pretty little house itself was huddled down in the lowest part of the valley just out of reach of the stream which in warmer weather ran busily at its feet. There were two barns; one a large stone building which bore the name *Warren Barn* in faded whitewash, and the other a low tumbledown structure which looked like one more bad storm might be enough to crush it entirely; and as I approached, I wondered how it was that Jamie Donald had managed to end up in such a place. As far as I knew, he had never been a farmer; but as I drew closer, I answered my own question.

Clearly visible behind the car and the open barn doors lay woodworking benches and tools which swiftly reminded me of the Inspector's description of *joiner*. The rough unfinished skeletons of gates and doors lurked in the shadowy interior, and Jamie had, I realised, been employed by the Estate to make the endless repairs that were essential for keeping the livestock in, or keeping unwanted visitors out.

Watching the car cautiously as the track brought me nearer, I saw two men climb out and I could see another down at the house. They planted themselves in my path with unwarranted authority and, naturally on edge, I halted, keeping a wary eye on them both. There was little doubt that these brutes were the Irishmen from Matthew's story.

One had a face which was curiously slack and devoid of expression, and he looked as though he depended very heavily on his companion for instruction. There was no mistaking his animal strength however, and I did not doubt that he was the sort to react swiftly and brutally to anything he did not understand.

The other must have been Matthew's gunman; he had great hulking shoulders and walked with the heavy stride of solid muscle, and he had thin lips which he now licked speculatively:

"What do you want? This isn't a public road."

"Afternoon, I haven't met you before, have I? I'm just riding through," I explained politely, catching a movement behind them as the man from the house began hurrying over.

"Well, this here is private property so I suggest you simply turn about and take your pretty little self back the way you came." His voice was hard and dry, the words more a blur that had lost a few crucial vowels and consonants, and I brightened inwardly, knowing that I had at least solved the mystery of their origins.

"I just need to get through that gate and then I'll be out of your way." I gestured to the small gate below the house which led back into the woods and gave what I hoped was a very sweet smile. "I've not got far to go then you see. Sir William—"

"What you *need* to do, lass, is turn about."

"Oh, come off it," I said with the beginnings of impatience. A leer had spread across the other's slack mouth and gathering myself together, I gave a click of my tongue and urged the pony forwards.

As quick as lightning a hand flashed out and caught at my pony's reins. I gasped and swore uselessly at the silent brute, suddenly realising my folly as he held my pony fast.

"Let go of my horse!" I squeaked, not even pretending to be

87

brave any more. No amount of tugging on the reins would release them.

Casting an approving glance at his fellow, the talkative one stepped in and thrust his broad face up to mine. "I've asked you nicely to turn about and now I'm telling you, this is private property and you're trespassing. Unless, of course, you'd like to stay and keep us company?" Then he reached up and touched my hair.

I knew it was a ploy. I knew it was just a joke at my expense playing on the stereotype of countless gothic dramas but all the same I could not help batting away his hand in disgust. He gave a laugh.

Then a voice I recognised spoke with forced authority from somewhere close behind;

"What is going on? Let that woman go! *Miss Phillips?*"

Relief flooded in and with it came anger and the abrupt return of my pony's reins. I straightened up to my full height and looking straight over the nearer man's head, fixed the estate manager with my most disapproving stare. "Mr Hicks, these men were attacking me. Kindly inform them of who I am."

There was an unpleasant pause. But then, with a scowl at me, the nearer one turned away to launch into a furious but muted argument with Hicks, which involved much gesturing and shaking of heads. The silent man continued to stare at me with a disconcerting kind of blankness, almost as if his mind were just resting there for want of anything better. Ignoring him, I strained my ears to listen but I could catch nothing beyond the occasional oath from the brute and a spluttering protest from Hicks. Eventually, however, the manager seemed to gain his point and, hastily flapping his hands to silence the last protest from the other, he finally approached me with a cringingly deferential air.

"Miss Phillips, let me apologise. These men are just trying to protect a crime scene; you'll have heard about that sad business? But of course you may take your usual ride through the park. Sir William would be most upset to hear about this."

"Yes, he would, wouldn't he," I said acidly, thankful that my voice held no trace of a tremor. I turned my gaze to the two thugs, "What are your names?"

They exchanged glances beneath lowered brows. Finally, the man who'd argued with Hicks spoke sullenly, "What do you want them for?"

"Miss Phillips," Hicks interjected hastily, "I'm sure we can resolve this matter ourselves. They meant no harm and, as you know, Sir William is not in the best of health …"

"Your names," I snapped. "I have never in my life been spoken to as you just have and I may wish to take this matter further. Your names, or do I have to tell Sir William that his estate manager was condoning a friend being attacked by his staff?"

I glared down at them as they fidgeted sulkily. They looked to Hicks but he held up his hands helplessly. He looked scared and I wondered who was actually in charge here.

"Davey Turford." There was an unexpected mumble from the less alert one and, judging by the expression on his fellow's face, this had the misfortune of being the truth.

I turned to the other. "And you?"

It looked for a moment that he might refuse but then, with a brief show of teeth that passed for a smile and was all the more sinister for it, he growled, "Simon."

"E's my brother," offered Davey, again surprising us all. Simon Turford shot him a loaded glance and he shut his mouth quickly.

"Right then, Davey and Simon Turford." I settled back in the saddle with the applied authority of a school ma'am, "Do you apologise or do I need to make a formal complaint?"

I wondered if I had gone too far when I saw their mouths tighten. But then at long last their thin lips formed something which may have passed for an apology and I was able to nod and gather up the reins. "I will let this matter drop this once, but if either of you so much as think of bothering me next time …" I let the threat hang.

Then I turned to the beleaguered manager. "Mr Hicks, would you be a dear and open the gate?"

Chapter 12

My mood could only have been described as buoyant as the ponies laboured their way homewards towards the glistening village; so much so that I couldn't help hallooing jovially as we trudged past the Manor driveway. John was standing watching his grooms as they fiddled about inside the smart horse lorry with its Daimler engine, and it seemed that they must have been changing the partitions because I could see great panels of plywood being nailed to hollow frames in the workshop nearby. He looked up as I called my greeting and lifted a hand. Then he beckoned.

With a fleeting regret for the post-drama exuberance which had inspired my greeting and would now cause my delay, I turned the ponies into the drive.

"Afternoon," he said as we drew near.

His greeted was rather lacklustre and it became instantly apparent that not everyone was having quite such a successful day. I noticed then that his expression was clouded and with a sudden rush of care, I said, "Why, John, what's the matter?"

He mustered a cheerful enough smile. "Oh, nothing much, just the usual. How are you anyway? Forgiven me for invading your peace yesterday?"

"Of course, but have you forgiven me for being so cross?"

He gave me a tired grin. "I don't suppose you have time for a

91

cup of tea? I could do with a break, and you'd make the perfect excuse. You could put your ponies in a stable for five minutes, couldn't you? Please?"

I very nearly refused and made my excuses but he looked so much in need of a friend that I felt guilty for even hesitating and so instead nodded my agreement. "That would be lovely, thank you."

The Manor stables were amazing. They had been built into the remains of the old tithe barn and many of the original oak beams still hung gracefully overhead. The air had that wonderful sweet horsey scent mixed with straw and, as we clopped our way quietly along the row, twelve eager heads appeared over their half-doors to investigate the newcomers. They were each magnificent beasts, tall and strong, designed to carry men over mile upon mile of uneven ground in pursuit of the unlucky fox and I was swiftly reminded of my youthful adventures on the similar horses that my father had kept. It was pleasant to indulge in these memories and I could do so without any trace of regret – somehow I had never quite embraced the rough and tumble of the hunting field, though I had been fearless enough, and I had given up jumping perfectly readily with the acquisition of the problematic but inspiring Beechnut.

Hanging the small saddle over a convenient bar, I shut the stable door on the three little curious faces and turned to follow John back along the row towards sunlight, greeting the residents as I passed. The stables were always clean but this time I noticed a hint of shabbiness in the chipped paint and tatty buckets which had not been there before and I wondered what his father said about this. Keeping up appearances was paramount to the Colonel.

"He's off next week, now that the weather forecast claims to be improving at last." John had stopped by an elegant dark bay thoroughbred who lipped politely at his proffered hand. I gazed thoughtfully at the horse's sensitive face, taking in his dark eye and supple mouth as he investigated me in his turn. "You remember him, don't you? Union Star – your father broke him in for me, so you should remember."

I nodded slowly, thinking, but any need for a reply was stolen by the horse suddenly sniffing hard and taking hold of my pocket in his teeth. He gave a sharp tug and tasting success, pulled harder, drawing a startled squeak as he made me stagger against the stable door, jamming my hip painfully against the wood as he worked to get at the cubes of swede I kept in my pocket.

"Gerroff!" snapped John, giving him a smack that sent him rushing to the back of his box. He looked at me in concern, "Are you all right? That's unlike you to take cheek from a horse."

"I must be losing my touch." I gave a slightly unsteady laugh. "My fault for keeping treats secreted about my person. Anyway, you were saying – he's going somewhere?"

"To America of all places. I've found some crazy fool out there who wants to use him as a stud horse. He's a half-brother to National Spirit you see, so this fellow wants to use the bloodline even though he never raced. Anyway, I'm not going to sneeze at the money he's offering."

The horse gently nosed between us again and I stroked his forehead to show he was forgiven.

"Tea," John said firmly and led me across the gravel into the house.

The house always inspired awe in me. It was a huge old manor house which, so I was told, had foundations dating back to Saxon times. For the most part however, the house was a mixture of Tudor and Jacobean with lovely stone windows filled with tiny diamond panes of glass to match. At the front of the house, facing south and furthest from the church, this crumbling and antiquated elegance had given way to a thoroughly Georgian addition but in spite of its inconsistency, I had always loved this easternmost wing with its light and airy views over the fields as they sloped steeply down to Washbrook.

It was into the last of these rooms that we now settled and, ushering me into a comfortable armchair while the housekeeper discreetly set cup and saucer by my side, John drifted over to the spirits counter.

"Brandy?" he offered, pouring himself a measure. "Ah, you may well look disapproving, my young friend, but if you'd had the morning I've just had you'd be beating me to it, I assure you."

He walked into the deep bay window and as he stood moodily contemplating the bright valley that stretched away below with its hard pockets of glittering shade, I found myself covertly watching him over my cup of tea. This unprecedented inspection was inspired, I suppose, by the recent recurring mentions of his name but regardless of its cause I was suddenly aware that I had never really acknowledged the transformation of the boy that had featured in the best of my childhood adventures into this person who was now very much a man.

From as far back as I could remember, our summer holidays from school – him from a boarding school, me from the one in the next village – had been spent in grubby companionship on the hunt for frogs and other delightful things in the stream that ran along the bottommost boundary of the Manor estate. Now he was taller, perhaps an inch or so above my houseguest's height and lighter in his build, though not nearly as underfed, and these days, with all the advantages of adult sophistication, his mother's dark hair and the piercing Langton blue eyes, he was undeniably very handsome.

And yet, odd as it might seem, even after all our years of closeness and in spite of that constancy of friendship which should probably have marked him out from the start to become my unrequited childhood sweetheart, I had never doubted myself. Quite contrary to the goaded accusations I had recently received from another.

I gave a sudden start at the unexpectedly vivid turn my mind was taking and, dragging myself hastily out of thoughts that could only confuse me, I said; "John? Do you know the Turford brothers who are staying over at Warren Barn currently?"

He thought for a moment, watching a cock pheasant as it beat its way clumsily past the window. "I don't think so. Should I?"

"Not really, I was just wondering, that is all. I think they're working for Sir William, and I wondered if he'd said anything about them."

"Not to me he hasn't. You can always ask my father."

I grinned to myself, knowing that it was the last thing I would want to do. "No, it's fine. Just idle curiosity, that's all."

There was a pause while we both stared out at the fields below, each lost to our own thoughts. But then John took a great gulp of brandy and said, "Do you know, I really hate that man."

I stayed silent, trying not to stumble into saying something blunderingly stupid. But then he continued, venting the frustration of a very bad day in one short revealing burst; "Are you actually aware of just how much trouble he has caused me? I'm days behind on my work and it's all because I'm having to spend every waking moment poking about in grubby corners on the hunt for that hateful man! When I find him, I'm not sure I'll be answerable for the consequences."

I must have made a noise because he cast me a glance over his shoulder, "Oh, don't mind me, I'm just fed up. I don't mind helping the search, of course I don't, but after nearly two months of digging out the lane and now my father nagging me to lend Sir William my best men, it's all starting to get a bit much. Life doesn't just stop, you know, the horses still need exercising, the lorry still needs its refurbishment and it has to be ready for Tuesday. I don't mind telling you that this search has cost me a damned fortune and Sir William doesn't give a fig of course, the likes of him never think about us lesser folk. 'No expense spared!' and all that rubbish." He turned to face me and sighed, adding in a more sedate tone, "Although in this instance I'm not sure I should blame him."

He gave me a rueful smile. "I was in a tediously long finance meeting but when I got Sir William's frantic telephone call to say that the police were swarming all over his land, of course I had to just drop everything and dash over there. He was in quite a state I can tell you – I thought he was going to have a seizure!" He turned back to the window. "And then we would have had another death to add to Croft's account."

I tutted sympathetically, "And the Colonel? Was he very upset too?"

John gave a dry laugh, "When is my father ever anything else? We were at least spared the full force of his furious observations, but rest assured that he made extensive use of the telephone to transmit what he couldn't say in person."

"Oh dear," I said, with genuine feeling. "It must have been a very shocking experience for you all."

John's profile was obscured by the turn of his head but I thought I saw him smile. "You call it a shock? I call it a tragedy. My uncle was practically having a fit, I was running around like an errand boy and the police were locking down the Estate like it was a prison with no one allowed to go anywhere, let alone near that wretched farmhouse, and all because Jamie Donald took it into his head to get himself killed ... Sorry, that's not a very respectful thing to say about the newly deceased is it?"

Shaking his head, he turned to move towards a chair and I gave a sudden exclamation which made him look up at me in surprise; "John, you're limping!"

He settled himself into the window seat and gave me a wounded puppy kind of look. "Another cost of this manhunt – my leg is playing up again. It always does in winter but it is worse today ... must have been all that pointless walking about the countryside yesterday. Next time I shall lurk at the end of a telephone like my uncle, not giving a damn whether it is twenty yards or twenty miles."

"You didn't find anything then?"

"Not a trace. He can't have vanished into thin air, and the police don't think he's left the area so he must be hiding somewhere. There are reports that he was shot so he'll be suffering a bit by now. Although of course we may be lucky and he's lying dead in a ditch somewhere … It'd be a shame because I would *really* like to be the one to catch him, but it saves hanging him."

I found myself repeating Matthew's words. "You're taking this a little personally, aren't you?"

"Shouldn't I be?" He flicked a glance at me; he seemed faintly surprised by my question. "The truth is I never liked him – he's … well, I don't need to tell *you*, you know better than anyone what dependence can be placed upon his character. The Law wants to catch him and hang him, and if my efforts make that happen I will be a very happy man. He's a jumped-up little farm boy who should know his place and honestly it pleases me to think he's finally slipped up. Very unchristian of me, I know, and I'd like to pretend I'm doing it for King and Country, but I'm not." He could have easily added "*so there*" and thereby completed the schoolboy rant but he didn't and instead fiddled with the cord that drew the curtains.

There was a pause while I sipped my tea and tried not to think of Matthew or what dependence I was placing on him. Instead, I fixed my gaze firmly on the wonderful view framed by elegant windows and sophisticated furnishings which were, I realised, the enduring legacy of John's mother. The Colonel was far too precise and masculine to pick a floral fringe for a dado rail and before the room had taken on its present incarnation as the son's office, this must have been her domain to have retained the pretty trimmings of her feminine tastes. I wondered whether the perfect room and its idyllic view had gone some way towards compensating for the deficiencies of her spouse.

"I was going to ask you to marry me, you know," John said suddenly.

I jumped guiltily, wondering if he had been reading my thoughts. "Oh John," I said sadly.

"Don't worry, I've thought better of it. You would have said no anyway, wouldn't you? You're too damned independent, that's your trouble. Nobody can get behind that tough façade." He gave me a cheery grin to show that he didn't mean to offend. "Anyway, onwards and upwards, that's my motto. I've got plans, you know."

"Plans? How exciting!" I said brightly, and realised that I sounded far too keen to change the subject.

"Yes. This horse going to America is the start of new things for me. You'll be surprised by what the future holds, Ellie, you really will." He finished the remains of his drink and climbed rather gingerly to his feet. I felt a rush of sympathy at his poor damaged leg but as he set his glass down onto the table with a firm click, I saw him glance thoughtfully at the decanter on the cabinet and a different kind of concern took hold.

"Look at that," he said, oblivious to my thoughts and gesturing at the newspaper which lay on the table by my side. "Some people are so idiotic."

I picked it up and scanned the opened page. "What am I looking at?" I could only see the usual reports on food shortages, the escalating row about electricity outages and the sorry state of the economy. The paper was last week's edition of the *Telegraph*, from the morning that had brought the storm.

"There at the bottom – pathetic, isn't it ... What kind of person would do something like that? I mean you'd have to be pretty damned idiotic, wouldn't you?"

I hastily rescanned the page and then finally found what he must be talking about:

"Police were swiftly called on Wednesday when Messrs Wyatts and Clarke of Cirencester Auction House unexpectedly identified Lot 216 as a miniature known colloquially as 'The Idle Hands'. The painting by an unknown Dutch artist along with a private collection of etchings and watercolours vanished from the home of Lord and Lady _____ of Lansdown Place, Cheltenham in December 1940 during that brief period of despicable looting which still shocks the residents to this day. The identity of the would-be vendor is still unknown."

"You see what I mean?" he asked, pacing to the window again. "If you're going to do something like that, at least have the sense to sell it in a different county to the one you stole it from." He laughed.

"I remember when that happened," I said, recalling the shock of the residents after the criminal events which had followed in the wake of Cheltenham's single night of German bombing. "People can be so cruel, can't they? Imagine having your home destroyed and your lives blown apart, only to then find that some disgusting lowlife thinks he has a right to your few surviving possessions. I find it hard to believe that anybody could do that to their fellow Englishman."

"We Englishmen are not such a saintly breed as we would have you believe, I'm afraid, Ellie." John smiled gently and then moved to give me a friendly embrace as I rose to go. "Anyway, enough of these depressing subjects. This pathetic example of an Englishman was wondering if you'd decided about the dance on Saturday, now that it looks hopeful that I'll be able to get the car out? Strictly as friends of course, but I think it might be nice. What d'you say?"

He looked so adorably eager that I hadn't the heart to say no and so, laughingly, I agreed. But later, as I walked steadily up the sodden lane with my ponies, I had to wonder how on earth I had let him charm me into going. I hadn't worn a dress in a very long time.

Chapter 13

Freddy had been a good boy and had brought in all the ponies bar Beechnut who whickered her greeting softly as I approached. Her stable was ready and all I had to do was sling a blanket over her and slip her meal of chaff and waste vegetables – because access to animal feed was heavily regulated – through the door and then I was done. The sun had dipped below the horizon and it was sending a last incredible burst of light up into the sky to reflect crimson off the streaked pattern of the fields. There was no breeze and already a few stars were blinking on. There would be another heavy frost overnight and, putting paid to anyone's hopes of taking a car anywhere, today's thaw would be an ice rink by the morning.

There was no one in the kitchen, no lamps were lit bar the usual glow from the hearth and I wondered for a moment where they might have gone. It could not have been long because there was a pan steaming gently on the hot plate by the fire. Next I thought that someone must have come and breathlessly scanned the room for signs of a struggle, but finally, more calmly, I realised that the chaos was just Freddy's usual detritus. Then I registered the distant tinkling of the piano in the back room.

Notes were forming haltingly in the air, untrained fingers stumbling along something I ought to have recognised only to be brought to an abrupt stop by youthful eagerness.

"I bet it was fun joining the army."

Silence, and then the same keys but struck this time with the fluidity of experience. "Yes, there was a certain fun in it. You get a strong sense of camaraderie – sorry? Oh, I mean brotherhood or friendship. I met some good people and there is a lot of tomfoolery and humour amongst soldiers." There was a fresh whisper of notes from the piano; they must have been his as Freddy's fingers never moved so smoothly. "But, in truth, it wasn't that great. Going to war is not fun; you have to leave your home and … people. And when you start to lose your friends to enemy bullets, the joke suddenly wears very thin. Go on, try it again from the beginning."

A memory tugged at my mind and then receded again. The back room, which would have been the front room had we used the main door as we ought, was really my store for saddles but there was still a little space for the old instrument and the few other items of furniture that had become too tatty for use elsewhere in the house. Behind the closed door it was almost possible to feel Freddy's effort as he mimicked the notes he had heard and I was both impressed and unreasonably irked that Matthew had managed to inspire this level of interest in the instrument in a matter of hours when I had spent four years of trying with very little success at all.

Then a finer hand joined the other and suddenly my ears made sense of the clumsy music. The melody curled about me, enfolding me in its embrace and its memories. I knew it now of course; they played to a more cheerful rhythm than I had previously known so that the Northern folk tune took on a sweet romantic lilt that was wonderfully warming. *Oh, the snow it melts the soonest when the winds begin to sing …*

My father had tended to retreat to his piano when my mother had taken some silly misdemeanour in its worst possible light and scolded him mercilessly, and I tried to recall how long it had been since I had last heard him play. Was it fair, I wondered, that

101

having already shown myself a bitter fool once today, I should now be confronted by the happier past as well?

I had an awful flashback to our last meeting. I wasn't thinking of my father now. *He* had not yet received his call-up papers but he had known they were coming. I had been eighteen and about as unreasonable as an eighteen-year-old in love can be, whereas he had been hatefully calm and sensible, and I had raged and stormed at him until he had finally lost his temper. He always was more eloquent than I could be – his eight years' more experience of the world had given him the ability to turn any argument of mine into the silly ramblings of a child; and his brutal angry words as he forced his point home had cut me to the core. He could not love me too.

"It was Eleanor, wasn't it, the 'people' you talked about." An uninvited mirror to my memories, Freddy's voice drifted through the wall. I had barely noticed that the tune had ended.

"What makes you say that?"

"I just guessed. It's the way she looks at you, only then you say something and she gets cross."

Matthew laughed. "You think you're very smart, don't you? Well, unless you want her to be cross with you too, I'd keep your guesses to yourself." There was a creak of a chair as he stood up and a murmur about dinner getting burnt, and then I was frantically retreating down the passage by the dairy, cuffing imaginary tears from my icy cheeks and praying that the forgotten saddle over my arm wouldn't jangle. I think I must have just wrenched open the door and slammed it noisily shut when he appeared in the kitchen.

We both froze. We stood there in the half light, barely yards apart, and for a horrible moment I feared he knew that I had been listening, but then he smiled and when he spoke his voice betrayed no sign of suspicion.

"Hello, you're just in time for tea."

I mustered what I hoped was a convincing smile in return and stepped into the room once more. "Mmmm, smells good. You managed to corner him then?" My voice sounded brittle and I tried to keep my head turned away so that I would not have to meet his eyes.

"What? Oh, you mean the renegade cockerel?" He laughed. "I didn't even try, you'll be pleased to know. It's rabbit."

"Oh," I said lamely, feeling horribly like I might crack after all.

"Eleanor, are you all right? Only you look like you've seen a ghost."

"Do I? No, I'm fine thank you." A lamp flared into life as he set a match to it and I blinked rapidly in the amber light, turning hastily to busy myself with hanging the saddle over a chair-back, desperate to avoid any kind of interrogation. "Must just be the cold air outside."

My hands finished smoothing the old leather of the saddle flaps and then, not even thinking that I might be betraying a lie, I asked, "Did you know that was my favourite?"

He didn't need to question my meaning. "I did. Your father taught it to me once, and I remember your delight as he played it."

"Oh." In my surprise my voice came out as a flat croak and I cursed myself for somehow managing to sound cross, even when I truly was not. Somehow I had turned to face him once more. "I mean—"

There was an impatient yell from next door. "Is anyone going to answer that telephone?"

Even as Freddy spoke, I heard it. A bizarrely distant ringing penetrated with all the subtlety of a bludgeon and the peculiar stillness between us abruptly vanished to the echo of the telephone's shrill urgency.

"Oh!" I cried, feeling very strange in a way I couldn't even begin to describe. Squeezing past the table and Matthew, I hurried across the room to answer it.

"Hello?"

"Hello?" came a quavering voice in return.

"Hello. This is Eleanor Phillips, who am I speaking to please?"

"Oh hello my dear."

This really wasn't going well. I waited for the person to continue and after a rather long pause the woman spoke again. "Oh, er, well. Mavis is here with me."

Wondering whether it was too soon to be rude, I said, "That's good. Can I help you?"

"It's Mary Croft, dear. How are you?"

I was suddenly acutely aware of Matthew's presence as he turned to lean against the doorframe, observing me while the remnants of the moment before still played behind his eyes.

"Hello Mrs Croft. I'm very well, thank you. How are you?" I said carefully, watching his face.

He gave a little start and, with a sudden intensity of concentration, moved closer to perch on the arm of the settee.

"Oh dear me," said Matthew's mother breathlessly, "I've just had the police round to see me again. They were very kind of course, but they were saying such horrible things; such awful things. Mavis – my sister, do you remember her? – wouldn't let me stay on my own so she's here too which is very kind of her. But I can't put it out of my mind. Have you heard?"

Turning away so that Matthew could not see my face, I answered cautiously, "I've heard, Mrs Croft. I had the police here yesterday myself."

"It's just awful, isn't it? They were asking me such questions; I hardly knew what to say. Of course my boy hasn't got a history of violence! What a thing to ask! And then they were asking whether I'd seen or heard from him. It was just horrible."

I made a sympathetic noise, feeling a deceitful fraud and barely knowing what I should say. Finally, I managed limply, "Yes it is terrible, they asked me something similar. Is there anything I can do?"

"Bless you, dear, you always were a lamb. But no, nothing, thank you." She hesitated, then added, "I just feel so awful. It's in

104

the press and everything, and they're saying such hideous things about him. They're saying that there is enough evidence to hang him if they catch him, but I know he didn't do it, he can't have done. Not my Matthew. Why he's the most kind, most wonderful ..." There was something that sounded horribly like a sob.

"He's ... um, he always was nice, Mrs Croft."

It sounded painfully lukewarm, even to me. I felt torn, desperately wishing to give her the comfort she needed but crippled by the embarrassment of being asked to speak in such personal terms of the man who had once introduced me to her as his future wife – hard enough in any circumstance but presently made infinitely worse by the knowledge that the very same man was at this moment listening intently to every single word that I said.

Matthew made some involuntary movement on the settee and I glanced back at him. He looked terrible, pale again, and the hard line of his mouth clearly betrayed his miserable frustration at the grief he was causing to his mother. His gaze flicked up to catch mine and seemed to understand what I was thinking, and the expression in his unhappy face appeared to only convey compassionate gratitude that I should be saying anything at all.

Shame hit me hard again and suddenly my selfish discomfort vanished. I said what I ought to have admitted days ago.

"I don't believe what they're saying for a moment, Mrs Croft. I don't need your description of his good character to know that it's just not possible. I *know* he is innocent."

"You do?" All of a sudden, her voice brightened to show only a faint tremble of emotion. "Good girl, I'm so glad to hear that. You make me feel braver already. If he's not entirely friendless, there's hope yet, isn't there? There has to be."

"Of course there is," I said crisply. "And he certainly isn't friendless."

She gave a soft little sigh that was terribly sad. "I'm really calling because I couldn't rest without finding out whether he has been to see you. I know he can't come here, but he was talking about

105

you only the other week, about how he wanted to, although you might think he shouldn't, and he was going to anyway; and I kind of hoped he might have done."

Her words had blurred into a garbled rush and it took me a moment to decipher her meaning.

"Have I seen him?" I repeated slowly, looking at Matthew. His gaze lifted to hold mine and he gave a single shake of his head. "No, I'm sorry, Mrs Croft, I haven't. But I'm sure he's coping. He's a very resourceful man, remember, and I'm sure he's fine, wherever he is."

"Yes dear, I'm sure you're right." She sounded so painfully uncertain.

"I know I am. He's quite capable of looking after himself, isn't he? You can trust Matthew to not do anything foolish."

"I'm sure you're right," she repeated and then hesitated. "But they're after my darling boy with dogs and guns ... *Guns!*"

I thanked all the lucky stars in heaven and all the lesser saints and their cherubim that the report of him being shot did not appear to have reached her. "I'm sure he's perfectly safe, you know," I said decisively. "Any sensible person can see that he didn't do it, it's just the press blowing it all out of proportion. The police are being very thorough and I'm sure they'll get to the bottom of it soon."

"Do you think so?" She suddenly sounded much more cheerful. "Oh goodness, there's the operator, no, I won't have another three minutes. I'd better go, my dear. Do look out for him, won't you? And if you happen to see him, tell him I ..." The telephone went dead as she panicked and cut herself off.

I set the receiver back on its hook and slowly turned to face the room once more. I was somehow feeling incredibly exposed again, without even quite knowing why.

In his own face there was something of the expression that had met me that morning, something like caution and vaguely wary. He said quietly, "This doesn't seem to have been said enough recently; but thank you."

"She's all right, Matthew. No, really she is. Her sister is with her, and she sounded fine. I think she just wanted to do her bit to counter the newspaper reports."

"The hacks have taken hold of it, have they?" He made a fist and then forced himself to release it, looking suddenly so utterly defeated that I forgot restraint for the moment and went over to cover his determinedly relaxed hand briefly with mine.

"It'll work out," I said as he looked up and gave me a small lopsided smile that didn't reach his eyes. "It won't be long before we've found the truth and then everything will be just as it was."

"Yes," he confirmed and his hand flexed in his lap again.

"And besides," I added, folding my arms and staring regally down my nose at him. "I won't let them hurt you. They'll have to get past me first."

This feeble attempt at a bit of silver-screen bravado did at last have the desired effect and finally I saw a more convincing smile pluck at the corners of his mouth.

"Oh!" I exclaimed, suddenly enthusiastic. "I haven't told you about my day! I found out something which will cheer you up. Can we have tea and I'll tell you about it? Currently I'm too weak from hunger to get my thoughts into anything resembling a logical order."

"Wait for me! Don't say anything interesting until I'm there!" Freddy's voice came as a wild shout from the other room.

Matthew's smile suddenly widened to real warmth as he climbed to his feet to move past me towards the fire. "You two really brighten an otherwise dreary existence, do you know that?"

"What with all the yelling, unpredictable outbursts and everything?"

He laughed as he lifted the lid of the pan. "Particularly with those. They remind me I'm alive."

Rabbit stew proved to be remarkably tasty if a little gamey and it was only as we set about our second helpings that I was finally able to spare a thought for the day's events.

"Their names are Davey and Simon Turford," I announced, smugly dipping a piece of bread in the remains of the sauce before waggling it at them, "and they are brothers. I also suspect that they are from Yorkshire, although the accent is too diluted to determine which part."

"How on earth did you discover all that?" Matthew's incredulity made me laugh. Freddy was staring at me with new-found respect.

I quickly told them of my adventure, glossing carefully over Simon Turford's unpleasant allusions for Freddy's sake, although I suspected that the other was not fooled by my light-hearted tone. Any particular upset for me was long past anyway, and the stupefied silence which followed the conclusion of my tale was worth a thousand such brutish run-ins.

"Well," said Matthew after a long pause. "That certainly gives us something to go on."

"It does?" Freddy asked.

"Why yes, Freddy, it gives us a lot. We now know their names, that they're northern men – which may tell us something in itself – and that they're here with the express permission of Sir William's Estate. That alone must be quite significant."

"Hicks didn't seem very comfortable with ordering them about though." I sat back, finally allowing the very undignified feelings of triumph to begin to fade. "I'm not sure what that means, but I feel that it means something. He almost seemed *afraid*."

"Perhaps they don't answer to him. Could they answer straight to Sir William?"

"You're wondering whether he was the man on the other end of the telephone?"

"Whoever it was, he was clearly the boss of them. Simon, who definitely isn't an Irishman as we now know," a nod in my direction, "was reasonably polite and even called him 'sir' at one point. Although I can't quite see what would motivate Sir William to require that one of his own tenants be murdered."

"But then we already know Jamie tried to tell you something he shouldn't. It must have been a pretty terrible secret to push them to murder."

"You think so? Perhaps Jamie was simply messing about with his usual shady dealings and got on the wrong side of them, or rather, their boss. After all – as I think you've already experienced, our two Turford brothers are pretty rough customers and I'm not sure it would take much to make them violent."

"Yes, but it is a big step up from violence to murder, Matthew, really it is. Think about it – someone can be bullied into silence easily enough, but to deliberately order their killing is an entirely different matter. You've got to deal with the body and not to mention you then have the police crawling all over the place, poking their noses in to just the thing you were desperately trying to keep secret."

"So it is something big."

His wooden insistence left us mute and we sat for a minute, dismally meditating.

"There's something else too." The sudden sound of Matthew's voice made me and Freddy both jump.

"There is?"

He smiled as the boy and I spoke in unison. "Yes. All this time I've been thinking that they're just hanging about at the farm to see if I turn up again, but that's illogical. Why wait there, exactly where I know they'll be, when they could be looking for me at any number of other more likely places?"

"But surely that's the point? With John …" I felt a strange hesitation to use his name again. "With John and his men looking under every stone for you, and the police searching everywhere else, there's little use in their trailing about the countryside as well. You've been back once already, who's to say you wouldn't again?"

"True. Damn, I hadn't thought of that." He thought for a moment. "But what if … what if we're going about this all wrong. What if it truly doesn't have anything to do with me at all? Perhaps what we should actually be trying to work out is what's keeping them there in the first place, I mean specifically *there*. After all, something must have been going on long before I stumbled onto the scene. Yes, I know they might be on the lookout for me, but what if that is secondary to their primary motive?"

"Which is …?"

"To guard something."

"What like? *Treasure?*"

A laugh. "I knew that would get your attention, Freddy. But for the sake of argument, yes; why not treasure, although drugs or restricted foodstuffs are equally possible. You did mention a secret: Maybe they're not waiting for me at all, maybe they're guarding the farm *from* me. Hicks told you they were guarding the crime scene – perhaps he wasn't wrong."

I mulled this over carefully. "So you are involved."

"Well, me and anyone else who happens to be riding by," he corrected with a smile. "I think they can safely presume that after trying to pin his murder on me, I might take a certain degree of personal interest in exposing them. The silly thing about it is that all they've achieved by bullying you is to draw more attention to themselves."

"Tea," I said firmly into the pause.

Freddy entertained us while the kettle boiled with excited musings on what the treasure might be, if it could really be gold and whether they might notice if we took some of it. "We'd hand the rest in to the police, of course," he finished piously.

"Of course," confirmed Matthew dryly.

My fingers accidentally touched his as I handed him the milk. It was only a simple everyday sort of contact but even so it made me give an involuntary flinch as though my skin had been singed. He only seemed to grimace a little as he took his hand away.

"You mentioned Sir William, what of him?" I asked, focusing very hard on my role as his assistant.

Matthew smiled wryly, perfectly ignorant of the nameless disquiet

110

in my idiotic mind. "Well, he's a true brother of the Colonel – believes he rules by 'Divine Right' or some such nonsense, doesn't he? I passed him in the street just after I was demobbed. There I was walking home for only the second time in just over six years with my kit bag in my hand, feeling disorientated because even though you expect time to have stood still, it most definitely hasn't, and he practically drove the car over me yelling 'Out of the way, boy!' as if I were still fourteen years old and stealing apples from his tree. Only I wasn't fourteen, I was thirty-three and pretty tough looking with my close-cropped hair and battle-worn scowl."

"I didn't know you lived in Miserden!" Freddy gave an excited squeak. "How come we've never happened to see you?"

Matthew shifted uncomfortably in his chair and flicked a little glance towards me. I found a remarkable interest in examining the dregs of my tea.

"Oh!" Freddy suddenly turned beetroot. He coughed, "Ahem. Anyway, what were you saying about Sir William?"

Matthew picked up the thread very smoothly. "Trying not to show my prejudices here, I think I can safely say that Sir William is a stereotypical example of a rich man too much used to having what he wants, all silken charm to his friends and a bully to everyone else. That being said, I'm not sure I'd go so far as to claim I've witnessed any true villainy – any thoughts, Eleanor?"

"I'm sorry, but I feel duty bound at this point to admit that much as I'd like to lend evidence to your assessment I've only ever personally encountered the neighbourly side of the man, with particular reference to the steadiness of his attentions to my father. There are rumours that the Langton Family is struggling financially, but really, who isn't at the moment? I suppose if their situation were particularly bad, as the head of the family Sir William might take it upon himself to do something drastic. I certainly wouldn't like to trust to his general benevolence if something occurred to make him truly angry, particularly if whatever I'd done was making claims upon his public standing, but even then, it's his brother that has the reputation for decisive action, not him."

"Hmmm," was all Matthew said in reply. Then, "Well, we're not going to get anywhere unless we know what it is that the Turford brothers are trying to hide."

I looked up sharply, suddenly wary of what he was hinting at. "You're not going up there again?"

"I'll help," Freddy immediately piped up.

Matthew caught my glance. "No, Freddy. Thank you but there's no need. I was just getting carried away."

"Oh." Freddy looked instantly crestfallen, clearly seeing his chances of fame and fortune vanishing before his eyes.

"Oh indeed," I said firmly. "Time for bed I think, young man." Freddy whined. "Not fair."

Matthew laughed. "Off to bed with you. I've got a special task for you in the morning, anyway."

"Really?" Freddy brightened immediately.

"Yes, really. Now goodnight."

Disappointed to be dispatched off to bed like a child, Freddy trudged his way upstairs, huffing and puffing as he went and I watched him go with affectionate amusement; he really was a lovely boy. But then Matthew must have shifted in his chair because all of a sudden I was acutely aware that we were alone, and the realisation was absolutely, overwhelmingly terrifying.

I got up abruptly to fuss unnecessarily with boiling water for a drink I didn't want. I felt unbalanced and on edge again, and although there was a certain irony in the discovery that once more I was resorting to tea-making as a defence against his presence, above it all I was aware of the fact that if he so much as moved a muscle I would have no choice but to turn and run from him as I had done only the night before.

As I say, it was utterly absurd.

"We-ell," Matthew said slowly and I suddenly realised he was feeling just as uncomfortable as I, although obviously for entirely different reasons. "I think I'll turn in myself."

"Yes, good idea," I said vaguely, fiddling aimlessly with clean crockery. Typically the lowermost hinge to the cupboard door chose that moment to finally lose its battle with gravity and I caught it in my hand, hoping he hadn't noticed. I hid it in the breadbin.

"You're in my bedroom, my dear."

There was a crash as I dropped a cup. It promptly smashed across the kitchen floor and I hastily bent to gather up the scattered pieces, ducking my head so that he wouldn't see the unpleasant blush that was heating my cheeks. "Sorry, sorry, sorry."

"Here." He was holding out a piece of broken ceramic. Amusement was just beginning to touch his mouth.

Still crimson, I gingerly took it from him while carefully avoiding touching his fingers. I put the pieces into a pot to be disposed of in the morning and having done that, with my dignity in tatters, I moved hastily towards the door, muttering as I went an almost unintelligible, "G'night."

"Goodnight, Eleanor."

I stopped at the foot of the stairs, the open door in my hand, and turned to him again. He paused in laying out his blankets to look at me enquiringly.

"You're not really planning to go over there again, are you? It's dangerous."

"We'll talk about it in the morning," he said, turning back to making up his bed. "Goodnight."

"Goodnight, Matthew."

Chapter 14

I could not say what had woken me, only that some sudden sound had jerked me out of slumber to lie there with my heart beating wildly and my ears straining to listen. Nothing, no sound at all followed whatever it was that had disturbed me.

I lay there waiting for sleep to return but it stubbornly refused. Some sixth sense told me that it hadn't been my imagination and finally, reluctantly, I gave in. Climbing sluggishly out of bed, I set about dragging some clothes on in the darkened room with the resigned view that I would at least have to go and check, otherwise I would just end up lying awake staring at the ceiling, worrying sleepily until dawn.

I tiptoed down the stairs, anxious not to wake Matthew – Freddy, I knew, could sleep through anything – but I needn't have worried. As I slipped out into the faint glow of dying embers in the living room, I was stopped short by the realisation that the settee was empty. The blankets lay in disarray as if he had leapt up suddenly and I wondered if the noise I had heard had been him leaving. I very nearly went back upstairs to alternately fret and sulk in the comfort of my bed but some other instinct made me slip my bare feet into frozen boots and slide soundlessly out through the kitchen door. As I went, my fumbling fingers met and then lifted down the heavy torch from the shelf above the coat-rack, although I didn't light it.

Outside, the clear night sky had been consumed by dense fog and there was nothing to brighten my way as I stumbled along the path. I stopped at the road, listening as my breath merged gently with the icy air around me. Nothing. Nothing but the crisp silence of a windless night and the occasional rustle of a small creature in the undergrowth.

In the near-black ahead I could just make out the darker shadow of the covered-yard where I stored bedding and fodder. I couldn't even see the faint stain of its rotten tin roof set as an outsized lean-to against the crumbling workshops higher up the hill, and to its left, the low range of my stables was only discernible by the comforting sound of rhythmic chewing from the undisturbed inhabitants. Then something moved in the darkness and, cautiously, I slipped across in its wake.

The covered-yard was truly pitch-black and before I had gone many paces my foot painfully struck something solid. Biting back the hiss of pain, I fumbled with the torch but before I could get it lit, I felt the shockwave as a rush of air lunged towards me across the darkness. It struck my arm, turning me forcibly about before snatching me back, and I would have cried out in fright but that another hand clamped down hard over my mouth.

"Be still, you fool," hissed a low voice in my ear. His arm locked in a tight embrace, crushing me against his chest. I lifted my foot to stamp down onto his but he hissed again; "Eleanor! It's me!"

Matthew? Instantly I stopped fighting and went slack, breathing jerkily into the hand which smothered my mouth and nose, and slowly, once he was sure that I wouldn't scream, he relaxed his hold although his arm still held me close. The torch was eased from my fingers and noiselessly set down somewhere behind him.

"No, don't speak," he breathed by my ear. "They're here."

Who's here? My eyes futilely scanned the darkness as I tried to make sense of what he was saying.

"Come," he breathed again. Taking my hand, he led me blindly

115

along the wall and up the stone steps which rose to the old stone workshops at the side. Once there, concealed within the chill blankness of an alcove, we had a vantage point over the entire yard and through a rusting gap in the tin, I saw where the faintest cast from the moon lightened the roofline of the stables. I could hear Beechnut moving restlessly in the corner.

I looked up at Matthew in silent enquiry as he held me fast against the icy stones. He glanced down and put his lips to my ear. *Wait.*

We waited and I began to think he was mistaken when suddenly, out of the corner of my eye, I caught something moving through the gloom across the banked snow and cobbles. A stable latch squeaked as it was drawn back and then the shadow moved on along the row.

I made an involuntary noise and felt Matthew's body tense beside mine; the soft murmur of unshod feet on the frozen yard was loud in the heavy night-time silence as my ponies began to explore their unexpected freedom.

Suddenly a match flared and I saw Simon Turford's face glow grotesquely in the little red circle of light.

No, no, no!

My voice was lost in breathless horror as I realised what was about to happen. I tried to push Matthew away but my struggles might have been no more than those of a fly, so easily did he hold me back against the wall as he watched what was going on below.

Simon Turford had wound a rag around a broom handle and this flared to blinding life as he set the match to it. The breath caught in my throat.

"Stay here," Matthew hissed. "I'll go. But please, just stay here!"

Then silence as he slipped soundlessly down the steps into the darkness.

The flaming torch glided smoothly across my yard. It was borne along by Simon's ugly bulk through the growing herd and I had the sudden sharp shock of realisation that the cost of Matthew showing

116

himself to these people could well prove to be considerably more serious than the burning of my stables. Cursing myself and desperately regretting the burst of idiotic agitation that had made him go, I peered into the gloomy shadows hoping to somehow remedy this disaster but he had masked his movements too well and I could not find him. A splinter of stone broke off the wall beneath my hand.

The stab of pain to my clenched fingers jolted me into a decision. Recklessly and without much care for silence, I flew down the steps after Matthew and on into the blinding darkness of the covered-yard.

I don't know what would have happened if I had burst out into the open as I think I was intending, but just as I was stumbling through the darkness, two things happened. The first was that as I raced across the floor, I was suddenly caught and held by strong arms once more; the second was a great clattering of angry hooves followed by a high-pitched shriek of terror.

"I *told* you to stay put." There was a sharp hiss beside my ear. "*Ah* ..."

In the end I needn't have worried, Beechnut solved it all for us. They had made the unfortunate mistake of opening her door and as Simon Turford prepared to toss his burning rag into a stable, she charged.

A shrill scream split the night sky as he dropped the burning handle and clutched at his head in a desperate attempt to protect himself. She reared up over him, front hooves flailing violently and I thought that was it and he was dead, but he was lucky. The falling broom hit the ground in a great flurry of sparks and, with a guttural roar which seemed impossible to have come from a horse, I saw Beechnut twist and spin away, eyes rolling wildly in her head.

For a moment Simon Turford stood transfixed by horror. He was frozen like a statue and as the seconds ticked onwards I wondered if he would have time to remember his failed plan. But then, quite suddenly, his nerve broke and he turned and bolted for the muckheap. He threw himself up its steaming banks and vaulted clean over the wall even before Beechnut had time to wheel about and face him again, and it took barely another second for his vanishing figure to become little more than a shadow dwindling into the fog.

An unexpected moment of peace followed this where I had time enough to register Matthew's arms around me and begin to grow embarrassed. Only then there was a flurry of movement within the milling herd of ponies and Davey, his mouth silent working "*oh, oh, oh!*", sprinted clumsily across the yard to throw himself bodily over the closed gate into the road. He barely cleared it before Beechnut slithered to an angry halt behind him, her chest pressed hard against the wooden bars. She looked wild and I thought for a moment that she might try to jump it, but then, as the second man disappeared into the darkness, she simply gave a triumphant toss of her head and turned to trot sedately back to her fellows.

In the same instant, just as soundlessly as that man's departure, the tight hold about me abruptly released and Matthew disappeared, leaving me to stand alone and reeling in the icy shadows.

I must have been staring stupidly at the flaming torch for a good few minutes before a shrill flirtatious squeal from one of the ponies reminded me of my duties and I finally managed to drag my mind back to something resembling sensible thought. I doused the flames with melt-water from the trough before even attempting to make order from the mêlée of ponies and typically it was the smallest of them all that was the most trouble. He seemed to have remembered the days when he was still entire and my feet were stepped on so many times that I lost count, not to mention all feeling in my toes. Eventually, however, he was successfully prised away from his miniature harem and I had them all safely back in their stables, and seemingly none the worse for their adventure bar the odd superficial cut here and there.

Beechnut, in fact, seemed extremely proud of herself. She returned to her stable with great dignity and although she simply appeared to be her usual affectionate self as she politely questioned my claim of empty pockets, I could not help reliving the terrifying vision of her raging fury as she pounded down the yard towards the two men. Running my hand down the soft arch of her neck, I finally came to the happy conclusion that this was one of those rare moments when there was a very definite advantage in being a woman.

"All set to rights?"

Matthew cheerfully loomed out of the darkness beside me just as I was giving them all a final pat. He sounded slightly out of breath as if he had been running.

I nodded and the nearby pony confirmed it by giving a great lazy sigh and turning back to his hay. "Wherever have you been?"

A brief hint of a quiet smile. "I just wanted to check that they really had gone. Didn't you hear the car? They had it hidden in a gateway towards the village."

"Is that what it was? The roads must be improving then," I said stupidly, and then shivered suddenly as the adrenalin left me.

"You're cold. Here, take my coat, sorry, your coat." He shrugged his way out of the big black coat and slung it around my shoulders before starting to steer me back across the road towards the house. "What on earth were you doing out here anyway?"

Hugging its second-hand warmth about me, I cast a quick glance up at him. He looked invigorated and alive, and not at all how I expected him to be. "I heard you go out. I thought … Well, I don't know what I thought, but I couldn't just go back to bed and pretend nothing had happened, could I?"

He reached past me to feel about in the gloom for the door handle. "No, I guess for you that would be impossible."

"Matthew Croft! That almost sounded like an insult."

"Maybe it was." The door swung open and he grinned down at me out of the darkness. "Why you couldn't just do as you were told and stay put like a good girl …? Anyway, let's get out of this fog. I think the drama is over – for now at least."

I led the way inside, muttering darkly to myself.

I think it was only when I was back in the warm comfort of the kitchen that the full magnitude of what had happened finally hit me. My fingers were trembling as I lit the stove and he only needed to see me fumbling with the tea caddy to take it out of my hands and firmly order me down on the settee near the fire. It felt like barely a moment later that he was putting a steaming cup into my hands and I hardly noticed when he set about dragging the heavy armchair closer.

He settled himself into it and fixed me with an appraising look. "You're shivering. Are you cold?" He got up again to drape a blanket around my shoulders while I watched the flames in the hearth lick hungrily at the logs he had placed there.

There was a pause. Then he said with increasing concern, "You're still shivering. Are you hurt?"

"No."

"Scared?"

"No."

"Well, what is it then?"

I turned my head to look at him properly for the first time. "I'm not scared, Matthew, I'm livid."

He gave a laugh then, and leaned back in his chair. "You really are quite something these days, aren't you? The girl I used to know would have been frightened, upset, confused, but no, not you – you're *livid*."

I flinched from his humour, voice rising testily. "Don't laugh at me, Matthew. Whatever you do, don't laugh at me!"

"I'm sorry. I'm not laughing at you, not really," he said, trying to suppress his smile. "It's just that you constantly surprise me, that's all."

Grudgingly, I let that one pass.

We sat in silence for a while, staring at the fire and each of us lost in thought before a sudden realisation gripped me that beat aside my flimsy bravery in an instant. "What were they doing here?

120

Do you think that they've found you?"

"I don't think so," Matthew said slowly, clearly thinking. "When I tailed them to the car they were talking about you, not me. And it didn't sound like they were under orders either …" His gaze lifted and, whether he meant it or not, his next words were brutal. "You must have really made an impression."

I swallowed painfully. It wasn't easy to feel so very clever about the afternoon's little adventure anymore.

All of a sudden, Matthew reached out and put his hand over mine where it rested in my lap. "I won't let them hurt you. You do know that, don't you?"

Unlike mine earlier, there were no clichéd film-star heroics in his words, only absolute certainty, and I couldn't help the little shiver that ran up and down my spine. His thumb moved lightly across the backs of my fingers.

"I'm definitely going to go and have another look around tomorrow; see if I can't figure out what they're up to." He was speaking very steadily and clearly as if expecting an argument and doing his level best to pre-empt it. "Tonight's unpleasant little episode has decided that for me."

"Yes," I said, equally firmly. "And I'm coming with you."

Very abruptly, he released my hand. He leant back in his chair once more, whistling softly through his teeth.

"Agreed," he said at long last. "But on one condition."

"What's that?" I asked suspiciously.

"You do as you're told. If I say stay put, I mean it."

"But I was only …!" I stopped when I saw his eyebrow lift. "All right. Sorry. I'll do as I'm told."

His mouth twitched at my contrite expression. "Good. In that case, I think we should try to get some sleep. Off to bed with you, young lady."

I disentangled myself from the blankets and set my empty cup down on the table. When I looked back, his mouth had set into seriousness once more and he was staring intently at some fiercely

121

private thought. I meant to just slip meekly away but as I made for the stairs, something made me pause, and barely turning to him, say, "Goodnight, Matthew, and thank you."

His head lifted in surprise. "Thank you? Whatever for?"

"For not treating me like a helpless girl and telling me to stay at home."

"I wouldn't dare," he said with a smile. "Goodnight."

Chapter 15

The day dawned warmer than on previous mornings, the fog clinging in a sodden blur about the head of the valley and I wondered if more snow was expected. My brain felt utterly numbed by the disrupted night and I had obviously slept later than I thought because when I finally got downstairs there was evidence that Matthew, and even Freddy – who was not known for his early rising – had breakfasted and were already outside somewhere.

They had left me the crust of the bread and I nibbled this thoughtfully as I leaned comfortably against the fireside, looking out through the window towards the road. The trees at the top of the hill were bare of their muffling burden of hoarfrost and birds were flitting about in the dirtied crust at their roots, squabbling and chasing each other; they seemed noisier than of late and I wondered if I was wrong after all and this miraculous little thaw truly was going to prove to be a forerunner of the belated spring.

Finishing the dregs of my tea, I crossed to the kitchen to retrieve my boots. It was only after I had dragged on the first and was halfway through the second that I realised I was resting against the broken chair. Which seemed suddenly to have become undeniably solid. On an impulse, I went to the cupboard with its broken hinge.

Perfect.

Outside, the yard showed little evidence of the drama which had unfolded in the middle of the night, although the burnt remains of the broom handle still lay where it had fallen. Scatterings from the muckheap were weaving a trail across the road and where Davey had thrown himself desperately over the gate, I found a little snag of blue cloth hanging gently in the still air. Of Freddy and Matthew there was no sign.

I wandered down the little line of stables and barns, greeting the residents as I passed and noticing that all of a sudden the yard was somehow looking considerably less wintery. It was almost as if the season had abruptly come to a decision; the snow was rapidly retreating, my neat little swept-up piles were shrinking to leave slushy puddles and a treacherous lake across the cobbles in their place, and, defying my doubts about the weather, water was running off the rusting roof with such vigour that it was creating a glittering little cascade into the trough.

I was just sliding the last bolt home on a happily breakfasting pony when I heard a muffled crash from one of the old cow-sheds that lay behind the stables. It was followed by a steady stream of swearing and, slipping up the three steps out of the far end of the yard, which once must have led into another building but now acted as a minor waterfall whenever it rained, I finally located Matthew.

He was irritably waving a bashed thumb in the air to cool it while Freddy hastily folded away the hinged bonnet of my father's old car with the very apologetic air of one who had just accidentally knocked its support. Beside them, the tatty old tarpaulin which normally protected the car lay in an untidy heap and beyond, in the gloom of the mouldy old cow-shed, I could make out the dull gleam of leather seats behind the dirtied glass.

"Were you going to ask, or did you just presume that you could use it?"

Matthew looked up sharply from his inspection of the engine to find me watching from the doorway. He gave a sheepish grin. "I've already taken so much from you, I figured what was one more thing."

Returning his smile shyly, I moved closer and peered down into the engine. "What are you doing to it?" I had just noticed the blanket lying folded on the back seat. He had not made it far then, when Freddy had taken to sneaking out with the remains of our supper.

"Well, being a conscientious person, your father, whenever he last used it, drained the radiator and isolated the battery which by the mercy of heaven still has some charge. All I have to do is give her a bit of a clean-up, a dash of oil and she'll be good to go."

I nodded, implying I knew exactly what he was talking about. My father had insisted that I learn to drive but in the years since his death I had been perfectly happy to leave the car slumbering in the shed to dream of its youthful adventures. I was far more comfortable with the living warmth of horses than the roar of engines, but the remembrance of my father's abiding love for the machine and the sentimental feeling that it somehow kept me closer to him had, until recently, made me ignore the rather more practical demands of living on the cusp of poverty. I suppose, put simply, it represented some of my most tender memories, and it was one of the few things of his that I had been determined to keep until necessity had at long last forced a decision.

Now though I realised that I was looking upon it quite without sadness or loss and I was startled to discover that something had changed. I could recognise that I no longer needed to live on the memory of family to preserve my happiness, and could even revel in the solitude of my future. But, beyond that, there was another influence that I had not even realised was missing. Something altogether more fleeting and hesitant – vaguely familiar, but entirely unexpected. Matthew.

"Is this what you wanted?" Freddy emerged from the gloomy interior of the shed. He was dragging a large petrol can behind him and it was clearly very heavy, but I knew better than to injure his pride by offering to help.

With one gruff word of thanks from the man, the boy almost burst with cheerfulness, and I suddenly realised that Matthew must be the first male influence in his life who was actually bothering to treat him like an equal. No one knew where his parents were and his uncle had been an indolent man whose sudden and unexpected fits of fury were hardly likely to inspire much affection. Whereas now Freddy was moving around Matthew with the same sort of wide-eyed admiration as might be expected from someone mixing with a member of the nobility. The slightest hint of that man's approbation was enough to make the boy positively glow with joy, and, I realised with some irritation, Matthew had exactly the same effect on me.

"Hello?"

A voice drifted up from the yard. It was accompanied by a crash which could only have been Beechnut's teeth lunging over her stable door and my eyes were wide as they turned to meet Matthew's sharp questioning glance. Without a word, he slipped away into the thick mouldy dark of the cow-shed.

"Hello?" called the voice again and I hurried towards the steps. A familiar head popped through the gap. "Here you are, Miss Phillips – I hope you don't mind the interruption?"

Before I could deflect him back down onto the yard, Inspector Woods had stepped up through the old weathered doorway.

"Good morning," I said cheerfully, fervently hoping that my voice would not betray my sudden tension. "What can I do for you?"

He cast a nervous glance over his shoulder as the fury in her stable crashed about her box again. "I just wanted to ask you a few more questions. I hope you don't mind?" He came closer without leaving me time to form an answer. "Well, well, is that a Morris Minor? A 1930 saloon …? Lovely – I think my wife used to have one of these." The Inspector pushed past me to run his fingers along the edge of the bonnet, taking in the style of the running boards and the square cobwebbed grill.

Then he looked up to smile across the engine at Freddy. It was his light genial smile and instantly my nerves were on edge. "What are you doing with her?"

Freddy flushed crimson. "We're just fixing her up …"

I interrupted smoothly, harmlessly chattering, "I've just sold it, you see, so we're making sure everything is as it should be before the new owner comes to collect it. Don't worry though, he's bringing his own fuel. We've no intention of running foul of the rules about sharing rationed petrol!"

"Ah, I see. Well, Freddy … it *is* Freddy, isn't it?" The Inspector gave him a warmer smile and I had the very strong suspicion that he was recollecting the Colonel's description of *Idiot*, and quickly forming his own judgement.

Freddy nodded warily. "Yes sir."

"Freddy," I said sternly, "would you go and check whether the ponies have finished their breakfast, please?" I tried to keep the urgency out of my voice, but even if I had, the heightened colouring to Freddy's cheeks as he eagerly grasped at this escape was probably enough to give us away. A hard chill began to settle in the pit of my stomach.

"No, wait a minute." The Inspector stopped him with a smile like that of a benevolent grandfather. "We didn't get a chance to speak the other day. I'm Inspector Woods. Miss Phillips may have mentioned me? No? Oh, er, well, I'm the man in charge of the hunt for Jamie Donald's murderer and I'd like to ask you a few questions if you don't mind. You do understand that you must tell the truth to the police, don't you, Freddy? You can get into a lot of trouble if you lie."

Freddy shot me a nervous glance. All at once, he looked suddenly painfully young. "Yes sir."

The Inspector nodded approvingly. "Well then, have you seen anyone hanging about looking suspicious?"

"Suspicious, sir?"

"You know the sort, skulking about, looking like they're up to

127

no good."

The boy shook his head mutely, making a small uncertain scuff with his shoe against the tarpaulin by his feet. The heavy ancient canvas creaked noisily. "No, sir, nobody."

"You do know we're on the lookout for a murderer, don't you? Have you seen him anywhere?"

There was the tiniest of hesitations, then the quiet voice said, "I don't think I've ever seen a murderer, sir. I wouldn't know what one looked like."

Oh God, Freddy, don't get smart with him.

The Inspector gazed at him steadily, assessing this response while the boy fidgeted about like a hare in a spotlight. Then he calmly said; "Have you seen Matthew Croft recently, Freddy?"

The boy jumped like he had been stung. Then his eyes turned to mine and they were white and wide with fear. My heart sank.

"It's all right Freddy. Just tell the truth."

There was a long pause, then at last, reluctantly, a very indistinct mumble of; "Yes sir."

If anything the Inspector's smile only grew friendlier. "And when was that, Freddy?"

There was a crash as I knocked the support out from under the flaps of the bonnet.

"So sorry," I said hastily, trying to fold them out of the way again. As it happens, it had actually been completely accidental but I could not have been more obvious if I had tried. Terrible, inescapable, there was a desperate feeling that the game was well and truly up.

The Inspector's hands reached past me to twitch the support back into place. The amiable smile had not altered, but he was watching my face with those intelligent grey eyes under the unlikely forest of eyebrows and he said, "I've noticed something, Miss Phillips. Something you've said and now Freddy has said."

"What's that, Inspector?" By sheer strength of will I kept my voice calm and my gaze steady.

"You both happily tell me that you haven't seen the murderer."

"That's because we haven't."

"Most people say that they haven't seen *Matthew Croft*. But I notice that you don't … At first I thought it was just the phrasing, but I'm beginning to think that your choice of words isn't quite as accidental as you would have me believe."

I said nothing.

"Miss Phillips," he said flatly. "Do you believe that Matthew Croft is our man?"

I had to speak then, and at long last I said, "No, Inspector. I do not believe he is a murderer."

I think that even though he had been expecting my answer, he was still surprised. Those thick eyebrows rose a fraction. "Do you disregard the reports of what happened, Miss Phillips? Have you not seen the terrible story in the press?"

I had the strong impression that although he was talking quite normally, his brain was making some extraordinarily rapid calculations. I spoke slowly and very deliberately. "I don't take a paper, Inspector, and I sold my wireless, so I don't know what they're saying – although I can imagine it isn't pretty."

He gazed steadily at my face before suddenly dropping eye and hand to the oily rag that lay abandoned across the radiator grill. He straightened it into tidy folds. Then he looked up at me again, saying, "That's very interesting, Miss Phillips. So on what are you basing this opinion?"

"On what I know of him."

"Even though you told me that he was nothing to you?"

"Even so, Inspector," I confirmed woodenly.

He gazed at me thoughtfully through narrowed eyes and I felt my cheeks flush. He was not smiling any more and when he spoke it was intensely muted as though he were speaking only to himself. "Interesting … I *had* been given to understand that you were inclined towards another. But perhaps I was mistaken …"

My lips compressed into a tight line at this. I would have liked to have pretended that I didn't understand him, but I grasped his meaning only too well. My heart was beating in slow painful strokes. I knew I had to make some answer, or at least shrug it off with a laugh, but my mind was scrabbling desperately to find what I could possibly say to this without adding to the wealth of evidence he was collecting against me. And all the while, at the back of my mind I was wondering if Matthew was listening. Surely he would have had the sense to disappear … *Surely*.

With the calm precision of a hunter closing in for the kill, the Inspector said, "So, Miss Phillips. Back to the original question …"

And stopped.

With scarily uncanny timing, a car's headlights turned into the sodden trackway behind the stables, momentarily glaring white off the moisture-rich air before grinding to a noisy halt at the end of the row of cowsheds. I could not honestly say which it was that hit me hardest, whether relief or crushing dismay when I recognised it for John's car. He climbed out; he was wearing an immaculate pair of pale trousers and jacket, not obvious attire for trapping a fugitive, and with a cheerful lift of the hand, began picking his way through the mud and slush towards us.

The Inspector stayed silent. He was observing John's approach with what could only be described as mild disinterest and my nerves frayed a little nearer to the very tip of hysteria as that man took all the time in the world to reach us, all trace of the limp gone.

Finally he arrived and, somehow, I managed to greet him quite sedately. "Good morning John. You've met the Inspector before, haven't you?"

John smiled and nodded his hellos, casting a curious glance at me which took in my flushed cheeks and far too cheery smile. After the briefest of hesitations, his gaze slid smoothly onwards, across Freddy and beyond to the Inspector; "Am I interrupting?"

To my absolute stupefaction given how much I must have given away, the Inspector gave a shake of his head. He smiled benignly. "Not at all, Mr Langton. In fact," here he examined his watch, "I must be off. Goodbye Freddy, Miss Phillips; I'll go this way if I may – I don't like the look in that horse's eye. Mr Langton."

With a merry smile to Freddy and a nod which encompassed the rest of us, he turned and set off down the track behind the stables. I stared after him, watching him blur a little as he worked his way through the puddles, barely breathing while re-running and re-examining everything I had said, only to come back again to the one peculiar question of: *he's leaving?*

For a moment exposure had seemed inescapable. And yet now he was going, abandoning his advantage ... Was it possible that John's arrival truly had been enough of a distraction?

Even as the hope touched my mind it faded again. Of course he knew.

And what now? A pouncing crush of policemen, an arrest and an agonising wait for the inevitable ... execution.

Think, Eleanor. Think. The tumult of fears span ruinously in my mind and only one thought would surface from the chaos time and again: failure.

It was a few moments before I realised John was attempting to quiz me about the Inspector's visit.

"So, Eleanor, what did he want? Checking up on you? Checking that you aren't fraternising with murderers after all? I'm afraid I let slip about your shady past with Croft." John was teasing me, his open expression friendly and quite understandably amused, and yet equally, knowingly straying so close to the raw truth as to be almost hateful.

I snapped at him distractedly, actually brought to laughter by the frustration of it all. "Oh John! I do wish you'd stop going on about that, it was a very long time ago and really doesn't matter any more." I wasn't really thinking about what I was saying, although for once it was the happy truth. The Inspector had just reached the end of the track.

"Yes, I can see that it doesn't," John said slowly. He was looking at me again, thoughtfully examining my face as though he was

131

reading something there, although Lord knows what he was finding except a person whose nerves were being stretched to the very limit of endurance. He flashed his bright smile. "You seem different somehow, you know. You look softer around the edges, and very pretty if you don't mind me saying. Ellie, can I just …?"

"Sorry, just a minute, John," I cut across him impatiently. "There's just something I need to quickly ask … Inspector!"

I very nearly ran as I splashed away down the track after the retreating man. As I drew closer I noticed that a shabby police car was tucked inconspicuously in the lee of my stables and it was apparent that its driver had been undertaking a certain amount of illicit snooping while his superior had been keeping us neatly out of the way. The Inspector paused to wait for me, lifting his hand to the other in some sort of signed question and I thought I saw the uniformed policeman give a faint shake of his head. A negative.

I slithered to a soggy halt. "Sorry, Inspector … I just wanted to ask you something."

He turned to face me with the air of one who had been held up one too many times already today. "About the case?"

"Not as such, no." I paused to catch my breath; oddly I felt a little faint. My heart was racing now, beating wildly in my throat. I coughed and tried to calm myself; "Have you heard anything about a Simon Turford, Inspector? Or a Davey Turford for that matter?"

He was too experienced to permit himself to look puzzled, but his usually smooth façade clouded a little. "Turford? No, I don't think so. Should I have?"

I hesitated, then plunged in headlong. "They were here last night messing about. I … I seem to have got on the wrong side of them."

"And this worries you? Are you …?"

"No – no, it's not that exactly, Inspector. It's just that I have never seen them before, I don't think they're local, and now suddenly they're working in the Park." I paused, still struggling to control my breathing. "It just seems a bit odd, that's all."

"Ah." I saw him drop another glance down to his watch. I was not convinced that he had actually been listening at all. "I will add them to my enquiries. Try not to worry, Miss Phillips, they're probably just migrant farm labourers with too much time on their hands. And now—" A brief fleeting smile that faded as he gazed at me, "may I ask you something?"

I swallowed, then nodded. My throat was dry. "Of course."

"Do you know where Matthew Croft is?"

He fixed me with those kindly grey eyes and stared straight into my mind.

"No, Inspector. I do not."

Well, it wasn't really a lie, he could be anywhere.

He gazed at me appraisingly. The assessment seemed to last forever. But then, all of a sudden, with a sharp nod, he simply turned and walked away to the waiting car.

The slush reformed behind him, swallowing his footsteps and shining brightly against the blank seamless sky. It swam and shivered, blurring before my eyes as the tatty police car veered out onto the road and then was set at the hill. All that was left for me now was the shattered state of my emotions, the ruins of a morning, and a faint, fragile glimmer of hope that through this desperate trade of ideas, I might have just bought us a little more time.

Chapter 16

I would have given almost anything just then to have been able to take myself off somewhere to sit in a cool and quiet corner, but instead I walked slowly back along the track towards John and Freddy who were peering down into the engine compartment of the dusty black car. As I watched, John climbed into the driver's seat, turned the key and pulled the starter button. The car gave a cough or two before spluttering into life.

"Turn it off!" I yelled breathlessly over the roar of the engine, having covered the last few yards at a run. "Turn it off!"

John grinned up at me like an excited child at Christmas before seeing my expression. "Sorry, I couldn't resist. She's lovely, isn't she? Practically a miniature!"

"Yes, very nice. But we haven't checked the oil yet, you'd better not have done any damage."

"Oh, I won't," he said carelessly, climbing out of the car again. "Anyway, Freddy said I could."

"Sure he did," I said, trying not to laugh at the schoolboy comment. "Do I have to sound like your mother and scold you for telling tales?"

John looked askance at my humour and turned to poke into the engine. He peered down at it, reaching out now and then to test the fit of some socket or other. "Hmmmm, I see. Very interesting.

Overhead camshaft, dynamo here …"

I really did laugh then, "Oh, come on, John, you don't know any more about cars than I do."

John was not impressed. He frowned. "Is Freddy your mechanic then?" He cast an ill-concealed look of surprise at Freddy who was hovering nearby, once more looking flushed and awkward.

"He does well enough. We've only got to get it moving." I told him about Mr Dixon and the offer he had made last Easter then again in the autumn, and the exchange that had at long last been agreed for next Tuesday.

"Is he? That's nice," John said vaguely, not really sounding like he was listening. Then he suddenly snapped, "Don't do that! If you don't know what you're doing, don't do it at all."

I put a protective arm around Freddy who was trying rather forcibly to turn the oil cap the wrong way. "He's only trying to help, aren't you, Freddy. Oh, John, you'll get oil on your clothes, don't mess about in there – I must say you look very smart for visiting farm girls. Where are you off too? Oh, come away do, Freddy can manage much better without an audience."

"Just the usual monthly meeting with the bank, nothing special." Finally John turned to follow me and I led him down through the old doorway onto the yard only to instantly regret it as Beechnut kicked up a fuss.

"You should never have taken on that horse," he commented, amiably enough. "She's a true chestnut mare, isn't she? All fire and brimstone and," he added, sensibly stepping back a pace, "teeth."

I picked up a couple of headcollars and slipped them onto the heads of a pair of waiting ponies before replying, "She's certainly quite feisty when men are around, she's as soft as anything the rest of the time though."

"Fascinating. Well, you know what they say about animals and their owners …"

"No, what?" I said, more crossly than I intended. The day had only just begun and I was already feeling exhausted.

"Oh, nothing," he said with a gentle smile. "I'm just teasing, don't mind me. Are you still coming to the dance tomorrow?"

I nodded, letting the ponies out of their stables.

"Good. I'll pick you up at about six then, shall I?" He stepped backwards out of my path, narrowly missing the muck barrow so that I had to hastily smother another laugh; I knew from fond experience that the spoilt boy of my childhood still lurked in the man somewhere only waiting for an excuse to come out. Unfortunately, however, this was then swiftly followed by the unhelpful impression that to compensate for my mirth, I had been far too bright in giving my reply, because the look he shot me as he left was alarmingly proprietorial. It had been something akin to the looks I had observed him make at whichever pretty woman was the current object of his determined courtship, and it worried me.

It took me an hour to get back to the car. A soft plaintive bleat as this latest visitor drove away was enough to bring me sharply out of my thoughts and back to a sense of my real duties, and it came as a shock to realise that the poor goats had been neglected yet again. In spite of my guilt, however, it was almost pleasant to be reminded that whatever else happened, the animals and their needs never changed, and the sun had reached its uncertain heights in the sky to cast a strange halo through the white blinding haze before finally I was able to slip back to the car and whisper into the darkness.

"Matthew?"

There was no reply.

Reaching across the engine, I lowered the bonnet carefully, finding it hard to feel reassured by this latest disappearance. The car and its maintenance could wait, but my fears for the man were only growing and as I stepped down into the yard it was to be met by a fresh concern.

Freddy had long since given up pretending that he knew

136

anything about the mechanics of the thing and was, I saw with dismay, now mucking out the stables with an angry vigour that I had rarely seen. I realised then that what with Matthew's dramatic arrival, my recurring histrionics and this latest upset of the Inspector's excruciating questions, his life had been rather unusually disrupted; and now, it seemed, the poor boy had quite simply had enough.

With a last glance behind me into the shadows, I carefully shelved my private alarms, stepped down through the old doorway and out onto the yard.

Freddy was forking soiled bedding from a stable into a barrow and when he saw me coming, he hurried over to the muckheap, setting about levelling it vigorously.

"Freddy, are you all right?" I asked. He turned his head away so that he could pretend not to have heard and then hurried back to the stable again.

I followed. "Has something upset you?"

No reply.

"Freddy?"

He barged past me back to the muckheap again. I trailed doggedly after him, refusing to be put off. "Is it the questions the Inspector asked you? Because I think you did very well."

"It's not that."

If I didn't know any better, I would have called his tone surly, and he was clearly very determined not to look at me.

"Then what is it?" Silence. "*Freddy!*" I begged helplessly. "Is it John? Because I'm sure he didn't mean to snap at you."

"It's not that," he muttered again, still refusing to look at me.

"Is it something *I* said?"

Staring at the back of his head, I saw his shoulders lift in a tiny shrug and at last I began to feel that we were getting somewhere. "What did I say?" A little trail of manure rolled past my foot in a miniature avalanche, disturbed by the boy's frenetic levelling. "If you don't tell me how can I make it better?"

"You can't make it better!" Freddy suddenly shouted, stepping back from the steaming heap and throwing his fork to the ground. "There is nothing you can do. Nothing at all! You're going to marry Mr Langton and live with him in his big house and have babies, and … and …"

He stopped. He stood there, an angry child glowering furiously with clenched fists and breathing hard while dismay rose within me. For eight long years people had been linking my name with Matthew's. It had been painful and occasionally extraordinarily distressing; and typically now, when it could not possibly be worse timed, everyone seemed suddenly determined to link me with John.

I said quietly, "Freddy sweetie, I'm not going to marry John, really I'm not."

"You're just saying that."

His voice came as an unhappy whine through his flushed scowl and on a sudden impulse, I stepped closer and pulled him into a gentle bear-hug. There was a moment of resistance but then, with surprising fierceness, his arms came round me and we stood there, hugging each other in the middle of the yard while stray drifts of fog parted from the mass to lift and curl around us.

I stroked his hair and realised suddenly that he was crying. I felt like joining him. Instead I said, "Freddy, love, don't be sad; you can believe me, you know. I really am not going to marry John. Whatever gave you that silly idea?"

He pulled away, blinking at me through puffy eyes, "You promise?"

I nodded, smiling at him gently. "So come on, spill. What made you get all upset like this?"

"You said it didn't matter."

"What didn't?"

"You said that Matthew didn't matter! You did, I heard you." He started crying again. "And it's not fair, I like him. Why do you have to like Mr Langton? He … he … he's *rich*."

"That's not a crime, Freddy," I said very gently indeed, and then pulled him back into my determined bear-hug. "I don't know what to say, Freddy. There's nothing I can say other than to repeat that I do not love John, not in that way at least, and I am not going to marry him."

"And Matthew?" His muffled voice came from somewhere near my right shoulder.

After a short silence, I said with difficulty, "It isn't fair to ask me that."

There was a pause and then his voice rose again into anger. "You're going to leave, aren't you? You say that you won't, but I know you will. You're going to sell this farm and move away and marry someone and then I'll be all alone!" His voice cracked a little and then he added on a whisper, "I don't like being alone."

"Oh, Freddy," I said sorrowfully. I tightened my arms again. "I won't let you be alone, you matter far too much to me. And who would I get to muck out as well as you? Sorry, that was a very bad attempt at a joke." I felt him close his grip on my jumper. "But in all seriousness, I promise that whatever happens, you're still my number one man and you've always got a place in my house and heart for as long as you want it. Do you hear?"

The brave words ought to have sounded painfully hackneyed but every single one was meant, truly. I gave him a squeeze and finally he nodded into my shoulder. "Now dry your eyes and pick up your broom. Come on, we've got jobs to do."

I helped him finish the stables, giving him little nudges every once in a while and chattering incessantly about the plans we should make for the coming spring. Eventually I was rewarded by a return to something like his customary cheerfulness. It was a relief to know that regardless of what followed, I had at least managed to successfully avert one little disaster this morning, and it was still more of a relief to at long last see him walk happy and smiling back into the house.

The same could not be said for me, however, and watching him go, I felt a sudden desperate urge to regain some tranquillity of

139

my own. Despite my concern about where he could have got to, I was really quite relieved not to have to talk to Matthew. After such a morning, I knew it would only need one minor misunderstanding to break my remaining self-control, and with my emotions already whirling in a senseless chaos, I suspected that it would not take much beyond that to tip me over the edge into a total screaming mess.

But Beechnut, my ever-present source of comfort and peace, seemed of all the residents of my farm to be perfectly cheerful, and she inspected my pockets carefully as I lifted the saddle onto her back and reached under her belly for the girth. She kindly lowered her head to accept the bit before lipping up the last few strands of hay while I fiddled about with the stirrups and then finally, after an infinite number of other tiny adjustments, we were ready.

I led her over the road into the small dirt paddock that doubled as a school. The snow had been laboriously and regularly cleared from this little corner, or at least cleared as much as it was possible to be in that incessant wind, and so there were only a few areas that were thick with slush. Even more impressively, the thaw was actually quite advanced here and the saturated ground had finally softened enough to give a little, although thankfully it had not yet turned to clinging mud. Giving the girth one last tug, I clambered up onto the gate and swung my leg over her back.

Our warm-up unfolded a little inconsistently. The horse's attention strayed every time something caught and glittered in the blinding light – which given the conditions was pretty much every other yard – and I was about to start being a little irritable with her when I realised that I could not expect her to concentrate if my own mind would persist in wandering. It was going over and over what Freddy had said in an everlasting cycle and I wondered what I would do if everyone thought the same. And by everyone I meant the Inspector, John and ...

I halted, put myself into a more correct posture and then started again.

"*You angel.*" Beechnut rose fluidly into a collected trot, her back lifting as her weight settled onto her hind legs. To encourage her to relax – she always was a worrier – and to open her shoulders, I sent her moving diagonally across the school in a half-pass and was rewarded with a more expressive trot than I had felt in a long time. My body relaxed into her movement as if it knew what was intended before even my mind had formulated the instruction and the feeling of power that lifted through the saddle brought a smile to my flushed cheeks. We cantered and she lifted sweetly from my leg to carry the contact into my hand; it is hard to describe the joy that is inspired by riding to such an intense level of communication, but as we settled back from canter into a steady trot it was as if all the stresses and strains of the past week had become simply a distant memory.

A hard splutter of gunfire brought me sharply down to earth. The sudden clenching of my fingers on the rein snatched Beechnut to so harsh a halt that she almost sat down. Then the distant shotgun fired again. I bit my lip.

All happy schooling was over. I led Beechnut back across the road and lifted the saddle down from her back. Using a twist of straw, I wisped the sweat from her coat before slinging a blanket over her. It took a while, and I had to tidy her bedding and replace the hay in her stable before, at long last, the horse having relieved my pocket of all its treats, I had nothing left to do but to collect my tack and carry the saddle into the house. I dreaded the emptiness of the kitchen.

Taking the turn from the passage into the house, I very nearly dropped the saddle on the floor. Matthew was standing by the stove with my kettle in his hand seeming perfectly at his ease and he turned to greet at me calmly, quite as if nothing was amiss. Instantly flooded with an overwhelming sense of relief, I could have laughed aloud. Instead, rather more sensibly, I said, "That wasn't you then?"

"Eh?" Matthew looked completely taken aback.

"The guns," I said hoarsely.

"What? Oh, no, pheasants, I think."

"Oh."

It was only when I saw him begin to look faintly bemused and then lift a questioning eyebrow that I realised that I was staring dumbly. I must have been standing there for a good minute before I recollected the saddle in my hands.

Swiftly, I swept away into the back room. Once there and safely out of sight behind the door, I finally set the saddle down and covered my mouth with my hand. I allowed myself one long trembling breath, my eyes screwed tightly shut. Then, forcing a cheerful expression onto my reluctant cheeks and making myself turn back to the open door, I walked out and across the room towards him.

He was spooning loose-leaf tea into the pot. "Not too much," I said, tension making my voice coming out in a kind of complaint. "We can't have any more for another week."

I smiled to show I did not mean to sound so stern but he had turned away and did not see. Instantly that unpleasant tightness closed around my chest again, making my heart beat uncomfortably, and in an attempt to remedy the situation I propped my elbows on the sink beside him, saying casually, "Where did you disappear to then?"

"Langton's place. I couldn't miss a perfect opportunity to have a look round." His voice sounded oddly flat and he barely acknowledged me as he made me step aside so that he could rummage in the drawer for a teaspoon.

"And did you find anything?" I asked politely, trying hard to keep the surprise out of my voice.

"Nothing." He was lifting cups down from the rack.

I raised my eyebrows. "Well, you needn't sound so disappointed."

"You seem very determined to discount him," he observed curtly, somehow managing to pour tea through the strainer into the cups in a manner which implied thinly veiled impatience.

"And *you* seem determined to convict him," I replied, beginning

142

to lose my cool. At long last he turned to face me and something in his unsmiling expression prompted me to add, "And it is very unfair, you know. If I believed you, I can certainly believe *him*."

That really did not come out how I had intended. I tried to find words to remedy it but before I could speak he had snatched up his cup from the counter and left the kitchen. I expected to hear the front door slam but it shut quietly, which was even worse.

Chapter 17

Freddy was happily watching the stew cook on the hotplate by the fire. I had prepared him a meal just in case Matthew was not so angry as to go alone to Warren Barn. I sincerely hoped not, but he had been outside for a long time and I fidgeted and waited and fussed around the house until Freddy finally lost patience and told me to go away and mess about with the ponies. Taking orders from Freddy was a new one and I realised that I really needed to pull myself together.

Matthew was bending over the engine again and he barely even glanced at me as I stepped up through the doorway. I let my hands rest on the grill at the front of the car and concentrated hard on keeping my voice level.

"Are we still going?"

"You still want to come?" he asked, without lifting his attention from the nameless piece of metal that was being worked beneath his oiled fingers. His voice was as flat as mine.

"Matthew! *Please!*" I begged, losing all pretence with a rush.

He looked up at that. For a moment his face looked hard and full of icy feeling, only then it softened. "I'm sorry, Eleanor – I'm not really angry with you, it's not your fault. It's just that all this skulking around in the shadows is getting a bit much, that's all." He reached out his hand and it hovered above mine for a moment.

There may have been a light whisper of contact from the very tips of his fingers but then the hand clenched into a ball and dropped away again.

Finally he said in a carefully measured tone, "I'd appreciate it if you came. You'll make a much more credible witness than I could."

I hung about while he finished the car, but he didn't speak again. The line of his jaw seemed fixed by the unhappy tension that had settled about him and although it lightened a little as I curiously set about examining the contents of my father's ancient tool box, his mouth sharply contracted again when, with timely irony, it transpired that John's playful interference had drained what little power was left in the battery. Shamefaced and quietly cursing that man's name, I sought out the crank, passed it to him and then climbed silently into the driver's seat.

The handle jumped sharply as the engine kicked into life and Matthew had to hastily snatch his hand away before it could batter his fingers. I was ready with my foot to depress the accelerator but it still took a token cough and a splutter for the car to settle to a steady rumbling, and I climbed out again to hover nervously beside a newly arrived Freddy while Matthew gave it one final check. With a light touch to the pedal, the engine picked up and as soon as he was satisfied that it was running smoothly Matthew stepped out, closed the bonnet and beckoned me towards the car once more.

Leaving Freddy as a lookout, I drifted over only to stop, my eyes running from him to the open door and back to him again. He was looking at me expectantly.

"Hang on a minute," I said, backing away in genuine alarm. "You never said anything about making me drive."

Behind me, I heard Freddy stifle a giggle and there was a momentary lightening of the serious mood as he firmly guided me into the driver's seat. He shut the door. "I'm sure you'll be fine – just don't let it stall …"

Matthew climbed in through the passenger door onto the pokey back seat and then settled himself low so that he could just see the road ahead but a casual passer-by would be unlikely to notice him. *Not likely*, I thought grimly as I put the car painfully into gear, *they'll be too busy leaping for cover.*

The car, in a moment of charitable kindness, did not stall. It took me a while to get the hang of smoothly depressing the accelerator but I managed to navigate the bends through the inexplicably busy village without killing anyone so personally I was quite impressed. Leaving the cluster of mercifully distracted old ladies, their stray dogs and a suicidal cockerel behind, we swung past the empty gates of the Manor without seeing a soul and then we were streaking down the steep hill into thicker fog towards the Washbrook junction at the bottom. The road was awash, melt-water and ice running in great sheets down the crude metalled surface and I wondered if Matthew had been correct to decree that we would go this way, avoiding the risk of exposure by a brief stint on the main road.

"Er …" Matthew said hesitantly from somewhere near my left ear. The car was gaining speed at quite a rate and I had to fling the wheel hard over to make the first of the many bends. "The gate? … *Eleanor!*"

As we flew down towards the next corner I saw it and remembered at the same time. Somehow the fact that this was a gated road had completely slipped my mind. I stamped on the brake and the clutch and the wheels locked, wearing millimetres of tread on the ice-damaged surface as, with a horribly high-pitched whining sound, the gate raced upwards out of the white glare to meet us.

"You can open your eyes again now." Matthew's voice was slightly less controlled than usual. "We've stopped."

My fingers were gripping the steering-wheel so tightly that my nails were digging into the palms of my hand and, rather unsteadily, I slipped the gear into neutral before reaching to open the door.

Matthew's arm shot past me as he lunged for the handbrake. "I'll put that on, shall I?"

I threw him an evil look.

The drive to the bottom of the hill went considerably more smoothly, despite the river that appeared to be running down the roadway, and the gate at the bottom was opened and closed without so much as turning a hair as we rolled on towards the descriptively named Washbrook. This stream, swelling grossly with the newly melting snow, had escaped the normally shallow bounds of its crossing and was dirtily fording the road with intimidating force, but I managed to ease the car through without either flooding the engine or grinding to a halt in the middle. Quite impressive I thought, although the occasional sharp intake of breath by my ear suggested that my companion was not quite so admiring.

The run up the hill was relatively easy by comparison, snaking past the Keeper's Cottage with its tidy allotment garden and up onto the level road that formed a branch of the ancient ridgeway. The surface was drier here and the fog less oppressive, and the surrounding landscape seemed suddenly awash with colour as we cruised past the impressive Park gates and then turned off to swing down the winding road that would eventually lead to the village. There, at long last, the road turned onto the rough farm track, steeply dropping below the invisible gaze of the house high on its cloud-bound ridge and winding round the hill and out of range onto the Warren Barn fields at its feet.

I slowed to a crawl as we neared the farm, dimming the headlights and trusting on nothing unexpected meeting us on the trackway. The dripping roofs of the stone barn and crumbling outhouse were just visible as shapeless masses over the brow of the hill and I could see Matthew's nose out of the corner of my eye as he scanned the terrain for a suitable place in which to conceal ourselves.

"There," he said, pointing into the wooded copse beside us on the hillside.

I eased the car past before reversing back up the narrow dirt track into the trees. Although he said nothing, I felt rather proud of myself for not veering off into the undergrowth and, killing the engine, I turned in my seat to look at him expectantly. His eyes were narrowed as he surveyed the muted scene. Then, abruptly and without a word to me, he folded the passenger seat forwards and climbed out.

"Stay here," he mouthed through the glass as if I had any intention of wandering. I settled down in my seat to wait.

The straggling array of farm buildings lay about three-hundred yards away just beyond the shoulder of the hill and through the unhelpful blur of thickened haze I could just see what might have been a gleam of grey metal nosing out of the darker shape of heavy barn doors. The house lay further downhill and only the very faintest suggestion of its roof could be made out from behind a fringe of trees, and that only because I knew it was there. It was eerie waiting alone in the car, trying not to think about it and yet knowing all the while that two men, armed and lethal, were still about somewhere. The whole place seemed dead and abandoned; there were no signs of life except for that same raven which was somewhere nearby, calling hoarsely, and the few pheasants which were scuttling about in their brainless fashion on the grass. I suppressed a cold shiver of apprehension. It was hard to resist the urge to keep turning around to check that the two men were not behind.

Not surprisingly, I very nearly screamed when the car door opened and Matthew climbed in beside me. I hadn't heard his approach at all.

"Any sign of them?" I asked, somehow managing to sound much more nonchalant than I felt. "I saw their car."

"Yes, they're here; in the barn as before – which pretty much tells us where to concentrate our search."

"It does? Oh. Good." A pause. "What do we do now then?"

"We wait. They must eat sometime; my guess is that they go somewhere else."

"Oh," I repeated lamely. We sat there in silence, saying nothing and doing nothing except listening to the car tick as it cooled. A rabbit hopped by and it reminded me of dinner.

The sun was dipping lower in the sky so that the effect of its muted halo was barely showing at all anymore across the streaked and snow scarred grass, and I hoped it would not turn to a heavy frost when night fell; my toes were already feeling chilly. There were sheep droppings everywhere but no sign of the culprits; evidence, I presumed, that the fields were let out to someone else as Jamie most definitely had never been a farmer.

"Stop fidgeting," Matthew suddenly said, making me jump. He had spoken quite coolly without taking his eyes from the ghosted barn but a faint smile was threatening to show at the corners of his mouth and I had to resist the urge to stick my tongue out at him.

We sat there for a while longer, watching nothing happen, before I finally broke the impasse. "So did you look in the Colonel's rooms too?"

"No." His gaze didn't falter from its attention on the vacant trackway. "His office was locked."

"Oh," I said uselessly. I might have added 'You didn't bother, did you?' but I held my tongue.

An uncomfortable silence yawned between us once again. An owl twitted shyly and I waited for the usual quavering *twooo* in reply from across the valley. Instead, its muted question was answered by the coarse cooing of a woodpigeon and judging by its volume, it was thoroughly determined to make its presence known before the day was finally forced to surrender to the growing dusk.

"What do we actually know about your John?"

Matthew's abrupt question shattered the tentative peace completely. I looked at him in surprise, forgetting to correct him on the '*your* John'. "What do you mean?"

He kept his gaze level on the unmoving car but his fingers were fiddling with the window catch as he expanded on his query. "Where did he fight, for example?"

"He didn't fight. He was signed off as unfit for active service."

"Was he?"

Matthew's voice was perfectly level but the increase of tension in the car was palpable and I realised with a sinking feeling just where exactly this line of questioning was going. I said; "Don't you remember what happened to his leg? It's amazing he can even walk."

Matthew frowned. "He doesn't look particularly lame to me. In fact I don't really recall him ever being that badly hurt. Is there a chance – no, listen for a minute – a chance that Jamie found out it was a lie? Perhaps Jamie found evidence that he had forged his injuries. Maybe that was what he wanted to tell me. You can go to prison for that, you know."

"And then what?" I asked, struggling to keep my tone light. "John murdered him to save his own skin?"

"You have to admit it's a theory."

"A pretty lame one," I said. His frown deepened at my poor attempt at a pun and I sighed. "Fine. There are several reasons why this theory is utter rubbish. One – I saw John's fall from his horse and it wasn't pretty. Trust me when I say there was bone, and it really wasn't where it should have been. He was in hospital for a very long time, but you won't remember that because you were away in London doing your studies. Two – I thought we were here to find out what it is that those two are hiding which, although I may be being presumptuous, I imagine is a touch more valuable than a pair of crutches. And three," I took a breath before finishing, "I should have thought that you of all people would know better than to be accusing perfectly innocent bystanders on utterly flimsy grounds. Particularly when that person was elsewhere at the time. With witnesses."

This time it was Matthew's turn to say, "Oh."

There was another very long pause, then he said, "But what if …"

I cut across him quickly. I was getting heartily sick of being put on the defensive about John. "Look; I don't mean to be rude, but John is one of my oldest friends and I think I can safely say that he's not prone to murderous tendencies. Can we just leave it until we get some tangible evidence?"

"Of course. I'm sorry. I was forgetting that he was one of your particular friends."

There was an unpleasant emphasis on the 'particular' and I very nearly snapped at that. Instead I pressed my lips tightly shut and concentrated hard on simply breathing. I felt like screaming at him. It was unfair, and utterly absurd that having so ruthlessly denied me the comforting prop of my own resentment, he should be subjecting me to the worst of his. I opened my mouth, not to scream, but to say something, anything that might defuse the tension but when I dared to glance at him, his expression was so formidable that the words died on my lips.

Jealous ...

The thought came unbidden and was dismissed just as quickly. I stared hard out of the window once more but there was still no sign of life at the barn. The pale outline of the sun had very nearly vanished behind the valley ridge that flanked the farmhouse and the air was noticeably cooler though it was not yet dark. Another rabbit, or possibly the same one, hopped by completely oblivious to our presence; I was surprised that it couldn't sense the tension.

Finally, I said rather cautiously, "Can we talk about something else?"

"Of course." His reply was a little abrupt but then, after a moment, he turned to look at me and with an effort to sound pleasant, said, "What are your plans for the future?"

I think that the question had been meant innocently enough but I was feeling so sensitive about any possible reference to John that like a fool I snapped some curt meaningless reply.

Matthew blinked at my spiteful tone. Then his mouth curled into a sneer and he turned back to gazing at the barn again. "Sorry. As you've already told me, it's none of my business, is it?"

Shame hit me painfully in the stomach once more and made me forget my reserve long enough to touch his arm briefly with the tips of my fingers. "No, *I'm* sorry, Matthew. I didn't mean that.

151

I'm just not used to having to talk about myself." I gave him a weak attempt at a smile. "I'm so used to being limited to 'Yes, Mrs Whatsit, your boy will make a *fabulous* rider' and the weather that I'm out of practice with talking about personal things. I truly am sorry; I didn't mean to be rude."

His frown faded then, genuinely. "All right. We'll start with something easy and you can tell me to push off if it gets too personal. Will that do?"

I nodded my agreement, feeling a different little flutter touch at my core.

"Where did you learn to ride like that?"

Modesty made me want to misunderstand his meaning but with a great effort I decided to be honest instead. "Dad taught me. You remember that Dad was a northern lad? Well, before their war, and when he was still a young man, he found a job with a stud in Cheshire. They used to import mares from all over the place and he was sent to France to find some new blood. He liked it so much out there he ended up staying over there for five years and was lucky enough to fall in with a man from the Cadre Noire – the French Classical riding school – lucky man. You wouldn't know it but he was a fabulous rider, my father. He would have taught me too but unfortunately there isn't much demand for hunters trained in the classical style so I had to glean what knowledge I could on the unschooled youngsters. But now I have Beechnut. She's the first horse I can call my own and so I'm finally getting to put it all together. There are a lot of gaps though, and of course Dad's not around any more to ask."

I stopped, suddenly embarrassed. "Sorry; I bet you didn't expect a great monologue. I told you I was out of practice."

"You're doing very well," he said soothingly. "Ready for the next question? Do you plan to carry on with the ponies, or will you get back into horses now?"

"Now?"

"Er, now that the war is over."

I had the very strong impression that wasn't what he had meant, but I wasn't brave enough to broach the subject of John again. It was ludicrous, I thought in frustration, that I was allowing the myth to become the acknowledged truth simply because the idea of talking about it to him of all people was so laughable that my mind would not even begin to find the words.

"Now that the war is over," I said carefully, without betraying the thoughts in my mind, "I honestly don't know. Ponies are easier to care for, cost less and don't tend to injure themselves on the tiniest little thing so potentially the profit, although small, is more reliable. But, and this is a big but, what I'd really like to do is start breeding and training riding horses. Not hunters, you understand? Proper riding horses, and hopefully grow a reputation for producing dressage horses. It's a bit of a remote dream though."

"Your dad would be really proud of you, you know."

His words sounded startlingly sincere. I shot him a stealthy glance, feeling uncertain again as I found myself saying; "Flatterer. Anyway, enough about me. What about you – what do you plan to do now?"

"Now? As in now that the war is over? Well, I don't know. Hard to say really, I haven't …" He stopped. "Sorry – I'm obviously out of practice too." His mouth twitched. Then, with a return to seriousness, he added, "Though if I have to be perfectly honest; at the moment I'd settle for taking a step out from under the shade of the gallows. But presuming that all this is just academic however … I don't quite know. I love my job and living here, but … well, let's just say my plans aren't fixed. I might move away, or I might not. It all depends."

If ever there was an invitation to say "on what?" this was it, but unfortunately I was too busy trying to interpret my own reaction to manage to speak and I missed my chance.

When I didn't ask the invited question, the frown slowly reformed on his face and he turned back to staring out of the window once more. His eyes were fixed upon the faint gleam of the unmoving car but I was not sure that he was really seeing anything at all in the steadily fading scene. I watched him mutely; his averted profile was dark and shadowed against the black metal of the car door, unnaturally amplified by the approaching dusk as it betrayed all the strain of his present situation and with a rush of compassion, I almost put a hand out to him. But then he blinked and shifted uncomfortably in his seat and I had to hastily look away in case he thought I was staring at him.

I felt myself cringe at what would have been an embarrassingly telling gesture of care, and then flushed again but this time with self-righteous indignation at being made to feel like this when, all along, all I had ever wanted from him was to be allowed to give my help. It was becoming increasingly apparent, however, that this assistance was neither useful to him nor wanted and by this frayed impatience, he was making it abundantly clear that he would have much rather been anywhere else but near me.

Muttering a silent tirade at myself for believing it could ever be otherwise, I fixed my own gaze with renewed concentration upon the smudge of farm buildings with every intention of discovering that I didn't care to help him so very much after all. In fact I was sure of it. He really was almost hateful and it was clear now that I ought to save us both from this unpleasantness, and find some excuse so that I could simply go home and leave him to deal with his future and his frustrations alone.

Just to torture myself with the hope of proving myself indifferent, I couldn't help daring to glance at him again. His thumb was tracing a line along the doorframe as he gazed steadily at the dead scenery. The act was abstracted, introverted, and I think it was that very fact which made me finally acknowledge the truth. With a sudden jolt, I saw that the unhappy set to his jaw was not a result of the extraordinary stresses of his fugitive existence at all. *That* was like a charade agreed between strangers. And he was sustaining it for *me*.

I took a deep breath.

"Freddy got upset today," I said, all of a sudden being very brave indeed.

"Did he? What about?"

"He wouldn't tell me at first, but eventually I got it out of him. The silly boy had convinced himself that I was planning to marry John!"

"Did he indeed?" His reply was flat and disinterested as he tirelessly watched the silent barn and from his tone, it would not have seemed that he was paying the slightest bit of attention. But his thumb had frozen in its endless sweep of the doorframe.

"He got himself so worked up – I don't think he likes John very much and it really scared him – but all was soon set to rights." My voice sounded unnaturally false and high after the stifling silence but I persevered doggedly. "I don't know how he came to that conclusion, I really don't."

"Do you not?"

An owl hooted in earnest in the fading light. "I can't say whether John truly wants me, although I can see why Freddy might have thought that, but as to me liking him in that way. Well, it's just impossible." I snatched a hasty breath, catching myself before I could run on in that same silly voice.

"It is?" The chair springs gave a squeak as Matthew turned towards me. I could feel his eyes resting watchfully on my face but it was impossible to meet his gaze.

"It is?" he repeated. "Why do you say that?"

"Well, er ..." I swallowed nervously, realising suddenly that here we were straying into something truly dangerous. "John and I have been good friends for a long time, and I'm sure he's very attractive, but love him? No. I don't. I couldn't. Not when I —"

I stopped. I was too scared to continue. The car seemed very, very small all of a sudden.

"When you what?" Matthew was still watching me closely. His manner was strange. "Eleanor, when you ...?"

"Look out, they're moving!" I cried suddenly.

"What? I just … *Oh!*" His head snapped round as comprehension dawned.

They were indeed moving. Lit by dirtied headlights, the battered grey car had nosed its way out of the barn and, creating a distraction that could not have been better timed, was now heading along the road straight towards us.

"Get down!" snapped Matthew, dragging me sideways before dropping over me himself. From within the peculiar cocoon of his folded body, I heard the car rumble slowly by. For a horrible moment I thought that they had seen us and were stopping but then the rough roar of the engine passed steadily onwards.

Finally Matthew released his hold. I sat up slowly, feeling more than a little shaken, though at what I did not truly know. I peered out of the window, trying to make out where they had got to.

"Looks like we're on," Matthew said, all attention now focused on the red taillights that were rapidly dwindling into fog. I waited, expecting a sharp instruction to make for the barn but to my surprise he got out, ran round the car and dragged open my door.

"Shift over," he ordered. "We've got to find out where they're off to first of all."

Obediently I slithered across into the passenger seat as he urged the car into life. Thankfully the battery had regained some charge and the car lurched forwards as he threw it into gear.

But no sooner had we roared into action than Matthew had to step on the brakes. The grey car was gently climbing the hill into the village with all the casual air of one that was out for a pleasant Sunday drive and as we lingered in the shelter of the woodland, there was a pause just long enough for me to be grateful that I was no longer the designated driver, and to be just a little bit startled by the all-consuming concentration that had settled on my companion's face. Then the car bounded forwards once more and all thought ceased as the nervous thrill of the chase caught me so that I too must have seemed just as intent and focused.

Matthew had to wait until the car was nearly out of sight and into the village before daring to charge up the slopes after them. A tall and willowy maple tree stood in the middle of the road to form an impromptu roundabout and our little car had to instantly slow to a crawl again, negotiating it carefully before plunging wildly after the other car like a stone from a slingshot past the public house and on towards the school. It was hard to imagine what possible destination there could be along this gentle country lane that might have any connection with their crime. A nearby village perhaps, or further? Whiteway? Cranham? Or beyond to Stroud and Gloucester ...?

None of them, it seemed. I very nearly hit my head on the windscreen when Matthew braked sharply and swung the car into a space behind a chimney-sweep's van.

"What are you doing?" I asked in confusion as Matthew silenced the engine and leaned across my lap to see around the parked van.

"Don't you recognise where we are?"

I peered at the muffled road ahead. At first I could not make out the grey car at all only then I spotted it on the small driveway of a converted outhouse.

"Oh!" I exclaimed uselessly.

"Oh indeed. My house."

We watched as the two burly Yorkshiremen climbed out of their car and went along the short path to the front door. I remembered now that the outhouse had been part of old Mr Croft's farm complex and had been little more than a crumbling machine-shed back then. But then he had died, the farm had been sold so that Mrs Croft could move to be nearer her sister in Gloucester and, unwilling to surrender the village he had loved as a boy, Matthew had bought back the crude building before painstak-ingly converting it into a very sweet and very stylish little cottage. Looking at it now, I could recall in perfect detail the beautiful view from the kitchen window where it backed onto the fields that his father and grandfather before him had worked and tended. I could also remember the uproar it had caused when Mrs Croft sold the farm to a distant cousin rather than to the Estate as was expected.

"I wonder ..." I began but before I could translate the embryonic idea into coherent words, it was stopped in mid-thought by the sight of the Turford men opening the sturdy wooden door and disappearing inside. I looked at Matthew.

"Did they have a *key*?"

He shook his head grimly. "I don't think locked doors matter much to those two."

They were gone for about ten minutes. When they emerged there was some kind of ragged bundle cradled in Davey Turford's thick arms. It looked like a large shapeless mass of curtain fabric, but I didn't have to see the furtive manner in which it was concealed in the boot of their car to presume there was something more valuable wrapped within it than a few yards of faded upholstery.

"Did you see what that was?" Matthew's voice was very soft.

I shook my head. "Did you?"

"No," he said slowly. "I can't imagine what they would find in there to be worth stealing ... Oops, look out – they're coming. Sorry about this."

"What ...?"

This was all I had time for before I was roughly grabbed and pulled towards him. I think I gave a startled squeak, instinctively putting my hands to his chest almost certainly with the intention of pushing him away ... But I did not. He held me fast as the sound of a car crawled past. It seemed to take forever. A lifetime of racing senses and heartbeats, and the crush of unexpected contact. Then there was a wolf-whistle, a shout of obscene congratulation and finally the car was gone.

He lifted his head. Mesmerised, I simply lay there, head against the turn of his shoulder, and watched as his eye traced the course of the car through the small rear window while it drifted around the tree and back down into the park. My lips burned where he had touched them; although this abrupt handling certainly was not likely to be the fulfilment of my most tender dreams – it was only a cover after all – my mind had frozen and I really couldn't tell whether I was supposed to be affronted by his uninvited closeness, or charmed.

Then the heady mixture of musty car and his warm skin gently filled my nose. As all my senses abruptly made a return, I suddenly found myself very aware indeed of the texture of his coat where it pressed beneath my fingers. The coarse fabric was lifting slightly to the steady rhythm of his breathing.

He glanced down at me still imprisoned within his arms; "Sorry about that, couldn't think what else to do." He released his hold and, as I straightened, he started the car.

"A touch on the clichéd side, don't you think?" I said, considerably more steadily than I felt. "You need to work on your secret-agent routine."

He gave a laugh as he turned the car around and sped after them while I concentrated very hard on trying not to think about the feel of his mouth upon mine. It was a cover, just a cover, I reassured myself as he span the car around the tree and raced back down into the park once more. I stole a glance at him and he was grinning.

I had to hang onto my seat as the little car plunged down the unkempt road after the others. "There!" I cried.

"I see them," said Matthew as he swung the car in a right-hand turn away from Warren Barn and onto the rough frost-damaged drive that led across the park. There was a brief impression of grey between the black trees as the other car went round a bend, then a resounding crash as our car hit a pothole and I swear we were airborne for a moment.

"If you break my car, I'll kill you."

"Sorry," said Matthew ruefully, while not actually looking remotely sorry.

I saw the brief flash of light ahead as their headlamps bounced back at us against the deepening gloom; the grey car was already halfway up the far slopes of the valley side, casting a ghostly trail through the fog as it followed the snaking road towards the hilltop. We rocketed over the little stone bridge in pursuit. I cast a quick sideways look at Matthew; he was wearing the most remarkable expression.

He shifted down a gear to set the car at the incline. Then he glanced at me and, seeing me staring, said, "What?"

"You're enjoying yourself, aren't you?" I said accusingly.

A corner of his mouth twitched. "Let's just say it is nice to play the hunter for once."

The road was very dark under the trees and still driving necessarily without lights, I was amazed that Matthew could see well enough to make the tight turns. The Eagle Gates loomed above us through the heavy canopy of bare branches, the great white stone birds standing silent sentry over the road, and then we were up and out in the open, running along under the trees of the long avenue that would lead us to the main gates.

Then the road straightened and Matthew eased the car back to a steady crawl; even with the fog, it would be simple enough to see which way they turned with the yellow glare of their headlamps catching on the drooping branches as they passed.

But to my considerable surprise, instead of passing through the tall metal gates and out onto the road, the grey car slowed and then drew clumsily to a halt by the gatehouse. Matthew braked instantly and silenced the engine, and we watched as the two men, recognisable by their bulk even in the low light cast by the nearby windows, stepped out and walked into the house. Clearly this door posed no difficulties either.

Without a word, Matthew allowed the car to coast backwards down the incline before swinging it into a vacant field gateway. He stepped out. I hesitated to follow but at his expectant expression, I swallowed my half-formed excuses and hastily gathered my courage, climbed out of the car and joined him in the sudden chill of the wood-scented driveway.

I took my lead from him. We hurried along, me trailing feebly in his wake, passing silently under the still arch of the trees and onwards until we were met by the deeper shadow of the house. Until then I hadn't realised just how thoroughly night had settled but now I saw that the fog had thickened abruptly to swallow any hope of a starlit sky and without even the faintest of halos from the moon to lighten the sober dark, I was very glad of the faintly greenish sheen of the driveway between white verges as a guide.

With a lift of his hand, Matthew instructed me to wait and I lingered nervously while he crept forwards to the first window. A dull glow from the heavily curtained glass lit his features as he paused, head tilted slightly, listening. He slipped along to the next and I saw his posture change as he suddenly tensed. Then, after what seemed like an age, he finally beckoned.

Reluctantly, I crept forwards. He gave a slight nod of approval as I settled next to him, crouching under the low sash of the window and we huddled there together under the stone windowsill, watching and waiting, and listening intently. I could just make out the dark gleam of his eyes where they stared thoughtfully at the stone wall standing inches from his face.

For a while I could not hear a thing above the sound of my own hushed breathing. But then, all of a sudden, my ears made sense of the muffled sounds and abruptly I was able to distinguish a rough growl from Simon Turford. It was followed by a rather softer murmur in reply and, stupidly, it actually came as a shock when I recognised the muffled voice as belonging to someone still more familiar: Adam Hicks. This then was the estate manager's home – as if on any normal day I would not have known from the start – gifted to him by the Park and his for as long as he held the post; which given that he was an honest and dependable man, would probably be until old age or infirmity took it from him. Honest and dependable, excepting of course that he was now fraternising with murderers.

Matthew glanced at me and, giving a quick hint of a reassuring smile, cautiously raised his head to peer over the sill. I held my breath waiting for a cry of surprise and flurry of action from within but nothing came and so slowly, and violently wishing that I had stayed at home, I too lifted my head.

We were shielded from view by grubby netting which hung limply behind the dirty green of the gaping curtains and beyond it, lit by a couple of standard lamps, I could just make out the ugly profiles of Simon and Davey Turford where they sat at a heavy wooden table. The aging estate manager was pouring whiskey into some glasses at the sideboard. His wife, a fifty-something housewife complete with apron, ugly floral housecoat and spectacles hanging from a string about her neck, marched in clutching two steaming bowls which she set down with a brisk clunk on the table and, judging by the quick guilty glance her husband gave her from across the room, it seemed that she had been very unwillingly relegated to this role of domestic servant. Certainly, the two men barely acknowledged her before snatching up their spoons but, as she turned to go, I felt the cold night air catch in my throat. The pinched look I had seen in her face was not that of grudging hospitality at all, but the white grimace of a woman functioning on the very edge of fear.

Matthew's eye flicked left to me in a brief flash of shared concern before grimly fixing once more upon the remaining occupants of the room. We listened for a while, hoping that their talk would turn to something of interest but as seems to be the case with all master criminals when being watched, their stilted conversation consisted of nothing more incriminating than the dangers of such a rapid thaw and the possibility of further bad weather. Finally, however, the pitch of their voices shifted and here was something. It was not the wished-for confession of all their plans but nevertheless I felt a little tingling flare of tension as Hicks began to fret about Sir William. "If he hears that you've been up here …"

"Sir William," Simon spat the words, "is more clued-up than you think, old man. Just keep your mind on your job, and your thoughts on what we're paying you. We wouldn't want your wife to have to worry about how we'll take it all back again, would we?" He let the threat hang.

The silence was palpable. I glanced wide-eyed at Matthew, an unspoken question hovering electric between us while, in the background, Hicks noisily slammed the rapidly diminishing whiskey bottle down on the table. I thought I heard a snigger. Then I was sure of it and I had to hastily look back as Matthew tensed and sharply caught his breath. But thankfully, whatever ideas of rebellion had briefly flickered across the aged estate manager's mind, they were evidently gone now and instead I was just in time to catch the blur of his movement as he turned to shuffle quietly back to the armchair in the corner.

I turned my gaze to Matthew again and at long last, with a hint of a nod, he indicated the dark silence of the avenue behind. I cannot describe how glad I was to slip away from our station beneath the window towards the comforting isolation of the trees and on to the cold and stony gaze of the Eagle Gates beyond.

Chapter 18

We hid the car behind a hedge near the main road where it was less likely to be considered out of place if it was spotted before hastening down to the farmyard. The track with its worn Cotswold stone surface contrasted brightly with the darker tone of the patched hillside and it was only when at last we walked into the silent stone barn that I realised that I should have brought a torch. It had seemed dark enough outside, the smudged outline of the buildings looming like giants out of the night, but inside, the darkness was almost complete and, before I had gone many steps, I crashed noisily into a workbench. Matthew's hand shot out to grip my arm as he steadied me.

"All right?" The word was a low breath on the air, nothing more.

"I can't see a thing," I hissed back, rubbing the spot where my thigh throbbed painfully. "And why we're whispering I don't know. If there was anyone here, they would have heard that."

"Force of habit," he returned softly. I heard a faint trace of a laugh.

"Do you often go sneaking about in the dark like a …" I searched for the word, "like a Lothario?"

"All the time." He seemed to be fumbling his way along the workbench. "Anyway, what do you know about Lotharios?"

"Nothing," I whispered cheerfully. "Nothing at all." My foot nudged something and it gave a faint rattle as it rolled away.

"What, no lovers knocking at your door in the dead of night?"

"Not even a sonnet whispered under my window as I sleep," I said, concentrating hard on not crashing into anything else.

"There'd be no point if you were asleep." His muted voice came from somewhere over to my left.

"As I rest my eyes then."

"And such pretty eyes they are too," he said and then struck a match. "Here we go, I knew I'd seen a lamp somewhere."

The ancient paraffin lamp spluttered reluctantly as it was goaded into life. It guttered and faded before growing again to cast all manner of crazy shadows across the barn as Matthew lifted his hand high and gave a slow turn.

There were three workbenches, the one I had already encountered and two others beyond, which were covered in an array of off-cuts and what appeared to be the beginnings of a hunting gate. A great stack of crude timber was leaning casually against the wall by the door and an assortment of tools lay strewn about, becoming a shocking reminder that until a week ago this barn had been in daily use. The compacted earthen floor glinted occasionally here and there, showing where a nail had fallen and been forgotten, but I could see nothing that remotely resembled the treasure of Freddy's eager imagination.

With unvarying determination, we checked all the cupboards but bar finding something that looked like the broken-off corner of an old gilt frame and some tins which initially excited our interest before turning out to contain turpentine, the contents of each were resoundingly innocent. We even went up the ladder into the roof beams in case there was something hidden up there but again we found nothing except a few boxes containing what looked like the stained and pitted metal plates from an old printing press. I had joked that perhaps they were printing money but in reality the plates were probably for leaflets from some old political campaign.

Feeling increasingly despondent, I perched precariously on a stool while Matthew shone the lamp into the corners once more. Nothing. Perhaps we had been wrong after all. It was terribly hard after the optimism of feeling like we were getting somewhere only to return to the depression of knowing that now we had nothing once again.

Refusing to completely surrender to the gloomy thoughts, I drifted idly along to some wooden crates which were stacked in a grimy corner behind some half-made doors and, lifting a pile of rags and rubbish, I peered inside. Steadfastly ignoring the instinctive recoil when a large spider darted angrily for cover, I saw that the mess lay above a cluster of tatty rolls of paper and more from a desire to be doing something than any real interest, I reached in to pick one out. In the dim and flickering light I couldn't make out anything bar a few lines here and there; it looked like it might be one of Jamie's designs for his doors and I was just moving to put it back when Matthew appeared beside me.

"Anything?"

I shook my head, showing him the paper. He peered at it under the lamp before handing it back to me with a shrug.

"I can't make anything out," he said, and then added a soft long drawn out, "*Oh.*"

"What?" I whispered anxiously, wondering what he had seen. But he was not looking at the paper in my hands. Instead, he was lifting the lantern, casting its light along a shelf, across a few empty tins and finally onto the dusty reflective sheen of a photograph.

"How odd," he said vaguely, reaching the curling and creased image down from the shelf. He was staring at it blankly and, curious, I peered over his arm. I understood then just why he might be feeling a little distracted.

The photograph was a torn and tattered print in grainy black and white, and it showed what appeared to be a typical military steel girder bridge across a non-descript river in what was probably Flanders, but may have been any flat part of the Continent given how little I actually knew about Europe. It was made more interesting by the dusty column of armoured vehicles that were labouring past with their heavy loads, complete with British and American insignia and some very fearsome weapons. But what brought the odd tightness to my throat was the sight of a pair of wearied and dishevelled soldiers standing grinning in the foreground, both stained and dirtied almost beyond recognition but nevertheless perfectly unmistakeable.

"This was taken after a particularly hairy incident at a particularly unpleasant spot for bridge-building near Lanaeken, as I recall," he said slowly in a voice filled with wonderment. "How odd to see it again."

"How so?" I asked hesitantly, unsure of whether to pry or not.

He glanced at me and then smiled gently, "No reason. It just explains a few things, that's all."

He turned it over and showed me the inscription written on the back in his own distinctive hand: *Donald, Count on me to return the favour some time.*

I understood then, and felt a wave of sadness for him and for his lost friend. "I see," I said feebly.

Matthew set the photograph carefully back up onto the shelf. "Damned shame that I didn't manage to, don't you think?" He spoke with an edge that went far beyond grim purpose and then, as he felt me stiffen beside him, added; "What is it?"

"Did you hear a car?" The lamp was doused immediately and the sad little photograph with its record of a life saved was forgotten in the sudden urgency of our own immediate danger.

"Come," Matthew whispered, taking hold of my arm and tugging me after him to the door. In the sudden darkness the paler outline of the doorway was both a guide and a blind as the flimsy light cast all kinds of improbable shadows. It rendered the solid barriers of the workbenches entirely invisible; we both stumbled in our haste, reeling clumsily through the maze of tools and obstacles, and the crash of something heavy hitting the ground reverberated deafeningly behind us. But then we were safely though and I felt a waft of colder air across my face as the night and freedom rushed forwards to meet us.

Unexpectedly, Matthew stopped abruptly in the doorway and he had to put his arm out to prevent me from tumbling out past him into the open. I staggered and gasped but he held me back. A blinding glare of headlights through fog hit the sky briefly as the car rounded the top of the rise, much closer than I had realised, and then there was the low hiss of tyres as it cruised steadily towards us.

"Not enough time!" Matthew turned sharply back to look into the barn. I suspect that had he been alone, he would have chanced the dash across the wide expanse of open grassland surrounding the barn but encumbered with the responsibility of protecting me, he must have known that the bare rolling hillside could hold no hope of cover for someone so wholly untrained. Perhaps I ought to have decided for him in a demonstration of all I had learned since my early days of youthful feebleness, but I remembered my promise that I would defer to his judgement and my body ached at the idea of trying to outrun the car and that gun.

"In there. Quickly!" Matthew almost bodily shoved me into the dark void behind the door created by the lengths of rough timber that leaned there.

Matthew squeezed in next to me and I shuffled back as far as I could in the hope that he would be protected, but it was a painfully narrow space and I feared what would follow if they happened to look too closely. My breath was coming in short uneven gasps. They sounded deafening in our cramped shelter and as the car rolled to a halt nearby, I fought desperately to calm myself.

From the darkness, I felt Matthew reach silently for my hand. It was only when the intense gloom was punctuated by an odd crinkling noise that I remembered the paper still held in my fist and I am afraid to say that with every instinct still urging useless panic, it didn't even occur to me to be brave. Instead, I hastily stuffed the roll into my waistband before finding his hand again and clasping it tightly.

The engine's dull roar was followed by an unbearably long period of suspension. The air was so still and dry that it felt like we might suffocate in our dusty little cocoon and I could not see a thing except for the faintest impression of Matthew's profile silhouetted against the paler wood. But in this weak light he seemed startlingly calm and where I caught the soft whisper of his breathing, the slow intakes of air were perfectly steady. I tightened my hand again and his thumb stroked mine soothingly before stilling abruptly as heavy footsteps scuffed the rough gravel outside.

"That man Hicks is such a jerk."

The sudden rare sound of Davey's voice came so close to the raw timber by my ear that it felt like he must be in our little space with us.

"*Jerk*?" A snort from somewhere outside. "Been spending much time with Yankee GIs, have you? But yeah." His dull sneer floated in on the breeze. "Stupid fool, wittering on about that girl – as if that stuck-up bitch could make trouble for us. I plan on paying her another little visit before we go, and maybe not just to mess about with the horses ..."

Davey gave a horrible little laugh in reply and Matthew's hand closed painfully on mine. In the muddy gloom I could just make out a muscle working in his jaw; he looked angry and, I realised with a jolt, extraordinarily dangerous. Suddenly I did not feel quite so afraid.

"At least we shouldn't have to wait too much longer; we'll be out of here soon enough. Although if the boss hadn't lost his head and caused all that mess," a scuff of Simon's feet as he stepped inside and then a pause while he spat, "we'd have been out of here long ago. Bloody amateurs." The acrid scent of a cigarette being lit was followed by an odd rasping sound as he inhaled deeply.

Then there was a pause, a very long pause, and a sharp curse as the match burnt his fingers. I flinched from the sudden snap by my ear as another match was struck and then, after an impossibly tense silence, Simon's voice came on a soft note of enquiry. "What have we here?"

The temperature dropped by about ten degrees.

"Did you do this? Did you knock this over?"

Footsteps drifted past barely an inch from where we were hiding and Matthew's hand held mine in determined calm. I could feel the flicker of his pulse beating beneath my fingers, definitely stronger now but still unhurried.

"Dunno. Don't think so."

"Someone's been here." The voice lowered to an ugly snarl. "That damned Croft – He's been poking about while you were making eyes at Hicks' wife. Find him. Find him and then finish him. Preferably slowly."

"Er …"

"Use your brains, man!" snapped Simon impatiently. "You check the road and I'll check the house. Now move!"

There was a creak as the car doors were opened followed by the startlingly innocent sound of a shotgun being broken, quickly loaded and snapped shut. Then a door slammed and the muffled sounds of their heavy footsteps softened as they touched grass, separated to a whisper and then slowly receded convincingly to silence. Somewhere, quite oblivious to the hunt, a fox screamed for its mate.

I felt horribly afraid that somehow they were still waiting outside but clearly made of sterner stuff, Matthew slowly released my hand and slid noiselessly out from behind the timber to peer cautiously around the door. "Come," he breathed.

I eased myself out of my cramped position and followed as closely as his shadow as he slipped out of the barn to crouch behind the car. He touched my hand and pointed across the grass to the dip with its great oak trees and dry streambed which I knew led down to the ford near the old bridge. The expanse of open space was still wide and deadly, and I loathed the prospect of trying to cover the distance with those men and their guns so close by, but our car was uselessly hidden far along the roadway and with the path past the house equally impossible, we had very little choice.

There was no sign of either man as we darted out from our hiding place. Keeping low, we ran soundlessly across the grass, compromising between stealth and speed, and were very nearly at the trees before a bellow told us that we had been spotted.

The car's headlights flicked on and for a moment I was hopelessly disorientated as my shadow plunged ahead of me. The sudden brightness bounced back off the fog and thinly streaked snow, distorting the ground horribly and throwing deep shadows so that I stumbled and would have fallen but that strong hands caught me and heaved me back to my feet again. Then we were in the shade of the dip and gratefully scrambling for the shelter of a broad tree-trunk where we could pause for a moment while Matthew squinted into the light, trying to spot our pursuers.

The hard report of a gun broke across the open space like a thunderclap. A shot whipped past making Matthew jerk sharply back with a curse. Then a shadow lunged across the grass, stretching long and deformed towards us as a figure passed in front of the headlights and, distinguishable even at this range, I could see the dark line of a gun-barrel hanging blackly from his hand. Matthew muttered something under his breath and, turning, took my hand once again and tugged me after him down the gully towards the deeper cover of the strip of woodland below.

At some point the fog must have broken a little because through the thinning trees I could see pale moonlight glinting off the overflowing waters of the ford and I don't know why but in my mind I had marked this out as some kind of boundary, beyond which we would be safe. I was wrong of course.

As we splashed through the knee-deep icy water, Matthew tripping and nearly taking me down with him, a great roar betrayed Simon's close pursuit behind. The crude animal cry came from the rough woodland above the river and I realised, with a frantic reawakening to fear, that he must have predicted our path and was gaining on us with unrelenting ruthlessness. There was a crash and a sharp twang of wire as he leapt the flimsy fence and then a scattering of dirt as he plunged recklessly down the steeper slopes towards the grassy clearing by the ford. He was nearly upon us.

With a sob of dread, I scrambled up the scrubby valley sides towards thicker woodland and a distant hope of escape. Matthew's hand was firmly on my hip, keeping with me and pushing me ever onwards, but I heard the splash as Simon Turford hit the water no more than twenty yards behind and I knew he was far, far too close.

Then, unexpectedly, there was a foul oath and a crash and, daring to throw a glance back over my shoulder, I saw that he had missed his footing as he leapt for the bank. The sodden earth had given way beneath him, sending him sprawling painfully facedown onto the grass. But it wasn't enough. Even as I turned once more to the tangled chaos of young and mature trees ahead, he was pushing himself up onto his knees again and then the gun lifted to glint black and deadly in his hand. I was running to the very limit of my endurance but I knew even that would not be enough to outpace the bullet that must surely follow.

Suddenly Matthew's hand was hard on my elbow. Moonlight and darkness blurred into a dizzying spin as his grip snatched me round into the cover of an ancient beech. Then his arms came protectively around me. They closed tightly and my head buried into his shoulder just as the gun fired.

The sharp report was not the dull crack of a shotgun. It was the angry snap of a rifle and the bullet smacked past us to leave devastating silence in its wake. The gun fired again, and then twice more making me flinch and cry out with the expectance of sudden pain. Only then there was nothing. Nothing but the sound of my breathing and the crush of Matthew's arms holding me close.

The woodland was stunned to silence, no birds or animals moved, no sounds except my own but then, slowly, horrifically, I became aware that a coarser breathing was matching mine. The hoarse and laboured panting seemed to be nothing more than an extension of my own rapid breath but twigs cracked beneath a stealthy tread and the sounds grew louder as Simon stalked steadily closer. I felt Matthew prepare himself for renewed flight, his stance shifting into a state of readiness for the necessary ambush, and the thought of what little he would be able to do against such a man very nearly made me cry out again in terror. But then his hand soundlessly tightened in my hair where it rested on the back of my head and the shock of his warning was enough to silence the sob that threatened to escape.

The stealthy footsteps stopped. There was a pause, an endless wait filled with that irregular coarse breathing as he listened for us to give ourselves away and it felt like I only had to open my eyes to find him standing there, staring at us with that ugly smile playing about his mouth. I kept my eyes pressed tightly shut.

Then there was a crash and a distant bellow, and Davey's voice penetrated the agonising silence. "You got him?"

A pause, then a reluctant growl, "No. But he's in here somewhere, I know it. They dived behind the trees just as I got the gun aimed and knowing that slippery little devil, I'll have missed."

The answering voice gave a sympathetic curse and then, puzzled; "*They*?"

There was a crack of dead wood under foot as Simon stepped cautiously closer. "They," he confirmed gruffly. "Some young lad by the looks of him."

Still that horrible rasping breath grated near my ear. He didn't move; he seemed to have stopped and it took every ounce of my remaining self-control to suppress the flinch of apprehension that threatened to betray us. My cheek was stinging where it pressed tightly into the rough fabric of Matthew's shoulder.

Then suddenly and with a great angry roar, Simon unleashed another two shots.

"CROFT! Show yourself!"

He fired wildly and at random into the silent trees. His guttural challenge was resoundingly brutal and it seemed for a moment that it was impossible for anything to be worse than this. But then, appallingly, I knew I was wrong. His voice dropped to a hoarse whisper:

"What was that? Did you see that?"

A long pause filled with that terrible breathing. And then, at last, a low triumphant growl:

"Got him ..."

I almost didn't manage to stop the panic that time. But somehow, through the living heat of his body and sheer power of thought, Matthew managed to urge me to stillness. With my forehead pressed into his shoulder and my eyes kept tightly shut, I forced my wavering mind to concentrate my ragged breathing, and waited.

It seemed an eternity. Every nerve stretched almost to breaking before I realised that the coarse echo of my breathing was fading and receding. It seemed impossible, a fantasy of terror, but the sound did indeed gradually become softer and more muffled as whatever he had seen led him away from us in an endless sweep, moving further and further until eventually they were both gone and we were left perfectly alone in the shocked woodland.

We waited a long time before Matthew released me enough to cautiously look out from behind the tree, although his arm never left my shoulders.

He turned back to me and gave a little smile but I didn't notice; my gaze was fixed and unmoving on the deep gouge of fresh wood which gleamed whitely against the darker bark of the trunk barely inches from where his head had been. His eyes followed mine and instantly his body shifted to cover the mark but I stood as if transfixed, just staring, trembling and shivering uncontrollably.

"Look at me," he urged gently. "Eleanor, look at me."

I couldn't move. For the first time in my life, I think I was very near breaking down completely. But then his finger touched my cheek and he lightly tilted my head until I had no choice but to do as he asked. His eyes were very dark and they broke through

174

the blinding chaos in my mind to hold my gaze steady in determined reassurance.

"Hey." His voice was very gentle. "You're all right. You're all right, my love."

I blinked and it was like I was drawing breath for the first time in minutes. I felt a roaring in my ears as the blood rushed back to my limbs and I almost fell but his arm held me secure. I blinked again and managed a very weak smile.

"That's my girl," he said softly. "Do you think you can manage to move?"

I nodded slowly.

"Let's get away from here, shall we?"

And he shifted his arm to hold me gently around the waist, and helped my clumsy limbs carry me up the slope, through the trees and on towards home.

Chapter 19

It took an age to reach the lower limits of my land. I think I was a terrible hindrance to him but he bore it all patiently as he nursed me across tumbling walls and swollen streams on our route to safety.

I was exhausted and very cold, and I felt that I had never appreciated the warmth of a wood fire as much I did that night when we finally opened the kitchen door onto the reassuring comfort of my peaceful home. Freddy was already in bed and while I suspected that he had fully intended to wait up for us, I was thankful for it; I desperately wanted to be allowed to just rest and sleep, although I feared that the rough sound of Simon's heavy breathing would haunt me even there.

"Sit," Matthew said, ushering me over to the settee. He knelt down and tugged at my sodden boots and I am afraid to say I just sat there like a lemon while he fussed around me, wrapping me in blankets and stoking up the fire.

"Drink," he said firmly, thrusting a steaming cup into my frozen hands. I drank it automatically, uncaring and unthinking, and it was only when I finished the second cup that I finally came back to life sufficiently to make my brain formulate words into a sensible order.

"I'm sorry," I eventually said. "You must think that I'm an idiot."

"There are many things I think of you," he replied gently, adding a smile, "but that is definitely not one of them." He stretched his feet before the fire and looked so utterly relaxed that it seemed impossible to believe that we had just been within a hair's breadth of total disaster. "Hungry?"

Even the idea of feeling anything so mundane as hunger was inconceivable after all that fear and exhaustion but just as I was about to decline, my stomach forced me to admit that actually, I was ravenous. "Has Freddy left us anything?"

Matthew climbed to his feet and went over to peer into the pot which stood by the side of the stove. "Some left. It's not very hot though."

"At the moment, I really couldn't care less."

We ate in silence. Conversation was impossible; to re-live the night's events was a terrifying prospect and to chatter about anything else seemed nonsensical, but eventually the tasteless meal was finished and with it, grudging warmth began to creep back into my frozen limbs. My mind, however, was still entirely numb; I would probably have dropped my forgotten bowl as I slipped back into staring vacantly into the fire except that, with unvarying kindness, Matthew climbed to his feet once more and took the dish away to set it down upon the table.

When he came back, however, he surprised me by sitting next to me on the settee rather than on the armchair where he had been before. He stretched his arm out along the back of the chair in comfortable ease and it felt only natural that I should shuffle closer to lean my head on his shoulder. Oddly, there was a very brief moment of what seemed like caution in spite of this having evidently been his intention but then his arm gently came around me and, at long last, I felt myself begin to relax as the warmth of his body seeped slowly into mine.

I almost jumped when he spoke, the stubble of his chin brushing lightly against my hair. I had been fiddling absentmindedly with the fraying edge of the blanket, barely thinking of anything at all, and it was a shock to be forced back from comfortable oblivion by the unwelcome intrusion of memory and reality.

"How are you holding up?" he asked gently, preserving the dreamy haze after all.

I leaned a little closer, tucking my damp feet up under the blanket. "I'm fine, actually," I admitted with perfect honestly. It was impossible to feel anything else when in the warm protection of his arm.

"I shouldn't have let you come. I'm sorry." His hand tightened momentarily where it rested above my elbow. "Are your feet thawing yet?"

"Getting there," I said, wondering if the evening had almost been worth it if it meant I got to be so close to him without the usual accompaniment of awkwardness or impossible arguments. "Anyway, I asked to come. I don't think I quite realised what would be involved."

Suddenly and unavoidably the night's events flashed back through my mind; the long wait and the listening, the smell of the timber and Simon's rough voice as he spoke from the darkness. I sat up with a gasping breath and fixed him with a wide-eyed look that betrayed my very real fear, "You don't think they'll come after us, do you? Do you think that they'll come here?"

His arm tightened as he gently pulled me back down into his embrace. "No, they won't," he said firmly against my hair. His hand gave me a reassuring squeeze. "I didn't get the impression that he recognised you; he thought you were a boy, do you remember? And I suspect they'll be rather preoccupied with finding a new hiding place for whatever it was that they were guarding." His cheek brushed lightly against my hair. It was extraordinarily comforting, and his voice had a lovely soft timbre to it that was warm and soothing as he added, "You were incredibly brave, my dear. I've seen hardened troops show less nerve than you."

There was a pause and then he spoke again, this time in quite a different tone; "I know I promised I wouldn't fling unreasonable demands at you, and I won't. But I will just say this: I'm very proud of you. Do you know that?"

Suddenly shy, I gave something that was halfway between a nod and a shrug, but a smile could not help breaking the dry line of my lips.

Matthew seemed to be smiling himself and his hand tightened briefly in affirmation of his words on my arm. Then he gave a funny little sigh and allowed his head to fall back against the cushions, saying in a more regular tone of voice, "More than ever now, I refuse to believe they were simply waiting there just in case I turned up. I wish we had found a clue as to what it was."

"I think you'll find that it was me that thought they were hiding something, actually," I said, with a trace of my usual self putting in a brief appearance.

He tutted. "You can say that as much as you like but it doesn't change the fact that you're wrong, I was definitely the one that came up with that idea. Ouch—" He laughed. "Langton was right, you *have* changed. You used to be such a delicate little thing. But don't worry; I like this version too."

I could have prodded him again for that but that, still laughing, he deftly fielded the next blow and then, ignoring my token resistance, firmly returned my hand to the warm straightjacket of my blanket once more.

"So you *were* listening," I said accusingly from within my cosy little bundle. "I thought you were. I could have fainted when Freddy took me literally and started telling the truth."

"I suspect, my dear, that you're not the fainting kind," he said cheerfully, giving my thoroughly entrapped hand a condescending pat. "Anyway, it's your own fault. Freddy has only learnt what you've taught him. Hoist by your own petard I believe is the appropriate saying."

I grinned, relaxing happily into the curve of his arm. The fire flickered gently and, staring into its depths in a comfortable silence, I found my mind drifting wonderingly on to this surreal discovery of sudden ease. It seemed incredible now to think that only a week ago I had still been cursing his name, if I could be brought to mention him at all. Only seven days ago I had been struggling out into the snow to find him injured and raving, and tonight ... Tonight, here I was nestling cosily into the turn of his neck while fantasising about the kiss he had stolen in the car earlier ...

"My dear, you're snoring," he said gently, jerking me guiltily out a confused but pleasant dream. I hadn't even realised that I had fallen asleep. "Time you were in bed, I think."

For a wildly nervous moment I thought he was suggesting that he should follow me. But then my brain clicked out of that particular haze and I walked dreamily past him to the stairs. At the door I handed him the blanket and then, without really knowing what I was doing, I turned, stepped closer and in one breathless movement, reached up and kissed him lightly on the mouth. The touch was soft and very fleeting, but his lips were warm and, I thought, not entirely displeased.

When I stepped away he looked thoughtful, but it seemed to me as if some other expression was beginning to lighten the surprise behind his eyes.

Instantly flushing crimson, I flung a hoarse farewell at him and fled for the stairs. "Goodnight," he whispered softly after me, and there was a smile in his voice.

Chapter 20

I woke to bright sunlight. Not actually that bright, as it was overcast and still vaguely misty, but what I mean is the bright light of a day well into the morning, and not the dull lightening of dawn that it ought to have been. With a cry of horror, I leapt out of bed and grabbed what clothes I could, and very nearly tripped headlong into the door over the pile of still damp clothes that I had sleepily discarded in the night.

Kicking them carelessly out of the way, I dashed down the stairs only to find when I got there that Freddy and a young boy were sitting at the table sipping hot milk with as much ease as if they did this every morning.

"Why didn't you wake me?" I cried, trying to pull on my boots and only succeeding in hopping about crashing into things.

"Because he said to leave you," Freddy said calmly, infuriatingly unconcerned. "He left you a note."

I stopped hopping as it finally dawned on me that Matthew wasn't there. The boy was staring at me as if I were a madwoman and, feeling rather flushed and more than a little flustered, I snatched up the paper and carried my boots over to the settee where I perched on an arm to read it.

To the lovely Miss Phillips,

When I knocked on your door this morning with a cup of tea, you were so completely dead to the world that I hadn't got the heart to wake you. So Freddy and I have fed the ponies (even the fiery Miss Beechnut – I'll let Freddy tell you about that one), and milked the goat. Fearing your wrath if any harm should come to it, I've gone to retrieve the car if I can and I thought I'd take a look inside my house – see if I can work out what our friends from the farm were doing there. I'll also see if our theory is correct and they've moved their "treasure". Unfortunately, this all means that I probably won't see you before you go to the dance so I'll wish you a good night now, and I promise not to be too bad tempered on your return.

M.

P.S. If Freddy has remembered my instructions he should be handing you a cup of tea about now.

I looked up to find Freddy hovering with a steaming cup in his hand. Sheepishly returning his grin, I took the tea and thanked him before giving the letter another read. I would have liked to have treasured it always as if it were a disclosure of his undying love, but the sensible person in me remembered that technically I did not know where he was and so instead I put it in the fire.

"Go on then," I finally said. "How on earth did you manage to feed Beechnut?"

Freddy giggled smugly and squared his shoulders as he sat at the table in a remarkably passable imitation of Matthew's straight posture, "It was brilliant! We hung the bucket on the end of a pole and dangled it near her nose until she sniffed it. Then he just dived in and slid the bucket through the door before she noticed."

"And that actually worked?"

He giggled again at my incredulous tone. "I think she was so surprised that she didn't remember to kill him until he had got away and then I think she just decided to make the best of it, seeing as the food was already there." Then he added with an admirable burst of honesty, "It was all Matthew's idea really, I was too scared."

At the mention of Matthew's name, I suddenly recollected the boy sitting very quietly at the table and felt an instant sharpening of concern for our carelessness. But Freddy saw my look and in an abruptly adult moment seemed to understand. "This is Charlie. His mum sent him down, said you'd asked him to come. He's only been here for about half an hour …"

Good, so he wouldn't have seen Matthew and it could be hoped that he would not remember the name enough to give us away. I smiled. "Good morning, Charlie, pleased to meet you."

He shook my hand with all the gravitas of a boy trying very hard to be grown up and I suppressed another smile before adopting a more serious tone as befitted one adult speaking to another; "I'm glad you could come down today. You can help us turn out the ponies and then I'd like you to take Whisper around the fields on a little hack, Freddy will go with you on Fly. Once you've ridden, you can get started on the mucking out. Think you can manage all that?"

He nodded mutely.

"Good. If your mother can spare you, and you do a good job, you can come and help out on every Saturday if you'd like to. I'll pay you three shillings a day, how does that sound?"

Three shillings may not sound much but believe me when I say that to a boy of his age it was a princely sum only to be dreamed of. Suddenly his face cracked a bright smile, "Ooh, yes please!"

The telephone rang and for once I was able to drift over to answer it with casual cheerfulness. It felt like today was going to be a good day. "Hello?"

"Hi Ellie, it's Lisa."

"Lisa!" I exclaimed, realising to my shame that I had completely forgotten about her, "How is it going in the world of telephones?"

183

"Not too bad, thank you. I'm ringing about that number you asked for."

"Yes?" I prompted eagerly, barely keeping the excitement out of my voice. "Did you manage to trace it?"

"No, not yet I'm afraid."

"Oh," I said, instantly deflated. Realising how rude this sounded, I hastily tried to cover my disappointed gloom and said lightly enough; "Never mind, thank you for trying though."

I don't think Lisa was convinced by my tone; she spoke with motherly reassurance. "Well don't give up just yet. The one remaining girl that may have taken the call is in later today, so I'll ask her just in case she remembers. Is it important?"

I was going to be polite and say no, but instead I said, "Actually it is rather. If she has any ideas I'd be really grateful to hear them."

"Okay Ellie. I'll see what I can do. Oops, better go – the boss is coming over. Byeee!"

In the end, I wasn't entirely sure the day exactly satisfied all my ideas of a good one, but it did at least prove to be busy. Apparently, now that the weather was improving, all the other mothers in the neighbourhood were equally keen to send their children out for the day and at about midday a cluster of children arrived on my yard, demanding their long neglected riding lessons. This ought to have meant an afternoon spent barking instructions to confused children on bored ponies as they trudged or sometimes, inadvertently, careered around the school but with half my mind half a valley away, I couldn't face it and so instead we invented gymkhana games. These probably didn't quite satisfy the remit of informing the innocent mind of the child and moulding them into the prim little riders they were supposed to be, but it was fun and thankfully no one fell off or burst into tears, so in many respects the session could be counted a resounding success.

It was already getting quite late when the ponies were all finally put to bed, a tired but smiling Charlie had been packed off home and I had set the pot on the fireside hotplate to heat for Freddy's tea. My hair had to make do with a hasty wash in lukewarm water and a careless air dry as I rummaged in my drawers for stockings and delved into the wardrobe for the one dress which was smart enough for a dance. The simple frock was a pretty dark green and at some point it had endured my clumsy alterations to make it fit my rather slimmer form now that I could no longer lay claim to the feminine curves that I had enjoyed in my teens. Somewhere I had a sash which would cover the uneven seam at my waist.

Always quick to heal, the bruises about my wrists had faded, and on my right it was so pale as to be barely noticeable. But on the left, the unsightly stain was still vivid enough that finger-marks were clearly visible and there was no way I would be able to pass it off as an incident with a horse. I sat down on the edge of the bed and cupped the bruise in my hand for a moment, examining it and feeling a peculiar mixture of emotions at the way my week had been shaped since that day. Then, crossly reminding myself to stop wasting time when my driver was likely to arrive at any moment, I rummaged in my drawers again and pulled out an old heavy bracelet to clasp it about my wrist. All I needed then was to twist my unfashionably long – and rather too straight in a spends-to-much-time-under-a-woollen-hat kind of way – hair up into a loose bun at the base of my neck, add a flash of red lipstick and I was ready.

I need not have hurried as it turned out. John was half an hour late and seemed harassed as I climbed into the car beside him. He was suitably complimentary about my appearance, however, and it was only as he swung the car into yet another bend with far too much vigour that I finally spoke up.

"Are you all right? You seem a little stressed."

"Sorry," he said, allowing the car to slow down. "Was I scaring you?"

"Not at all, I like hanging on to my seat by my fingernails."

"Sorry," he said again, casting me a little sideways glance. "It's

185

just the usual joy at the impending return of the prodigal son, you know how it is."

"Oh dear," I said sympathetically. John was in the unfortunate position of being the younger of two sons and I knew full well just how uplifting an experience it was for him when his father and brother got together.

"Oh dear indeed. If Dear Papa mentions one more time how he wishes I could have gone into the army too, because then he'd have two sons to be proud of, I shall do something reckless."

I laughed. "Don't do that. I'll never be able to visit you in prison."

"I'll try to control myself," he replied soberly.

The house looked spectacular in the heavy dusk, with light blazing from the great latticed windows and a steady stream of cars drawing up before the porch on the wide gravel driveway. Music and chatter drifted out in waves from the open doorway and before we had even entered I could pick out the carrying boom of the Colonel's loud guffaw. John tried to take my arm but I pretended to fuss with the wrap around my shoulders.

We received our greetings from Sir William and his wife and passed through into the hall to join the crush of people that had gathered around the perimeter of those who were already dancing. The band was playing all the old favourites – by that I mean the really old tunes which were tame enough to avoid offending the sensitive tastes of the older guests – but the sweating musicians did at least seem to be inspiring enough enthusiasm in the younger generations to keep them from becoming restive. The loud chatter from those who preferred to linger around the edges consisted almost entirely of indistinguishable nothings about the contradicting forecasts for the morrow, quite as if two months of very little else ought not to have been enough to satisfy even the English appetite for talk on the weather.

Never one for idle conversation, however, John barely even allowed me enough time enough to deposit my wrap on a bench before whisking me onto the dance floor. He seemed to have developed an unprecedented enthusiasm for the exercise and I wondered what had inspired it until I spotted the Colonel bearing down on us with all the subtlety of a bull rhinoceros. He was deflected however by the determined attentions of an elderly widow who appeared to have rediscovered her coquettish streak. Amazingly, she actually seemed to be attempting to flutter her eyelashes and to my intense amusement, the Colonel's normal shade of puce deepened considerably.

I will admit at this point that I was not entirely insensible to the charm of gliding about the floor in the arms of a confident man. I had not been to a dance in years and I couldn't help laughing as John navigated an intricate path between the jostling and bumping couples. We turned and span, and all the while, the complex pattern of our movement was accompanied by the lively rhythm of the music. Gradually however, I began to develop a faint suspicion that it was not just chivalry that motivated John to hold me close as he whirled me about the chaotic room. He seemed to be giving me the full high-voltage benefit of his piercing blue eyes and kept holding me much more tightly than I liked, but I am afraid I just laughed and pushed him away. He pouted but then grinned and loosened his hold.

We danced for a good few numbers before thirst drove us to the drinks stand. The brief moment of alarm caused by a hint of overstepping the established platonic bounds of our friendship had already faded beneath the happy glow of dancing and under the easy comfort of his conversation, it became increasingly likely that the only fault had been with my imagination. But then, whichever way John's intentions transpired to have truly been, I swiftly came to the realisation that the Colonel had no doubts. And equally clearly he was seriously displeased.

The Colonel had successfully extricated himself from the lady's enthusiastic conversation and now cornered us by the punch bowl where we had no chance of salvation. As soon as he even opened his lips, I knew that I had been extraordinarily naïve in hoping that our evening would be allowed to pass in simple uncomplicated friendship. I watched helplessly as John's mouth settled into a petulant frown and then my heart sank. If this was a sign of how the evening was going to progress, I thought, looking about me futilely for some hope of escape, it was going to be *fun*.

The two Langton men were eyeing each other with what could only be described as a deep-seated distrust and I quietly sipped my drink wondering if the bonds of long-term friendship meant that I shouldn't just slip silently away. But before I could even formulate a plan, the Colonel had turned to me and, fixing me with a stern look, said:

"Well, well, Miss Phillips. You managed to leave your animals alone long enough to dress up, did you?"

I really couldn't be bothered to be offended. I laughed instead as if he had made a particularly witty joke and said with a cheerful smile, "It was close, but thankfully John was held up so I had just enough time to run in and brush the straw out of my hair."

Unfortunately I then developed a horrible suspicion that I had somehow dropped John in it because the Colonel's frown deepened and he fixed his son with a penetrating stare. "Held up, were you?"

John smiled but his eyes were wary. "Just tidying a few loose ends."

I realised then that the cause of his earlier mood had been more than just the imminent return of his brother; they must have had a blazing row and, knowing John, it was probably about money. At best their relationship was always rather thorny and if John's various frustrated outbursts over the years were anything to go by, his father appeared to consider him nothing more than a steward to the family estate in the stead of the heir apparent, rather than the hard-working and much loved younger son that by rights he ought to have been. Whether or not the Colonel truly believed him to be little better than a failing employee I could not say, but certainly he was now glaring at his son with the full spectrum of emotions that paid tribute to his own unique grasp of parenting skills; disappointment, contempt and a startlingly intense dislike.

I felt a rush of protective care for my friend. "Lovely room this, isn't it?" I said brightly, but I needn't have bothered. It was as if I did not exist except as an accessory to their quarrel and the Colonel was not to be deflected.

"Loose ends, eh? Well, if you kept your mind on your job," the Colonel said sternly, "and didn't waste your time chasing about on every whim of some cheap baggage, we wouldn't be in this mess."

Apparently I was her. He couldn't have made his meaning more clear than if he had come straight out with it and accused me of being a gold-digger. Well it didn't suit me to play a bit part in some family feud, particularly when one of the main players felt he should put his arm around my waist and vehemently defend my honour.

"Look here, Father. Ellie and I …"

"Are just good friends," I interjected smoothly. I really didn't want anyone hearing him bracket my name with his. Tongues would get wagging in an instant and I had experienced quite enough upset from people gossiping about me as it was. "Is that Sophie Green? I haven't seen her in years. Excuse me would you? I'd better go and say hello."

I set my glass down and turned to make my escape, but my way was blocked.

Oh joy.

"Ah! Miss Phillips," said Sir William, smiling genially down at me. His gaze drifted beyond me and clouded slightly as he took in my two frowning companions but the smile only grew more beaming as he looked to me again. "Tut, tut, eh, Miss Phillips? What say you and I leave these two dogs to have their quarrel alone?"

To my intense surprise, he held out his hand. Even more surprisingly, his offer was apparently serious and I had to rapidly blink away my disbelief before my hesitation could extend into insult. With a nervous laugh to John which was met by a stony glare, I swallowed my puzzlement, reached for the proffered hand, and allowed the old man to lead me back out onto the dance floor.

Sir William seemed oblivious to the curious stares he was attracting by this unusual choice of partner and instead authoritatively led me straight into a waltz with square-backed precision. Trying very hard to pretend that this kind of honour was a perfectly unexceptionable occurrence, I concentrated on keeping the conscious blush at bay and my feet to the rhythm, and determinedly ignored the weight of his heavy hand at my back.

"So, my dear," he finally said in his distinctively lazy tones, rolling an amiable eye down at me as we wove our way slowly across the dance floor. "We get to have our chat at last."

"Our chat, Sir William?" I was distracted by the sight of a familiar pair of eyebrows in the crush at the edge of the room but before I could confirm my suspicions, the dance had swept me onwards.

"You like my nephew."

Were all the Langton family made of the same mould? Friend to my father or no, this went beyond any normal claims on politeness and when I spoke it was with managed reserve. "He is a good friend, Sir William."

"Ah." Whatever he wanted from me, this was clearly not the reply he had been seeking. He changed tack. "I was surprised to hear you were riding out alone the other day. Weren't you afraid?"

"No. Should I have been?"

My partner appeared to be waiting for me to say something more and with a considerable effort I applied my mind to his recent question. I wondered what he had been told about my encounter with the Turford brothers and thought I might pursue my own subtle lines of enquiry. "I had their apologies, Sir William, I don't think it needs to go any further."

There was a barely perceptible pause before Sir William said mildly, "Eh? Oh, you mean those fellows at Warren Barn … John told me that you'd been asking about them – labourers you know; just doing a few odd jobs on the Estate." He dismissed the topic

190

with his customary ease but, I thought with a sharpening of interest, he had at least understood the reference.

"But no, dear girl, I didn't mean them." He fell silent as he led me in a languid turn past a rather flamboyant couple, then added, "I meant with that man on the loose, what's his name …"

"Matthew?" I offered distractedly as a face loomed through the crowd and I had my fears confirmed. Our turn had brought the Inspector into sight once more but thankfully he appeared to be deeply engrossed in conversation with a woman I faintly recognised from the next village and I clung to the hope that he wouldn't see me. If reports of the anticipated conclusion to my intimacy with John had reached his ears as I thought, my dancing with the uncle could only be seen as a confirmation … Although why the thought of the Inspector believing this should matter even more than my normal loathing of gossip I did not know. But it did. Very much.

"You can call him by his name? After what he's done?" Sir William's stark tone brought my mind sharply to heel and my eyes to his face.

"Force of habit, Sir William," I said quickly with as much careless ease as I could muster. "I did very nearly marry the man, after all."

"And thank heavens you didn't, eh?" He took my agreement for granted and I suddenly realised just how peculiar it was to be dancing close to this old man after all I had seen and heard in the past few days. He was familiar to me, a man who had been present throughout my entire life and yet, apparently, not someone I could be confident I knew. Like all the Langton men, he must have been a handsome man in his youth, with the same blue eyes as his nephew – although now faded through age. His cheeks still held the strong structure typical of the family but unlike the Colonel's his complexion was not marred by purple rage. The lines and creases of his face were softer with an implied joviality that matched the lazy warmth of his eyes; and those eyes were now fixed in almost paternal concern upon my face:

"But since you've mentioned marriage, it reminds me of

something I wanted to say to you."

"What is that, Sir William?"

For the first time in my life, I saw him look a little uncomfortable and, for a very fleeting moment before he mastered himself, something that could only have been distaste flickered across his face. He said, "Your father has been dead for what, five years?"

"He has," I confirmed cautiously, wondering where this might be going. We made another sedate turn and unconsciously my gaze fell upon the crowd again but the man and his eyebrows were gone.

"And you're finding it hard to manage alone, aren't you? Your house is falling apart, things are wearing out … and it is getting worse, isn't it?"

I do not believe I had ever heard him speak so bluntly before.

"Who told you that?"

He flushed and blustered a little at the sharpness of my question, adjusting his hold on my hand. "My nephew did, but you mustn't be cross with him, my dear, you have nothing to be ashamed off." The ill-concealed quiver to his mouth said otherwise and I had to bite my lip to suppress the retort that might have followed. "Only last week I heard him say that he was shocked to see what deterioration has occurred in recent months. Cupboards falling off the walls, furniture collapsing and a general air of mouldering decay … it concerned him … and it concerns me too. Why I quite look upon you as part of the family you know." Geniality returned with a rush, "And there is a very simple solution to this little embarrassment of your deteriorating circumstances …"

"And what is that, Sir William?" I had myself under control again by now and there was nothing in my tone that could betray the heat that burned within.

The old man was too well bred to be vulgar so he hinted by allusion. A fleeting reference to care and comfort passed his lips. A suggestion of safety and security, and of protection from loss. Gratitude featured too, but the overwhelming message was of wealth and financial succour – with the power and might of the

192

Langton family at my back, what heights of glory might I not achieve?

So I was to be cast as the gold-digger after all. It didn't seem to occur to him that the trivial little matter of love might in any way influence me in this arrangement, or that money might not be as much of an inducement as he supposed.

"Any woman would, I am sure, be proud to be welcomed into the Langton family," I said carefully, "but I do have to wonder what incentive there is for that dignified family to overlook my – how did you put it? – deteriorating circumstances?"

Sir William was wise and decided to be frank with me. The grey eyes were all at once very unsmiling as we made a slow graceful loop across the room. "My brother is a stern man but he's no fool. He'll come round very quickly when he sees what a positive influence you are; particularly when his son's, shall we say, youthful excesses and exuberances are tempered under your improving influence. And when you are secure under the protection of the Langton family, and have learnt to hold all its concerns as near to your heart as your own ..." here we get to the crux of it, I thought, "... Any doubts you may have fostered in the wake of that unpleasant little incident you experienced at Warren Barn the other day will have dwindled into insignificant memory. Regardless of who is asking the questions."

Ah.

So wealth for me and silence for them, and any other unpleasant little incidents such as the trial and execution of an innocent man would pass us by unnoticed in a haze of unrepentant marital bliss.

Sir William's beam widened once more, as warm and confident as ever. "I can see that you are an intelligent young woman, and I am sure that you'll make the right decision. All you have to think, my dear, is what would your father say?"

The music stopped. I was glad to be released. I only had to resist the urge to wipe my hands clean of his contaminating contact. '*Sir William knows more than you think, old man.*' Simon's words echoed in my head and I stared at my partner with new eyes and new trepidation.

I gave him a smile that was perfectly unambiguous, "I always do, Sir William."

"Good girl. Your father would be proud of you I'm sure. He was a good friend to me, you know, a very good friend." The band started up again and he nodded towards the wings. "I think I should sit this one out. That's the wonderful thing about being old, you can say and do whatever you like and no one dares to pass comment ... Ah, and with perfect timing here is the man himself. John – come and save your pretty little friend from the confused wanderings of a foolish old man. Goodbye, my dear."

And with that he walked off, leaving me to meet the quick interrogative gaze of his nephew alone.

Chapter 21

It was a long while before the tumult of my own mind faded enough for me to notice that the mind of my partner might not be any more composed than mine. But suddenly I was very aware that my partner's steps were stilted, the hands now guiding me around the dance were hard and unyielding, and when I glanced up into his face, I was startled to be met by eyes made grey by cold and consuming fury.

He blinked himself out of his thoughts and caught my gaze. A smile touched his lips that was devoid of any mirth but when he spoke it was carefully light and teasing. "Nice of you to swan off onto the dance floor when you knew that Father was working himself up into his usual fury. What were you two talking about anyway? It can't have been particularly pleasant judging by the expression on your face."

Wisely I held my tongue. He would not thank his uncle, I think, for trying to force his suit and I had no intention of discovering whether John believed there was a suit to be made.

John frowned. "You mean to keep it to yourself, I see."

"Oh John," I said with a sigh, reading the danger signs and knowing that he wasn't far from one of his pettish rages. Normally I greeted his little tantrums with affectionate understanding but at this particular moment, with my head full of his

195

uncle's unspeakable bargain, I was dangerously close to throwing a tantrum of my own.

He continued in a sulky monotone; "I see that I'm going to have to leave it to my imagination to decide what could have possibly held you so enthralled."

I sighed again. Sometimes I felt more like his mother than his friend. "Actually, John, I can tell you something of what we spoke about." I waited while he arrogantly swung me into another turn before continuing; "Sir William believes my house to be an example of mouldering decay. Who could have given him that idea, I wonder?"

He blinked and then smiled, his anger evaporating in the face of mine. "Ah. Sorry. I gather he was not very sympathetic."

"Oh no, he was perfectly sympathetic, John," I said sweetly. "What I want to know is what possessed you to tell him about my, and I quote, 'deteriorating circumstances'?"

"Oh Ellie, I am sorry. I didn't think. I didn't want to upset you, I really didn't." He smiled with uncomplicated charm as he led me, more gently this time, into another turn. "And anyway, don't be unhappy, it's easily remedied after all."

"It is?" I asked, very cautiously indeed.

"Of course it is, Ellie. Why don't you borrow one of my men for a day? I meant to suggest this when I nearly landed on the floor after that dining chair collapsed but it slipped my mind. You told me that you're selling your father's car – how much will you get for it if you don't mind my asking?"

I waited while he steered me past a rather sluggish couple before answering, "Fifty pounds."

"Well then!" he said cheerfully. "You'll be perfectly able to pay his wages then, won't you?"

I took a breath before saying with a careful smile, "Thank you, John. You're very generous, but it won't be necessary."

He frowned again, his voice now tinged with exasperated humour. "There is no need to answer me like that, Miss Disdain;

you know full well if I'd offered my man for nothing, you would have been even more offended. You never let anyone help you, not even me, and you're just too damned proud to admit that you can't always cope alone."

The frustration in his words was palpable and the stupid thing about it was that he was right; I would not have liked him to have made a gift of the man's time. But was it pride alone that made me fiercely preserve my independence even to the point of rudeness? Or was it from the sheer impossibility of a spinster daring to be indebted to a man; even to one who was as old a friend as John?

Being a single woman of dubious financial standing and therefore vulnerable to the very worst of social judgements, I had always worked hard to retain my integrity. One of my guiding principles had always been a rigid aversion to obligation, it had been one of the few things I had managed to stand fast to throughout all the past years of solitude. And now, when that same friend's uncle appeared to have taken to striking untenable bargains in his name, it suddenly seemed that I had every cause to be thankful.

No, definitely not just pride. Self-preservation.

Perhaps rather unkindly I swallowed the apology that had formed on my lips and said instead, "Actually the chair was repaired yesterday." I gave him a teasing smile, "You see – my circumstances are not so much in a decline as you believed, are they?"

"Hmmm," was his grudging reply, concentrating instead on leading us safely through a press of dancers. I felt a little pang of guilt for goading him when he clearly wasn't having a very pleasant time of it with his father but although I felt sorry I couldn't help hoping that having survived Sir William's manoeuvring and his bad humour I might now finally be due some respite of my own. But unfortunately for us both, nothing ever seemed to quite go as it should.

As we floated into an uneasy truce and another dance I became uncomfortably aware that the Colonel was watching us again with blatant displeasure etched across his crimson features. We moved on, whirling deeper into the crush of dancers so that the blur of angry redness was lost for the moment, and I hoped fervently that my partner hadn't noticed – his head had been turned towards the band as we swung past. It was a futile wish of course.

John betrayed his awareness by fixing me with a glowing smile that ought to have melted my bones, but didn't, and then he allowed his hand to drift slightly lower on my back. I stepped away, forcing him to lift his hand and giving him a sternly disapproving look, but as soon as I stepped back into his grasp again, his hand began to creep once more.

I would normally have felt sympathetic solidarity at the realisation that if I found the two old men, the Colonel and his uncle, and their meddling difficult, my feelings were nothing compared to his. Nothing he ever did was allowed to go unobserved and even the matters of his heart were not free from their unwarranted and damaging interference. But another turn brought another glimpse of the Colonel's face glowing pink from the side-lines and, with a bright merry laugh as if I had made a joke, John held me closer. I resisted and pulled away but his hand tightened authoritatively on my waist, showing that he was fully aware of what he was doing and, equally clearly, taking a rather malevolent pleasure in it.

This was too much. Sympathy evaporated and conscience asserted itself so that I stopped dead, insensible to the startled looks from the other dancers and fixed him with a deathly stare that I hoped would put an end to his antics. My voice was tight and sharp as I said, "I would like a drink. Shall we go and find some more punch?"

He indicated his agreement and tried to slip his hand around my waist as he followed me from the floor.

"John Langton, are you actually trying to seduce me?" I said, softening the stern tone with an exasperated laugh.

"Is it working?"

I glowered at him, wishing that I had been truly stern and marched ahead towards the punchbowl. Typically, and perfectly matching the way this evening had gone so far, I saw his father move to intercept us, and as soon as he arrived, barking: "John? What the devil are you playing at?" I simply handed John a glass and left him to face his father's wrath on his own.

Refusing to feel remotely guilty about abandoning him this time, I marched off with the intention of resuming my hunt for the girl that I had faintly recognised. But before I could break through the crush to find her, I heard someone speak my name and felt a light touch upon my arm. "Miss Phillips?"

I turned to face him with every outward sign of unvarying delight at the prospect of yet another attack on my tranquillity, and even managed a decent show of surprise. "Inspector! What are you doing here?"

His eyes crinkled a little at the corners. "Even policemen are allowed a night off, Miss Phillips. I'm here with my wife; she's over there somewhere chatting to Mrs Sir William – I can never remember her name. They were at school together back in the last Ice Age and these sort of social gatherings are vital to their friendship, or so I'm told."

I had to laugh at that. "So you're telling me you're off duty? I don't believe it for a moment. You'll be catching me unawares in a minute and getting me to confess to some heinous crime that I don't even remember committing."

"That's your guilty conscience speaking," he said coolly, and I wasn't entirely sure he was joking. Then he smiled and the kindly crinkles reappeared. "How is Freddy? He seems like a good boy."

"He is," I said confidently. There was a momentary glimpse of Sir William beyond the crowd and as the press of people moved and shifted again, I caught him staring. He gave a satisfied little tilt of his head before turning away.

"And are you having a nice evening, Miss Phillips?" The Inspector spoke in a kindly tone that thankfully showed he was oblivious to the words which were raging savagely in my head. "Who did you come with?"

"I came with John Langton," I said, feeling horribly like I had been caught out on a lie. "Although I'm beginning to regret it."

"Regret it? How so?" He looked only politely interested, but there was an almost audible click as the policeman came back on duty and I had the distinct impression that something was riding on my answer. I could not even begin to fathom what that was.

I smiled. "I've somehow managed to feature in a family row as the gold-digging baggage. Not a part I intended to play, I assure you. So I drifted over this way in order to declare my non-mercenary intentions. In fact to wholly convince you of my innocence I will admit that my devious plan is to introduce John to … that girl over there, who I hope can be counted on to divert all attention her way."

The Inspector turned to look at the woman in question. "A most interesting prospect," he observed dryly, "I wish you luck with your diversion." He turned back to me and for a moment I wondered if he was intending to say something else but then he simply gave me one of his farewell nods and walked quickly away to reclaim his wife.

Thankfully John was nowhere to be seen as I finally made my way over to where Sophie was standing. She was watching the dancing with absorbed interest while the older couple beside her sipped their drinks and kept up a steady flow of chatter over her head without seeming to pause once for thought or breath. I think I joined them somewhere between a debate on the delights of the decorations and the extraordinary lightness of the wine.

"Sophie? Sophie Green?" I said as I approached.

She turned and looked me up and down before finally settling on peering closely into my face. "Ellie? Oh my, I didn't recognise you!"

There was a whisper of sophistication and a gentle waft of her fragrance as we daintily air-kissed cheek to cheek before, linking her arm affectionately through mine, she led me away to a less crowded corner.

"How are you? I'm fine, though sick of this winter, of course. Did you hear that Sammy got killed? Devastating, isn't it. Oh and poor Carrie got into trouble, if you know what I mean – with an *American!* You aren't married, are you? Last I heard you were stepping out with that man, whatshisname – Matthew Croft, that's right. But isn't he the one they're all after? That must feel a bit odd, mustn't it? To think you've been *kissing* a murderer! Only of course that was years ago, before the War. Which no one seems to want to talk about either. Have you noticed that? You've changed, haven't you? David says that I still look just like I did when we were at school but I guess when a person works outside all the time like you do, one would look older. That's a pretty frock, don't I recognise it? Mine's new – do you like it? – David only bought it for me last week; got it from a spiv in London of course, clothing vouchers get absolutely nothing in the shops, do they." She paused to draw breath.

I should explain at this point that Sophie was my friend at school, or to be more accurate, we caught the school bus together on the run down to Gloucester. She was the sort of friend that thought you were wonderful and admired the ribbons in your hair (though not as nice as hers of course) right up to the school gates. Then of course you miraculously became '*just a girl from the next village*'. This all sounds terribly like bitterness but that's not what I mean. I liked Sophie, I just didn't bother to pay much attention to what she said, that's all.

"I'm fine, thank you, Sophie. You look well."

"So who did you come with?" Suddenly she focused on me and I could tell she was having the age old worry of whether or not she would still have the best. She peered round the room as if she might spot my partner just by his appearance, perhaps she was looking for a tell-tale trail of manure. "David couldn't come, he's still away on a business trip. We're getting married in April. Did you know that?"

"Congratulations," I said cheerfully without even a trace of the envy she hoped for. "A spring wedding, how lovely."

"So who *are* you here with?" She wasn't going to be deflected.

"Ah John, let me introduce Sophie Green. Sophie is an old school friend. Sophie, this is John Langton. He's from the Manor." John had shown his usual panache for turning up whenever he was being talked about and was now standing with a palpable air of martyrdom beside me. I felt a momentary wave of guilt for abandoning him, but only for a second.

Sophie seemed to grow about two inches as she greeted him and, if it were possible, her dress actually shrank across her breasts. John eyed her appreciatively over the rim of his glass and I suppressed a smile. Stage one of my diversion campaign appeared to have been a success.

Stage two got well underway even as I watched.

"I've heard of you, of course," she purred. She was smiling her lovely big smile and I felt it would only take another comment like that for John to forget me completely. She always did this whenever in the company of an attractive man, particularly if that man was loosely connected to someone else. I don't believe that she ever did it maliciously; she just naturally exuded an alluring feminine loveliness that delighted in tempting susceptible men into flirting with her only to then show them that their hopes were exaggerated, and that she was still very definitely out of their league. Flirtatious she might be, but she certainly was no fool and it would do John good, I thought, if he were humbled a little by one such as her.

"Of course ..." John smiled suddenly, his lethal bright handsome smile designed to make the recipient's heart miss a beat, and at that instant even I could appreciate why women fell at his feet with alarming regularity. "Have you danced yet?"

Sophie beamed at him, "I haven't actually. But aren't you with Ellie? Would you mind very much if I stole him, Ellie? Just for a minute, naturally."

I smiled happily, "Oh don't mind me. I'm starving. I barely had time for lunch today what with all the mucking out and things.

I'll go and see what there is." This was a bit of a lie but, I felt, perfectly reasonable under the circumstances.

John held his hand out to her and, carelessly thrusting his empty glass into my hands, swept her off without so much as a backwards glance. Just before they disappeared into the crowd I thought I heard her say:

"Poor dear. I bet she'll be glad of a bit of free food, if what I heard is true. Not exactly plump, is she?"

And John's bright laugh drifted back at me over the music and the crowd's noisy chatter.

Chapter 22

It was irritating that the success of my little plan did nothing to improve my mood. I had an overwhelming urge to just go home, but the flaw with dressing up in a flimsy frock, stockings and satin shoes is that the option of walking far is rather firmly closed, so instead I had to console myself with wandering about in reflective solitude. But at least I finally had some peace and I drifted my way through the rooms in a haze of relative contentment until at last I found the buffet table.

The array was spectacular, and looked worthy of a pre-war party rather than the restricted menu of the ration book. I wondered if Sir William's whims bent to a little black-market dealing and picked up something that looked temptingly like a sausage roll, but in the event – and proving once and for all that he had paid for nothing but the innocent talents of a good caterer – tasted strongly of cauliflower. I have always hated cauliflower.

As I reached for a pastry something-or-other I accidentally brushed hands with Mrs Woods, the Inspector's wife, who was still being talked to death by Mrs Sir William. The lady's voice was as steady and somnolent as her husband's and as carrying as the Colonel's, so that I couldn't help but overhear:

"Oh my dear, I'm so tired that I might not last the night. Would you believe we've been either out or entertaining almost every day for the past month."

"You poor thing, so very tiresome," murmured her friend with ready sympathy as she reached for a dainty morsel.

"It is, it truly is. I never get even a moment's peace. In fact, just this morning as I was taking breakfast we had the news that whatshisname – that awful man, you know the one they're all looking for – broke in to one of my husband's barns last night. He was scavenging for food, we think." She selected a misshapen morsel and cautiously nibbled at it before changing her mind and depositing it onto a vacant tray. Perhaps it too had contained cauliflower. "A sign that he's getting desperate I suppose; he's probably starving by now and thought he would chance his luck … Oh, but I wasn't supposed to tell you, Bill told me not to speak of it!"

I bet he did, I thought darkly. Mrs Woods made sympathetic noises before reaching gamely for another treat from the waiting trays. "That sounds so awful. You poor thing, and poor dear Sir William. And of course you mustn't talk about it, if you'd rather not."

"Oh, but it upsets me so. No matter how hard one tries, it is impossible to be strong all the time." The lady of the house blinked rapidly and fixed a heroic smile on her immaculately made-up face, and I had to swiftly turn my head away as her gaze scanned the room to check that everyone was noticing just how brave she was being. Satisfied, and with a belated nod to secrecy, she lowered her voice. "We're not even safe in our own home now. That revolting man obviously has no respect for the lives of perfectly innocent people, no respect at all. The men my husband hired to keep us safe went after him of course but he got clean away."

"Oh my dear! That's just ghastly. Did Sir William—"

"I know I shouldn't ask," she swept on seamlessly, "but does the Inspector really have no idea of where he is? Bill says this nightmare really can't carry on much longer. That odious man! Of course he is the son of that horrible woman, so I suppose one shouldn't expect much better – to think that we went to school with her … Ugh, it makes my skin crawl! Dear Bill still smarts about what she did … By the way, thinking of Bill, did I mention our plans? The dear man thinks that we'll finally be able to get the summer drawing room done up in the new style …"

I couldn't listen to any more. In daylight I might have found her silly fussing amusing but now feeling tired and I suppose rather lonely, I really didn't want to hear it and so instead, abandoning the cauliflower delights, I took myself off to find my wrap.

Hugging the soft woollen shawl about me, I slipped away from the unpleasantly overheated rooms, out under the arched arcade with its impressive wide terrace and sloping beds, and down onto the sodden lawn. The dark night sky was thick with cloud and there was a smell of change on the air. Drifting past a few people smoking cigarettes, I found myself in the lower garden and, heedless to the icy wetness beating through my flimsy shoes, I wound my way down to the cold seclusion of the boundary at the bottom. A slim mulberry stood overlooking the low boxed hedge, growing cheek by jowl with two great sculpted evergreens which formed a gateway at the limits of the garden. It waited there, silent and inviting, and, leaning back against its solid trunk, I took a deep steadying breath of the crisp night air; and with it drew in the sickly sweet smell of the nearby yew. I shut my eyes and allowed my mind to still for a while.

A delicate little thing, he had called me; the sort that wouldn't say boo to a goose. Perhaps he was right. Perhaps I had been younger and more dependent than even I knew. And perhaps the dreadful prospect of his own future had been enough to make him feel unable to face the responsibility of deciding mine. It was suddenly easy to perceive that if I had listened, had truly listened, I might at the very least have proven myself ready to cope with more than he believed. I could still remember his face as he said:

"A penny for them." No, that definitely wasn't it. He had said …
Then it dawned on me that this was not memory, but had come

very softly from somewhere to my right.

"Matthew?"

"No, don't look round. I wouldn't want you to get a reputation for having liaisons with dubious men."

I leant back against my tree again and smiled. "Trust me, I've already been labelled a mercenary baggage tonight; one more mark against my character really wouldn't make one jot of difference."

"Poor girl," he said, but I could tell he was smiling too. "But you are enjoying yourself?"

"Which would annoy you more? My enjoying myself without you or that I want to be at home with you and I'm stuck here?"

"Definitely the former."

"In that case – I'm having a wonderful time, thank you." I jerked suddenly out of the pleasant haze that seemed like an extension of last night's dream and dragged myself rather painfully back to reality. "But what are you doing here?"

"You have previous form for avoiding crowds if you recall. I thought I would take a chance that some things haven't changed."

"I …" Surprise made me falter. But then I mastered myself. It pleased me that he remembered. "What if they see you?"

"Worrying about your honour again?"

"The Inspector is here."

"Ah."

I shivered suddenly. My wrap was rapidly proving to be very little protection against the breeze wafting across from the woodland now that the uncomfortably heady heat from the stifling rooms had faded. And now that I was fully immersed in the present.

"Are you cold?"

"Oh no, not really."

"Liar." His voice came from the depths of the evergreen. "Close your eyes."

"Pardon?"

"Close your eyes. Go on; I'm serious as it happens. I want you to be able to honestly say that you haven't seen me."

207

Hesitantly, I shut my eyes, feeling absurd as I stood there leaning against my tree. My fingers jumped as they were caught in a warm grip. Then, with a fresh admonishment to keep my eyes shut, I found myself being tugged away from my tree and on into the lee of the nearest yew.

The scent of the tree was sharper here. I was caught and firmly enfolded in the flaps of a coat and somehow, with my eyes closed and my cheek turned against his shoulder, it didn't feel so strange anymore to be close to him like this. Hands rested lightly on my waist as he held the coat around me and the touch was a world away from the calculated grasp that I had recently received from another.

"There. Is that better? Good. Now we can talk properly. I've got the car back, by the way, so you don't need to kill me."

"That's a relief. It would be messy." My voice was muffled by his shoulder; I felt him smile a little against my hair.

"I dropped in at the farm too and we were right; they've moved. There was no sign of the Turford boys, in fact I would be hard pushed to prove they'd ever been there at all. I couldn't tell if anything had gone, things looked pretty much as they were last night. Something *was* different but I couldn't for the life of me tell what it was; it's very frustrating. Oh, but I did find one item of interest."

You did? What was it?" I could smell the sweet scent of horses on the rough coat that had belonged to my father and was now becoming Matthew's.

"I went to my house."

"And you found out what they've taken?"

"I think so, but this isn't that." His hand lifted from my waist to reach into a pocket. "Turn around. Be sure to keep those eyes closed, mind."

Clumsily, I turned my back to him and wondered what he was going to do. Then my skin shivered sensitively as I felt his arm come around me; it was followed by the sudden cold shock of metal against my throat and I gasped and lifted a hand. It found a thin cold chain with a tiny pendant hanging loose. His fingers lightly brushed against the hairs at the back of my neck as he fastened the clasp.

"What is it?" His grip felt warm through the fabric of my dress as he turned me back to face him.

"Can't you tell?" He was smiling again, I could sense it.

I ran my hands over the necklace again, trying to remember. The pendant wasn't metal, it was smooth and rounded, like a pebble. A *pebble* … I remembered then. "But this is my necklace …"

My father had given my mother this necklace when they were married. It held a stone from the beach where they had met, he had carried it as a little treasure until the day she became his wife and then, when she died, I had kept it and loved it almost as much as she had. It was a beautiful little stone, dark and speckled like an egg, worn smooth by tide and skin.

"Where on earth did you find it?" I stepped a little blindly as he drew me gently back into the warm folds of the coat once more. "I lost this years ago."

"Well, you didn't actually lose it," he said slowly. Oddly, he sounded faintly guilty. His mouth was muffled against my hair as he quietly added, "I found it a few days after you … After we parted that final time. I had always intended to give it back but somehow it came with me to France. It's silly really but I carried it all the time I was out there. It kept me safe, and reminded me of you."

I could not speak. I just stood there, leaning into his shoulder, with the little pebble warming in my hand.

"I found it today as I was looking over my house; I had forgotten that I had it. I was just shifting my kit bag and it fell out onto the floor – I thought you might like it back."

After a very long time, I finally found my voice. "I do, I do like having it back. I can't believe you took it all the way to France."

"You're angry with me."

"No!" I said emphatically into the coarse fabric at his shoulder.

I lifted my head and almost looked at him but then I remembered and simply allowed my cheek to touch briefly against the rough texture of his jaw before speaking again. "Never angry, not that."

Then absurdly, irrelevantly, I added, "Are you enjoying the life of a vagrant too much?"

"Pardon?"

I smiled at my own flustered nonsense. "You haven't shaved."

"Ah, I see." He laughed suddenly. "No, I'm just not man enough to brave your father's lethal blade. In actual fact I've collected a few things – razor included – from my house so I should be more presentable by the next time you see me." His hands shifted to my arms and he held me away from him a little before saying lightly, "Whereas you look very presentable right now. Very lovely indeed, in fact."

I felt myself instantly become shy and, ignoring the rush of cold against my skin, turned aside for a moment. "Hardly," I said tightly, suddenly feeling oddly sad.

"My dear," he said gently, "I don't want to embarrass you, but with a figure like that …"

I turned away completely so that I could open my eyes. The dim shape of the valley with its thin silvery strip of the last lake was just visible under the heavy cloud. "… I could get mistaken for a boy, I know."

I could sense that he was close behind me. He was standing so close that I could almost feel the warmth of his body against mine. If I leaned back I would be able to rest my head on his shoulder; if I turned, I …

A sudden noise from somewhere near the house made us both jump. Matthew gave a soft laugh.

"Well, I think that's a sign I had better slink away like a thief into the night. I presume you're staying?"

Then, in a totally different voice, he added, "I wasn't teasing just now. One day very soon I'm going to make you take a good long look at yourself."

And on that patently threatening note, he stepped away.

I stayed blinking at the distant valley for a moment and then suddenly remembered. I turned and made an urgent whisper into the dark. "Matthew?"

But my only companions were the heavily scented yew, the distant sound of music and the bright shimmering lights from the house with all the impenetrable mess of its tangled secrets.

Chapter 23

It was probably just as well that Matthew left before I could tell him what had been said; he would almost certainly have tried to stop me from going back into their lair. But given that as soon as I rejoined the heat of the crowd, I was passed and beamed at by Sir William and then passed and scowled at by the Colonel, to have so conspicuously fled would have been incriminating in the extreme. So instead I simply watched the dancers in a dreamy daze and my only worry was that I had to keep reminding myself not to toy unnecessarily with the necklace.

I danced with an old friend from school and a farmer's son from the village, and suddenly, unexpectedly, I was in grave danger of actually starting to enjoy myself. It was funny how much pleasure there was in the spinning and whirling confusion of the dance floor when partnered by one who knew how to politely place his hands. On that subject, I caught a glimpse of John and Sophie very occasionally, mingling with wine in hand or dancing. Every time I saw them it seemed like it must have been mere moments after he had said something amusing because she was constantly laughing and looking up into his face with the same wide-eyed adoration that was typical of his usual conquests. She looked lovely and every bit the perfect companion for him; I pitied poor David wherever he was.

As the evening wore on however, my tolerance for insubstantial chitchat and loud music wore rather thin and I drifted through the thinning crowd, idly wondering just how rude it would be to ask the farmer's son I had just danced with to drop me home. With this thought in mind, I allowed my feet to weave a path towards the entrance hall but as I waited for a tangle of people to organise themselves into their coats and out of my way, I felt a light touch upon my arm.

"Miss Phillips. Have you time for a quick word?" It was the Inspector once more.

Mutely, I followed him away from the noisy mêlée. My nervousness increased tenfold as his route took us to a secluded corner near the coat rack. He turned to face me and this time his demeanour was much more businesslike, with lowered brows and grey eyes that were scarily alert. The policeman was most definitely back on duty.

"Miss Phillips. I have to thank you for your information of the other day. It has proven to be very useful."

"I am pleased to hear it," I said. "What information was that?"

"Would it surprise you to learn that Simon Turford spent a good few months of his younger life at a prison in Hull? And that although his brother has never been convicted, it is widely believed that whatever the one does the other is sure to follow?"

My throat went dry. I said hoarsely, "And what is it exactly that they do?"

The Inspector looked at me appraisingly, hesitating. Then he sniffed and said; "He was convicted of a minor arson, but there was some evidence that a spate of violent robberies were by his hand. I'm not telling you this to scare you, understand, particularly given what you told me about their little visit, but I did think you might be interested to know that this new information has cast serious doubts as to the validity of my two most important witness statements ..."

I had the strong impression that our earlier conversation had gone some way to making up his mind to tell me this. I said cautiously, "They were the people that found Jamie's body." I already could guess at the answer.

"The very same." He nodded approvingly. "They reported the incident, and when we arrived they told a very convincing story."

"And has no one else been able to confirm what they said?"

"No other witnesses have come forward to corroborate their account, other than to give statements about Croft's recent movements; certainly nobody else was at the scene. And to further compound the mystery, when I interviewed them I was not given Turford as a surname." The eyebrows contracted abruptly. "Since learning this, I have had my detectives visit the address they gave, and guess what they found."

"That it was wrong?" I was a little late in asking the required question. The gift of this information was making me increasingly apprehensive. I did not know what he would want in return.

"More than wrong, Miss Phillips – the address I was given was 42 Norfolk Street in Gloucester and this house, as it turns out, was something akin to a brothel before it was reduced to rubble in the blitz." The Inspector's jaw set into a rare frown as he added, "Our Turford brothers have been making a fool of me, Miss Phillips, and that will not do. That will not do at all."

I could well believe it. Finally I plucked up the courage to ask, "Why are you telling me this, Inspector?"

In an instant, his attitude snapped from hawk-like consideration to lax inattention and he was suddenly giving a very good impression of one who was just passing the time of day. "No reason really, I just thought you would be interested to hear." He flicked another glance at me and smiled. He seemed to become peculiarly interested in the condition of his fingernails as he added, "I'll be stuck in my office all day tomorrow, you know, from about nine o'clock. I'm at the Gloucester branch."

He paused, now seemingly fascinated by a scarf hanging on the rack behind him. Finally he said indifferently, "It is a shame that no one knows the whereabouts of your man Croft. In light

214

of this new information, it really would be very interesting to speak to him …"

"It would, wouldn't it," I agreed weakly, trying frantically to decide if his use of the term *my* man Croft had been accidental. On the whole, I suspected not.

He reached out suddenly and patted my hand. "Ah well. I'm glad we've had this little chat, Miss Phillips. I'll doubtless be seeing you again soon. Goodnight."

"Goodnight, Inspector."

I emerged from the coat racks in something of a shaken state. After an evening of upset and insult, the sudden hope of Matthew being believed after all was a delight I had not expected. And yet, for some indefinable reason, I felt more afraid for him now than I had ever been before. Surely the Inspector meant what he said. Surely this could not be a perfectly laid snare with me playing the part of the naïve and unwitting decoy …

"What did he want?" John's demand cut crossly across my apology as I almost walked into him. His face bore that sulky scowl once more and I wondered with a faint impatience what had put it there this time. Then I saw that Sophie was standing with him and, I noticed with some concern, not looking nearly so blooming as she had been. Her lipstick was smudged and she wore an agitated air as she pushed past me to retrieve her coat.

"Just letting me know that he's closing in on where Matthew is," I said lightly.

"Ah? Is he indeed?" John didn't look quite as enthused by this as I would have expected but then, given his mood, most likely nothing could have impressed him. "Are you ready to go? I'm sick of this place."

I nodded. Sophie reappeared beside me and my suspicions had been right – she didn't look very happy at all. It may have been my imagination but her large eyes glistened wetly and I was suddenly very aware that in spite of her alluring smiles she was, like me, just a simple farm girl at heart.

"Are you two leaving?" she asked brightly. "I'm leaving too as soon as I can find the others. I mustn't be tired tomorrow as David is coming home; I told you about our plans didn't I, Ellie?"

I was hit by a sudden and consuming rush of guilt; my little scheme had not included upsetting her. "You did. It all sounds lovely and I bet you can't wait until the spring."

She smiled suddenly and very genuinely. "You know? I really can't. Goodbye, Ellie, so nice to see you again."

She whirled off trailing coats and scarves behind her. She had barely looked at John and now he was watching her go with a very unpleasant smirk etched across his face.

"What on earth did you say to her?" I demanded more crossly than I intended as we climbed into the car.

"I don't know what you mean," he said, sounding amused. "Why? Are you jealous?"

"Not at all," I said levelly, looking out of the window as the car pulled away with a crush of gravel under the tyres.

He gave a dry laugh. "Of course you're not. She's just some silly cheap bit anyway; there's no competition."

I was suddenly bitterly regretting not begging a lift home from someone else. His driving had not been improved by the evening's dramas and a small squeak of alarm escaped as we shot around a corner narrowly missing a couple who were walking home. I twisted in my seat to look back at them in case they were hurt but bar an angry fist waving in the air at our wake, they appeared to have escaped unscathed.

I braved a glance sideways at him as we accelerated along a straight stretch which was still banked by high discoloured drifts. His face seemed flushed and distorted in the pale reflected light and the aroma in the car only confirmed what I already suspected. He was drunk. But I was not sure that he was so drunk that he was not fully aware of what he was doing and, unhappily, revelling in the barefaced recklessness of it. A flash of white caught in the headlights as we raced around a bend – the first long-suffering snowdrops to show their faces and a tentative sign of the belated spring.

"Did you have to say that?" The sudden snap of his question made me jump.

"Why? What did I say?" I asked, forcibly keeping myself from squeaking again as the car hurtled into another tight turn. When I looked over at him, his knuckles were white where his hands gripped the steering wheel.

"What you said to my father. About us just being friends."

"But we *are* friends."

"Yes, but it wasn't a very nice thing to say was it? You made me look like a fool." His tone was increasingly hard and I began to watch the road ahead with renewed enthusiasm as houses loomed in the headlights. A smithy smacked past; we were fast approaching the tight series of bends into Winstone.

Not far now, I thought as we span left and then sharp right. I was becoming increasingly aware that I really didn't like him very much anymore; if his behaviour to me had not been enough, the look on poor Sophie's face had decided that.

"I'm very sorry," I said carefully. "I didn't want to upset you."

"Too late for that," he snapped. "Although it's not as if Father needs any excuse to be disappointed in me. I manage that all by myself."

"He's annoyed with you?" I was playing for time, hoping to appease his anger and distract it from me until we got home. I wasn't very optimistic about my chances.

"Of course he is. You heard him tonight. What Father wants, Father gets. Unless there isn't the money to do it, then he gets cross. He and my brother are both the same. They go off to fight their damned expensive wars and it's the rest of us poor beggars that have to foot the bill. Have you any idea of how tight things are for me at the moment? And now dear brother Richard needs funds …" Here he uttered an ugly curse as a rabbit raced for safety.

"I had no idea things were so hard for you currently," I

murmured sympathetically. This, it turned out, was a mistake.

He fixed me with a furious stare and for a painful moment I thought he wasn't going to look back at the road ahead again. But then, with an angry jerk of the wheel, the car twitched back under control once more and away from the hedge.

"Hard for me – you don't say. You and your ponies and that idiot boy live an idyllic existence; you couldn't possibly imagine what it is like for me." The dim lights of the Mason's Arms shot by as we launched out onto the brief stretch of the main road without so much as a glance to check for traffic. We sprinted past the dirty hulks of impossibly high drifts then we took a hard swing left onto the road towards home. He spoke again, his voice rising to a fevered pitch and blurring incoherently, "How would you feel having every move dissected, every hope crushed and every plan ruined? Taxes are sky high to pay for the fallout from that blasted war and I'm still being told that somehow it is all my fault. We're practically bankrupt, you know."

There was a certain grim irony in this given Sir William's attempt at bribery, although I was in no mood to appreciate it.

John continued his wild monologue with full red-blooded ferocity. "And dear darling Uncle is no better, though he tries to help with his petty interferences. But all I hear is Bathurst, Gatcombe, Badminton, in an endless drone of social ambition. It's driving me insane!"

After all that anxious watching of the road ahead, I hardly noticed when we stopped outside my house. I was watching him with a grim sort of fascination as he ranted out his fury.

"And you – you sit there judging me, don't you? Admit it. Just because some silly girl got upset when she got burnt. She should know better than to play with me. Silly bitch." I had a feeling that this last comment was directed towards me.

He turned to face me, his eyes glinting in the darkness and I stared at the man before me with his angry tone of injured complaint and downturned mouth, and wondered how I had been so stupid as to ever think that I understood him. I waited for him to continue in a mesmerised trance, knowing with dismal certainty what he was going to say and likewise knowing there was absolutely nothing I could do to prevent it.

"We've been friends for years, you and I, and I've watched and waited while you mourned for that man. Patiently. Like a saint." He smiled mirthlessly at some private joke.

"John, I—" My attempt was as ineffective as it was weak. He swept on as if I hadn't spoken. "Only you're not mourning any more, are you?"

I had feared it might come to this. But no matter what I had expected, I was not remotely prepared for the violence of his next words. He delivered them in a breathless roar that actually made me flinch. "I love you, Ellie, and I mean to have you. By God I do!"

He glowered at me, breathing hard with hands clenched in his lap looking so absurdly like a child in a fit of the rages that I might have laughed had it not been so extremely genuine. Instead, in defiance of the fury that lurked behind his eyes, I managed to force myself to speak.

"No, John," I said with gentle firmness, much as an old friend might. "That's not going to happen, I'm sorry."

He nodded sagely, seeming to be taking in what I had said. His stillness gave me courage. I began to say something else, probably an innocuous attempt at a peaceful exit, but even as I started to frame the words, he made an odd little throaty noise and lunged at me, and crushed my mouth with his.

"Oh, Ellie …"

For a brief stupid moment I was so paralysed by shock that I didn't move. But then, with a sudden urgency of strength, I managed to shove him away.

"What the hell are you doing?" I demanded shakily, wiping my mouth on the back of my trembling hand.

"Nonsensical girl." He gave me a silly drunken leer that conflicted oddly with the force of his presence. "You can't tell me

219

that you haven't wanted this too."

This time his lunge was more determined. With a strangled cry, I shrank painfully back against the doorframe. I put my hands to his chest, trying to ward him off but his weight crushed me so that I was pinned between him and the cold hard metal of the door as he leaned closer. Desperate, I gave a frantic twist and succeeded in wrenching my head aside so that his lips fell across my cheek. He pulled back, looking faintly confused ... or was it offended? As I supposed he might. I doubted that many women had ever rebuffed his advances before.

Looming over me in the cramped space of the car he seemed for a moment affectionately amused by my resistance. He flashed me a big smile. "Now, Ellie. Don't play coy."

His mouth twisted to kiss me again and, panicked, I said the first thing that came into my head.

"I know about Union Star!"

He froze, with his lips barely a millimetre away from mine. "*What did you say?*"

"Union Star. I know you switched him."

Abruptly he sat back into his seat. He took a deep breath. "And how did you figure that one out?"

"John, my father broke him in for you. I think I would remember him." I was too upset to worry about what I was saying now. "Why did you do it?"

"Observant, aren't you," he said slowly. His voice was low and had an unusual note to it, and he suddenly seemed very sober indeed. "I wondered why you let him snatch at your pockets like that, and now I know. What else did you notice?"

"What do you mean?" I said helplessly. "I understand things are tight for you but why sell a dead horse? He *is* dead, I presume?"

"Oh yes, he's dead. Damned thing dropped dead of a heart-attack last August. But because I had to pay for my father's stay in London while he watched my brother butter up the men at HQ by pretending to be a war hero, I'd let my insurance premium

220

lapse. Clever, eh? So then the damned horse dies and with just perfect timing I get some American with more money than sense wanting to preserve the bloodline. What would you have done? No, don't answer; we know what Miss Prim would have done." He gave a hard little laugh. Then he frowned again. "I found this beast at an auction. He looks the part and my American is never going to tell the difference so I just went ahead. Can't see what the problem is really. Everyone gets what they want."

"Do they?" I asked quietly. I moved my hand slowly to the door handle. I really didn't care about the horse; I just wanted to get out.

"He told me I shouldn't have you, you know." His tone was suddenly lighter, it was almost conversational and I floundered in my desperation to keep up with the shifts and pitfalls of his mood. "Father said that tonight – he actually came straight out with it and told me that I should aim higher." He laughed and, oblivious to the insult, I only wished that his mirth was a sign of an improving temper. "But interestingly Uncle says different, and for once I have to agree with him ... He said—"

He stopped, casting a little sideways glance at me as he paused to focus his thoughts.

I realised then that I had never stood a chance, not when my only armoury was of stern looks and careful distance. No words of mine could have ever hoped to combat the power of his uncle, or the deep-driven urge to contradict his father. That was an impulse far more enduring than any claims of adult accountability. And now, all I had left were the ruins of a friendship and a pointless wish that I had not gone at all, had left with Matthew; that I was, in fact, anywhere but here.

He spoke out of the silence, a faint shadow of that hideous undertone still lurking in his voice. "I didn't have a choice about the horse, you know."

"I understand, John, I really do. I'd have done the same."

"You're a bad liar, Ellie," he said, finally sounding calmer. I said nothing. "This has ruined any chances I ever had with you, hasn't it? You'll never have me now, what with your damned high morals. You sit there in judgement, I know you do."

"I don't, John, really I don't." I started to ease back the door latch.

"Oh, shut up," he snapped, anger flaring again in an instant. "I've noticed your habit of collecting those you deem needy and worthy, that idiot boy and that wretched horse being prime examples, but you've never bothered to extend that care to me, have you? And why? Because I don't fit your special little ideas of *purity*? Is that it? You have no right to judge me, you know, little Miss Superior – you've got more vanity than anyone. You hide yourself away behind all that ridiculous reserve and believe we don't notice that all the while you're *thinking*. You disgust me. In fact, I think I might hate you after all."

"I'm sorry you feel like that, John," I said quietly. The door catch lifted.

He threw me a wild look. "I don't hate you, Ellie. Really I don't. Oh, Ellie …"

I threw the door open and practically fell out in my haste to get away as he lunged again. His kiss fell on empty air and he stared up at me, open-mouthed and ugly as I carefully shut the door and turned away. I walked quickly. It took a lot of self-control not to break into a run but as I reached the shadows of the kitchen door, I heard a reassuring roar as the car kicked angrily into life. I turned and caught the reflected blaze of red as his lights finally sped away towards the village, and it was only when the sound had faded to silence that I briefly allowed reaction and cold to have its say. I stood there for a few precious seconds, staring vacantly into space while my body was wracked with a violent and uncontrollable shivering. Then I straightened my flimsy wrap, brushed the hair back from my face and wiped the smudged lipstick from my mouth. I wondered if Matthew had been watching out for the car to pull up and if he had seen what had followed. I dreaded to think how it must have looked if he had.

I took a deep breath and opened the door.

"You're back!" yelled Freddy. "Just in time to join us!"

They were in the living room. Matthew must have repaired the gramophone because Freddy was vigorously giving the handle a turn so that one of my father's old records blared out. The sudden heat of the fire and the deafeningly crude music were such an assault on my senses that I almost staggered but instead I stopped and put a supporting hand on a chair-back.

"Oh Freddy, that's wonderful!" I cried merrily, while feeling anything but. I desperately wanted to know if Matthew had seen but I couldn't bring myself to look at him. Instead I fixed a bright smile on my face and walked steadily over to Freddy and his gramophone.

Matthew had started up when I had come in but almost immediately returned to his position near the fire where he was now leaning a shoulder in easy comfort against the wall. I could feel his eyes on me. Determined to avoid him, I beamed madly at Freddy and picked up the record sleeve to examine it with concentrated interest only to have to swiftly put it down again when my hands almost betrayed me.

"Did you have a nice time?" Freddy asked. I couldn't help glancing at Matthew then, his face looked shuttered and carefully wiped of all feeling. He had seen, oh, he had definitely seen.

"Freddy? Isn't it time you were in bed?"

Matthew's suggestion was ignored by both of us, Freddy because he wanted to stay up and play with his gramophone and me because I couldn't bear to be left to face this argument alone.

"I danced with all sorts of people tonight, Freddy. You would have loved it." I was speaking to the boy but I couldn't help the snatched glance that fell once more on Matthew. He had been true to his word and had shaved and changed his clothes, and suddenly the man in my house was very much like the man I remembered, only older, wiser and considerably more ... formidable.

I felt wretched. And hid it with a smile. "By the way, the Inspector gave me a message for you, Matthew."

Matthew roused himself at this and pushed himself upright away from the wall. "What did he say?"

"That the Turford brothers gave a false statement. He wants to see you to hear your side of the story. He'll be in his office from nine tomorrow." I spoke quickly and eagerly.

"Can we trust him?" His tone betrayed nothing.

"I think so. He sounded genuine."

"Well, this is good news then, isn't it? This could all be sorted by this time tomorrow." His voice lifted to sudden warmth and he actually smiled. "Your life could get back to normal before you know it; you've been wonderful as usual."

He was trying to be kind and I knew it. His voice held that hideously positive note of one who was deeply disappointed but was trying very hard to hide it; he would not forgive me for this.

Before anyone could say anything else I lightly said, "Yes, well, I'm only the messenger. And anyway I'm feeling very tired so I'll go to bed now. Goodnight all."

Freddy was oblivious to anything but the wonder of the gramophone and I heard him start it up again as I ran up the stairs. The door shut and I threw myself down on the bed; I would have sobbed my heart out but for the fact that the tears just wouldn't come. Instead, with my face pressed to my pillow, eyes tightly shut, I lay there and hit it repeatedly with my fist while I concentrated really hard on not screaming.

Chapter 24

The house was quiet. Freddy had stumbled up to bed nearly an hour ago and in the peace that followed in the wake of the music, the house had settled gently to a slumbering silence. If I had not been desperately thirsty I would have stayed hidden away in my room, but telling myself that Matthew was bound to be asleep, I braved slipping soundlessly down the stairs and out into the light.

He wasn't, of course. He was sitting at the kitchen table waiting for me.

I walked past without even a glance. "I just wanted some water."

The chair creaked as he stood up and then quiet footfalls recorded his progress around the table until they came to a stop somewhere behind. There was a pause while I fiddled about with a glass but then, in the silence that followed, I heard him give a little sigh.

He spoke with concentrated patience. "Are you going to tell me what happened tonight?"

Defeated, I set the glass down somewhere quite without thought and turned to face him. Nothing could have made me brave enough to meet his eyes so instead I fixed my gaze feebly on a spot on the floor. Putting my hands behind me on the counter for its meagre support, I steeled myself to meet the final stage of a terrible evening.

"I don't know what you mean," I said weakly.

"Oh, come on." His voice was rough and exasperated and I looked at him then. I think my heart broke, he looked so remote. I looked down to the floor again.

"I thought you were protecting Freddy just now but you weren't, were you? Don't shut me out. Not this time, please. You keep doing this – and I think it is high time you started being honest with me."

I still couldn't bring myself to look at him. I heard another suppressed intake of breath and then, "Right. Let me help you get started. Did Langton do that?"

Instinctively, my hand flashed across to cover the bruise. I had removed my bracelet earlier and the marks were clear against my icy skin. I said stupidly, unthinkingly, "No, of course not. You did. Out in the snow. When I found you."

No reply. Then, abruptly, in the wake of an even more formidable silence, the words burst out in a helpless rush. "I didn't want to it to happen like that. You have to believe me. It's not what it looked like, it really isn't! Please don't be angry. He was being strange so I got him to dance with Sophie Green – I used to catch the bus to school with her, and ... oh, that doesn't matter – only John upset her and then I spoke to the Inspector and then we came home only he was drunk, and he was angry and ranting about his father and ... and other things. Then when we got back he kissed me. *He* kissed me, I didn't kiss him, I really didn't. I didn't want to. So I told him about the horse to make him stop and then I ... No, please don't say you don't believe me! If you'll just listen, I ..."

He made an impatient gesture that silenced me and jerked my attention up to his face. His eyes were black. "You're not listening to *me*. I know what I saw."

I waited for the words that would finish me.

They came in a voice that was held low and steady in spite of the wearied undertone of long suppressed impatience, "My dear, I very nearly marched out there and hit him. In fact I should have done, and if you had stayed in that car with him for a second longer, I most certainly would have, hunted-man be damned." A grimace. "Believe me, I was halfway through the door as it was, and only the knowledge of what it would cost you if I exposed what you've done for me held my temper in check even that much."

His words had fixed my eyes upon his face only I couldn't quite grasp his meaning. His eyes were still dark and he was frowning a little in that controlled unreadable way of his and I bit my lip, feeling every kind of misery as he gazed at me steadily, seemingly waiting for me to make a reply.

Then, suddenly, his expression transformed and he gave a very exasperated reproof of "*Eleanor!*" and took a sharp step towards me.

Looking back, I think he had intended to enfold me in his arms. But there must have been some caution still lurking at the back of his mind of the uncertainty of his right and so instead he froze, his hand hovering in mid-air somewhere near my cheek and his eyes watchful in softly delivered enquiry.

There was a brief numbing moment of stupidity as I stared at him blankly. But then, gradually, my tired mind stumbled back into life and I began to make some sense of the words he had spoken.

Oh.

He gave a gentle smile then and very slowly as if he was afraid the moment might break and I might flinch away from him, he lifted his hand. His touch lightly grazed my cheek.

"You thought I wouldn't believe you?" I couldn't have moved even if I had wanted to and I stared up at him, breath and heart-beat stilled to silence as his fingers caught at a strand of hair to delicately lift it aside. Seemingly concentrated on this little act of tidiness, he lightly said, "My darling girl … *really?*"

I think I managed a faint shake of my head and my heart rushed to piece itself back together again as he stepped a little closer. Then his gaze touched upon my lips and if my pulse had stopped before now it raced with terrifying urgency as he tentatively and very gently leaned a little nearer.

After a very long time he pulled away. His hand was warm against my cheek and his eyes were smiling down at me. Feeling suddenly very giddy indeed, I found a wobbly little smile of my own, and with a brief close of his eyes he stepped in again, gathered me into his arms and kissed me.

Chapter 25

I woke to the soft gloom of a night heading towards dawn, wrapped tightly in my blankets and with the memory of his arms holding me close still lingering on my skin. The interval between then and now seemed to have passed in a brief dreamless blur and yet I was sure that I hadn't imagined that last teasing smile as he deposited me at the foot of the stairs. Or, only a short time later, that I had found myself being sweetly but cryptically reminded that there were things that needed to be said, and that now was not the time, and then dispatched firmly up the stairs to my bed, alone. And that being so, I was a little surprised when I opened my eyes to find him there.

"What are you doing?" I asked in a hazy glow of warm confusion. He was fully dressed and standing beyond my little bedside table, and the sudden unexpected change of the lamp being lit must have been what had woken me.

At my words he turned to me and he looked almost unearthly with the thin inky amber of the oil lamp touching his hair and the side of his face to healthy colour, and casting a pale shadow beneath his jaw.

"Good morning sleepy," he said, and the brief appearance of a smile brought a rush of warmth to my cheeks that had its origins somewhere down near my toes. "I hate to talk business so early in the day but can you explain how you came by this?"

"I don't know," I said dreamily, showing that I really hadn't yet registered the decidedly formal air of this invasion into my room. But then I saw that he held a crumpled piece of paper in his hand, angled so that he could see it better by the sooty ball of light on the table and, giving myself a shake, I tried to assume a more workmanlike air. "Where did you find it?"

He smiled at my tone, undoing all my hard work in an instant. "I took the liberty of coming in with a cup of tea for you and tripped over a little pile of clothes – we really are going to have to talk about tidiness, you know – then this fell out. Where did you get it?"

Reluctantly I sat up, tucking the blankets carefully around me for modesty and for warmth, and blinked at him blearily before finally my brain decided to come to life. Cursing my carelessness, I saw that the pile of clothes by his feet were the same ones I had been wearing that night when we had fled from Simon's gun, and which I had left in a soggy heap ever since.

"I guess that must be the paper from Jamie's barn. A design for a door or something, isn't it? I still had it in my hand when we were hiding so I stuffed it into my waistband. What of it?"

He stepped around the little table then and, handing me the paper, sat down quietly beside me on the edge of the bed. His arm was resting behind me in easy comfort as he shared my examination of the document and unlike me, he was clearly far too preoccupied to notice the sudden intensity that this previously unexplored level of closeness inspired. I took a calming breath and, with a very great effort and a certain amount of suppressed disappointment, finally managed to force my mind to focus.

The paper was still rather damp and what looked like faded watercolour had run badly to blur the lines that sketched lazily across its surface into barely intelligible disorder.

"How odd," I said, trying to make it out. "Is it some kind of artist's impression?" I made to hand it to him but he pushed it back.

"If I say 'tiger, tiger, burning bright'; what does that mean to you?"

"A poem," I said vaguely, still attempting to match the sweep and curve of the lines to any kind of doorframe I had seen. "Byron, no that's not it. Blake?"

"Got it in two, my dear … In what distant deeps or skies; Burnt the fire of thine eyes?"

"Is that what this is? A poem?"

I peered doubtfully at the stained paper in my hand. I was being very slow on the uptake, but in my defence I had just woken from what had turned into the strangest night of my life so far to find myself suddenly being expected to rise to intelligent thought.

"Not quite, no." He was smiling at me, I knew, but then his thumb moved against my back and for a moment my brain switched off again. Eventually however, light dawned;

"Is this one of Blake's illustrations?" I could see it now, a bizarre drawing of a sweeping frame of open curtains – the doorway of my imagination – and a faded figure striding away between them like some kind of monstrous character from a disturbed dream complete with protruding tongue and a murderer's eye. There may once have even been a shower of yellow stars rushing to greet the ugly form but the ford had ruined its detail. The style of the creator's hand was unmistakable however, and it was very clearly not just a replica.

"The Ghost of a Flea." His tone was very dry. "No, not the original. That's a painting and housed in the Tate, or at least it was when I last saw it. This must be a preparatory sketch of some sort."

"But that's impossible! How could Jamie afford a William Blake drawing, even a minor one? They've got to be worth a fortune!"

Matthew smiled and, proving he was not as unaware as I had thought, lightly touched his lips to my shoulder before saying, "Definitely worth a penny or two, I should say."

I gaped at him, finally understanding what he had been hinting at all this time. "Freddy's treasure! Oh my!" I covered my mouth to smother a giddy laugh. Managing to sound calmer, I added, "Good Lord. And there's a whole box of them too."

"Was," he corrected. "They've moved it now." Then he quoted very softly, "*The flea. Inhabited by the condemned souls of blood-thirsty men ...*"

Something flicked through my mind and I touched my hand to his in sudden eagerness. "Hang on a minute; this reminds me of something ..."

I quickly told him of the newspaper article I had seen. "I don't remember any mention of a looted Blake drawing though ... But it did say something about the collection including etchings. I *suppose* this could be described as a print ...? I don't know anything about them; you don't think—?"

Matthew nodded slowly. "It is all too much of a coincidence wouldn't you say? Though whether Lord and Lady Anonymous of Lansdown Place, Cheltenham will be pleased to have this one back is another thing. Not exactly in mint condition any more is it, thanks to its brief encounter with the ford."

"Oh dear," I said, with feeling. "Do you think our Boss character was trying to sell the painting that got found in the auction house? John said ..."

I stopped. I really didn't want to talk about him, I realised.

"Go on, what did John say?" He caught my glance. "I don't know why, but I feel so at peace with the world today that I can even bear to talk about him. I couldn't possibly explain how that could be. Can you?"

I returned his grin shyly and indulged in a little happy lean into his side as his arm tightened. Finally however, he released me and allowed me to collect my thoughts.

"Well ..." I began dazedly, drawing a fresh grin, "All he said was that you would have to be stupid to sell something like that locally to where you stole it from."

"Though it pains me to admit it, he's actually right on that one."

A thoughtful silence followed this admission. And all the while,

232

the ghoulish figure leered back over its shoulder from the page, mocking us.

Beside me, I saw Matthew give a faint grimace, his mouth tightening at one corner in sudden seriousness; "This is all very interesting isn't it, though I'm not entirely convinced that it gives us much more information about our villains."

He frowned again only to follow it with a deliberately brighter tone as he added, "But at least it gives me plenty to tell the Inspector; and hopefully swings the evidence a little more firmly in my favour …"

"So you really are going then?" I asked, trying to hide the quick quiver of fear at the risk he was taking.

He nodded and gently took the valuable ruins of the paper from my hands to place it on the cabinet. "Got to face the music some time."

He settled back against the pillows with a sigh. There was a brief moment of awkwardness while I smiled shyly down at him but then, in a deliciously natural assumption of right, he simply reached out a hand and dragged me down beside him.

I found my cheek being happily crushed against his warm shoulder as he wrapped his arms around me and the heavy folds of my blankets. His comfortable ease with our newfound closeness felt wonderful, I could have stayed there for hours but then, with a bit of a shuffle, he twisted onto his side and propped himself up on his elbow to gaze down at me. His hand sent little shivers running up and down my spine where it touched the hairs on the back of my neck.

"I will go soon. But first of all …"

He took my hand and threaded his fingers through mine as they lay across my stomach. A corner of his mouth gave a little twitch; "First of all, when you—" The words faded. He was toying a little with my fingers where they rested under his and oddly, I seemed to suddenly lose him to his thoughts. His eyes were downcast and he appeared to be turning something over in his mind, adjusting his thoughts just as his fingers rearranged mine. Then his hand stilled.

When he continued, it seemed to me that he had taken a slightly different tack. "Last night, when you told me how you got these marks, I thought that was it; I had just handed you one last insurmountable bit of proof that I shouldn't be trusted. Only somehow, for some unfathomable reason, it seems that you decided to talk to me after all and seeing as you have, I must tell you that I absolutely refuse to let you go again. For better or for worse you can rely on me this time ..." The impossibly dark eyes lifted abruptly to mine. "Presuming, that is, that you still want to?"

I didn't entirely understand his meaning and he seemed suddenly so uncharacteristically unsure of himself that for a moment I was robbed of speech. Finally however, I found my voice. "I do, I do want you," I said, giving him a silly smile.

There. It was done. I had admitted it. And the ludicrous thing was, after all that fear and wretched distance, it had barely been terrifying at all.

Chapter 26

On days like these I was profoundly happy for the necessary routine of the horses. Beechnut was willing and I was determined and, oblivious to the gusting breeze that was bringing in more heavy cloud, we ambled along the streaming road trailing our steady company of ponies. A raven gave its usual greeting of a croaking bark and I watched as it flew away hopefully searching along a tree-line.

The morning's chores had whistled by in a haze of warm recollection and ignored foreboding until, having finally exhausted these tasks and still desperate for any distraction, I had been forced to resort to heartlessly chivvying Freddy into coming out on a ride with me. I couldn't bear to sit at home simply meekly waiting until my car reappeared … or not, and even milking the goat had been unfortunately brief. The poor thing's routine had been so extraordinarily disrupted in the past week that judging by the drastically reduced yield delivered into my pail, there was every likelihood that she was drying up.

"Will he come back to live with us after he's finished with the police?" Freddy's voice suddenly broke in from somewhere behind.

I smiled to myself. I had necessarily explained the reason for Matthew's dawn departure but the depth of our late-night rediscovery of intimacy was a secret I had yet to share. "I don't know,"

I said truthfully. "After all this is over he might prefer to spend some time on his own."

"I don't think he will," Freddy said rather firmly. "He likes it with us, he told me so."

His words made me smile once more in spite of the persistent shadow of tension and when the raven called again as I flung open the uppermost gate on the road up the hill from Washbrook, it appeared to almost be trying to confirm his view that everything was going to be all right.

"He can always have my room, you know." Freddy's voice drifted up the hill once more as we climbed towards the village.

I twisted in the saddle and grinned back at him. "But where would you sleep, eh? And what about all your things? I doubt very much that he'll be quite so keen when he sees what squalor you call a bedroom."

"I could tidy up; we could share," he repeated stoically. "Or we could build a new room or something – he is an archee … um, a designer after all." I laughed and he persevered doggedly, "*If* he wants to stay, will you let him? Please? I'm sure he'll be quiet and not cause any trouble."

"He's not a pet, Freddy," I said, laughing. "You sound like you're asking for a new kitten … But yes," I added, quickly pre-empting his protest, "If he wants to live with us, of course he can. I couldn't think of anything better. And no, I don't think you'll have to share. I suspect I can find a more suitable arrangement."

"Really?" Freddy's tone brightened enormously, but then, clearly thinking deeply about the practicalities, he added, "But where? He can't live on the settee and he won't want to share your room, yours is worse than mine."

"It isn't!"

Freddy sniggered from the safety of his distance behind me. "If you say so."

"Good morning."

The voice most likely to wipe the smile from my face interrupted our happy little bantering and I twisted jerkily in the saddle towards it. I hadn't noticed that we had entered the village but as I gave a startled turn, I recognised the wide expanse of the driveway to the Manor as it swept away from the road to our left; and beyond, through the dense scrub of dormant shrubs on the level ground before the front door, I could just make out the red and green livery of the horsebox, with John standing nearby.

"Good morning, Ellie."

He repeated his greeting loudly, accompanying it with a cheerful lift of his hand and I had to wonder whether he even remembered his actions of the night before. On the whole, I suspected not; his jaunty walk as he sauntered over to intercept us was not quite in keeping with one who had anything playing on his conscience.

He skirted past a thick patch of particularly slushy ground and smiled. "On your way back from a ride?"

"As you see," I replied, rather coolly. I wasn't really sure how to play it. I knew I could no longer count him as a friend, but I didn't think that I actually wanted open hostilities with him and I was thankful when Beechnut did her job nicely, and a toss of her head was enough to stop him from coming too close.

"Did you have a nice time last night?" John's expression was the very essence of guileless innocence. I stared at him in amazement, wondering if he was being deliberately crass or truly had been very, very drunk. But then he blinked as he realised my mood and suddenly gave me a disarmingly sheepish smile. "You're cross with me."

"I wouldn't say that, John." I gathered up my reins. "But I do have a lot to do today so we'll be on our way."

"Wait a minute, Ellie, don't leave it like that." He made to step closer but then saw the look in Beechnut's eye and thought better of it. "I behaved very badly last night and I want to have the chance to explain myself. Surely you can give me that at least, can't you?"

I glanced at Freddy who was watching us curiously and knew that whatever John was going to say, I really didn't want the boy's delicate young ears to hear it. "You go ahead Freddy, I'll be home very shortly."

With a frowning look at me that was intended to communicate his intense distrust, and a scowl at John that was meant as a warning but only looked adorably fierce in the manner of a very small lamb, Freddy took the ropes I held out and trotted away up the road with my little cluster of ponies trailing obediently along behind him. I watched him go, calming Beechnut's impatient stamp and wondering why politeness had made me choose to stay for an explanation that I knew could not bring me any cheer.

"Oh, don't look like that, Ellie, I'm not going to bite," John said wearily. He turned to lead the way back down the drive again and reluctantly I followed, reminding myself that regardless of what had come over him last night, I didn't need to actually be afraid of him. But all the same, I was very glad of Beechnut.

I drew the horse to a halt by the lorry with as detached an expression fixed upon my face as I could manage, implying, I hoped, only aloof disinterest, and waited for the apology that was unlikely to save our friendship. To my surprise, however, instead of seeming appropriately contrite as I expected, or even remotely humbled, when he finally turned and looked up at me, he actually laughed. "Honestly, Ellie, you do make a fuss. It *was* only a kiss."

I scowled at him silently and eventually he gave in, lifting his hands in a mock gesture of surrender. "All right, fine. I'm sorry. I behaved very badly and I'm a cad. Will that do?"

I shrugged. I had a horrible feeling that I was coming across as an old prude. "It'll do," I admitted grudgingly.

"Good. Now, will you come in and have a cup of tea? I can't stand talking to you with you towering over me like that, particularly when that damned beast keeps looking at me with a hungry look in her eye."

I shook my head. "I must get back."

"Ellie," he said sternly. "Don't tell me that you're the sort to bear a grudge. Just come in for five minutes, surely you've got the time for that. You could put that horse in a stable, couldn't you? I'm sure she wouldn't mind."

I shook my head again; I had no intention of going anywhere with him. By way of distraction I said, "You've finished the horsebox?"

But John was prevented from making a reply by the brisk interruption of one of his grooms and although I was tempted to make my escape, I could see that John was keeping a watchful eye on me and would inevitably make a fuss. So instead I waited patiently while he finished his business and allowed my gaze to gently pass over the very neat little coach-built lorry by my side.

He had clearly completed the refurbishment and at the top of the modern ramp with its new hessian matting, I could see a hay bag and the assortment of other bits and pieces that were essential for transporting a horse. I nudged Beechnut forwards so that I could see fully inside and couldn't help admiring the new partitions which would nicely keep a pair of horses secure in their stalls during a journey along England's rough and jolting roads.

"Lovely, isn't she?" John had finished talking to his groom and had come as close as Beechnut's determined man-aversion would allow.

I smiled, making an effort to be pleasant, "Very smart. Are you taking it out today?"

He nodded and cast a glance up at the brooding sky. "I've decided to send the horse to Southampton now, before this next bout of bad weather comes. Apparently melt-water made the Thames flood at Reading the other day and if it tracks up as far as Cricklade like they say it will, we might not be able to get out on Tuesday and I just can't afford to lose this chance."

I frowned again at the mention of the horse; I really didn't like to be reminded of how we had last spoken about it, and I didn't like that he could apparently mention of it without any shade of embarrassment.

"Oh, for goodness sake!"

John was suddenly and very genuinely exasperated. Repressively, his hand touched to his forehead, pinching the bridge of his nose before he dropped it again and looked up. "Haven't you *ever* done anything that you were ashamed of? I got carried away, that's all, and if you'd just stop sniping at me for a moment and get down from that blasted horse, we could talk about it like civilised people."

He might have been about to add something else but at that very instant the grey-haired housekeeper hurried out and came to a breathless and abrupt halt in front of us. I believe she actually bobbed a very small curtsey.

"Yes?" snapped John impatiently, barely turning his head. "What is it?"

"It's the telephone, sir."

"Well, tell them I'll call back, can't you?" John crossly flapped her away as he turned back to me. He blinked. "What was I saying, Ellie?" Then he frowned as he remembered.

"But sir …" The housekeeper had not gone. She was a small timid woman who, as I had discovered over the years, it was impossible to be kind to. She responded to any attempt at friendly interest with exactly the same blank deference that she used to greet the Colonel's barked commands. From as far back as I could remember, she had busied herself in unobtrusively hovering on that man's periphery with servile hands clasped in front of the inevitable grey dress that fastened tightly at her neck, and it seemed to me that her whole life would be spent in waiting for whatever was next in his long line of abruptly delivered instructions. Whenever I met her I found it hard to decide if it was compassion, frustration or pity that most dominated my thoughts and now, as she stood there, blinking owlishly and anxiously lingering in unhappy defiance of the son's sharp words, I still could not truly tell.

"What is it?"

John's eyes had followed my gaze past his shoulder and he now twisted to face her when it was apparent that she wasn't going to leave. "Do I have to do your job, too?"

240

She tightened her linked hands across the starched breast of her dress, looking very shocked by his tone. Her chin wrinkled a little as she persevered, "It's not for you, sir … It's for Miss Phillips."

Both faces lifted in perfect unison to look up at me. One was very slightly flushed, the other pale.

"It's definitely for you, Miss," the housekeeper insisted, anticipating the obvious.

"Well then, you'd better come in and take it, hadn't you," John said waspishly in the face of my confusion. "Put your horse in a stable, she'll be happy enough for a few minutes."

If John hadn't looked as equally surprised as I felt, I would have never believed the housekeeper. But finally I had no choice but to give in to the inevitable and slither down from Beechnut's back. It only took a moment then to knot the reins securely on her neck and leave her merrily flirting with the would-be Union Star, and then I found myself following a pointedly gracious John into his office to take the waiting call. He left me by the drinks stand and, feeling absurdly nervous, I walked over to the desk.

"Hello?"

"Hello?" A woman's voice answered. "Ellie, is that you?"

"Lisa!"

I caught John's interested glance and turned away so that I had a little privacy. I lowered my voice. "What on earth are you calling me here for?"

"I called you at home but Freddy said you were there, so I thought I might as well try. You *did* say it was urgent."

"Well, yes, I did," I said very cautiously indeed. I didn't want to give anything away to my listening audience; *that* was an explanation I couldn't even begin to conceive. "Did you manage to track it down?"

"I did and it took me a while, I can tell you. You wouldn't believe what trouble you've cost me, I almost feel like becoming a private eye – I've shown some talent, I should like to think." She laughed and I think I managed to raise something in response.

"Chasing that girl all over the place I was. And then, whenever I managed to corner her, the boss would appear and tell me off for gossiping during work time! If I'm dismissed over this, you'll be the one who has to cover my wages."

"Ha, ha," I said weakly, wishing she would just get it over with. "Lisa, did you get the … what I wanted, then?"

"I did! And you'll never guess what."

"What?"

"You're speaking on it."

Chapter 27

I stood there for a very long time simply concentrating on breathing. I must have set the telephone down because I found that my hands were empty but I don't remember actually doing it and it is quite possible that I didn't even say goodbye. Random thoughts were flitting through my mind, all disjointed because I couldn't finish the last one before another thought burst in. Nothing was making any sense, but then, horribly, painfully, it did. It made a lot of sense.

I suppose if I had been a true friend I would have naturally assumed that the Colonel was the man, but as it was I didn't even waste a moment in denials or forming useless explanations. There was no point, not when I remembered that the Colonel had been in London with his other son on that fateful day.

John must have moved or said something because suddenly the room came sharply back into focus.

"Ellie? I said, are you all right?" His voice came from what felt like a very long way away.

I blinked and forced my shaken brain to concentrate. Whatever happened I knew I mustn't let him find out what I had heard, mustn't let him guess what I knew. All I had to do was be polite, make my excuses and leave. Surely nothing could happen while the housekeeper was nearby.

I took a deep breath, fixed a smile upon my face and slowly turned to face a murderer.

He was still standing by the drinks stand, with a bottle of something in his hand ready to pour. I put my hand out behind me and it met the reassuringly warm wood of the big oak desk, giving me strength and support.

"Fine, thank you," I said and I was amazed to find that my voice showed not even the faintest tremor. "That was just Lisa, she's been trying to get hold of me for days."

"Oh?" he asked pleasantly. Looking at him now as he stood there with the same brilliant smile that he always wore, it didn't seem possible to believe he had ever killed someone. But I had Simon Turford's words as a dismal echo in my memory. The boss had caused all this by *losing his head*. "Anything important?"

"No. Not really." My voice squeaked a little, but only so that I would notice.

He had straightened up and was walking slowly towards me. He still had the bottle in his hand and I wondered if he was drunk again; what it might mean if he was, and whether he would be easier to get away from, or worse ...

Sharply I dragged my thoughts back to safer footing and forced my mind to focus. I said, "She just needed to talk, you know how it is."

"No, I don't know," he replied patiently. His eyes were that brilliant blue that mesmerised. "Why don't you tell me."

I slid casually along the desk away from him, wondering if I could back all the way to the door without him noticing. "Oh, she likes to catch up occasionally; we were at school together." I was chattering gaily as my mind feebly did its best to keep up this façade.

"Were you?"

The bottle glinted in his hand as he tilted it and suddenly I realised, with a horrible tightening of my throat, that he wasn't pouring the contents into a glass.

"Yes!" I said. It came out as a strangled croak. "Anyway, I'm sure this isn't remotely interesting, and you must have a lot you need to be getting on with."

"Not particularly." He was closer now and I cast a quick anxious glance about in case there was anything I could pick up as a weapon. There was nothing. "Tell me more. I'm still curious as to why she bothered to call you here."

"Oh, er ..." I gabbled frantically. I was closer to the door, with less than half the room to go before I would be out of there. *Perhaps he only means to scare me*, I told myself optimistically as I edged along the length of a chaise-longue. The light from the tall Georgian bay window was picking up the dust on the floor beneath it and I wondered if he knew that his servants were being so lax. *Concentrate*, I snapped at my wavering mind.

"She ... er ..."

He carefully set the bottle down on a table and took another step nearer. "Why did she call you, Ellie?" Suddenly his voice wasn't so mild, although his manner was still convincingly friendly. "What did she have to tell you that she needed to call you here?"

"Nothing!" I squeaked the word far too eagerly. A chair brushed the back of my legs, but I managed to avoid falling onto it. "Nothing at all! Anyway, is that the time? I really must be going. Goodbye!"

I turned and ran then, all pretence abandoned.

There was a crash behind which must have been from the chair being thrown over, then, before I had even cleared the next obstacle, his hand landed heavy on my shoulder, dragging me back. I gave a short breathless scream, half falling, half twisting away in a desperate move that had nothing to do with sensible thought. There was a great tearing as my coat tore at the collar and using my momentum to drag my arms free, I slipped out of the sleeves and then I was up and onto my feet again, and running.

A loud thump followed behind as he tangled with the ruins of my coat. I heard a curse and a mutter of pain and another sound of tearing but I didn't bother to check where he was. The door loomed white from the wall ahead of me and I lunged madly for the handle.

Magically, before I had even laid a finger on it, the tall wooden frame began to open. It yawned wide and for a moment I enjoyed the wild belief that someone had heard, had come to save me, but the chest I ran into and the hands that caught and held me were not those of a tiny aging housekeeper but those of a great brute of a man. My enemy.

"Well, hello, lass," said Simon Turford thickly and a nasty sneer spread across his face, widening into a grimace that passed for a smile as I tried uselessly to free myself. Then he must have lost patience with my feeble wriggling because he tightened his grip upon my arms and suddenly gave me a vicious shake that made my head reel.

"No!" I begged, shrinking back from his leering, brutal satisfaction. The room span nauseatingly as he shook me again and his unforgiving eyes rested on my face in unashamed scrutiny for a moment before coolly flicking up over my head to look behind me.

"In your own time, sir," he said calmly.

In the blinding chaos of panic, the thought finally crossed my mind that I should scream but even as I drew breath, I felt John's arms come around me. His cheek touched to mine and then, with deliberate precision, he covered my mouth and nose with the cloth in his hand. I thought for a moment that he intended to suffocate me and very nearly took the frantic gasp that would have ended it, but the odour on the rag made my eyes water and then, with a final crushing rush of horror, I remembered the bottle.

Fighting every impulse, I held my breath and tried to wrench my head away, and might have managed it but that he shifted his hand and I was held still in a cruel grip that hurt.

"Go on. Breathe in, Ellie, my dear. Get it over with." John's voice was soft in my ear. "There's no use fighting."

I kicked hard, my foot swinging back with all my might, and

246

it connected.

John gave a sharp hiss of pain and his hand tightened horribly over my nose. "Bitch," he said calmly.

I held on for what seemed like an eternity. My lungs ached to be allowed to breathe but still I refused to give in, jerking uselessly and painfully in their vicelike grasp, and never even gaining a millimetre. Then my ears began to ring and I knew I was beaten. I tried so hard to fight the defeat back, but then finally, agonisingly, I lost control and at last my desperate lungs drew in a great breath of air. And with the air came the sickly sweet smell of chloroform.

It was only a matter of moments then. With a terrifying succession of shuddering breaths, I plunged recklessly down into the clinging, clawing blackness of oblivion, and as I fell, numb now to the pain of Simon's grip on my arms, I heard a murderer's voice in my ear.

"Good girl, breathe deeply. Goodnight, my dear ... and sweet dreams ..."

Chapter 28

There was a cold hard surface at my back; the sound of horses moving restlessly nearby. I tried to open my eyes but like my limbs, they seemed leaden and unresponsive. After a futile effort to make anything, even any muscle at all move, I gave in and simply hung there, helplessly immobile, as my fogged brain tried to remember what had happened.

I could hear an irregular tapping like fingers drumming idly on a table, only softer. A vague memory of being on Beechnut flitted through my mind and I wondered if I had taken a fall. Then the rhythmic chewing of hay caught in my ears and when the sweet scent of manure pricked at my nose, the spinning sensation of cold suddenly solidified and I realised abruptly that I was not out on a ride at all but was on my back on the hard stone floor of one of my stables. With a rush of frustrated irritation, I wondered why on earth Freddy was just messing about out there, playing games and tossing grit up onto the barn roof when surely he must have noticed that I hadn't come in for some lunch. Or had we already eaten lunch? I tried to make my mind dredge up a memory but after a very brief effort it gave up and wandered off.

I heard voices coming closer and the soft whisper of hooves on grass. Here he was then, finally. All I had to do was lie here and he would find me.

The sounds came closer. There was a clattering of unshod feet on wood and the ground seemed to shift and tilt. I heard the voices more clearly now and suddenly I knew something was wrong; this was not Freddy, this was not my yard and I was not at all sure that I should want them to find me. Then the clattering approached nearer, alarmingly so, coming to a stop very near my head, and despite this, still my body refused to work.

"She's in, sir." I knew that voice. How did I know that voice?

"Well done." It all came back to me then, in a rush which made my head hurt. John's voice was very near and I gave up trying to move and concentrated very hard on staying very still indeed. Overhead, the soft drizzle continued to patter monotonously on the hard metal of the lorry roof. "And no one saw you put *her* in, did they?"

"No," Simon replied in his gruff northern accent. "No one was about. We'll be on our way then?"

"Yes. But I nearly forgot; did you get what I wanted from his house?"

There was a brief flurry of action filled by Simon yelling at Davey to fetch whatever it was from the car, followed after a short while by, "There you go, sir. What are you going to do with it?"

I listened intently, wondering what new clue Simon might be about to betray. In hindsight, I don't think my brain had quite processed the fact that I wasn't exactly in the position to be playing detective, as all I thought about was what information I might be able to give Matthew when I saw him later, quite as if the very serious reality of my own situation didn't exist at all.

Either way, I was not to learn and instead all I heard was John's casual reply of, "Nothing much. Just a little bit of harmless incrimination to send that damned detective trotting off in the right direction."

Simon laughed, then abruptly stopped. "Did she just move?"

There was an agonising sharp intake of breath. All thoughts of investigation stopped and my brain screamed *No, no I didn't!* But wood creaked as someone climbed into the horse lorry beside me and then John's hand was tilting my head.

My eyelashes must have flickered because he said, "Well, hello, my dear. Not quite asleep, are we. Fetch that bottle, would you?"

There was a steady crunching of gravel underfoot as Simon walked away. I felt John's hand shift to my throat; for a terrifying moment I thought he was going to strangle me as I lay there, but he was just checking my pulse. I must have regained some coordination because my hand feebly tried to push him away but it was perfectly easy for him to take hold of my wrist and then, surprising me with his gentleness, carefully press my hand back down onto the cold mat floor of the lorry once more.

The rough sound of footsteps and a trace of that familiar breathing announced Simon's return and then his distant voice said, "Here you go, sir. Be careful how you go with that though. Too much and you'll kill her."

"I'm well aware of that, man," John snapped curtly, before adding in a softer tone, "I have no intention of killing you, Ellie, not if you behave yourself like a sensible girl. How would I complete my little scheme if you were dead?"

My eyes suddenly flicked properly open and I stared up at him mutely as he tipped the bottle over to allow some drops to fall onto a fresh scrap of cloth.

John smiled down at me humourlessly. "You did me a good turn by turning up here, you know – you saved me the job of having to come and get you." He smiled again, gazing at me for a few long seconds before flicking a glance over his shoulder at Simon. "She found out about the horse, you see. Knowing her and her damned principles, I can't trust that she'll have the sense to keep it to herself if the wrong people happen to start asking questions. It'll be much safer with her out of the way. And, perhaps more vitally, it is my profound hope that the girl's disappearance will flush that idiot man out into the open once and for all."

I must have unconsciously made some sound because he turned

back to me and then his smile grew. "Oh, yes, Ellie, you're the perfect weapon, didn't you know? We don't know what you feel about him, do we, my dear?" He patted me on the cheek. "But we know that he's still sweet on you."

There was a pause while he stared thoughtfully at the bottle in his hand for a moment before tipping another drop onto the cloth, "He warned me off you, did you know that? It was months ago now; I ran into him when he was out walking and I couldn't help but goad him, he looked so … so, what's the word? I don't know, so much like he just didn't give a damn. There I was with some fellows from the shoot and he just said good morning and went to walk on by as if he was one of us! One of *us?* I remember when he worked his summers in my uncle's fields for goodness sake! Long before he got his so-called education and came back acting like he owned the place, jumped up, smug bastard. So I decided to set him down a little. He pretended that it didn't touch him of course, all calm and detached, but he didn't like it so much when I mentioned you. Didn't like it at all."

He laughed and it was a silly little sound of boyish delight. "There is a certain ironic symmetry to it all, don't you think? Just when my plans were all coming to fruition, who should turn up to play scapegoat but my own personal little nemesis; our favourite ex-farmhand, Matthew Croft?" He grimaced slightly. "That man presumed, wrongly, to set himself against me and later, while you are sleeping your way to Southampton, he'll be finding out just how much I am his superior in every possible way."

He gave another ugly little laugh and slowly moved to lean over me with that hateful cloth ready in his hand.

"So now you see why I suddenly stepped up my courtship of you? I was reasonably content to let our friendship drift along before, but since he decided to meddle in my affairs, the temptations of my pretty little childhood companion suddenly seemed so much more … pressing. Particularly when marrying you will make the perfect coup-de-grace for the condemned man." He paused,

251

still smiling. "And you will marry me, my dear. You really don't have a choice, not if you want be able to watch Freddy grow up ..."

I barely managed any resistance at all this time when he placed the rag over my nose. He watched patiently for my numbed body to make its second surrender to uninvited sleep, and as he waited, he spoke over his shoulder, "I want her back in one piece, do you hear? Dump her nag or kill it, whichever you choose, but if you lay a finger on her I'll kill you, or even worse than that, you won't get paid. Understand?"

And the faint echo of Simon's reply gradually faded to nothing until all that remained to penetrate the smothering embrace of unconsciousness was the light patter of rain on the roof and the ugly rhythm of a man's coarse breathing.

Chapter 29

I could feel the warmth of his body against my back and I could only marvel at the fact that he had found me so soon. I murmured something sleepily and his arm tightened. Eleanor. His voice was a whisper in my ear. Eleanor … Eleanor …

Ellie.

"No!" I cried and suddenly the noise in my ears was only the deafening roar of tyres on wet road.

I sat bolt upright and stared about me in a bewildered panic. Two horses were peering down at me with steady interest as they swayed to the jolting movement of the lorry and I blinked stupidly up at them through the fog of drugged and fearful mindlessness.

Oblivious, Beechnut blew gently down her nose in greeting and only then, with a sudden painful rush of nauseating relief, did I realise that no one was holding me at all. She seemed surprisingly unconcerned as she chewed steadily on a mouthful of hay but a telltale crust of dried sweat had dulled her coat and I tried to get up to see what they might have done to her to get my lovely horse to load into the lorry. I very nearly made it.

With a sickening jolt, the lorry rocked over a pothole and my legs gave way beneath me so that I sat back down again with a crash. Then, just as abruptly, all thoughts of her were put out of my head. My body reacted violently to the poisonous effects of the chloroform and for a horribly memorable stretch of minutes, I was left incapable of saying or thinking or doing anything else at all.

It was an extraordinarily unpleasant interlude but at last, gasping and coughing for breath, I managed to get my unhappy stomach back under something like control. Slowly, gingerly, I propped myself up to lean against the wall of the box. I was freezing cold and shocked and utterly weary, and as I fought to suppress the vicious trembling that wracked my body, I discovered that I knew some very choice words with which to describe my feelings towards my former friend. It seemed to be a long while before I recovered enough to be able to lift my head and attempt a second look at my surroundings.

The gloomy interior of the lorry was as impressive now as it had appeared when I had last seen it; the wood-lined box was well built and looked very robust, and if I could have found any fault it was in that the little jockey door could not be opened from the inside. The ramp, of course, was equally impossible.

The new partition between the horses was impeccably designed – thick and sturdy with a metal breast bar that would hold the horses safely in place if there was a sudden stop – and each horse looked remarkably comfortable as it stood rocking gently within its individual compartment. I had been laid in the small space in front of the bar where their hay bags were slung and I could feel where occasional wisps had escaped from a steadily chewing mouth to drift down and tangle in my hair.

Beechnut looked perfectly relaxed, particularly when she stole a mouthful as it dangled from the stallion's mouth, and I wondered whether they had drugged her too to get her into the box. Perhaps she had been blindfolded; I certainly doubted that even her new gentleman friend would have been enough of an incentive to set aside her usual hatred of all things man-related. At that thought, my mind vividly replayed John's last instructions to Simon Turford and I suddenly struck the wall with the heel of my hand. It was a burst of fury of the like I have rarely experienced; the sensation was intense, extraordinarily heating and regardless of the impossibility of escape, I absolutely refused to just sit in helpless submission while others plotted away her life. And mine. And, with a gasp of pain, Matthew's.

Slowly, grudgingly, my brain got to work. It was inconceivable that John had orchestrated this entire nightmare purely for the purposes of damning Matthew and marrying me. And, lovely as he was, surely it could not be possible that the horse was so valuable as to be worth all this risk. No, even the original Union Star would have been worth only a tiny portion of the rolls of paper we had discovered and as my poor befuddled brain struggled back into some semblance of life, I became certain that the unlucky horse's imminent emigration had to be a convenient cover for the real ambition. It seemed perverse that what had been meant as a casual criticism should in the end prove to be the key to the whole thing, but if John was right and a person would have to be a fool to try and sell looted artworks in his own county, the thought finally occurred to me that perhaps it could be presumed that this rule stretched to countries, too.

With sudden vigour that denied the weakness of my drugged limbs, I set about exploring the turbulent and swaying space of the moving lorry. The horses' stalls, the Luton space above the cab and even the hay bags were all examined in great detail but after I did it for the second time I had to accept it. There was a big fat nothing.

But I couldn't be wrong. Surely?

Think Eleanor. Think!

I found myself sitting on the hay-strewn floor leaning against the wall once more, with my hands pressed tightly to my eyes. My enfeebled mind was complaining bitterly at this final assault on its weakened powers and, staring defeat in the face, I lifted my head to look up at Beechnut in the hope of finding some glimmer of cheer to save me from the fast approaching grip of bleak and unanswerable despair. She flicked her ears at me before vigorously scratching an itch under her mane on the edge of the partition.

"Beechnut!" I cried, making her jump in surprise. "You clever girl!"

She didn't quite know what she had done to deserve this praise but nevertheless accepted it with good grace. It was so obvious when I thought about it, this sudden urgency of refurbishing the lorry when he was constantly reminding me of his financial difficulties. Why so urgent unless it would be carrying a priceless cargo?

With a sudden burst of wild enthusiasm I began examining the smooth wooden surface of the upright that secured the new central partition and held the breast-bar. My fingers ran down its length in search of any loose trimmings that might conceal a void in which to secrete the papers. Then I stopped and did it again. There, definitely there, just above the fixing for the bar, something moved.

I tugged at it and pushed and pulled, and I believe at one point even kicked, but the odious bit of wood would not budge. With a cry of rage I threw my weight against it – and immediately had to stop with a curse and say "*Ow!*"

A splinter had caught in my hand. However the sudden shock of pain steadied me in my rising hysteria and as I sucked the tiny bead of blood away, I was able to examine the strip of wood more calmly. It had been tacked on with long nails and no amount of cursing at it would draw them out; I needed some leverage. There was even a gap of almost a finger's width behind it where a knot had broken off and if I could just find something to jam in there I suspected it would not take much to pull it away.

I searched about determinedly. There was nothing in the Luton other than an old blanket which smelled of horse and the rest of the box contained only me, the horses and the hay. That was it; nothing – nothing that would be strong enough to part the nails. I felt my pockets, my clothes and about my body, and then, abruptly, all thoughts of the search were forgotten. My heart stilled and suddenly, completely, nothing else mattered.

My necklace was gone.

It was ludicrous that such a small object should have been the thing that finally broke my fragile resolve but suddenly the fight went out of me and I sat down and cried and cried until my eyes hurt. Somehow the necklace had come to symbolise everything about my newfound hope for a future and the loss of the necklace made me suddenly realise the loss of the man. If he should fall into John's trap while I was stuck here in this awful prison of a horsebox, if he should die and I was not there …

I stopped that thought very sharply. I wasn't prepared to give up on him just yet. Tremblingly, I forced my brain to focus and as I began to feel about myself once more and my searching fingers found my waist, I suddenly discovered my much needed inspiration.

The belt was perfect and its long metal buckle seemed almost designed for the task as it slipped easily into the gap. I pushed with all my might against that strip of wood and by some miracle the buckle proved stronger than the nails. Then, with a great tearing sound, the nails ripped free and with tidy efficiency as if mocking my former despair, the wood pulled away, and fell neatly into my hand.

I was right, the partition was hollow and there was space enough inside for all the papers. There was just one problem; they were not there.

I looked and peered from every angle, but nothing made any difference. The papers truly were not hidden here.

"Dammit!" I threw the strip of wood to the floor in useless fury. Then, cursing again and with more venom at my own stupidity, I had to scrabble about under the stallion's legs to retrieve it – the protruding nails would be a terrible danger if he were to step on them.

I placed the piece up into the Luton above the cab so that it was safely out of their way before attempting to reawaken my eagerness for my foolish little mission. I was beginning to suspect that I had latched upon this task purely to keep myself from collapsing into a sobbing hysteria but as I stood winding the belt about my waist once more, I felt my brain tentatively give another little nudge.

The floor was covered in hessian matting to soak up any urine and to provide grip for their feet, and in the little space that I occupied, it was possible to convince myself that in the corner where the Luton met the jockey door, perhaps, just perhaps, the matting was not tacked down quite so securely.

Now an expert at prising things free, I bent down and tugged at the hessian with all my might. For a while it seemed like it might not give but then, with a wonderful fraying of threads, it finally surrendered and suddenly the whole portion ripped away from its pins in a great satisfying lump. I almost laughed as I looked down at the bare floor of the lorry. There, set into the plain wood panelled flooring, was a small hatch complete with little brass handles that had been laid flush with its surface. Their hinges squeaked as I lifted the cold metal loops.

Defying tradition, the hatch lifted smoothly clear without even so much as a murmur of resistance and there, below me, in a recess in the floor with the road roaring past underneath, lay my papers.

Chapter 30

Angels and gods and gurning serpents; I was so mesmerised by the crazed illustrations unfolding from the grubby rolls that for a moment I did not register the change in pitch of the road noise. A sudden crash as we went over a dip in the road caught my attention however and then, with a sharp rush of fear, I realised that we were slowing.

Hastily, I stuffed the papers back into their hold and rolled the hessian back. One corner would not lie flat and I flung myself down on it as the lorry rolled to a shuddering halt. The engine sounded louder than ever before as it idled and after the steady roaring of the road, its changeable tone felt horribly menacing.

A sudden thought occurred to me. I leapt up again to snatch the nailed strip of wood from the Luton just as a door in the cab slammed shut. There was barely enough time left to arrange myself in a pose of sleepy carelessness before the jockey door was wrenched open and then abruptly my darkened little world was flooded with the blinding brightness outside.

His head was silhouetted against the open doorway as he peered in at me. I stayed very still, miming out the part of one who was still drugged to stupidity in the hope that he would just shut the door again and leave me, but then, with a leap that defied his heavy build, Simon Turford climbed in.

He was huge. His vast bulk filled the doorway and as he towered over me in my little huddled corner, I suddenly realised how very, very small my space really was. Beechnut shied away from him, her agitation making her throw herself against the partition until it cracked alarmingly under her weight but he didn't seem to notice. Completely unconcerned, he stared down at me with such an ugly expression on his face that I feared what he might do. But all he did was laugh and turn away, seemingly satisfied.

Beechnut flinched away again, throwing her head wildly, and he batted his hand carelessly at her face as he prepared to climb down from the box once more. His hand was gripping the frame to the jockey door, bracing himself for the leap and he had almost done it when he suddenly, terrifyingly, stopped. For a long agonising moment he stood quite still, simply staring at the mat by his feet but then he turned back and looked at me.

I blanched and shrank feebly back into my little corner.

"Just what have you been up to?" His low demand came as an incredulous snarl. I couldn't answer.

He stared down at me for a moment but then he took a step back into my space and reached for me. I gave a short strangled cry and cringed away as he took hold of the collar of my shirt but all he did was snarl again and then, oblivious to my pathetic attempt at resistance, gave a heave and dragged me bodily to the open doorway.

Frozen by sheer paralysing horror, I had no time to repeat John's final instructions or to remind him of my immunity from harm and quite without thinking, I swung the strip of wood I held concealed in my hand. It connected. With a bellow of pain he flung me away and then I was airborne for a moment, rushing through the damp air only to crash down heavily onto my side on the cold soaked grass of the verge.

Winded and very scared, I blinked painfully up at him through eyes that ached after the darkness of the box. With barely a thought, he wrenched the nails out of his sleeve and as he tossed the wood

260

aside, I suddenly realised just how foolish I and my burst of reckless defiance had been. I think my legs tried to push me away through the mud and grass but I didn't get far.

With a roar he leapt down and took hold of me again. The suddenness of his movement made me cry out and he gave a guttural sneer at my hopeless attempts to shield myself from him as I recognised the full force of his violent intent. He drew his huge fist back ready to strike.

"Car!" yelled Davey from the cab.

Fist still held high and threatening, Simon lifted his head and sought out the black shape that had appeared on the horizon. He stared at it for a few long agonising seconds as it wound its way closer down the hillside before he finally lowered his hand, and then, with a sharp curse, he dragged me painfully to my feet and thrust me towards the cab.

"In," he growled and wrenched open the door. Davey slithered over into the middle of the bench seat and I was practically thrown up into the space he had made. The door was slammed shut and then I was abandoned to the leering stupidity of Davey's care while Simon inspected what I had done to their cargo.

It seemed to be a long time before he finally climbed down and set the lorry on its way once more.

I don't remember much of the journey that followed. We seemed to drive for hours, although it was probably only about fifty miles. The two men exchanged grunting conversation occasionally and once I feared Davey was going to touch me but for the most part they just ignored me and I was able to lean my aching head against the cold glass of the window while my closed eyes burned with the shock and pain of what had happened.

As far as I could tell through my distracted wanderings, their conversation mainly consisted of brutally mocking John's obsessive adherence to rank, and judging by their tone, I was not entirely sure that he was in nearly as much control as he thought. With a bitter twist of satisfaction it occurred to me that John's life would not be nearly as comfortable as he anticipated once the artwork made its destination and these two men laid on a tidy little bit of blackmail when the money started coming in.

"Don't know what's so special about her either," muttered Simon as we lurched across a busy crossroads. "Seems a hell of a lot of trouble to go through just for some girl. He should have finished her and had done with it; she's not exactly a prize amongst women, is she?"

"Dunno about that. I'd do her."

"Davey," Simon growled. "You'd 'do' anything if it wore a skirt."

I blinked and out of the corner of my eye I saw Davey's mouth stretch wide as he laughed.

"My guess is that the real story is she said no and he just can't take it." Simon gave a hard snigger. "Ah well, she won't get much say in it now – the other will be dealt with by the time we get back and I suspect her allure for our friend Johnny will end with him ... What a happy marriage that will be, makes you almost feel sorry for her, doesn't it? Although it certainly serves her right for getting smart with us, dumb bitch. If you ask me, they deserve each other."

I felt a shudder run through me that ought to have been one of sheer unadulterated horror, but somehow seemed to verge on uselessly murderous fury and I felt an unexpected touch of warmth to my limbs. In the wake of this momentary easing of my lethargy, the lorry checked and slowed and as a faint trace of intelligence began to hint at a re-emergence, I noticed that we were pulling in at a garage. With barely a lift of hope I wondered if I dared try to scream for help but Davey's forbidding presence remained inexorably by my side while Simon climbed out to rouse the pump attendant from his house and I knew that if I even so much as drew the breath to scream I would regret it.

There was an oddly comic moment when the two men scrabbled about in search of the ration book and as I lay with my head limply resting against the window, it occurred to me that John must have been using agricultural fuel to still have so many vouchers. Then I experienced a different kind of mirth at the realisation that I was actually marvelling at a man who was prepared to go to such lengths as these being equally unconcerned by the misuse of a few ration slips. I almost giggled at the thought and I began to suspect my mind was wandering completely but then all giddy humour abruptly evaporated as Simon climbed in to the cab once more and restarted the engine.

He leaned past Davey to peer at me. There was a fine mist of rain on his skin. "Has she said anything?"

"Nothing."

"She looks half dead, doesn't she; do you think the boss gave her too much of that stuff?" A hand reached past Davey to roughly shake my arm, "Hey? Are you still with us?"

I was not exactly acting when my head lolled against the seat-back and with a concerted effort, I turned my head look at him. Simon stared at me for a moment and then, with a dry laugh, let go of my arm.

"Water," I croaked weakly. "Do you have any water?"

I must have looked so awful with hay in my matted hair, swollen reddened eyes and a face that looked like death that for a moment I almost saw pity in his eyes. Then, with an irritated grunt, Simon climbed out of the cab again.

"Watch her," he snapped before marching off towards the office. Davey smiled at me and I grimaced, and turned my head away.

There was a sudden crash as one of the horses became impatient, swiftly followed by an unpleasant rocking of the lorry as it stamped about. The cab resounded with another crash and Davey looked at me in alarm. I ignored him and shut my eyes.

The lorry shook again and Davey swore nastily. Through lowered eyelids, I felt him throw another glance at me before he slipped across into the driver's seat and stuck his head out to see what was going on. Another crash was accompanied by what sounded horribly like splintering wood and this decided him. Lying limp and lifeless in my seat as Davey climbed out, I hardly bothered to notice when he took one last glance at my passive form before turning away. Clearly not nearly as stupid as he looked, he left the door swinging as a security against any attempt of mine to slip unheard out of the other side; but at last, after another crash sounded from the back, he finally stepped out of sight towards the rear of the box.

Instantly, my eyes snapped fully open and my heart began to race.

Nervous blood began pounding back into my exhausted limbs as I cast a rapid glance across the dripping forecourt towards the office. I could just make out Simon's shape behind the dirtied glass and my breath caught in my throat as I slithered very cautiously across into the driver's seat. I had to wait for long painful moment before I could eventually bring myself to muster the courage to slowly peep outside. Nobody noticed; Davey was peering intently at a bulge that had appeared in the side.

Trembling excruciatingly, I slipped the lorry into gear. He didn't hear the change in pitch of the engine as I depressed the clutch and after a brief fumbling search I found the hand-brake. Carefully, I eased it off. Davey seemed oblivious.

Slowly the lorry started to roll forwards and knowing that if I failed my death would certainly swiftly follow, I threw the clutch out and stamped my foot down hard on the accelerator. The engine roared and then gave a sickening cough that made my blood freeze. But then by some miracle it caught and suddenly with a crash of unbalanced horses, we were lurching violently forwards.

I managed to snatch at the door and drag it shut just as Davey lunged for it. I screamed at him as his fingers clawed uselessly at the glass; I do not think I will ever forget the look on his face as he tried to batter his way in. But then, flinging the wheel hard over, I swung the slowly accelerating lorry around the last of the pumps and we were grinding our agonising way past the office just as Simon ran out with a cup in his hand. He lumbered into my path, shouting something and looking impossibly deadly, and I am afraid to say that I didn't feel an ounce of guilt as the wing mirror clipped his head and he went down in a flurry of flailing arms and spilled water.

The lorry gave a great jolt as we hit the road surface and then all of a sudden we were roaring up through the gears and away in a great cloud of smoke. As we went, I could just see in my mirror the wonderful sight of Simon clutching at his head, Davey staring helplessly after us and lastly, the pump attendant plucking at his sleeve and gesturing at the disappearing lorry in startled and suspicious agitation.

Chapter 31

The hours and miles of the long drive home passed in a confused blur of exhilaration and worry that I would dearly like to forget. Directing the lorry along the undulating roads of Hampshire and Wiltshire was a nightmare of junctions and gear changes; every time I had to stop, I was terrified that the lorry would stall and every time I got to a straight stretch the frustrated cars behind would roar past in a whirlwind of spray and gravel. I wished that I dared pull in to a lay-by to gather my bearings but I had not even the smallest clue about how to start this great hulking machine if the engine died and I fervently prayed that nothing would happen now to force me to learn.

I had set off with my foot flat to the floor but a very scary incident when a corner approached much more quickly than the brakes could safely tackle with horses in the back had made me slow down considerably. On any other day I might have got a thrill out of handling such a vast machine but today, with my nerves hanging by a thread and any confidence in my judgement severely reduced, I was driving with cold hands fiercely gripping the large wheel and tired eyes fixed anxiously on the road ahead.

I think that we must have been very nearly at Southampton as it seemed to take forever for any signs to appear with a place name that I recognised. Junctions and their myriad of impossible decisions were navigated more by lucky guessing than any real idea of where we were and I found that the burst of adrenalin that had helped me make this crazed getaway began to abandon me as we rolled slowly across the high plains of Salisbury and on towards home.

I almost got the lorry stuck at a narrow turn out of a village that I vaguely remember thinking was one of the Winterbournes, but may have been any of the indistinguishable settlements that have since blurred to a nameless mess in my memory. The junction was wide and any normal lorry would have made the turn easily but with inexperience and a heavy exhaustion taking its toll, I very nearly took the side of a building away. It would have been a disaster and there was a terrible moment when I nearly disintegrated into a sobbing heap but thankfully with much enthusiastic waving of hands from a few pedestrians and a dark cloud of smoke from the exhaust we managed to extricate ourselves and set off once more on our long journey home.

Roads slipped by in a blur of routine. I don't believe that I thought very much at all as I drove along. I braked, changed gear and accelerated with regular monotony and when I felt something suddenly drag hard at the steering wheel, it actually made me jump.

I straightened the lorry again, setting it back on the road only to find we were sent firmly left again. Wearily, I dragged the wheel straight once more and with a shock that betrayed my alarming lack of attention to the road, I finally noticed that the hedges and bare trees lining the great sweeping hill down from Swindon were bowing and shuddering violently. Another gust hit us and then another, and we nearly veered into a ditch when a great bucket of windblown rain struck us hard across the windscreen.

In increasing desperation, I spotted a lay-by ahead. It was just beyond Cricklade, so regardless of the scene downstream clearly the Thames floodwater had not yet risen this far, and with a dubious show of gear-changing and indicating, I safely managed to navigate us to a halt on this narrow strip of dirt, blessedly without stalling.

The frantic search that followed was almost comic but finally after discovering all sorts of useless knobs and buttons I located not only my courage but the headlights too and, newly armed with these resources, I set the lorry back onto the road once more.

The wind had clearly been building for a long time in Cirencester. As we ground our way along the horrifically narrow streets and up through Stratton onto the last stretch of main road before home, I began to realise that the route ahead might yet prove to be too much. The road was strewn with broken twigs and branches dodged by other vehicles and when at last we crawled towards the final turning, I knew I could take the lorry no further.

There was no way that I was brave enough to face the narrow lane with its overhanging trees – we were being beaten about badly enough on the main road – and with a groan of exhaustion, I finally swung the lorry into the haulage yard that was linked to the Mason's Arms. Thankfully the sodden yard was reasonably wide and, equally mercifully, quite empty and just as I began to panic about how on earth one was supposed to park one of these great machines, the engine gave a great coughing shudder as I slowed and then, by way of having the last word, generously stalled.

Barely believing that we had truly survived the experience, I pulled the brake on with hands that were too leaden to tremble and then sat there for a moment just trying to come to terms with the fact that we were actually here. Outside it was wild; the rain cut instantly through my thin layers as I forced open the door to climb stiffly down. The loss of my coat meant more now than ever and I was quickly soaked to the bone as I fumbled with the fastenings on the ramp, although I was so numb by now that I barely felt it. I was moving deliberately and with exacting detail and, with as much care as if it were a climber's lifeline, I unlashed the rope that hung from the top of the ramp, took a step back and then pulled.

Nothing happened.

I stepped back a few more paces and gave another tug. Nothing;

it didn't even do me the credit of rattling slightly. I gave a dry humourless laugh at that. It really was too funny that I should be defeated by a ramp of all things after the day I had just had.

"Can I help you, love?"

A man's voice penetrated my lunatic mirth and I whipped round to discover a burly man approaching from behind. He had only shouted to beat the fierce moans of the wind and beneath the sensible raincoat, he wore the rolled sleeves and over-stretched waistcoat of a barman. He actually took a step back when I turned and I wondered what kind of vision he found before him; I could imagine I made quite a gruesome sight.

"Can I help you?" he asked again. The rain snatched away his words.

I actually managed a hapless smile. "I can't get the ramp down."

He hesitated but then came forwards and reached for the rope in my hands. The look he gave me as he took it was of one who knew he had offered but was equally sure he would rather hurry back inside to his cosy fire and a beer instead of stumbling about beneath the grey sky with a hopefully harmless but clearly unstable horsewoman. Perhaps he was worrying that I would expect him to offer us accommodation.

He prepared himself to heave. "Are you going far?"

I shook my head and stepped back as the ramp obediently lowered before him. "I just have to get them up the lane. Not far."

Both horses turned their heads to sniff at the strange blustery scene that had opened behind them and Beechnut whickered gently as I slipped past to unfasten the rope by her head. She was very sweet and quiet, and allowed me to shuffle her awkwardly backwards down the ramp until we were standing in the streaming rain. Then, with a stern command to 'stand', I looped the lead rope around her neck and climbed back inside to get the stallion. He had obviously travelled in the box before because the ramp presented no difficulties for him.

I gathered the thick ropes in my hands and turned to thank the barman who had been waiting uncertainly to one side. I must have staggered because he started forwards only to jump back again as Beechnut tensed and put her ears flat back.

"Are you sure you know what you're doing, love?" he asked after safely retreating to an even greater distance. "I could help, if you haven't got far to go?"

"No, no, I'm fine, thank you," I said cheerily. "But I don't suppose you'd mind putting up the ramp after I've got on?"

He watched me curiously as I made reins from Beechnut's rope and manoeuvred her into position next to the ramp. It took two attempts to leap from it onto her back but finally I was there and with my fingers knotted in her mane, the three of us turned away into the sodden embrace of the wind. I suppose I ought to have considered how sensible it was to lead a stallion from a mare's back but I didn't even think of it and it is a tribute to his exceptional manners that he took up his station by my knee as quietly as a lamb.

"Thank you," I called hoarsely over my shoulder as the man lifted the ramp and fastened it securely.

"Any time," he bellowed back. "Good luck!"

Luck. We had gone far beyond that, I thought.

The rain had actually stopped by the time we had slithered our way down on to my yard, although the storm was still building into great roof-rattling sighs. All the ponies were cosy in their stables and happily munching hay, and it didn't take long for even a person in my state to bed the two horses down and give them their feeds. To my relief, the stallion went into my only spare stable as if he had been there his entire life and set himself to the proffered hay with gentle enthusiasm. With its pokey corners and low sloping roof, it was a far cry from the positively palatial stables at the Manor but it would have to do and with a last pat I turned my tired aching body towards the house and went in.

I suppose I had never really quite come to terms with the idea that the kitchen would be empty; the ponies being in and fed had let my wearied brain believe that I would find them both there waiting for me as if I had only been away on a pleasure trip. But the kitchen was empty; dismally and hopelessly empty.

I am sorry to say that instead of being overcome with despair and collapsing into a weeping heap, I went to the toilet, washed the grime from my face, drank some water and even found the patience to snatch a morsel of food. I suspect that to a brain already numbed by shock after all the horrors of the past few hours, a bit more was nothing.

With automatic efficiency, I pulled on an old tatty coat and was surprised to find that the small amount of food I had managed to swallow had been enough to stop the trembling, and when I then spotted the note upon the table, I was actually able to read it quite calmly. It was in Matthew's quick hand and simply read:

Darling,
If by some miracle things are not as they seem and you get to read this, please, please come and find us before I do something drastic. M.

Clearly the trap had been sprung.

Chapter 32

Beechnut's saddle was, of course, still at the Manor where presumably it had either been hidden or destroyed. I contemplated taking one of the ponies instead but I knew she was the only one I could trust to carry me at the speed I needed. Lifting the stiff leather of an old hunting saddle down from the rack, I grabbed a bridle and without so much as a nod towards logic or good sense, hurried outside into the swirling chaos once more.

If Beechnut had shown any unwillingness to go out again, I would have taken the hint and gone on foot but her unsquashable nature meant that she greeted me with a cheery whicker and actually pricked her ears at the sight of the saddle. It only took a moment to sling her borrowed tack over her back and then I was scrambling on from the gate and turning her head in a flurry of windblown filth towards the village and away from home.

I always remember that ride as taking place in the dreary darkness of night, but I think it was actually just turning to dusk under the steely blanket of a featureless sky as we trotted steadily along the road towards the village. There was no one about as we slithered past the church to the Manor and I ought I suppose to have been afraid of what would happen if I should burst in to find only John, but the danger never even occurred to me.

The stables were in darkness as we slipped around to the front of the house. There, outside the door with a patina of twigs and matter resting on its roof, stood my car, waiting patiently where it had been abandoned. I leant down from the saddle to touch the metal of the bonnet. It was cold.

I nudged Beechnut onwards to the back of the house where the Georgian wing looked out over the valley. This leeward side was quieter, almost still and unusually the whole house seemed to be in darkness except for a light somewhere upstairs in the attic. Now I felt the danger as I peered in through the empty windows of John's office; I really didn't want to have to go back in there.

A sudden noise behind made me jump. It was the sort of noise a rabbit might make, or an injured animal, and already fearful, I twisted clumsily in the saddle towards it. There, in the gloom beneath the looming shadow of the house, I saw a booted foot snatch back under the cover of a bush and I had to stifle a cry. I knew those boots. My father's wireless had paid for them.

In a flash I was down from the saddle and pulling at the woody shrub. Freddy screamed a high girlish scream and tried to break away but I got a hand on his sleeve and called his name. It took two more calls before he would stop fighting with me and the bush but then suddenly he was in my arms and crying and hugging me with a fervour that took my breath away.

It was like soothing a small child as we sat together in the wet, the dirt and the ruins of the shrub. He sobbed and gripped and it was a long while before I could get any sense from him at all but eventually he was able to stem the flow of tears enough to catch his breath, and, still hidden in my shoulder, managed between gulps in a very cracked voice to speak.

"I thought you were dead," he said. Then he gave a fragile wail and disintegrated again.

I tightened my arms around him and rocked him gently. "I'm not dead, Freddy, darling, I'm fine, see? And I'm sorry that you had to go through that, but I'm here now." I took a little breath. "Can you tell me what has happened? Where is Matthew?"

"I don't know." The boy sobbed jerkily into my coat. "I got hit on the head and then I went all funny … and then I woke up under this bush and they'd gone."

I took a deeper breath and managed to stem the urge to panic. I wanted to beg Freddy to tell me quickly so that I could chase after them but I knew he shouldn't be hurried. Gently, as if I had all the time in the world, I asked, "Can you tell me what happened before that?"

Shakily, he found his voice. He began by describing the scene that Matthew had found when he had returned from his interview with the Inspector. This, as it turned out, had only occurred an hour or so earlier and I could picture Matthew perfectly as he parked the car and climbed out, utterly wearied and under police caution but cheerful and, most importantly, free, only to find Freddy going about his yard duties like a man possessed.

"I was a little bit scared of him." Freddy's voice was nothing more than a whisper. "Only a little bit, but he looked so *bleak* and it got worse when he realised where I'd left you. I told him that I'd tried telephoning the Manor when you missed lunch but they said that you'd ridden off on your own." His breath caught on a little hiccough. "The housekeeper told me that Langton had told you not to, that he'd said you shouldn't because Beechnut was still playing up like she was when I left, but you'd been your usual self and insisted."

I noted his adoption of Matthew's curt abbreviation of John's name. "And what did Matthew say to that?"

There was a pause, then: "I don't think I should repeat it; it wasn't very polite."

I actually smiled at that, although none of it was particularly funny. "Don't worry, I can guess. So then what happened?"

"We got in the car and drove straight down here to confront him. The place looked deserted, all scary and empty, and Matthew said that it was almost certainly a trap but there were bigger things at stake and we really didn't have any choice."

"He *knew* it was a trap? Why on earth didn't he just call the police?" My voice cracked impossibly loudly in the sheltered garden and Freddy's young hands clutched anxiously at my sleeve.

"He did! He *did* call them! He called the Inspector straight away but the desk sergeant said he had just left on a case and wasn't available, and anyway a person has to be missing for more than a couple of hours before they actually *are* missing. And then the policeman said that he'd had enough of rogue callers and he didn't care who he thought he was, whether Matthew Croft, the Mayor of Gloucester or even the Pope; the Inspector was still out on a case and *not available*." Freddy gave a fresh little shuddering gasp and then said, "So we cursed for a bit and then Matthew said we were going to look for you ourselves, trap or no trap, and anyway, he wasn't afraid of anything Langton could do."

I kept silent and simply tightened my arms to hug Freddy closer. My cheek was pressing against his hair.

"I think Langton must have been looking out through the back window because he whipped round when we burst into his study and dived towards his desk. We'd marched in through the front door, you see; I don't think he was expecting that. I didn't even realise that he had a gun there but Matthew did."

"Dear Lord," I said, but Freddy didn't hear.

"I thought he was going to kill him," Freddy whispered, "I really did. He looked like he could have done, but all he did was stand there, stand over him and demand to know where you were."

It may have been that Freddy's telling of it was enough to make it all seem so vividly real before my eyes. Or perhaps, having had my own horrific experience in that very same room only hours before, it was simply that my imagination could supply the rest. But either way, I could picture the two men as clearly as if I had been there; one sent down abruptly into an uncomfortable pose of reluctant submission on a chair, the other standing over him and wearing his own personal brand of terrifyingly calm fury.

Where is she?

Matthew's anger must have cut the air like a knife. And John's replies must have been perfectly pitched at that level of wounded innocence that implied considerable patience and just the right amount of concern as he hastily explained away my recklessness. If Freddy was to be believed, he might even have been convincing. Until, that is, he added a claim that he and I had lately reached some kind of romantic understanding. And even then it might still have gone either way. Right up to the moment that Matthew found my necklace.

"I failed him," Freddy whimpered into my shoulder, "I should have warned him, I was supposed to warn him. I should have stopped them or something, but I just stood there and let them do it!"

I tightened my arms again. "Oh, Freddy, darling."

"I was looking at Matthew and feeling very glad that he was on my side, because he looked so terrifying, and then all of a sudden the Colonel was there in the room with us with a shotgun in his hand. I thought he was going to shoot him!"

"But he didn't," I said firmly, forcing myself to focus on my need for information and not my growing sense of dread.

"No." Freddy's voice came out in a tiny frightened squeak. "Langton was just starting to look scared because he didn't know what the chain was and thought you might have dropped it weeks ago, only Matthew said you didn't have it weeks ago and the Colonel made a funny little noise; it was like a cat growling or something. Then he marched up to Matthew, turned the gun round and cracked him hard over the head with the butt. Matthew didn't even have time to *flinch*." The boy shuddered. I held him a little closer.

"They stood there, leering down at him and patting each other on the back as if they'd just won a prize, then they grabbed his arms and hauled him to his feet and away towards the door. I'd been as silent as a mouse until then, but I couldn't let them take him, could I? I just couldn't! So I jumped out."

"You went for them? Oh dear sweet heaven."

"I had to! They were hurting him, I know they were." He took a breath and his voice was very wobbly. "But it didn't do any good. The Colonel just cuffed me aside as if I was nothing and I fell into a sort of tangle and banged my head. Then he kicked me – not all that hard, I was in his way, I think – and I ended up behind a chair and just stayed there."

He paused and then added in a plaintive wail, "I failed him! They took him and I let them and it's all my fault!"

"Oh, Freddy, love." I felt a fierce rush of care for my poor darling boy, "You couldn't have stopped them. You really couldn't. If you'd tried to do anything else, you would have been hurt! Matthew would never have wanted you to do that. No," I said across his tearful protest. "You did exactly the right thing because you stayed here to tell me what happened and now you can help me."

"I can?" There was a faint lift of hope to his voice.

"Yes, Freddy, you can." I gave him a firm squeeze and then released him. "I'm going to go and find them. Did they say where they were going? No? Well, my guess is that they've taken him to Warren Barn given that's where this all started – I need you to call the police and tell them where I've gone. Can you do that? Don't let them fob you off, insist on speaking to the Inspector, tell them anything, tell them that the Inspector will have their guts for garters if you don't get put through. Got that?"

"Guts for garters," Freddy repeated seriously through a sniff, concentrating hard.

"And tell them to be quick," I said and climbed stiffly to my feet. Beechnut hadn't wandered far; she was happily pruning a decorative bush which I fervently hoped was not poisonous. "But first of all can you run and open that gate for me? Quickly now."

Clearly very much cheered, Freddy leapt up and dashed across the lawn. My own speed was equally vital if this was going to stand any chance of making a difference but I still made myself take a deep calming breath before approaching the horse. Keeping my actions fluid and steady so that she wouldn't pick up the state of my nerves, I put my foot in the stirrup and prepared to pull myself up into the saddle. As it was, however, I needn't have bothered trying to be calm; she knew full well that there was something afoot and was perfectly ready.

She gave an eager toss of her head, wheeling about almost before I had got myself settled in the saddle and then we were careering off towards the gate in a great scattering of mud and gravel. I gave a shout of thanks to Freddy as he flashed past in a blur. Then I gave a hard check upon the rein to steady her and set the chestnut at the steep banks and down the snow-damaged slopes towards Washbrook.

Chapter 33

The turf was slick as we slipped and slithered our way downhill but Beechnut plunged on regardless. Night had descended in the time it had taken to extract the story from Freddy, although I had probably only been sitting with him for a few frantic minutes, and in the gloom the slope had become shadowed and extremely treacherous. But the horse was unstoppable as if she shared the urgency that lurked fearfully at the back of my mind and I had to trust to her good sense as I let her pick her own route down the steep incline. Vicious gusts clipped us as we dodged the hazardous humps of anthills before crashing noisily through some brambles but then suddenly we were down into the comparative shelter of the level road and the shadow of the lower gateway was looming dully out of the darkness before us.

Beechnut paused long enough to let me open it before veering wildly through and impatiently stamping while I kicked the gate shut again. Then we were off; wading through the fiercely swollen Washbrook, staggering a little in its raging current but plunging on regardless. The gate into the lower meadows was open and she charged at it with her hind legs bunching for a gallop before I had even decided on our route.

I clung on like a burr as she sped across the flooding field, buffeted by wind and scared by her speed but doing nothing to check it. Barely able to see through eyes that were streaming, the sodden grassland flashed by in a featureless blur, but through the mist of wind-whipped tears, I suddenly became aware that we were not running alone. Grey against the seamless gloom, the fluid mass of a small herd of deer ran unexpectedly along with us like a bizarre extension of our shadow, and like a shadow they were entirely silent. I could hear nothing except for the steady thud of hoof-falls on saturated ground and Beechnut's rhythmic breathing, and the greyed figures of our companions were ghostlike as they floated alongside us across the wide gleaming surface.

We left them behind at the next gate and I steadied her there so that her feet would not slip as we negotiated the sudden change from grass to uneven forest trackway.

"Steady now, girl," I murmured and she sweetly settled to a short bouncy canter as we picked our path through grossly swaying trees and between the stones that protruded from the running hill-wash. We splashed deep through the ford and swung hard right to follow the track that ran under the copse and would lead us round to the farm. It was peculiar to find myself returning to the same place that Matthew and I had fled from only a few days before but, ever brave, Beechnut stretched forwards again and accelerated up the incline to burst through a rotting gate and out onto the pasture fields that surrounded the farm.

The wild air met us with a brutal blast. It stopped us in our tracks and with sudden concern, I threw a hasty look around in case we had been spotted, but I could see no one.

We jogged messily across the open ground to the barn, eyes scanning the black gaping doorway for any sign of movement other than the swaying undergrowth but it was clearly deserted. With a curse I used rein and leg to turn the horse and urged her down towards the farmhouse, careless now of any disturbance we made. But I needn't have worried; the farmhouse was similarly blank and empty.

I stopped for a moment, thinking furiously. Then inspiration struck and with renewed determination, I turned Beechnut about and let her fly again across the wide expanse of the open hilltop.

She stretched her neck forwards and lowered herself into the streamlined arrow of a racehorse as she sped across the curving grassland. We slowed briefly to navigate the spreading marsh of a thin stream and then, plunging through another open gateway and across the road that led to the village, we launched ourselves at the great grassy slope that climbed upwards to meet the summit of the high ridge.

It was impossibly steep and her laboured breathing became rough and irregular as she fought her way up the banks. But just as her great strength began to tire, the dark shape of the evergreen hedge loomed towards us and, giving her a moment to gather herself, I set her at the last slope and the low stone wall that bounded the open space of the drive near the rear range. She pricked her ears and I sat up to urge her on.

And very nearly fell off. There was a rough breath of air and a scattering of dirt as she locked her legs to slither agonisingly to an ugly stop. Her breast brushed the moss from the cold face of the wall and I would have fallen off but that she threw up her head at the last possible moment and by some miracle I managed to shove myself back into the saddle. With an angry snort she shied away and bunched to bolt wildly back down the slopes again but the hard hold I took on her mouth pulled her head round and held her panicked flight steady.

"Sorry, darling," I said breathlessly as I put a hand on her sweaty neck to calm her. "I'm so sorry, it's not your fault."

It occurred to me later that it was probably very fortunate that she didn't make the jump because if we had burst in on them like that, at such a maddened pace and so wholly unexpectedly, their reaction would have been purely instinctive and certainly devastatingly final. But as it was, her refusal checked my crazed headlong rush and instead we trotted relatively sedately along the wall to find the corner with its little gate that would lead us out onto the drive.

With limbs that were trembling from adrenalin and nerves, I slithered down from her back and led her carefully through the gap as the wind snatched open the gate and then swung it sweetly shut again behind us. Crossing her stirrups over the saddle and knotting the reins safely on her neck, I whispered a hard command of "Stand!" and, leaving her to forage for grass on Sir William's neat verges, I slipped soundlessly along in the lee of the bowing yew hedge, under the darkened wall of the house and onwards to the corner where the high gabled frontage met the gardens.

And all the while I was keeping up a steady silent prayer that this maddened race would not, with all the laws of logic, prove to be far, far too late.

Chapter 34

I do not believe that I even considered for a moment the possibility of finding that they were not there. Knowing John as I now unhappily did, I had already guessed he would not simply take Matthew away to dispose of him quietly in some secluded woodland spot. Equally clearly there had never been any intention of handing Matthew over to the police – with the danger of exposure creeping ever closer there was no likelihood of him making that mistake now. Instead Matthew's death would be as grandiose and as unnecessary as this crazed scheme with all its exhilarating risks could allow.

From the very instant that Matthew had unwittingly become involved, John must have allowed for this moment. With the same single-mindedness that had snuffed out the life of his uncle's joiner, I knew he would now act to remove any remaining danger of discovery and with it mark a final and emphatic conclusion to their absurd rivalry. And if I felt a momentary concern as to how effective I of all people might be in attempting to prevent it, my doubts were forgotten when at last I peered around the edge of the building.

Not far from me, on the level terrace that looked out over the spot where I had lingered in brief but wonderful respite from the pressures of the dance, stood the Colonel and Sir William. The two old men were standing side by side with their faces turned slightly towards me, identical coats lifting and guttering behind with each fresh gust, and where the dull cast of light from the house touched and coloured them, I could see the metallic gleam of a shotgun hanging in Sir William's hand. It was polished to a shine and he held it level at his hip with practiced ease. His finger was resting lightly on the trigger so that the long lethal barrel aimed casually down the stone steps to a point concealed by the bulk of a tall elegantly squared yew which, although bent out of all shape by the rising gale, was still entirely impenetrable.

Cursing the gardeners who had cultivated such an impossible blind, I forced my nerves to permit me to creep stealthily closer. I slipped clumsily under the light of a window and into the deep shadow of the high arches of the arcade and then, with my heart in my mouth, took that insane first step out of cover. With my fingers outstretched to ward off unforeseen obstacles, I slid along until I had moved beyond the very last column of the arcade. My awkward body came to rest in the woody stems of an overgrown creeper beside a bay window, only yards away from the unguarded backs of the old gentlemen, and where finally, and against every wish, I could see beyond the broken boxed yew.

I very nearly cried out. Not from fear or horror, although I could see in an instant that their treatment of him had not been kind, but instead from an overwhelming relief that whatever else had happened, I was not too late. He was still alive.

But this brief feeling with all the meagre comfort it could bring was quickly lost. He was kneeling in the soaked grass at the bottom of the steps with his head down and I could see a dark stain where blood had congealed above his eye from a cut that still bled a little. There was a graze on the back of his hand where it rested on his thigh and his clothes – the ones he had collected from his house only the day before – were torn and ruined. His breath was being snatched away by the wind but surprisingly, although I could see that it was strained and irregular, the little lifts of his chest beneath the open flaps of a mud-stained jacket seemed unhurried as John moved around him.

I watched as John gave Matthew's shoulder a shove. He had to fling out a hand as he was knocked sideways and slowly, and with what appeared to be a great effort, he righted himself. I wondered if they had beaten him.

"Not so cocksure now, are you?" The low hiss of John's voice was almost inaudible above the growing shriek of the wind. He was swaggering in a tight circle; he too held a gun, a shotgun I thought, although not a double-barrel. It hung loosely in his hand and I wondered just how much he craved to use it. "Still trying to pretend that you're innocent?"

I had to swallow another cry as Matthew raised his head. He had a cruel mark on his jaw but the pale face that lifted to meet his captors' did not bear the wavering gaze of one who was utterly weakened and defeated. With a sudden thrill of hope I realised that he was still very much master of himself and when he spoke it was with a thin fury.

"You can peddle your lies as much as you like, Langton – I just don't care. All I want to know is what you've done with *her*." The voice was cracked and faint, but his words broke through the racing air and flung his defiance at their feet with an almost physical force.

I saw John give an exasperated jerk of his head. He turned angrily away and I knew then that this strategic concentration of his remaining strength was how Matthew had managed to survive so long. He must have understood from the very first moment that his capitulation was the victory that John craved; and the denial of it, even as he slumped battered and bruised at the other's feet, was a challenge that would not be ignored.

"You can plead all you like, it won't save you." John spoke sneeringly and I wondered if he realised how this sounded when it was clear to us all that Matthew was still very far from any kind of pleading. Perhaps he did realise because then he turned to his

285

father and snarled, "We know he killed Jamie; he's almost certainly done away the girl and now tonight someone else has died by his gun, so what should we do with him, eh?"

There was an odd little silence while I had time to register the meaning of his words. *Someone else?* But then I had to shrink back into the shadows as John's gaze swept angrily across the vacant windows towards me.

Matthew's head drooped once more. From my useless position against the wall, I had the sudden horrible realisation that the effort of maintaining this last show of resistance was telling painfully. His head stayed down even as John stepped past him and I knew that if help didn't arrive soon to snatch him away from beneath the hungry gaze of those guns, he would lose this battle of wits and make that final admission that would unleash John's hatred. My ears strained keenly for the sound of approaching cars and our salvation in the form of the Inspector but the groaning embrace of the darkness behind was as uninviting as it was complete.

There was a crack of uneven paving under Sir William's foot as he shifted his weight. The gun twitched hungrily in his hand. "Who else has he killed?"

Gratified by his uncle's outrage, John smiled and indulged in a little self-righteous indignation. "Would you believe that he actually came to me, Uncle, trying to accuse *me* of doing something to harm that girl? Well, now we'll see who's boss, won't we?"

"*Who else?*" The Colonel cut across him sharply. Even in this meagre yellow light I could see the purple tinge to his features. "John?"

There was a sudden snap by my ear. It drew their attention as well as mine. I snatched back, nerves shrieking, into the creeper as their eyes jerked towards me. But even as I froze in immoveable horror, I realised that they were not staring at me but at the tall latticed window which had inexplicably opened barely inches from my side.

"Bill? *Bill!*"

The fleeting hope that this distraction would somehow prove to be a forerunner of the Inspector's judicious arrival was shattered by a woman's high girlish tones. So close that it seemed inconceivable that she didn't see me, Sir William's wife appeared in the vacant frame, swathed in a flapping, gaping dressing gown and grey hair escaping wool-like from a hideously frilly nightcap. In the guttering lamplight, her willowy figure cast a distorted and nightmarish shadow across the group of angry men.

"Bill!" she cried again, idiotically.

"*What?*" snapped her husband. "Can't you see we're busy?"

She flinched at his tone and covering her mouth with her hand, gave a sad little, "*Oh ...*"

Instantly Sir William's demeanour softened and, flapping a hand in hasty suppression of John's irritable mutter behind, he took a step towards her making an affectionate abbreviation of her name and restoring his usual genial tone. "What is it, my dear?"

She gave him a silly smile and I wondered whether she had even noticed that there was a man kneeling in the dirt at the foot of her steps with blood on his cheek and guns levelled at his head. "Oh, Bill, dear, it's just Lord Oakridge. He wants to know why the police have been calling on him to confirm he was with us that horrible afternoon. He said it was terribly embarrassing and that he hopes you won't be bandying his name about in future. I told him I didn't believe you ever bandied anybody's name about because you were above that kind of thing, but he wants to speak to you anyway. He's on the telephone."

Sir William shared an inward ferocious and silent exchange with his temper before forcing his mouth into a smile. "Tell him I'm terribly busy and can't speak to him now. And to be honest if that dratted buffoon can't even admit to the police that he likes coming here to share a sherry then he can just go hang and it's the last time I host his son's shooting parties. No, don't say that last. Just give him my apologies, would you? There's a dear."

With a simpering smile she span away, the window snapping

shut behind her and I knew then that I must be verging on total collapse, because the only thing I could focus on out of all the thoughts that were flying through my mind was the absurd realisation that yet again I had somehow failed to catch the woman's name.

There was a pause while each of us recovered from her bizarre interruption, then, coattails flapping, the old men turned slowly back again. The Colonel's eyes, narrowed against the storm, almost seemed to touch upon me for a moment, actually grazing my cowed figure where it pressed frozen against the woody stems of the creeper. But then it moved on and he too settled his attention once more upon the windswept figure of his son.

Sharp as a knife, the Colonel's voice cut across the horror of what might have been. "Who else has that man killed, John?"

John was staring blankly into space and it took another growl of his name before he blinked and managed to focus on his father. He lifted his head and said, confused, "Why, Hicks, of course."

"Hicks?" Sir William's hoarse croak fought a gusting sigh that rattled along the house front. "My manager? He's killed *Hicks*?"

"Yes!" John's enthusiasm revived again in triumph, "Hicks! And I've got his gun here, should we help him put it to one final use?"

He stepped smartly towards Matthew once more and gave him another vicious shove. My lip stung where I bit it and with a sudden bitter understanding of my uselessness, I peered fiercely into the darkness beyond the house wall and tried to force my brain to think of some diversion that might delay them until help came. I was listening feverishly but the wind had veered a little and the fresh rain that was now hammering down the length of the building oppressively smothered all else. I turned my eyes back to the men again.

"If you've ..." Matthew had eased himself upright again and was staring up at John. His voice sounded as if it was held level by a very great effort and it was betraying his fatigue. "If you've hurt her I'll ..."

John interrupted him with a laugh.

Matthew lifted his eyes to the two old men, "Colonel, show some sense – make him tell you where she is. *Please!*"

John's laugh transformed into a great sneer of triumph. "And finally *he begs* ..."

It took me a horribly long moment to realise what had happened. But even as I began to realise the significance of his words, I saw John stalk around the kneeling man in an arc that made my blood run cold. He came to a stop behind and smiled.

Matthew had turned his head to follow him. He was watching the other man out of the corner of his eye. Then John stepped a little closer. He bent down and, through the swirling tempest of freshly falling rain, I saw his lips move. "Don't look to my father for help, boy. He won't save you. He knows exactly what you are."

The expression on Matthew's face ought to have told me what I was too afraid to admit but then, with a savagery that brought realisation flooding painfully to my heart, John took hold of Matthew's hair. I saw Matthew's body jerk once in instinctive resistance but John simply adjusted his grip and in the stillness that followed it was clear that the man at his feet had nothing more to give.

John's next words were delivered in a gently spoken undertone and they were meant for Matthew's ears alone. "It's far too late for begging. Now you'll never know, will you?"

He pressed the cold mouth of the gun against Matthew's temple and cast a glance up at his father. There was loathing and need and not even the barest speck of pity in the Colonel's eyes as he stared down at the man held taut before him in cruel submission by his son's fist. Then the old man lifted his gaze to John's face.

John smiled. "I would say it was perfectly conceivable that overcome with guilt for this last despicable act he should contemplate suicide. Don't you?"

And slowly, almost imperceptibly, the Colonel gave a nod.

Chapter 35

"No!"

The scream flung itself gruesomely back at me from the high walls of the house. For a long terrible moment I thought the roaring in my ears was the report of the gun but then finally I managed to draw a gasping breath and I realised that the only sound I could hear was the sharp rattle of windblown rain against glass. I took a moment to steady myself, and stepped forwards into the light.

"I wouldn't do that if I were you."

There was a devastated silence. All eyes fixed upon me, each face pale and shocked as if I were a ghost, and perhaps I was. It felt so unearthly and cold that I might well have been dead.

But then the spell-bound silence broke. John let out a short choking gasp of a cry and took a staggering step backwards. Abruptly released, Matthew fell forwards in an ugly sprawl onto the lawn and he lay there, awkwardly propped on one elbow, head down and unmoving so that I almost wondered if I was wrong and I had spoken too late after all. But then I saw his soaked shoulders lift a little and he drew a long slow shuddering intake of breath.

I took another unsteady step forwards and found, insanely, that I was smiling. "Surprised to see me?"

John swallowed and put out a hand, half to ward me off and half as a vain attempt at casual greeting. "Ellie?" he croaked. "But

I thought …"

"What? That I was taking a Sunday drive?" I peered through streaks of rain-soaked hair at his father. "You might want to think twice before killing an innocent man, Colonel."

"Innocent? He's not *innocent*." Sir William was the one to find his voice first and it came with a spit of venom. No jovial friend to my father now; his mouth had twisted out of all recognition from its usual supine curve, his features laid bare by the toll of lately conspiring to exact his own extreme idea of justice.

"How exactly did Jamie die, John?" My voice was still possessed by that light unearthly tone; my body felt remote and alien as if I was merely an onlooker to a play and it seemed so numb as I took another step nearer that I actually had to question whether it was me that was moving at all. I gave my mind a shake and concentrated hard on keeping the creeping chill of shock at bay. "How did he die?"

Reminding myself that I knew how to breathe, I kept my gaze steady in a passable parody of a stare as John blinked and opened and closed his mouth a few times. He managed to sound relatively calm, however, when he answered, "How on earth should I know? I wasn't there, was I?"

"Oh, but you were, John." Behind him I saw Matthew stir slightly and felt my stomach tighten into an unhappy knot as his hand gave a tiny quiver. *Get up, please. Please just get up* I urged silently, wondering how long I might be able to sustain this madcap confession before someone thought to stop it.

It very nearly happened in the next moment when the Colonel climbed out of his daze at last. "Don't be idiotic, girl," he snapped. "John was in a meeting with Bates, our accountant."

I said weakly, "And does your accountant happen to work at 42 Norfolk Street, Gloucester?"

The Colonel looked utterly blank; although I was sure I saw a jolt run through John's body. Beyond him, Matthew's hand tightened to a ball upon the close-cropped grass but the Colonel was speaking again and I had to drag my attention hastily back to the old man's face.

"But Bates isn't from Gloucester. His office is in Cirencester; the Market Place, Cirencester. What on earth is the foolish girl wittering on about? John?"

John turned to him with a hapless shrug that reasserted control and dismissed me in an instant, "I don't know, Father. Perhaps she's taken a knock to the head. Croft's attack must have addled her brains, poor thing." He turned to me again and gave a sympathetic smile before speaking very slowly as if he were speaking to a child, or an idiot. "I've told you this once before, Ellie, if you recall. I was in a meeting all that afternoon – with Bates – and it has been investigated perfectly thoroughly. Your friend the Inspector told me so."

"Oh?" I asked politely. My voice was tight and very high. "Well, do you know what the Inspector said to me? No? He told me that he had two witnesses; that he had taken two statements – one from a Davey Turford and one from Simon – and that they were the only people who were at the scene. But what did you tell me?"

"What?" he asked patiently. "What did I tell you?" And passed a conspiratorial wink to his father.

"It took me a while to remember, but then I had a long time to think in that lorry, didn't I?" A gust buffeted me and I had to wait a moment while my lungs snatched for another breath. But then I managed to finish. "I think I quote accurately when I say that you told me you *saw Jamie's body and it was savage*. Just when exactly did you see him, John?"

John stilled and I felt the sudden tug as Matthew's consciousness focused on me for the first time.

"Eleanor …"

The sound was nothing more than a hoarse whisper cracked with strain but I could not look at him, I didn't dare. I kept my whole being focused on John. I said, "And before you say that you saw his body as it was being taken away by the undertaker, I'll

292

remind you that you specifically told me that no one was allowed near the site once the police had arrived." John snapped his mouth shut again into a tight angry line and, mercilessly, I forced my point home. "So when *exactly* was it that you saw Jamie's body? Can you answer that, John?"

He couldn't. He just stood there, staring at me while his father paled and swayed a little.

For an age nobody moved. We stood motionless while rain stung our faces and somewhere a gate shuddered and slammed shut like a pistol-shot. John was staring at me as though I were something very nasty indeed.

Sir William was the first to speak. "You promised me it was Croft. You *promised* me!"

"Well of course I did," John snapped impatiently and the barrel of the gun flashed in the light from the window as at last he tore his eyes from my face and turned them towards his uncle. Sir William was eyeing the weapon warily as John approached the foot of the steps. "I knew you were too much of a stickler for the rules to let that one pass, no matter how much your pocket might benefit."

"John ... what have you done?" The Colonel's voice was so weak that it didn't carry beyond a whisper. Rain flung itself across the paving slabs between us like a shower of hard pellets.

Oblivious, John leant against a stone pedestal. "Just a little bit of work in the art business, nothing special." He idly brushed the mossy grime from his sleeve. "A gentleman of my acquaintance had taken possession of some artwork in need of a new home but lacked the means of disposing of it properly. I was only too pleased to relieve him of it – it was an excellent arrangement, and will prove very lucrative." He looked up and gave his father a little smile. "Richard can keep his end up with the other officers now, Father."

"But I ... I don't understand."

"It really is very simple, you know." John spoke cruelly. "Our family is bankrupt. The Langton name is worth absolutely nothing. You and your other son swan about like royalty while I spend every second scrabbling about trying desperately to stop the ceaseless haemorrhaging of money. I certainly wasn't going to pass up a perfectly harmless business opportunity."

"But it wasn't harmless, John. A man *died!*"

Sir William broke in. "I lent you my barn, I covered for you!" Where before excitement had drawn his features into betraying an altered form of hunger, now he looked horribly like he was going to be sick. "I didn't sign up for *that*." His hand wafted whitely in the direction of the man who was still lying there half collapsed in the growing cascade of the steps. As we watched, Matthew slowly dropped his forehead to rest upon his clenched hand and took another very deep breath.

But the Colonel flinched and turned jerkily to his brother. "You *knew?*"

John laughed. "Of course he knew, Father. Who do you think provided the perfect alibi for my men while they guarded the hoard? He's been paying their wages!" He laughed again, although no one else found it remotely amusing.

There was a distant murmur that might have been a car but it was swallowed in a savage whiplash of air that smacked across the terrace. I glanced urgently at Matthew but he was gingerly pressing a hand to his temple and didn't see.

"And what about *your* alibi? What about Bates?" The Colonel looked like he would have liked very much to have sat down.

John shrugged, indifferent. "It wasn't hard to leave him – I just had to arrange for the housekeeper to fuss around him with a light tea. All he thought was that I had taken a business call in your office. A rather lengthy telephone call it is true, but he didn't question it and I had quite long enough to take my chance and slip away for a little while."

"To see Jamie ..." The Colonel was staring sightlessly.

"The stupid fool didn't have a single honest bone in his body."

John did not appear to appreciate the irony of this statement; "That was your mistake, Uncle, for treating him like your pet charity case and allowing him to settle there. All he had to do was keep his head turned the other way but the idiot man got greedy and actually tried to auction one of the paintings. Perfectly predictably, it was recognised and the damned fool very nearly brought the police down on all our heads."

I glanced at Matthew again but he was watching John carefully as he eased himself slowly up onto his knees.

"I went to see him." A hapless smile. "Jamie had actually called me you see, he actually came clean as if he expected me to give him a pat on the back and have a good laugh about it for old time's sake, but it finally seemed to dawn on him that he was in rather a lot more trouble than that. And then he told me he'd talked to *that one*. I only wanted to scare him." He looked up to his father and the tragedy of it was, I could see that he was telling the truth. "It didn't occur to me that he would actually *die*. But somehow it got out of hand. It only took a moment; he barely even struggled." There was a terrible silence, then John added, "Of course *he* was supposed to be caught in the act so to speak and neatly tidy up the loose ends, but you got away, didn't you? Like a worm you wriggled free."

He rounded on Matthew and spoke sneeringly, "And just where *have* you been hiding all this time? Down a rabbit hole?"

Matthew returned his glare impassively. But then, in an incriminating lapse of concentration, his gaze unconsciously flicked beyond the other man. In an instant he realised what he had done and looked hastily away again but it was too late. John's eyes widened as he slowly twisted to face me.

"*You?* You ... you *lied* to me?"

I flinched under the force of his revulsion before swallowing and finding my voice. I said quietly, "You're not the only one who has discovered a talent for stretching the truth."

John stared at me for a moment through the blurring sheet

of driven rain; a long, silent stare that drove a chill to my core before, with a particularly unpleasant smile, he suddenly thrust himself away from the stone pillar. Mud splashed under his feet as he started up the steps; I felt my heart painfully miss a beat as I unwillingly took a step backwards. I found myself pressing back against the cold hard wall of the house and shrank there, quivering, but he didn't come any closer. He had stopped just below his father who was staring at him as if he had never met him before. I felt an unexpected pang of pity for the old man.

"I did it for you, you know," John said quietly. "It was always for you. I just wanted you to be proud of me. Only you never are, are you? You're always running off after your other son."

The Colonel stiffened. "Why do you persist in dragging his name into this? He spent half of the past year in and out of hospital. Richard's injuries very nearly ended his career!"

John nodded slowly but then his lips curled into a malevolent leer. "And that would have made two of us. I knew you'd never be able to bring yourself to thank me. Why should you when I've only single-handedly dragged the Manor and therefore my dear brother's inheritance out of the hands of the debt-collectors." The Colonel squared his shoulders at this insolent speech but John ploughed on regardless. "Did you really think I was going to stand his steward for the next ten years while he drifts about planning wars and good marriages just so that you can hand it all to him on a plate when you finally get round to meeting your maker? I don't believe it was particularly wrong of me to want a little independence of my own, a little nest-egg to set me up in the world. *You* can't do anything for me can you? The younger son who never made anything of himself – why, you all but disowned me years ago!"

"*His* inheritance?"

The question stopped the tirade in its tracks. I saw a spasm flicker across John's face as he re-ran his father's words in his head and began to work out the connotations, and the possibility of a mistake. He floundered. "I …"

Unwittingly, my eyes moved beyond to where Matthew was still kneeling in the drowning grass. He was staring up at John with wearied concentration but he must have felt my gaze touch upon him because he blinked and suddenly his eyes flicked to mine in a little glance that seemed to communicate all the force of his mind in one intense, heating second. But then his gaze returned watchfully to John's pale face and I felt anew the icy chill of apprehension.

The Colonel was staring down at his son with something of the grit appropriate for a military veteran, although the purple tinge was noticeable absent, and it made him look very ancient indeed. "So you've decided to take matters into your own hands, have you? And now there's a second death; how do you plan to justify that?"

There was a tense little pause before Sir William said weakly, "But he said Croft killed him."

"Are you really that idiotic?" The Colonel rounded on him nastily, a trace of colour beating a return to his haggard cheeks. "He said Croft's gun killed Hicks – *that* gun in fact – not the man himself. Your age-old enmity towards that family has made you a pawn in his hands throughout this ridiculous scheme; and you're still falling for it. Do you honestly still believe that there is more than one murderer amongst us?"

Murderer. There was an ugly silence in the wake of that. No one had been brave enough to voice it before.

Then John said quite calmly, "He's right, you know. I thought you'd already guessed."

"But *why?*" Sir William's voice wavered, distraught and utterly confused. "Hicks was a good man. *My* good man. Why did you have to kill him?"

John gave one of his charming smiles but his eyes were sombre. "It's all Croft's fault, you know. You have to understand that I never meant for Jamie Donald to die, but once he had I thought it would all work out well enough when this man here conveniently set about incriminating himself. But the days dragged on and I realised that in spite of my best efforts, he was not dancing to quite the right tune. Then, just to crown it all, I found that our damned idiot Inspector was beginning to tire of the hunt and I knew it might not be long before he started to question the line I've been feeding him so carefully. It was perfectly obvious that something had to be done; what else was I supposed to do? Just sit by and watch all my hard work dwindle away to nothing?"

In the brief hush I searched in vain for the wished-for car but nothing penetrated the chaos of the shuddering landscape. I turned my eyes back to the group again and caught a glance from Matthew. It was meant as a question and we shared a brief flash of grim urgency which touched his face to shadows. He readied himself to rise but even I could see the numb weakness of his limbs.

John was smiling again. "It seemed like a good idea at the time. I wanted to leave irrefutable evidence that Croft was the culprit and what better way to do it than to use his own gun? It may perhaps smack a little of desperation, but Hicks knew too much anyway and now that he's dead, there is no one left who can lead the trail to me."

Sir William made an odd noise that was a sort of cross between a choke and a squeal. "To you? To *you*? No, but there is a trail that leads to *me*, isn't there, John? Good God, did you plan that too, just in case Croft isn't enough? Is that why the police are suddenly reviewing my alibis? Because they think *I* did it?!"

His voice had risen to hysteria and John gave a sharp laugh. "Don't turn squeamish on me now, Uncle. I've engineered conclusive evidence that Croft is their man; the police won't even think to question it. We just need to keep our nerve and follow it though, and by this time next month we'll be rich men. Rich! Why, even as we speak, the artwork is gently sailing its way to America ready to mark a change for all our lives."

Behind him, there was a blur of wet turf as Matthew made an attempt to stand but his foot slipped uselessly from beneath him and he had to throw out a hand to catch himself. It looked like it must have hurt. My tangle of creepers crackled beneath my hand.

"If we finish it now, *really* finish it I mean; if we put Croft down once and for all, no one will ever know. Heavens, given the family he comes from, it'll practically be an act of mercy." John waved a hand carelessly in Matthew's general direction as if to illustrate his point. "The girl will keep quiet – she and I have an understanding that will see to that – you'll work your usual charm and the police will be satisfied, the case will be closed and no one need ever realise just how close the Langton family came to the brink of ruin."

I almost laughed at this easy assumption of complicity; I had never known before what it was to truly hate. Then, above the steady pounding of my heart, I heard the sound of a car, a faint whisper of a motor carrying on a shriek of wind, and this time I was certain I saw a brief flare of headlights touch upon the heavy streaks above us. A fresh burst of hope brought a comforting breath of warmth to my frozen limbs and it lingered even as I drew my gaze back to meet the next stage of John's ugly persuasive argument.

"All we have to do is dispose of *him.* Give one final push now and by this time next week our ocean liner will have docked at Boston, the auctioneers will have met it and our artwork will be waiting to make the Langton family a truly staggering amount of money."

Warmth dissolved into horror as John's expression suddenly cleared to decisive action. With a wide unashamed grin, he turned sharply on his heel to march back down the steps; the gun glinted alive and hungry in his hand as he came to a halt at the edge of the lawn. Matthew must have been making one last concerted effort to stand because his hand was braced upon his thigh but even as he readied himself to make the final thrust, he looked up. The long black barrel lowered slightly in a tiny adjustment to its aim.

"No, John."

For a moment I thought it was my voice that had cut desperately across the scene but it wasn't. I found myself suddenly standing next to the Colonel where my frantic feet must have carried me and I watched dumbly as, with a gentleness that must have hurt terribly, the old man fixed his son with an expression that was entirely devoid of its usual hauteur. His hand was trembling slightly by his side as he spoke again "I forbid it."

John hesitated. I thought I saw him suppress a little shudder. The storm buffeted him, tugging at him and challenging his stillness. Then he turned again and looked up at his father with what can only have been stupefaction.

"You *forbid* it?" This change of tack had shaken him, I could clearly see.

But the Colonel's pride must have stepped in again at the sneer that was purely a front, because instead of maintaining this new sense of caring reason, the Colonel squared his shoulders and fixed his son with a new frowning stare. His posture now regained its parade-ground stature and when he spoke, it was with his habitual bullying force. "I do. I will not permit you to do this. Put the gun down and *come here*."

John actually swayed. I thought for a brief moment that he might obey but then the gun twitched angrily and I was suddenly very afraid indeed that John might shoot his own father. If the Colonel feared the same, he didn't betray it; he just stood stiff and tall while the gale snatched at his clothing, and stared down at his son in an unimaginable battle of wills.

Then John blinked. "Oh, damn you to hell!"

The next moment found me thrusting myself forwards across the terrace. He had turned again and as Matthew tried and failed to scramble desperately to his feet, the gun rose once more in his hand. With my heart pounding in my ears and a voice that quavered with fear, I raced past the frozen figures to the top of the steps and somehow, in a breathless jumble, managed to say:

"Actually your fortune won't be made in a Boston salesroom next week, John. The lorry should be where I left it, which is on the Mason's Arms haulage yard. Complete with horses ..." I had to pause to gather my nerves; and then committed myself to this fate.

"… And artwork."

What followed felt like an eternity of silence. In reality it probably only lasted for a millisecond. John took a few faltering strides towards me and then stopped, eyes glinting beneath dark streaks of flattened hair. The latticed glass in the windows made a crazed pattern across his face as he stared up at me. Then his mouth twisted strangely and with sudden terrible knowledge of what was to come, I took a few uselessly instinctive steps backwards.

A low murmur of engine noise washed across the wall of the house on the wind, in so fleeting a crescendo that it may well have been only in my imagination but then, whether truth or fantasy, it faded again, and with it took the last vestiges of hope. Desperate eyes flicked right to the Colonel but he was staring at his son with the blank mindlessness of shock and I knew that he would not help me. Sir William was simply gaping stupidly and I wondered if he was aware that we were still there at all. Matthew, I knew, had not even had strength enough to preserve his own life, he certainly had nothing left to offer for me and I do not believe I have ever felt so alone, flanked as I was by all those people and yet so very far from any kind of help.

Reluctantly my eyes returned to John's icy blue and suddenly my desperate burst of bravery seemed very foolish indeed. His eyes were wide and very light and when he uttered a strange strangled groan, I thought for an appalling moment that he was going to shoot me as I stood there. But then the gun flashed down into the grass and he started towards me once more.

"You little bitch," he said and closed the last few yards in a bound.

Chapter 36

I remember a confused blur; hands reaching for me, grasping and clutching. There was a hoarse shout of my name and then a piercing scream that could only have been mine but somehow seemed to come from somewhere else entirely. I hit out. I must have connected because he spat an oath but then he drew back and suddenly I was flung cruelly backwards to fall hard against the house wall. My head hit stone, painfully, then he was on me and I went down beneath him with a panicked cry and a disorientating flurry of dirt and stunted shrubbery. His grip hurt and there seemed to be a bitter sort of twisted irony that this story would begin and end with a man's strength easily imprisoning my hands.

I screamed again, uselessly, only to be sharply silenced as his fingers finally moved to my throat. I twisted frantically, desperately, but it was no use. The hand shifted, found its grip, and then with devastatingly practised skill, determinedly, agonisingly tightened.

An angry bellow from a gun penetrated the roaring by my ear. It was the sound of his breathing and the excruciating throbbing abruptly eased as an impossible pressure was dragged clear from my throat. My world span and my limbs were leaden, and for a moment it was all I could do to lie there, gasping painfully while grime and gutter water was thrown up in coarse clouds to crunch and splatter around me. It smelled of lavender.

A lump of mud, or a twig perhaps, struck my face, jerking me back to some sort of consciousness. Twisting, finding the boiling light clearing from my eyes, I saw the Colonel snatch the gun from Sir William's hands to throw it violently to the ground. Looking utterly and genuinely aghast, Sir William did nothing to stop him and as the black glint of falling metal drew my eye, I realised that the expanse of dappled window light that ran cascading down the steps behind them was empty. Entirely empty.

The sharp hiss of an ugly curse snapped my attention to the booted feet that had been scraping and straining unnoticed by my head for some time, and it finally dawned on me with a crushing surge of realisation that somehow Matthew had found the strength after all.

With the careful deliberation that comes from shock, I deduced that the gun had gone off instinctively, accidentally, at the very same instant that Matthew had plunged up the slope to crash bodily past Sir William and onwards to tackle John. With the same dazed stupidity, I noticed that fresh marks had streaked the stone stabs near my head from the spray of lead pellets. They almost made a pattern.

I came back to life with a jolt when the blur of wrestling men crashed noisily into the stone frame of the window above me. As a foot slipped in the wet to pass within inches, it actually tangled a little in the spread of my hair. The sudden unexpected sting of pain was the stimulus I needed and I managed to roll aside just as a clipped cry of pain overhead was followed by the tinkling crash of breaking glass.

Slithering back into my shelter of the creeper, I saw to my horror that it was Matthew who was being pressed painfully back against the buckling panes of the latticed window. But then his grip on the other's body shifted and then shifted again, and John was sent backwards into a stagger that very nearly left him sprawling on the terrace.

I heard Matthew's breathing, rough and laboured in the cold

night air as he lingered above me for a brief moment, fighting desperation and fatigue before thrusting forwards to meet the other's attack across the running surface. A knee lifted gruesomely, connected; John was fighting brutally and it was clear that he was perfectly determined to kill his opponent in any way he could. A fist swung for Matthew's jaw but the blow fell short to glance harmlessly off a shoulder and then John's foot slipped so that he had to flail desperately for balance and grip the person he was trying to destroy. In an instant Matthew closed on him and they both went crashing down in a rough scattering of mud and water so that for a moment I couldn't tell who it was that had the other held in a savage grip. But then Matthew managed to twist free and John's head snapped back and he fell away with a sharp animal cry of pain.

Matthew took a while to get up – too long, and I saw a flicker of triumph pass across John's clouded face as, muttering a lurid threat woven about my name, he stepped in to prepare another punishingly brutal blow. I screamed a warning, fingers tearing shreds out of the creeper as I dragged myself to my feet. It was only as I drew in another gasping breath that I realised that I had made no sound at all.

But whether by instinct or by luck, Matthew twisted aside in mid-rise so that I saw the kick cut a sodden arc to glide harmlessly past him and then he was on his feet again, stepping forwards into a determined lunge so that they disappeared together in another chaos of disturbed evergreens and straining limbs. They crashed down again, this time into one of the tall sculpted yews to carve a grotesque hole in the side before dislodging one of the stone urns in an uncontrollable dive that sent them both tumbling to the foot of the stone steps. Again, it was John who was first to stagger drunkenly to his feet.

Staggering myself as I took those first urgent steps away from the support of the sagging creeper, I saw that man, snarling, reach for his opponent's throat. His fingers worked with the same ugly confidence that had grasped at mine but he was not so bold when Matthew only stepped in and broke his hold with all the fluidity of experience. John gave ground, limping now as he slithered backwards down the slope of the mud smeared lawn and he seemed suddenly aware that as he tired, the distinction between murderer and victim became considerably less well defined. But then I noticed a black line in the rain-soaked grass behind his feet and as light burst from the house to cast their shadows long across the blackened hillside, I realised what he was doing. I set my dogged course towards it.

Light flickered again. It swung in a dizzying lurch across the bowing flowerbeds before fixing into a narrow wavering beam. Another joined it, swaying crazily from the other end of the terrace, and I realised that the lights were not coming from the house at all, but beyond from the sweeping driveway as, running with torches, the police finally arrived.

Hands touched me, gripping me as I reached the top of the steps and hung there briefly, gasping for breath and gripping the newly vacated plinth in my turn. They were patting me – the Colonel beside me with his brother just behind, checking I was unhurt I think – but their presence faded to nothing in my consciousness when beyond I saw John abandon the gun and break away to lift his head, listening. He took another clumsy step backwards, dodging Matthew's reach with a desperate snarl and then turned his head to listen again. Craning my aching neck past the old men, I tried to peer into the flickering darkness and it was only when a great shape detached itself from the shadows that I finally understood.

Spooked and maddened by the crush of approaching men who ran along behind her, Beechnut must have been sent on a frantic charge out of the driveway and around the far side of the house towards us. She jinked right, stirrups flapping and hooves scrabbling wildly for purchase on the slippery terrace before launching herself in a scattering of wind-ravaged buddleias over a flowerbed and down onto the greasy surface of the mud-scarred lawn.

Caught in mid-lunge, Matthew let out a cry as she crashed past him, sending him spinning aside from the force of her impact to land sprawling in the mud. John was more fortunate. Forewarned and already making a side-stepping evasion, John threw up his arms to ward her off and as she veered away I saw his hands stretch out and reach for the reins. She flung her head wildly, trying to tear away from him, but somehow he held her and even as Matthew scrambled into a desperate dive, he jumped and swung himself up onto her back.

The horse plunged and kicked savagely and I thought that he would fall but somehow he managed to force her up into the bridle to take her prisoner between hand and leg. He turned her in a spinning circle. It was very nearly a rear and as she shied from the spreading line of policemen, he dragged on a rein and at last released her to send her at a pounding gallop away from us down the slope.

She went at a maddened race. Her flying hooves sent up great clumps of earth as she charged across the slanting lawn towards the low hedge on its crumbling boundary that overlooked the great lake. It stretched black in the distance and suddenly I realised with a sense of numbing horror what was about to happen.

John was crouching low over her neck with all the precarious perfection of a racing jockey as he urged her ever onwards, and in that position he never stood a chance. As before she threw out her legs at the last possible moment and once again she crashed to a slithering halt so that her chest pressed brutally against the sharp evergreen of the box hedge and her muscles strained hard to hold her back. Her head dropped and then he was airborne, soaring high and far over the steep slopes of the black wooded valley. He seemed to hang there for an eternity, an unnatural creature snatching greedily at the sky. But then, suddenly, he lost his battle with gravity and at last, gracelessly, with terrible and devastating finality, he fell.

Chapter 37

I must have somehow staggered down the steps and onto the lawn because I found myself hurrying blindly across the dirtied ground towards Beechnut as she hovered by the hedge, nostrils flared and head flung high in wild agitation. The reins were hanging from her bit to trail about her feet as she anxiously stamped about and I desperately wanted to reach her before she could step on them and damage herself. But then, with a sudden and terrible awakening to fresh horror, I stopped dead, and try as I might I could not force myself to move any closer.

His heel, the booted heel of his foot was just visible above the low curve of the wall where it rested in unnatural stillness on the far pasture, and I knew with a terrible feeling in the pit of my stomach that I really did not want to see any more. I stood there, swaying gently in a helpless paralysis of horror, knowing that nothing on earth would be powerful enough to make me do it, and yet still trying to force my frozen limbs to carry me forwards to rescue my straying horse.

Then there was a wet crunch of footsteps behind and suddenly strong hands grasped my shoulders to pull me roughly round. My body obeyed helplessly and it was done with such insistence that I would have kept spinning but for his support. Raindrops streaked hard across the wild night air as with rapid breath and a ghostly complexion, his dark eyes stared down at me to intently search my face. There was fresh blood across his cheek and a weary line along his jaw, and when his questioning gaze finally came to rest upon mine, it brought with it such a powerful jolt of realisation that I actually felt as though it must be some kind of mistake.

"*Matthew* ..." I whispered in an agony of disbelief. For a moment he simply stood there, looking down at me, his exhausted face mirroring my own feeble doubts. But then, with a sudden contraction of his mouth, his hands shifted and I found myself being pulled into a tight embrace that was so very solid and so very determined that it seemed like I might never need to draw breath again.

It seemed to be hours later when I found myself dry and huddled warm under blankets, quietly listening to the steady pounding of rain outside. I was leaning against him in a drowsy haze of peacefulness on my settee; the gentle rhythm of his heart was regular now, settled and easy, and a world away from the rough embrace we had shared out on the windswept hillside.

My forehead had been buried in his shoulder then, and I do not believe that I had been capable of doing anything other than cling to him in determined oblivion, concentrating hard on the sound of his breathing as it gradually steadied. He had held me close and even when a police officer appeared by his side he had only lifted his head to confirm that we were all right before allowing his cheek to rest upon my hair once more. I was very cold, it must have been a long time before I could begin to control my shocked shivering and even longer before I was able to lift my head. But then at long last I did, and when I lifted my eyes to meet his, he lightly brought his hand to cover mine in a gesture of such tenderness that finally I was able to accept that his touch was real and he was definitely very much alive.

Now there was no doubt. His voice was warm and relaxed in my ear as he talked and the two police officers – who I suspected were Downe and Fleece only I couldn't remember which was which – were nodding seriously at us from their station near the fire. A fresh cup of tea materialised magically in my hands and reluctantly I roused myself from my cosy stupor enough to take it. Matthew paused in the act of taking his hand away and, gently, closed his fingers briefly over mine in quiet affirmation before turning his attention back once more to the patiently listening policemen. His other arm was wrapped heavily about my shoulders, pinning me against his side as if I had any intention of going anywhere, and occasionally, where he felt that he needed to expand on some particularly unpleasant point, his hand would tighten a little in its grip upon my arm. I gave a comfortable sigh and nestled a little closer.

The trip home had been a long blur of headlights and exhaustion, winding round by a long route to avoid roads closed by flooding and windblown trees, and that first step into my deserted kitchen, which still held Matthew's frantic note and the evidence of my hasty departure, had been the most bizarre kind of homecoming. Freddy, unfailing in his demonstration of the resilience of youth, was somewhere outside accompanied by a kindly policewoman as he settled a surprisingly sedate and blessedly unharmed Beechnut back into her stable. I had tried to insist on leading her back myself but Matthew's negative had been resoundingly firm and Beechnut had been so delighted to see someone she knew that she forgot to resist when he caught her and handed her to a ceaselessly euphoric Freddy.

That darling boy had arrived in the back of a police car looking anxious and deathly pale and, bursting heedlessly through the assembled policemen, had flung himself headlong at us with such energy that he almost knocked Matthew flat. The enthusiasm of their reunion had been wonderful and Matthew had smiled for the first time, a tired attempt at warmth, and enveloped him in a comfortingly smothering bear-hug.

And he was smiling now, a reassuringly familiar lift to one

corner of his mouth and I looked up to realise that one of the policemen had been speaking to me for some time. That smile grew wider as he mildly observed, "You're not really with us, are you? That was the Inspector on the telephone."

I hadn't even heard it ring.

The policeman beamed largely, seeming suddenly startlingly human behind the blank impartiality of his uniform. "The Inspector told me to give you his best, Miss Phillips, and instructed me to give you a severe dressing down for sending him racing away this evening, in this weather, all the way down to a poky little Hampshire police station only to discover once he'd got there that all hell was breaking loose back here ..." He grinned. "Oh and by the way, the Turford brothers send their best."

I sheepishly sat up a little straighter in my seat. "And how did he find them?"

"Bruised. And just a little bit confused."

The policeman's smile widened. It was a little startling how with the telling of my grim tale these two police officers seemed to have forgotten the normal bounds of their strict formality and were now treating me with friendliness, deference and a rather disturbing amount of frank respect.

The policeman's gaze sobered a little, lifting from mine to Matthew's face. "You will take good care now, won't you, sir? And you do know not to do anything stupid like attempt to take yourself away somewhere in the next few days, don't you ...?"

It appeared that whatever reply the officer read in Matthew's short laugh was to his satisfaction because he suddenly gave a nod that was startlingly like his superior's and shut his notebook with a snap. Then he smiled again and extended his hand, "I'm very glad you came to see us today, Mr Croft. Inspector Woods had already begun to suspect that the bleak picture being painted of your character was not entirely accurate, helped – if it's not too bold to say it – in no small part by the actions of this young lady, and he was glad to have it confirmed. No, don't get up either of you, we'll see ourselves out. The Inspector will drop in after a day or two if he may, just to complete his notes … And to see Freddy, of course. I'm not sure the desk-sergeant will ever be quite the same again after the tongue-lashing he received. Now remember what I said, sir; don't wander far."

Then suddenly, after a succession of vigorous handshakes, they left and it was disorientating after an evening of such chaos to abruptly find ourselves alone, in my house and after all that wishing. It seemed incredible; I might almost have become self-conscious but that, with a lazy sigh, Matthew stretched out his legs before the fire and gently tugged me closer.

All awkwardness forgotten, I rested there in a comfortable tangle of blankets and warmth, simply enjoying being able to watch the gentle rise and fall of his chest while drowsily wondering whether I was asleep already, but then, suddenly, Matthew broke the silence. His voice was heavy with exhaustion as he asked,

"I'm not dreaming this, am I?"

I had to laugh at this apparent symmetry with my thoughts but then, when I spoke, it was with gentle seriousness. "No, you're not. I'm here, you're alive; it wasn't a dream and instead of being lost, you've brought us back." I was rewarded with a squeeze of his arm and then silence again. Eventually I added in a whisper, "Back home."

The clumsily delivered allusion was followed by an unexpectedly loaded silence. He seemed to have frozen; the hand that had been lazily toying with a corner of my blanket abruptly stilled and I had the sudden bewildering confusion of whether I had somehow presumed too much.

But then he let out his breath in a low weary sigh. "Oh, Eleanor … Will you really make me the gift of that after all that's happened? I don't mean today, although Lord knows this is bad enough." His hand was suddenly beneath my jaw, tilting my face and I could only imagine what evidence he was finding there in the scuffs and bruises of my tattered appearance. "I mean for spending the past

311

week practically forcing you to confide in me when all the time I should have been telling you the truth."

His gaze flickered. Outside, something broke loose to bang noisily on the tin barn roof. His hand had softened against my chin and I drew away to lay my cheek against his shoulder once more. "The truth?"

He seemed to frown, knowing he had committed himself, but then his fingers tightened possessively on my arm as if he had something difficult to say and was afraid I might run away before he had finished. Eventually he said in a very measured tone, "All those years ago; that row. Do you remember?"

"Yes."

The word was a croak. My heart seemed to have stopped. It seemed he was going to make me admit my guilt after all. I desperately wanted to silence him, to stop him from reliving the hurt but instead I concentrated hard on the vital warmth of his nearness. And listened.

"When you came to see me that morning, you caught me at the wrong end of a week spent making my decision. So many men were marrying their girls just then for very little reason other than for the brief moment of personal gratification it would bring and it sickened me. You'd already lost a mother and your father was unwell; it was impossible for me to bind you to me with nothing to give in return but another death to bear." His voice was hushed against my hair. "But you ... you *fought* it. I'd convinced myself that if I told you calmly you'd understand and agree it would be better for us both – easier for me if we tackled it alone. But every expression of yours just proved that I hadn't explained anything at all. So I panicked. And then I took a different exit."

A log dropped spitting in the grate. It was sending golden flares racing up the chimney and, instinctively, I closed my grip on the fabric of his shirt. "You thought you'd disappointed me, didn't you? That it was simply because you were too young, too naïve; too gentle ... didn't you? This week, when you gave me shelter,

312

I felt so angry; so uselessly angry because I discovered my fear had destroyed that loving, darling young thing. I thought you'd become so *silent*."

His voice was darker now, rough and bleak. "But you're still you. You have no idea what it meant when I discovered that. I should have told you this long ago; I should have told you back then and I'm sorry to have done it like this, after such a day, when you're exhausted and I've already put you through enough." His tired voice grew hoarse, and then gruffly finished, "But at least now you finally know."

After what he had said, my speechlessness felt even more reckless than ever. I floundered, searching for what to say. Perhaps he understood my confusion or perhaps he was just unwilling to let the past go without fighting every last inch of the way, but regardless I was desperately relieved when he suddenly decided to speak again.

"Eleanor," he said bluntly, brutally clear at last. "I lied to you – do you understand me? I was lying when I told you it meant nothing, and I was lying when I let you think you weren't enough for me. You *were* enough. I love you."

He definitely misinterpreted the silence this time. His hand moved a little against my arm, the other closed restlessly in his lap. "You must hate me."

Finally I mustered the intelligence to shake my head. I heard his breath catch, and then he said quietly and very carefully, "Is it possible? Is it possible that, somehow, you still seem to want to offer me *this*?" His gaze turned away to run over the untidy clutter of my living room and for once he wasn't teasing.

Then his cheek touched to my hair again and his thumb followed, gently, to trace a line across my hand where it lay upon his chest, leaving a tingling trail of sensation before moving on to touch upon the corner of my jaw so that I blinked up at him, struggling to marshal my thoughts after such a giddying rush of awareness.

"Matthew, love …"

I managed to speak at last, somehow putting all the force of my care for him into that single utterance of his name. I didn't need to say more. Instantly and with an urgency that stole my breath away, he bent his head to kiss me, holding me and crushing me fiercely before pausing long enough to allow for a smile. It was followed by the possessive heat of his mouth against mine and a half-laughing sigh of relief, and then, drawing me into the safe shelter of his arms again, a calmer, more gentle touch of his lips to my hair.

Then silence. Nothing but the long comfortable silence of peace, broken, after a time, by a very faint murmur of; "Eleanor?"

"Yes?"

"Just …" He paused. "Thank you."

Later, drowsily leaning into his shoulder before the settling fire – having welcomed Freddy home, received the full account of his adventures and dispatched him tired but delighted off to bed – once I felt Matthew's relaxed body dip towards slumber, I made my own confession in a very private whisper to the silent room. "I'm glad you've come back to me."

I felt his arms tighten lazily, a little happy brush of his cheek against my hair and the slow steadying rhythm of his heart beneath my hand as his breathing drifted. Then, at last, taking in the soft familiar warmth of his nearness, I allowed my eyes to close and I too surrendered to the comforting lure of companionable sleep.

Acknowledgements

First and foremost my thanks go to Charlotte Ledger and the team at HarperImpulse whose enthusiasm at every turn has made my journey into print an absolute pleasure. Thanks also to Judith Samuel for her encouragement, Rob and Brenda Brookes for their interest and memories, Tony Curtis for his automobile expertise and to Malcolm Whitaker for permitting me to delve into his experiences of life on a 1940s Cotswold farmstead.

My thanks to George Booth of www.winter1947.co.uk for providing information on snow depths. Flooding patterns were taken from the 2007 RMS Special Report '*1947 U.K. River floods: 60-Year Retrospective*'. Finally, I give my eternal gratitude and affection to Jeremy Brookes for his time, patience and willingness to invent a solution for any problem.